IN A GLASS DARKLY

JOSEPH THOMAS SHERIDAN LE FANU (1814–73) was born in Dublin, the elder son of a clergyman whose Huguenot forebears had married into the Sheridan family. In 1826, the Revd Le Fanu was promoted Dean of Emly, and with his family went to live at Abington, County Limerick. Educated at Trinity College and the King's Inns, Dublin, Sheridan Le Fanu had already launched himself as a journalist and writer of fiction by the end of the 1830s. In 1843 he married Susanna Bennett, the daughter of a leading Irish Q.C. The 1840s proved a compromising decade for Le Fanu—a conservative by instinct and recent experience—for, in the wake of the famine of 1847, he found himself implicated on the fringes of the 1848 rebellion. After an unsuccessful attempt to get a Tory nomination in 1852, he withdrew into editorial work on the newspapers and into the tensions of a household increasingly affected by his wife's neurotic symptoms. Following her death in 1858, and his mother's death in 1861, Sheridan Le Fanu resumed fiction-writing with an Irish historical romance, *The House by the Churchyard* (1861–3); *Wylder's Hand* and *Uncle Silas* both appeared in 1864. The subsequent novels are less impressive, though *Checkmate* (1871) is an effective Victorian thriller-mystery. Throughout his writing life, Le Fanu published accomplished short stories and tales, the best of which are collected in *Chronicles of Golden Friars* (1871) and *In a Glass Darkly* (1872).

ROBERT TRACY is Professor of English and Celtic Studies at the University of California, Berkeley. He is the author of *Trollope's Later Novels* (1978), the translator of *Kamen'* (1913, 1916), poems by the Russian poet Osip Mandelstam, as *Stone* (1981), and has edited *The Aran Islands and other writings* by John Millington Synge (1962).

OXFORD WORLD'S CLASSICS

*For over 100 years Oxford World's Classics have brought
readers closer to the world's great literature. Now with over 700
titles—from the 4,000-year-old myths of Mesopotamia to the
twentieth century's greatest novels—the series makes available
lesser-known as well as celebrated writing.*

*The pocket-sized hardbacks of the early years contained
introductions by Virginia Woolf, T. S. Eliot, Graham Greene,
and other literary figures which enriched the experience of reading.
Today the series is recognized for its fine scholarship and
reliability in texts that span world literature, drama and poetry,
religion, philosophy and politics. Each edition includes perceptive
commentary and essential background information to meet the
changing needs of readers.*

OXFORD WORLD'S CLASSICS

═══

SHERIDAN LE FANU

In a Glass Darkly

═══

Edited with an Introduction and Notes by
ROBERT TRACY

OXFORD
UNIVERSITY PRESS

OXFORD

UNIVERSITY PRESS

Great Clarendon Street, Oxford OX2 6DP

Oxford University Press is a department of the University of Oxford.
It furthers the University's objective of excellence in research, scholarship,
and education by publishing worldwide in

Oxford New York

Auckland Bangkok Buenos Aires Cape Town Chennai
Dar es Salaam Delhi Hong Kong Istanbul Karachi Kolkata
Kuala Lumpur Madrid Melbourne Mexico City Mumbai Nairobi
São Paulo Shanghai Taipei Tokyo Toronto

Oxford is a registered trade mark of Oxford University Press
in the UK and in certain other countries

Published in the United States
by Oxford University Press Inc., New York

Introduction, Note on the Text, Select Bibliography,
Explanatory Notes © Robert Tracy 1993
Chronology © W. J. McCormack 1981 with
revisions © Robert Tracy 1993

First published as a World's Classics paperback 1993
Reissued as an Oxford World's Classics paperback 1999
Reissued 2008

British Library Cataloguing in Publication Data

Data available

Library of Congress Cataloging in Publication Data

Le Fanu, Joseph Sheridan, 1814–1873.
In a glass darkly / Sheridan Le Fanu ; edited with an introduction
by Robert Tracy.
p. cm.—(Oxford world's classics)
Includes bibliographical references.
1. Supernatural—Fiction. 2. Ireland—Fiction. I. Tracy,
Robert, 1928– . II. Title. III. Series.
PR4879.L715 1993 823'.8—dc20 92–18158

ISBN 978–0–19–953798–3

20

Printed and bound in Great Britain
by Clays Ltd, Elcograf S.p.A.

CONTENTS

CONTENTS

INTRODUCTION

SHERIDAN LE FANU's chief interests were Ireland and the supernatural, interests which often coalesced. Though a Dubliner for most of his life, he spent part of his boyhood at Abington, in County Limerick, after his clergyman father's appointment as Dean of Emly. At Abington he was exposed to the richness of Irish oral legend, especially the tales of a gifted local story-teller, Miss Anne Baily of Lough Guir. Supernatural stories described encounters with demons and fairies. There were also legends about the Irish past—the exploits of Finn MacCool, or of the more recent Cromwellian and Williamite wars, the latter ending with the siege of Limerick (1690–1), which marked the final defeat of the Stuart and Catholic cause in Ireland. Two of Le Fanu's historical novels have the Williamite wars as their setting, and describe their aftermath: the confiscation of Catholic estates, which were then granted to Protestants; the fate of the old families, who either fled abroad, or hovered dispossessed in the vicinity of their old homes.

Le Fanu was also a journalist, and for some years proprietor and editor of the *Dublin University Magazine*, a journal with some claim to speak for Conservative Protestant Ireland. Le Fanu initially had some sympathy with Irish nationalism, and was personally friendly with Isaac Butt, Parnell's predecessor as head of the Irish Home Rule supporters in Parliament. But he wrote no editorials on the chief crises of the late 1860s, the Fenian Rising (1867), and the Gladstone government's disestablishment (1869) of the Church of Ireland. Le Fanu seems to have sunk into a political apathy resembling the lethargy and despair that often afflicts the haunted characters of his supernatural stories. In their helplessness, those lethargic characters may in fact represent his response to Irish events, amid which his own class seemed less and less capable of preserving the power and privileges which it had once enjoyed, or of considering itself the 'Ascendancy' it had once proclaimed itself. Le Fanu's supernatural tales are among the best in this genre. But they are also at once personal confessions and expressions of political and social anxieties.

The supernatural tale, as a deliberate literary form distinct from the popular folk-tale, came into existence about the time the educated classes ceased to believe in ghosts and witches and so began to find them entertaining. The last English trial for witchcraft took place in 1712; the accused was convicted, but not executed. The last execution of a witch in Scotland was in 1722; in Germany a witch was executed as late as 1793. By 1764, Horace Walpole was ready to invent the gothic novel with *The Castle of Otranto*. His example was quickly followed by Clara Reeve, Ann Radcliffe, 'Monk' Lewis, and the writers of the numerous '"horrid"' tales Jane Austen ridicules, as she does their readers, in *Northanger Abbey* (1818).

The ghosts in these stories are real, usually appearing to right some wrong connected with the ownership of real estate. But Mrs Radcliffe had developed an important innovation as early as *The Castles of Athlin and Dunbayne* (1789). Her supernatural manifestations eventually turn out to be elaborately contrived frauds, concocted to terrify the heroine into surrendering her virginity, her property, her sanity, or even all three. In *The Monk* (1796), Lewis explored the tale of terror's many opportunities for sexual titillation, especially if the story featured monks and nuns.

Though *Melmoth the Wanderer* (1820), by the Dublin clergyman Charles Robert Maturin, enjoyed considerable popularity, the tale of terror as developed by Walpole and his successors had already ceased to attract many readers. Sir Walter Scott used the supernatural sparingly. By the 1830s it was clear that the writer of supernatural fiction needed a new method. Charles Dickens and Le Fanu seem to have discovered that method independently, at about the same time, though Dickens has priority. But the Irish novelist realized that Dickens's sceptical narration could be used not to undermine a supernatural story but to enhance it, to make it more mysterious and perhaps more terrifying.

In the fifth number of *Pickwick Papers*, published in August 1836, the Pickwickians hear a story about a bagman's encounter with a talking chair; in the tenth number (January 1837),

Mr Wardle tells the story of Gabriel Grub, the sexton carried off by the goblins. Neither story attempts to be frightening, and both are presented sceptically: the bagman and Grub have been drinking before their encounters with the supernatural. Le Fanu's 'The Ghost and the Bone-Setter', his first published story, appeared in the *Dublin University Magazine* in January 1838, to be followed by several other supernatural tales: 'The Fortunes of Sir Robert Ardagh' (March); 'The Drunkard's Dream' (August); and 'Strange Event in the Life of Schalken the Painter' (May 1839). In two of these stories, those who see ghosts have been drinking. In 'Sir Robert Ardagh' Le Fanu sets the folk legend against the 'true' story; each admits either a natural or a supernatural explanation. With 'Schalken the Painter' Le Fanu had clearly mastered a new kind of supernatural tale, which accepts and utilizes the reader's scepticism. Schalken's adventure barely allows for a natural explanation. He loses Rose to a sinister, rich, corpse-like old man; Rose flees from her husband, with an incoherent story, but then vanishes; later Schalken sees her, or thinks he sees her, living in a tomb. The sinister old man may simply be an old man, not an animated corpse; the frightened heroine may be hallucinating, or hysterical; doors can slam shut by other than supernatural agency; Rose may have leaped from a window to her death, not been carried off through the air; Schalken has fallen asleep before he sees her in the tomb. Like Schalken, the reader assumes the supernatural element, involving marriage with the dead, but we cannot be sure. The story marks Le Fanu's first completely successful use of the new method, building the story on both doubt and fear, leaving the supernatural presence unexplained and still powerful—or, in other words, creating a mystery and then maintaining that mystery. As with so many speculations about the supernatural, whether religious or merely superstitious, we finally do not know.

M. R. James (1862–1936), himself a distinguished writer of supernatural tales, considered himself Le Fanu's disciple. James has left us brief but valuable comments about the supernatural genre, drawn both from his work and that of his master. 'It is not amiss sometimes to leave a loophole for a natural explanation,' he remarks; 'but, I would say, let the loophole be so narrow as not to be quite practicable.'[1] Most of the stories collected under the title *In a Glass Darkly* include the narrow loophole, to tease us with its failure to reassure. There are demons in Le Fanu's world. We cannot always see them, but when we do, they take shape from our guilt, or from our obsessive fears. 'Can't you see them?' cries the haunted protagonist of T. S. Eliot's *The Family Reunion* (1939); '*You don't see them, but I see them, | And they see me*' (1. 1).[2]

Le Fanu usually hints at the possibility of hallucination, and of mental or even physical illness in his victims. '"I agree that ghosts appear only to the sick,"' argues Dostoevsky's Svidrigaylov, another haunted murderer, '"but that proves only that they cannot appear to anybody else, not that they have no real existence."' More flippantly, Scrooge tries to dismiss Marley's ghost as '"an undigested bit of beef, a blot of mustard, a crumb of cheese, a fragment of an underdone potato."'[3] Between them they more or less define the types of narrow loophole Le Fanu sometimes allows. Mr Jennings's apparition may be due to his addiction to green tea. Captain Barton and Mr Justice Harbottle have guilty consciences. They are all sick men, and suspect they are sick, for all three consult physicians, as does Laura in 'Carmilla'.

Le Fanu's early supernatural stories were supposedly drawn from among the papers of the Reverend Francis Purcell, an Irish Catholic priest who was also an antiquarian and folklore collector. Father Purcell's ghostly calling, and the association of Catholic priests with supernatural events in Gothic novels, suggest that the stories he has collected are true. *In a Glass Darkly* contains cases collected by Dr Martin Hesselius, a physician interested in 'metaphysical' medicine. Hesselius is

---

[1] M. R. James, introd., *Ghosts and Marvels: A Selection of Uncanny Tales from Daniel Defoe to Algernon Blackwood*, ed. V. H. Collins (Oxford: Oxford University Press, 1924 (World's Classics)), p. vi.

[2] T. S. Eliot, *The Family Reunion*, in *The Complete Poems and Plays* (New York: Harcourt, Brace, 1952), 232.

[3] Feodor Dostoevsky, *Crime and Punishment*, trans. Jessie Coulson, ed. George Gibian (New York: Norton, 1975), 244 (pt. 4, ch. 1); Charles Dickens, *A Christmas Carol*, in *Christmas Books* (London: Oxford University Press, 1974), 18.

willing to take seriously those who suffer from threatening apparitions—though he loses the only patient he actually treats. He is a doctor for the mind, a forerunner of the modern psychiatrist. As scientist he certifies the stories. But under certain circumstances he is willing to admit that supernatural forces can invade ordinary lives, that the barriers which normally separate us from the world of spirits can dissolve.

Strictly speaking, none of these stories are about ghosts. But they are about hauntings. Even though Beckett, in 'The Room in the Dragon Volant', encounters nothing supernatural, he is nevertheless haunted—tracked, followed—by Count and Countess St Alyre, and obsessed by the Countess's beauty. Jennings is haunted by a small black monkey, Barton and Harbottle by men they have murdered. As for Laura, Carmilla has apparently watched her for some time. In Ireland, incidentally, the word 'follow' is often used to suggest that a supernatural being is attached to a certain family over many generations: 'a banshee always follows the O'Sheerans.' As a descendant of the Sheridans, Le Fanu himself could claim a banshee.[4]

Le Fanu's ideas about the world of spirits, in so far as they shape *In a Glass Darkly*, are based to some extent on the teachings of Emanuel Swedenborg (1688–1772), the Swedish scientist, theologian, and visionary. After the death of his young wife Susanna in 1858, Le Fanu turned to Swedenborg's writings, which are reassuring about death by describing it as merely a change, to some extent a continuation of ordinary life. We can understand the comfort he found when we read, in *Uncle Silas* (1864), the description of the afterlife Le Fanu put into the mouth of the Swedenborgian Bryerly:

a beautiful landscape, radiant with a wondrous light, in which, rejoicing, my mother moved along an airy path, ascending among mountains of fantastic height, and peaks, melting in celestial colouring into the air, and peopled with human beings translated into the same image, beauty, and splendour.[5]

[4] Patricia Lysaght, *The Banshee: The Irish Supernatural Death-Messenger* (Dublin: Glendale Press, 1986), 124.

[5] Sheridan Le Fanu, *Uncle Silas* (London: Cresset Press, 1947), 45.

But there are less comforting visions and ideas in the writings of Swedenborg, and they shape 'Green Tea', 'The Familiar', and 'Mr Justice Harbottle'. Swedenborg taught that everyone has an 'inner eye', a non-sensual mode of vision. When opened, the inner eye helps us to read Scripture properly, to discern its hidden or non-literal meanings. The inner eye also lets us see into the world of spirits, which interpenetrates our own world, and even into the heaven of the angels. Swedenborg's religious teachings and his accounts of his visionary experiences depend on this inner sight, as do the visions of William Blake, at one time a reader of Swedenborg.

Le Fanu cites only one of Swedenborg's works in *In a Glass Darkly*: *Arcana Caelestia* (1749–56), a commentary on the books of Genesis and Exodus. Though the work is mentioned only in 'Green Tea', Swedenborg's ideas about vision also pervade the two following stories, and may play some part in 'Carmilla'. The *Arcana* also provides Hesselius with a literary model. It contains the biblical texts of Genesis and Exodus, Swedenborg's commentary on those texts, and from time to time descriptions of Swedenborg's own visionary experiences. Hesselius, we learn, 'writes in two distinct characters. He describes what he saw and heard as an intelligent layman might,' but then 'returns upon the narrative, and in the terms of his art and with all the force and originality of genius, proceeds to the work of analysis, diagnosis and illustration' (p. 5)—a double narrative, suited to stories where two worlds intersect.

Swedenborg's *Arcana* explains how we are to read Scripture, and how we are to read the world, texts we believe we can read with only sensual vision. Genesis is not just an account of man's origin. It is an elaborate allegory (*AC* 167): Eve represents self-love, Adam is the rational principle, the serpent is sensual rather than revealed truth (192, 196). The tree is intellectual as opposed to intuitive knowledge (202). Noah's flood was not an actual inundation but 'an inundation of evil and of the false' (660), which 'drowned' antediluvian man (257).[6]

[6] Emanuel Swedenborg, *Arcana Caelestia* (New York: American Swedenborg Printing and Publishing Society, 1870), 10 vols. Swedenborg's text is in numbered paragraphs, and the references are to those paragraphs.

The passage in 'Green Tea' that Jennings marks and Hesselius reads, expresses those darker teachings of Swedenborg which Le Fanu uses. We are born with both interior and external or ordinary sight. In most people, the interior sight or 'inner eye' is never opened. They see only the physical world around them. The inner eye, when opened, allows us to see the worlds of spirits which surround us, to peer into Heaven and hell, to enjoy intercourse with angels. But, as Swedenborg warns, if evil spirits become aware that they are perceived by—are in communication with—corporeal men, they strive to destroy them. This is apparently what happens to Jennings. Evil spirits take the form of savage beasts. The malevolent monkey has become aware of Jennings, and knows that Jennings can see it. Actuated by innate malice, it leads him to self-destruction—though Hesselius offers several other explanations for Jennings's fate.

'Green Tea'' emphasizes the arbitrary and apparently unprovoked nature of Jennings's visitation. His inner eye has been opened accidentally, perhaps by his indulgence in green tea. He is terrified by the spirit-monkey which haunts him with increasing frequency, interfering even with his religious duties, eventually driving him to suicide. Dr Hesselius loses his patient, partly because of his own irresponsible behaviour. Hesselius assures Jennings that he will be at his disposal, then disappears to a remote country inn to meditate upon the case, while Jennings's demon destroys him. Hesselius rather meanly excuses his failure by quibbling: Jennings was not yet really his patient, Hesselius's treatment—sure to succeed—had not yet begun. At the same time, he gives us too many explanations for Jennings's fate. Jennings drank too much green tea; his father had seen a ghost, and so Jennings had inherited a 'suicidal mania'; Jennings's studies in pagan metaphysics had made him vulnerable. In effect, Hesselius blames the victim.

Jennings does perhaps spend too much time in his study, where his interests resemble those of George Eliot's Mr Casaubon. Too much tea, green or not, can bring about a

[7] Information about any previous periodical publication of each story will be found in the Explanatory Notes.

nervous state. His studies have led him into pagan mythology, to half-realize that the gods and goddesses of Greece and Rome are metaphors for a sensuality he can neither accommodate nor confront: Venus is unbridled desire, Mars unbridled rage, Bacchus licentiousness, Pan sheer animality. His unintended invasion of the world of spirits causes him to see or imagine a metaphor for his own suppressed erotic self, his animal nature. When Stevenson's Dr Jekyll creates an alternate self so that he can indulge his baser nature while continuing to pose as a paragon of virtue, Mr Hyde is ape-like, with long simian arms. Hyde mocks and reveals Jekyll's repressions. Jennings's haunting monkey is an aspect of himself, from whom there is no escape—in Othello's words, 'As if there were some monster in his thought | Too hideous to be shown' (III iii. 106–7).

Jennings's monkey may reflect Victorian anxieties after Darwin's unwelcome suggestion that man was of simian ancestry. Crudely popularized versions of Darwin's theory served to argue that certain races—Australian Bushmen, sub-Saharan Africans, the Irish—were still close to their gorilla ancestors. Le Fanu would have been well aware of the simian Irish who were common in Victorian political cartoons, especially in the pages of *Punch*.[8] Supernatural stories often reflect their authors' own anxieties. Written shortly after an abortive Fenian rising, and in the year when Gladstone abandoned the Church of Ireland, and by implication the Anglo-Irish, to their fate, 'Green Tea' with its monkey may hint at Anglo-Ireland's anxieties about the unhyphenated Irish, their violence and probable malevolence. Members of Le Fanu's family had been attacked during the Tithe Wars (protests by Catholic tenants against being taxed to support the Protestant Church of Ireland) in 1832–6.[9] There was some monster in Le Fanu's thought, not too hideous to be shown but perhaps too hideous to be confronted directly.

Le Fanu titled his collection from St Paul: 'For now we see through a glass, darkly; but then face to face: now I know in

[8] L. P. Curtis, *Apes and Angels: The Irishman in Victorian Caricature* (Washington, DC: Smithsonian Institution Press, 1971).

[9] W. R. Le Fanu, *Seventy Years of Irish Life* (New York: Macmillan, 1894), 58–68.

part, but then shall I know even as also I am known' (1 Cor. 12). A clergyman's son, we can be sure he did not misquote scripture lightly. The glass of his title is not a window-pane through which we glimpse dim intimations of a spiritual world, or of divine truth. It is a mirror in which we glimpse our own darker nature.

Captain Barton, the haunted victim of 'The Familiar', has a cruel act on his conscience, and is perhaps more clearly responsible for invoking the footsteps which follow him, and the man shrunken 'in all his proportions, and yet [preserving] his exact resemblance to himself in every particular' (p. 54) who terrifies him. His approaching marriage suggests to him the memory of the 'guilty attachment' he had formed with the daughter of one of his own crew members, her father's resentment, and Barton's use of his powers as captain to destroy the man.

Le Fanu dates 'The Familiar'—a slightly revised version of 'The Watcher', a story he had published in 1851—with apparent precision, 'Somewhere about the year 1794', and places it in his own city of Dublin. The story gives him a chance to display his own knowledge of the city and its development. In *The Cock and Anchor* (1845), *The Fortunes of Colonel Torlogh O'Brien* (1847), and *The House by the Church-Yard* (1861–3), he recreated seventeenth-century Dublin and eighteenth-century Chapelizod, a Dublin suburb, reminding the reader from time to time that the seventeenth-century gallows stands where St Stephen's Green is later to be, and that outlaws frequent the wild acres of Phoenix Park. In 'The Familiar' Captain Barton is pursued through the laid out but as yet unbuilt streets of the city in which Le Fanu is writing the story. We know that *The House by the Church-Yard* is one of the texts underlying *Finnegans Wake*,[10] partly because of frequent references to the River Liffey in Le Fanu's novel, and partly because the novel is about different kinds of resurrection. Since *Finnegans Wake* is about the city of Dublin existing simultaneously at every period of its history, past, present, and

---

[10] James S. Atherton, *The Books at the Wake* (Carbondale: Southern Illinois University Press, 1959), 110–13.

future, it may also owe something to Le Fanu's phantom city of the future through which Captain Barton is pursued by his past.

Le Fanu's planned but partially unbuilt Dublin is historically accurate. There was a building boom, and considerable speculative building, in Dublin during the 1790s, when Grattan's Parliament made the city a true capital, in the period before the Act of Union (1800). Lady L——is genteelly poor, but nevertheless participates in the contemporary migration of the nobility and gentry from south to north of the Liffey. Barton lives in south Dublin, presumably in the then newly built Merrion Square—perhaps at Number 18, Merrion Square South (now Number 70), where Le Fanu was living when he wrote the story.

For *In a Glass Darkly* Le Fanu retitled 'The Haunted House in Westminster' as 'Mr Justice Harbottle', to place the emphasis on his protagonist and what he sees, or thinks he sees. The story is a drastically rewritten version—so drastically as to be almost a new story—of Le Fanu's 'An Account of Some Strange Disturbances in Aungier Street', published in the *Dublin University Magazine* in December 1853. The earlier version is set in Dublin's Aungier Street, where Le Fanu was married, south of the Liffey near Dublin Castle, in the oldest part of the city. Le Fanu is again meticulous about dates. The Aungier Street house 'was sold, along with much other forfeited property . . . in 1702; and had belonged to Sir Thomas Hacket, who was Lord Mayor of Dublin in James II's time.' Presumably the house was confiscated in the aftermath of the Williamite victory over James II, that is, at that pivotal moment of Irish history to which Le Fanu also returns in two of his historical novels. Many of his stories, supernatural or otherwise, portray the dispossessed Catholic gentry of Ireland after the Williamite triumph: 'The Fortunes of Sir Robert Ardagh', 'The Last Heir of Castle Connor', 'Sir Dominick's Bargain', 'Ultor de Lacy'. Charles Le Fanu de Cresserons, Le Fanu's ancestor, had fought for William at the Battle of the Boyne (1690), and the family cherished a portrait of the king which he was supposed to have personally presented to de

Cresserons,.[11] As Le Fanu contemplated his own class's loss of
power in the aftermath of Daniel O'Connell's successful campaign for Catholic Emancipation (1829), and increasing Catholic political and economic power, he seemed to imagine the
Ascendancy's future by examining the Catholic gentry's dispossessed past, to recognize that the Williamite revolution,
which had given the Le Fanu family lands and prestige, was
being altered by another revolution which would reverse the
earlier one. The rumoured Jacobite plot—a plot to restore the
Catholic Stuarts—in 'Mr Justice Harbottle' is an oblique
recollection of this historical obsession.

'Disturbances in Aungier Street' shares with 'Mr Justice
Harbottle' a cruel and sensual judge—Judge Horrock in the
earlier story—who hangs himself in a stairwell, where his
ghost re-enacts that hanging. But the story is primarily about
two young men who see the apparition, a century or so after
Judge Horrock's suicide. In 'Mr Justice Harbottle' this survives only in the lodger's brief account of what he has seen.
The story is really about Harbottle himself, and the way he is
either supernaturally visited or is worked upon by his own
guilt. He is certainly visited by the mysterious Hugh Peters,
and later the child sees the avenging Pyneweck, and the
kitchen maid sees a monstrous blacksmith. Dr Hesselius
comments on the 'contagious character of this sort of intrusion
of the spirit-world upon the proper domain of matter' to
explain these supplementary apparitions (p. 83). Harbottle
sees not only the apparition of his victim. He also has a
terrifying vision of his own cruelty, and must recognize his
own guilt, when he is judged by Mr Justice Twofold—a
crueller and more arbitrary image of himself.

In a Glass Darkly follows these three short stories with two of
considerable length, 'The Room in the Dragon Volant' and
'Carmilla'. Both differ drastically in kind from their fore-
runners. In the briefer stories, Le Fanu always supplies the
narrow loophole M. R. James recommends. Jennings, Barton,
and Harbottle may all have been hallucinating. All three may
have frightened themselves to death. Jennings may have

---

[11] T. P. Le Fanu, *Memoir of the Le Fanu Family* (privately printed, 1924), 28.

inherited a disposition to suicide. Barton may have died in terror because a pet owl invaded his room and his curtained bed. Harbottle may have examined—prematurely—Hogarth's *Industry and Idleness* (1747) and created, from the print depicting the Idle Apprentice's execution, a vision of his own execution. But at the same time, the stories powerfully suggest that some barrier between the natural and the supernatural worlds has been breached, that what Le Fanu's haunted protagonists see is real though uncanny.

'The Room in the Dragon Volant' is not a supernatural story at all, though the thieves who conspire against Richard Beckett pretend to necromancy to further their plot, and know that lodgers in a certain room at the Dragon Volant often vanish into thin air. 'Carmilla' is unequivocally supernatural, without a loophole. Carmilla really is a vampire, tracked down at last and destroyed in the tomb where she lies in seven inches of blood. But both stories retain the earlier theme of breached barriers between two worlds. Beckett swallows one of the mysterious draughts Hesselius cites in his preliminary note, draughts which induce a catatonic state resembling death. The names of such draughts combine natural and supernatural: *Vinum letiferum*, the wine of Lethean oblivion; *Somnus Angelorum*, the sleep of the Angels. Beckett is taken into the realm of the dead, if only a little way; he is undead, conscious that he is in his coffin but unable to move or speak, and aware that he will be placed in the grave. Carmilla is also undead. She moves easily between the world of the living and the world of the dead, at ease in both, in ballroom or tomb. Her freedom to disregard any boundary between life and death is what makes her terrifying.

Young Beckett, in France a few weeks after Waterloo, is eager for a sexual adventure and aggressive about seeking one. He is an easy mark for a gang of criminal conspirators, and the lovely bait they offer, the Countess de St Alyre—with its verbal overtones of allure. Beckett has brought his near-burial alive on himself, by his belief that he is irresistible as a lover, and by his willingness to run off with another man's wife. Unlike Jennings, Barton, and Harbottle, he survives his ordeal, rescued by a zealous French police agent. The official nature of his rescue is noteworthy. Jennings, Barton, and Harbottle represent three institutions that maintained Victorian Britain, the Church, the Navy, and the Law. None of these can offer protection against rampant evil. Perhaps they do order these matters better in France.

Though Beckett is explicitly described as an Englishman, he bears the name of an old and well-known Anglo-Irish family, of Huguenot origin like the Le Fanus. In his silence, impotence, and immobility it is tempting to see a foreshadowing of some of Samuel Beckett's themes and situations. Joyce, incidentally, drew on the story once or twice for *Finnegans Wake*: 'he urned his dead, that dragon volant' (25.05); 'Shutmup. And bud did down right well. And if he sung dumb in his glass darkly speech lit face to face on allaround.'[12] Le Fanu's subject, a sleep that is like death induced by quaffing a potion, anticipates the ballad of 'Finnegan's Wake' and Joyce's drunken, dreaming publican.

'Carmilla' is an undead survivor from the late seventeenth century, that period that fascinated Le Fanu because of the Williamite victories in Ireland. Her portrait, as Mircalla, Countess Karnstein, is dated 1698. Modern readers have often been surprised at the remarkably overt lesbian theme pervading this tale of a young woman threatened by a vampire—who is also a young woman. In fact, sexual anxiety pervades the whole story, and Le Fanu deliberately heightened this anxiety by introducing a kind of sex he would have considered illicit in order to emphasize the unnatural in his supernatural tale.

Laura, the destined victim in 'Carmilla', is troubled when she is suggestively embraced and kissed by Carmilla, more troubled when she begins to sense that she is the target of some mysterious and uncanny agency. Both reactions are plausible. But perhaps these anxieties at once suggest and mask Le Fanu's deeper anxieties. These anxieties are neither supernatural nor primarily sexual, though sex and a troubled religious faith play their part. They are primarily social and political, aroused as the Catholic Irish begin to assert themselves, especially in terms of the central issue in nineteenth-century Ireland, the

---

[12] James Joyce, *Finnegans Wake* (1939; New York: Viking, 1958), 25, 355.

ownership of land. Political issues can be rephrased in supernatural terms when religion is intermixed with politics. They
can be rephrased in sexual terms when racial tension is added.
Both factors were abundantly present in nineteenth-century
Ireland, to be encoded in Carmilla's pursuit of Laura.

The story is set in Styria, on the borders of Austria and
Hungary—traditional vampire territory. Laura, who tells the
story, begins by stressing her English nationality. Though she
has never been there, she thinks of England as 'home'. Her
father, also English, has retired from the Austrian service.
They speak English together, read Shakespeare to keep up the
language, and drink tea in the English manner. Their castle is
in the midst of a vast forest. There are no neighbours—that is,
no neighbouring gentry—and even the local peasantry are few
and far between.

The nearest village is roofless and abandoned, clustered
around a ruined church and the ruined castle of the Karnsteins, now extinct but once lords of the territory. Laura's dead
mother was related to the Karnsteins.

This insistent Englishness, their social isolation, strongly
suggest the lives of many Anglo-Irish landowners in the
eighteenth and nineteenth centuries. The abandoned village
suggests Ireland after the Great Famine of 1845–9. The people
have been removed by what Laura's father calls the 'infection'
of superstition, their fear of vampires—a recollection of the
fever that accompanied the Famine. Many have chosen exile.

In her introduction to a reprint of Le Fanu's *Uncle Silas*,
Elizabeth Bowen, herself an Anglo-Irish landowner, declared
that *Uncle Silas* is an Irish novel, despite its explicit Yorkshire
setting: 'The hermetic solitude and the autocracy of the great
country house, the demonic power of the family myth, fatalism,
feudalism and the "ascendancy" outlook are accepted facts of
life for the race of hybrids from which Le Fanu sprang.' Bowen
notes Le Fanu's earlier use of the *Uncle Silas* plot in 'Passage in
the Secret History of an Irish Countess' (*Dublin University
Magazine*, November 1838). She describes his choice of an
English setting as 'inscrutable', but the research of W. J.
McCormack has uncovered the reason. Richard Bentley, who
published most of Le Fanu's fiction after 1863, considered Irish

stories unpopular, and insisted on stories 'of an English subject and in modern times' (Bentley to Le Fanu, 26 February 1863).[13] So Mr Jennings, of Kenlis, becomes an English clergyman, Dublin's Aungier Street becomes 'a dark street in Westminster', Laura is settled in Styria, where Le Fanu had never been, but where he knew there was a popular belief in vampires. He drew also on the vampire tradition as it already existed in English literature: John Polidori's *The Vampire* (1819), written during that same competition to write a ghost story which produced Mary Shelley's *Frankenstein* (1818); and the interminable *Varney the Vampyre*, serialised in the early 1840s, and written by James Rymer or Thomas Prest. These in turn drew on the Balkan tradition of the undead, the vampire able to leave the grave at will, sustained by sucking the blood of the living, and apparently capable of sexual relations with the living.

Drawing on both the literary vampire tradition and the folklore tradition, 'Carmilla' in turn helped to shape *Dracula* (1897), by Le Fanu's fellow Dubliner, Bram Stoker (1847–1912). Both were 'Anglo-Irish', though Le Fanu's ancestry was French and Stoker's Dutch, and both were sons of Dublin's Protestant professional class. Stoker's short story, 'The Judge's House' (1914), draws on a situation similar to that in Le Fanu's 'Strange disturbances in Aungier Street'. In *Dracula* his Dr Van Helsing, scientist, physician, and vampirologist, is a more effective Dr Hesselius. Stoker had signalled his debt to 'Carmilla' in what was intended to be the opening chapter of *Dracula*, deleted because his publisher thought it revealed the vampire theme prematurely. In that chapter, Jonathan Harker, en route to Castle Dracula, wanders in the vicinity of Munich on Walpurgis-Nacht (1 May), when the witches hold their revels. He arrives at a great tomb, inscribed as that of 'Countess Dolingen of Gratz in Styria', who 'sought and found death, 1801.' An iron stake transfixes the tomb and the corpse inside. A violent storm arises, Harker sees 'a beautiful woman, with rounded cheeks and red lips, seemingly

---

[13] Elizabeth Bowen, introd. *Uncle Silas*, by Sheridan Le Fanu (London: Cresset), 8–9. W. J. McCormack, *Sheridan Le Fanu and Victorian Ireland* (Oxford: Clarendon Press, 1980), 140–2.

asleep on a bier,' and then a lightning bolt strikes the stake, rousing the dead woman 'for a moment of agony, while she was lapped in the flame, and her bitter scream of pain was drowned in the thundercrash.' The tomb is destroyed; Dracula himself must rescue Harker, partly by a timely telegram, but also by assuming the shape of a grey wolf and guarding him.[14]

Carmilla is at once vampire and Irish banshee, *ban sí*, woman of the *sí*, of the tumulus or mound—a woman who dwells in one of the ancient burial mounds so common in the Irish countryside, a woman of the dead.[15] In comparatively recent tradition, the banshee is a highly respectable appanage of certain old families, a wailing spirit who foretells or announces and laments the deaths of family members. In an earlier tradition, she is seen by doomed warriors on their way to battle, washing corpses or bloodied shirts. Other legends describe intermarriage between a mortal man and a woman of the *sí*. Conn the Hundred-Fighter is seduced by such a woman, as is Muircertach mac Erca and the poet-warrior Oisin. These relationships are seldom happy or long-lasting; sometimes the human partner begins to waste away.[16]

Sí (or *sídhe*) is usually translated as fairy, but Irish fairies are more sinister than Shakespeare's Mustardseeds and Peaseblossoms. They crave human beings, especially children, but also young men and women, luring them away to live a kind of half-life under the earth. In some way they live on—or through—these captives, as vampires live on blood. The *sí* themselves are not easily classified as living or dead. Like vampires, they are undead and hungry. Yeats calls them 'the unappeasable host'.[17]

---

[14] Bram Stoker, *Dracula's Guest and Other Weird Stories* (London: George Routledge, 1914), 9–11; A. N. Wilson, introd., *Dracula* (Oxford: Oxford University Press, 1983), pp. xi–xii.

[15] Lysaght, *The Banshee*, 30.

[16] 'The Adventures of Art Son of Conn', trans. R. I. Best; 'The Death of Muircertach mac Erca', trans. Whitley Stokes; 'Oisin in the Land of Youth', trans. Tomás O Flannghaile; *Ancient Irish Tales*, ed. Tom Peete Cross and Charles Harris Slover (1936; repr. New York: Barnes and Noble, 1969).

[17] W. B. Yeats, 'The Unappeasable Host', *Poems*, ed. Richard J. Finneran (New York: Macmillan, 1983), 58.

Carmilla has affinities both with the traditional banshee and the *sí*. Like the banshee, she is attached to Laura's family, and is her ancestress, though she does not limit herself to that family; the banshee is often assumed to be an ancestress of the family she warns. In some versions, she is an old woman, in others young and beautiful. Carmilla's beauty, white garments, and nocturnal habits are those of the banshee, and she is certainly a harbinger of death to the families she visits. In 'The White Cat of Drumgunniol' (1870), presumably drawing on oral tradition, Le Fanu describes a malevolent banshee eager to destroy the Donovans, whose ancestor wronged her.

In another traditional story he retells, 'The Child that went with the Fairies' (1870), set in County Limerick near Abington, the child is lured away by a beautiful lady in a coach, attended by servants with 'faces of cunning and malice'.[18] In the coach with the lady there is a 'black woman, with ... a sort of turban of silk striped with all the colours of the rainbow ... a face as thin almost as a death's-head ... and great goggle eyes, the whites of which, as well as her wide range of teeth, showed in brilliant contrast with her skin.' Carmilla arrives at Laura's door in essentially the same coach, with servants who look ' "wicked ... lean, and dark, and sullen." ' She too is accompanied by 'a hideous black woman, with a sort of coloured turban on her head ... with gleaming eyes and large white eye-balls'. The woman of the *sí* who seduces and destroys Muircertach mac Erca feeds him food that wastes him away, and further wastes his strength by sending him to battle blue warriors[19]—in Irish, for obscure reasons, a Negro is *fear gorm*, a blue man.

In her eagerness for a sexual relationship with Laura, Carmilla resembles the predatory *sí* of Irish legend, as well as the Balkan tradition of the vampire. Marriage with the dead is a common theme for Le Fanu, used in 'Schalken the Painter', 'Ultor De Lacy' (1861), and the 'fairy' tale, 'Laura Silver Bell'

[18] 'The Child that went with the Fairies' originally appeared in Charles Dickens's weekly *All the Year Round* (5 Feb. 1870), as did 'The White Cat' (2 Apr. 1870), followed (23 Apr.) by Le Fanu's 'Stories of Lough Guir'.

[19] Cross and Slover, *Ancient Irish Tales*, 524.

(1872), hinted at in 'A Chapter in the History of a Tyrone Family' (1839). For 'Carmilla' he adds the lesbian element.

At the same time, Carmilla is outside the banshee/*sí* tradition in certain ways. The *sí* do not suck blood, nor are they destroyed with stakes and bonfires. Le Fanu combined aspects of Irish tradition with his reading of Dom Augustin Calmet's treatise on vampires, and the other books of vampire lore which Baron Vordenburg lends to Laura's father, and with memories of Polidori and *Varney the Vampyre*. He recognized and used the sexual element that is so strong in both vampire lore and vampire fiction.[20] Freud's disciple, Ernest Jones, discusses the sexual aspects of the vampire at length in his *On the Nightmare*. 'The latent content of the belief yields plain indications of most kinds of sexual perversions,' Jones declares; '. . . the belief assumes various forms according as this or that perversion is more prominent.' Citing mostly German sources, Jones points out that 'Vampires always visit relatives first . . . The belief is, in fact, only an elaboration of that in the Incubus, and the essential elements of both are the same—repressed desires and hatreds.' Jones notes Freud's theory 'that morbid dread always signifies repressed sexual wishes . . . The explanation of these phantasies is surely not hard,' he concludes:

A nightly visit from a beautiful or frightful being, who first exhausts the sleeper with passionate embraces and then withdraws from him a vital fluid: all this can point only to a natural and common process, namely to nocturnal emissions accompanied with dreams of a more or less erotic nature. In the unconscious mind blood is commonly an equivalent for semen . . . in the Vampire superstition . . . the simple idea of the vital fluid being withdrawn through an exhausting love embrace is complicated by more perverse forms of sexuality, as well as by the admixture of sadism and hate.[21]

'Death and Love, together mated, | Watch and wait in

---

[20] John Cuthbert Lawson, *Modern Greek Folklore and Ancient Greek Religion* (Cambridge: Cambridge University Press, 1910), 415–16; Paul Barber, *Vampires, Burial, and Death: Folklore and Reality* (New Haven, Conn.: Yale University Press, 1988), 9.

[21] Ernest Jones, *On the Nightmare* (1931; rev. 1951; repr. New York: Liveright, 1971) 98, 102–3, 106, 116, 119–20.

ambuscade,' sings the seductive Countess in 'The Room in the Dragon Volant'; '. . . Burning sigh, or breath that freezes, | Numbs or maddens man or maid.' Laura is vulnerable because she is lonely, and dreams of a companion, perhaps a lover. To dream is dangerous in Le Fanu's world. Uncomfortable at Carmilla's embraces and ardour, Laura even imagines that she might be a man in disguise: 'What if a boyish lover had found his way into the house, and sought to prosecute his suit in masquerade?' (p. 265).

In 'The Circus Animals' Desertion' (1939), Yeats, remembering the themes of his early poems, calls them 'Themes of the embittered heart', especially 'The Wanderings of Oisin' (1889), 'starved for the bosom of his fairy bride . . . Heart mysteries there.' Le Fanu's wife Susanna, who died in 1858 at the age of 35, seems to have been the model for Maud Ruthyn in *Uncle Silas*, Laura, and his other lethargic protagonists. These women seem passive, without energy, half in love with easeful death. They are incapable of taking action to protect themselves—though Maud Ruthyn does rise to her final crisis. Susanna Le Fanu suffered from mysterious and probably psychosomatic illnesses, especially a nervous disorder which ended with her death during an attack of hysteria. She was morbidly afraid that anyone she loved would die, and had come to doubt both her husband's love for her and any religious promises of salvation.

In the weeks after her death, Le Fanu describes her in letters and a diary as 'so lowly in her thoughts of her spiritual state . . . so abject, so self-accusing, so prostrate in spirit . . . the idea of death was constantly present to her mind.'[22] In Le Fanu's description of her plight, we can recognize the mixture of fear and failure of nerve afflicting Mr Jennings and Captain Barton, the inability to act that grips Beckett in his coffin. We can particularly find a resemblance to Laura's mixture of fear and fatal attraction. Does Le Fanu represent his sense of his own guilt in Carmilla's mixture of sexual ardour and selfish

---

[22] McCormack, *Sheridan Le Fanu and Victorian Ireland*, 122–33. Not long before she died, she dreamed that her father, then dead two years, came smiling to her and said, ' "There is room in the vault for you, my little Sue." '

exploitation? Is he the 'boyish lover' in disguise, the blood-sucking and the suggestion of lesbianism masks for his own role as husband? To paraphrase Edgar Allan Poe, is this terror not of Styria, but of the soul?[23]

Victor Sage argues that the English horror story originates in Protestant doubt, and represents 'a form of "theological uncertainty", an anxiety which is recognizable at many different levels of consciousness.'[24] Le Fanu had witnessed his wife's anguished theological uncertainty, and turned, like Mr Jennings, to Swedenborg for possible relief. But 'Carmilla', which draws on Irish as well as Balkan superstitions, is not about theological anxiety. Le Fanu was creating myth, and myth often represents social anxieties.

In the threat that Carmilla poses to Laura, we can see a fear of female sexuality which reappears in *Dracula*. The tale also represents Le Fanu's anxiety about the future of his own class as Catholic Irish nationalists began to assume a dominant role, and reveal a new militancy. In the late 1860s his letters show an increasing fear of Catholic power; in 1868 he described Anglo-Ireland as resting upon 'a quaking bog'.[25] He was also anxious about money. The family fortune, never very large, did not recover from losses sustained during the Tithe Wars. He was worried about mortgages, which swallowed the income from the little land that was left, and even about his inability to pay the rent on his own Dublin house. These political, social, and financial anxieties—the latter connected with the loss of land and home—have some bearing on Carmilla and the threats she represents, as Le Fanu turns his anxieties into myth.

As *ban sí* and as member of the ancient family who once owned a great local estate, Carmilla is a native of the terrain she haunts. She is one of the ancient lords of the land, whose descendants, reduced to peasant/tenant status, often haunted

---

[23] In his preface to his *Tales of the Grotesque and Arabesque* (1840), Poe, remembering the popularity of German tales of terror, speaks of a 'terror . . . not of Germany, but of the soul'.

[24] Victor Sage, *Horror Fiction in the Protestant Tradition* (New York: St Martin's Press, 1988), p. xvii.

[25] McCormack, *Sheridan Le Fanu and Victorian Ireland*, 219–20.

the Anglo-Irish estates confiscated from their ancestors, which they considered rightfully their own. Carmilla threatens the new English landowners with death, with a kind of demonic possession, sexually with a kind of double miscegenation— basic fears among the Anglo-Irish gentry as they saw their control of Ireland slipping away. Though Le Fanu himself was not of the landed gentry, he had relatives who were. He tended to respect and defend the landowning class as Ireland's natural rulers; W. B. Yeats was to revere them as the natural arbiters and guardians of Ireland's culture. Carmilla will destroy these pleasant, well-meaning people, or enthrall them, or drive them away. In Ireland, as in the vampire legend's basic element, the past survives to torment the present.

In this context, the role of the antiquarian Baron Vordenburg is important. His 'curious lore' and knowledge of the past makes it possible for him to destroy the vampire and the threat she represents. Antiquarians are significant figures in Anglo-Irish fiction, beginning with the Prince and his daughter Glorvina in Lady Morgan's *The Wild Irish Girl* (1806) and Count O'Halloran in Maria Edgeworth's *The Absentee* (1812). These three, survivors of the old Irish Catholic gentry, study and preserve relics of the Irish past. Their role is to teach the Anglo-Irish to understand and respect that past. To do so is to legitimize the Anglo-Irish presence. By collecting folklore, or manuscripts, or studying the ruins of old churches and monasteries, the Anglo-Irish earn their membership in 'Ireland', restoring to the Irish their own lost past—a programme advocated, or embraced, with individual variations, by Sir Samuel Ferguson, Sir William Wilde, Douglas Hyde, Yeats, Synge, and Lady Gregory. In his 'Scraps of Hibernian Ballads', published in the *Dublin University Magazine* (June 1839), Le Fanu himself called his readers to 'the pleasurable and patriotic duty of collecting together the many, many specimens of genuine poetic feeling, which have sprung up, like its wild flowers, from the warm though neglected soil.' Baron Vordenburg, whose antiquarian lore saves Laura and destroys the vampire, hints at that commitment to Ireland and the Irish tradition which could help the Anglo-Irish to remain a vital force in Irish life.

But Le Fanu only half believes his happy ending. In a note to his poem 'The Host of the Air' (1893), Yeats tells us that falling 'into a half-dream' is characteristic of those who have been 'touched' by the *sí*. They 'grow indifferent to all things, for their true life has gone out of the world, and is among the hills and forts of the Sidhe.'[26] The lethargy, almost apathy of Laura, the 'touched' victim, seems a kind of death-wish. She is frightened and repelled, but she is also ready to yield—willing to die, the title of Le Fanu's last novel. A chorus in his verse drama *Beatrice* (1865) sings of 'Corruption that is beautiful, | And sadness that is splendid.'[27] Even after Carmilla has been exposed and destroyed, Laura thinks of her 'with ambiguous alternations' and sometimes hears, listens for, her 'light step'. In Laura's failure to resist we can perhaps discern Le Fanu's deepest anxieties about his own class, and his fear that the revenants of Irish history can never be laid to rest.

[26] *The Variorum Edition of the Poems of W. B. Yeats*, ed. Peter Allt and Russell K. Alspach (New York: Macmillan, 1957), 804.

[27] *The Poems of Joseph Sheridan Le Fanu*, ed. Alfred Perceval Graves (London: Downey and Co., 1896). 31.

A NOTE ON THE TEXT

THIS edition reprints the text of the first edition, published in London by R. Bentley and Son in 1872. However, punctuation and spelling have been revised to conform with modern usage. The first edition was in three volumes. Volume i contained 'Green Tea', 'The Familiar' and 'Mr Justice Harbottle'. Volume ii was the first twenty-three chapters of 'The Room in the Dragon Volant'. Volume iii contained the rest of that story, and 'Carmilla'.

In a Glass Darkly presents the five stories as cases collected by Dr Martin Hesselius, now edited and published by his literary executor. Hesselius appears as a character only in 'Green Tea'; otherwise he is simply a framing device to connect the stories and testify as to their sources. All of the stories appeared earlier in periodicals; information about these previous publications is given with the notes for each story. Apart from 'Green Tea', none of the stories were presented as from Hesselius's files when published in periodicals.

The 1872 text has been compared with the periodical texts of the stories, and corrected when necessary.

SELECT BIBLIOGRAPHY

THERE are facsimile first editions of virtually all Le Fanu's works, introduced by Devendra P. Varma (New York: Arno, 1977; 52 vols.). Most of his Irish fiction, also in facsimile, is included in the Garland reprint series 'Ireland from the Act of Union, 1800, to the Death of Parnell, 1891' (New York: Garland, 1979), with introductions by Robert Lee Wolff. There is a World's Classics edition of *Uncle Silas*, ed. W. J. McCormack, and several other Le Fanu novels are available in Dover reprints.

W. J. McCormack's excellent *Sheridan Le Fanu and Victorian Ireland* (Oxford 1980; 2nd edn. Dublin: Lilliput, 1990) is the only full biography. McCormack has discovered letters and documents, identified anonymous fictions as Le Fanu's, and placed Le Fanu in his Irish context. In addition, his bibliography supersedes earlier efforts to list all Le Fanu's work by M. R. James in *Madame Crowl's Ghost and Other Tales of Mystery* (London: Bell, 1923, 1925); S. M. Ellis in *Wilkie Collins, Le Fanu and Others* (London: Constable, 1931); and Michael Sadleir in *XIX Century Fiction* (London: Constable, 1951). W. R. Le Fanu, *Seventy Years of Irish Life* (London: Macmillan, 1894) supplies information about Le Fanu's youth and family background; there is extensive information about the family in T. P. Le Fanu, *Memoir of the Le Fanu Family* (privately printed, 1924). There are brief and useful biographical/critical studies by Nicholas Browne (London: Arthur Barker, 1951), Michael H. Begnal (Lewisburg, Pa.: Bucknell University Press 1971), and Ivan Melada (Boston: Twayne, 1987), all of which comment on *In a Glass Darkly*.

Though he is perceptively treated in Walter Allen's *The English Novel* (New York: Dutton, 1954), most English critics of the novel have ignored Le Fanu, or treated him as a sensationalist or an Irish regionalist. In two provocative essays, originally introductions to reprints of *Uncle Silas* (London: Cresset, 1947) and *The House by the Churchyard* (London: Anthony Blond, 1968), Elizabeth Bowen set out the case for considering Le Fanu primarily as an Irish writer; the first of these is available in Bowen's *The Mulberry Tree*, ed. Hermione Lee (London: Virago, 1986). In '*The House by the Churchyard*: James Joyce and Sheridan Le Fanu', Raymond Porter and James D. Brophy (eds.), *Modern Irish Literature: Essays in Honor of William York Tindall* (New Rochelle, NY: Iona College Press, 1972), Kevin Sullivan studies the reverberations of Le Fanu's novel in *Finnegans Wake*. There are brief comments about Le Fanu in Seamus Deane, *A Short History of Irish*

Literature (London: Hutchinson, 1986) and James M. Cahalan, *The Irish Novel* (Dublin: Gill and Macmillan, 1988).

M. R. James considers Le Fanu's contribution to the tale of terror in the prologue and epilogue to his edition of Le Fanu's *Madame Crowl's Ghost*. There are further discussions of Le Fanu in this context in Peter Penzoldt, *The Supernatural in Fiction* (New York: Humanities Press, 1952); Julia Briggs, *Night Visitors: The Rise and Fall of the English Ghost Story* (London: Faber, 1977); Jack Sullivan, *Elegant Nightmares: The English Ghost Story from Le Fanu to Blackwood* (Athens, Oh.: Ohio University Press, 1978); and Victor Sage, *Horror Fiction in the Protestant Tradition* (London: Macmillan, 1988). Several articles also survey Le Fanu's work in this category: Kevin Sullivan, 'Sheridan Le Fanu: *The Purcell Papers*, 1838–40', *Irish University Review*, 2 (1972); Jean Lozès, 'Joseph Sheridan Le Fanu: The Prince of the Invisible', Patrick Rafroidi and Terence Brown (eds.), *The Irish Short Story* (Gerrards Cross: Colin Smythe, 1979); Joseph Browne, 'Ghosts and Ghouls and Le Fanu', *Canadian Journal of Irish Studies*, 8 (1982); Jolanta Nałęcz-Wojtczak, 'Joseph Sheridan Le Fanu and New Dimensions for the English Ghost Story', Wolfgang Zach and Heinz Kosok (eds.), *Literary Interrelations: Ireland, England, and the World*, ii (Tübingen: Gunter Narr, 1987); and Patricia Coughlan, 'Doubles, Shadows, Sedan-Chairs and the Past: The "Ghost Stories" of J. S. Le Fanu', Michael Allen and Angela Wilcox (eds.), *Critical Approaches to Anglo-Irish Literature* (Gerrards Cross: Colin Smythe, 1989).

For discussions of *In a Glass Darkly* or the individual stories, see V. S. Pritchett, introduction to *In a Glass Darkly* (London: John Lehmann, 1947) and Pritchett's 'An Irish Ghost' in his *The Living Novel* (London, 1946). Neil Cornwell studies Doctor Hesselius in *The Literary Fantastic* (Hemel Hempstead: Harvester Wheatsheaf, 1990). Richard Dowling, 'The Only Real Ghost in Fiction', in his *Ignorant Essays* (1887), is perceptive about 'Green Tea', as is Barbara T. Gates, 'Blue Devils and Green Tea: Sheridan Le Fanu's Haunted Suicides', *Studies in Short Fiction*, 24 (1987). See also Ken Scott, 'Le Fanu's "The Room in The Dragon Volant"', *Lock Haven Review*, 10 (1968) and, for 'Carmilla', Arthur H. Nethercot, 'Coleridge's "Christabel " and Le Fanu's "Carmilla"', *Modern Philology*, 147 (1949); William Veeder, '"Carmilla": The Arts of Repression', *Texas Studies in Language and Literature*, 22 (1980); Ronald Foust, 'Rite of Passage: The Vampire Tale as Cosmogonic Myth', William Coyle (ed.), *Aspects of Fantasy* (Westport, Conn.: Greenwood Press, 1986); and Robert Tracy, 'Loving You All Ways: Vamps, Vampires, Necrophiles and Necrofilles in Nineteenth-Century Fiction', Regina Barreca (ed.), *Sex and Death in Victorian Literature* (London: Macmillan, 1990).

A CHRONOLOGY OF
SHERIDAN LE FANU'S LIFE

1814   28 August. Joseph Thomas Sheridan Le Fanu born 'at about half-past five o'clock AM' at 45 Lower Dominick Street, Dublin.

1815   With the appointment of his father as chaplain to the Royal Hibernian Military School, the family move to live in the Phoenix Park, west of the city.

1826   The family move to Abington, County Limerick.

1832   Entered the University of Dublin (Trinity College), primarily as a non-residential student.

1832–6   Persistent agrarian disturbances in County Limerick and elsewhere: Le Fanu's uncle, sister and brother gravely assaulted on separate occasions.

1838   (January) 'The Ghost and the Bone-setter', Le Fanu's first story, appears in the *Dublin University Magazine*: a further ten pieces are published before October 1840—these are posthumously collected as *The Purcell Papers*.

1838–*c*. 1841   Active in the Irish Metropolitan Conservative Association with Isaac Butt.

1840   Involved as proprietor and editor in various Dublin newspapers, notably the *Evening Mail* and the *Warder*.

1841   (March) Death of Catherine Le Fanu, his only sister.

1843   (March and April) Publishes 'Spalatro' in the *Dublin University Magazine*.

1843   (December) Marries Susanna Bennett, daughter of George Bennett, Q.C.

1845   *The Cock and Anchor*.

1847   Promised his support to John Mitchel and Thomas Francis Meagher in their attempts to unite Irish public opinion on the topic of Government's indifference to the Great Famine. Publishes *The Fortunes of Colonel Torlogh O'Brien*.

1848   (March) Mitchel prosecuted for sedition: (April, May, and June) Le Fanu publishes the three-part 'Richard Marston' in the *Dublin University Magazine*: (July) Rebellion in Ireland, led by William Smith O'Brien, M.P. for County Limerick.

1851   *Ghost Stories and Tales of Mystery.*

1852   Unsuccessful attempt to get Tory nomination for County Carlow.

1852   His wife's health increasingly affected by neurotic disturbance.

1856   Death of George Bennett.

1858   Death of Susanna Le Fanu (née Bennett), Le Fanu's wife.

1861   Acquires control of the *Dublin University Magazine*, despite personal financial difficulties: the bulk of his writing from this date appears in the *DUM*, including notably *The House by the Churchyard* (1861–3), *Wylder's Hand* (1864), *Uncle Silas* (1864), and a number of political articles (November 1865–September 1866)

1869   Sells the *DUM.*

1870   Publishes several stories utilizing Irish folklore material in Dickens's *All the Year Round.*

1872   *In a Glass Darkly.*

1873   10 February dies at 18 Merrion Square South, Dublin, formerly his father-in-law's home.

1873   *Willing to Die.*

1880   *The Purcell Papers,* ed. Alfred Perceval Graves.

1894   *The Watcher and Other Weird Stories.*

1923   *Madam Crowl's Ghost and Other Tales of Mystery,* ed. M. R. James.

IN A GLASS DARKLY

GREEN TEA

PROLOGUE

MARTIN HESSELIUS,* THE GERMAN PHYSICIAN

THOUGH carefully educated in medicine and surgery, I have never practised either. The study of each continues, nevertheless, to interest me profoundly. Neither idleness nor caprice caused my secession from the honourable calling which I had just entered. The cause was a very trifling scratch inflicted by a dissecting knife. This trifle cost me the loss of two fingers, amputated promptly, and the more painful loss of my health, for I have never been quite well since, and have seldom been twelve months together in the same place.

In my wanderings I became acquainted with Dr Martin Hesselius, a wanderer like myself, like me a physician, and like me an enthusiast in his profession. Unlike me in this, that his wanderings were voluntary, and he a man, if not of fortune, as we estimate fortune in England, at least in what our forefathers used to term 'easy circumstances'. He was an old man when I first saw him; nearly five-and-thirty years my senior.

In Dr Martin Hesselius, I found my master. His knowledge was immense, his grasp of a case was an intuition. He was the very man to inspire a young enthusiast, like me, with awe and delight. My admiration has stood the test of time and survived the separation of death. I am sure it was well founded.

For nearly twenty years I acted as his medical secretary. His immense collection of papers he has left in my care, to be arranged, indexed and bound. His treatment of some of these cases is curious. He writes in two distinct characters. He describes what he saw and heard as an intelligent layman might, and when in this style of narrative he had seen the patient either through his own hall-door, to the light of day, or through the gates of darkness to the caverns of the dead, he returns upon the narrative, and in the terms of his art, and with all the force and originality of genius, proceeds to the work of analysis, diagnosis and illustration.

Here and there a case strikes me as of a kind to amuse or horrify a lay reader with an interest quite different from the peculiar one which it may possess for an expert. With slight modifications, chiefly of language, and of course a change of names, I copy the following. The narrator is Dr Martin Hesselius. I find it among the voluminous notes of cases which he made during a tour of England about sixty-four years ago.

It is related in a series of letters to his friend Professor Van Loo of Leyden.* The professor was not a physician, but a chemist, and a man who read history and metaphysics and medicine, and had, in his day, written a play.

The narrative is therefore, if somewhat less valuable as a medical record, necessarily written in a manner more likely to interest an unlearned reader.

These letters, from a memorandum attached, appear to have been returned on the death of the professor, in 1819, to Dr Hesselius. They are written, some in English, some in French, but the greater part in German. I am a faithful, though I am conscious, by no means a graceful translator, and although here and there, I omit some passages, and shorten others and disguise names, I have interpolated nothing.

CHAPTER I

DR HESSELIUS RELATES HOW HE MET THE REV.
MR JENNINGS

The Rev. Mr Jennings is tall and thin. He is middle-aged, and dresses with a natty, old-fashioned, high-church* precision. He is naturally a little stately, but not at all stiff. His features, without being handsome, are well-formed, and their expression extremely kind, but also shy.

I met him one evening at Lady Mary Heyduke's.* The modesty and benevolence of his countenance are extremely prepossessing.

We were but a small party, and he joined agreeably enough in the conversation. He seems to enjoy listening very much more than contributing to the talk; but what he says is always to the purpose and well said. He is a great favourite of Lady Mary's, who it seems, consults him upon many things, and thinks him the most happy and blessed person on earth. Little knows she about him.

The Rev. Mr Jennings is a bachelor, and has, they say, sixty thousand pounds in the funds.* He is a charitable man. He is most anxious to be actively employed in his sacred profession, and yet though always tolerably well elsewhere, when he goes down to his vicarage in Warwickshire, to engage in the actual duties of his sacred calling, his health soon fails him, and in a very strange way. So says Lady Mary.

There is no doubt that Mr Jennings's health does break down in, generally, a sudden and mysterious way, sometimes in the very act of officiating in his old and pretty church at Kenlis.* It may be his heart, it may be his brain. But so it has happened three or four times, or oftener, that after proceeding a certain way in the service, he has on a sudden stopped short, and after a silence, apparently quite unable to resume, he has fallen into solitary, inaudible prayer, his hands and eyes uplifted, and then pale as death, and in the agitation of a strange shame and horror, descended trembling, and got into the vestry-room,* leaving his congregation, without explanation, to themselves. This occurred when his curate was absent. When he goes down to Kenlis, now, he always takes care to provide a clergyman to share his duty, and to supply his place on the instant should he become thus suddenly incapacitated.

When Mr Jennings breaks down quite, and beats a retreat from the vicarage, and returns to London, where, in a dark street off Piccadilly, he inhabits a very narrow house, Lady Mary says that he is always perfectly well. I have my own opinion about that. There are degrees of course. We shall see.

Mr Jennings is a perfectly gentleman-like man. People, however, remark something odd. There is an impression a little ambiguous. One thing which certainly contributes to it, people I think don't remember; or, perhaps, distinctly remark. But I did, almost immediately. Mr Jennings has a way of looking sidelong upon the carpet, as if his eye followed the movements of something there. This, of course, is not always. It occurs only now and then. But often enough to give a certain oddity, as I have said, to his manner, and in this glance travelling along the floor there is something both shy and anxious.

A medical philosopher, as you are good enough to call me, elaborating theories by the aid of cases sought out by himself, and by him watched and scrutinized with more time at command, and consequently infinitely more minuteness than the ordinary practitioner can afford, falls insensibly into habits of observation, which accompany him everywhere, and are exercised, as some people would say, impertinently, upon every subject that presents itself with the least likelihood of rewarding inquiry.

There was a promise of this kind in the slight, timid, kindly, but reserved gentleman, whom I met for the first time at this agreeable little evening gathering. I observed, of course, more than I here set down; but I reserve all that borders on the technical for a strictly scientific paper.

I may remark, that when I here speak of medical science, I do so, as I hope some day to see it more generally understood, in a much more comprehensive sense than its generally material treatment would warrant. I believe the entire natural world is but the ultimate expression of that spiritual world from which, and in which alone, it has its life. I believe that the essential man is a spirit, that the spirit is an organized substance, but as different in point of material from what we ordinarily understand by matter, as light or electricity is; that the material body is, in the most literal sense, a vesture, and death consequently no interruption of the living man's existence, but simply his extrication from the natural body—a process which commences at the moment of what we term death, and the completion of which, at furthest a few days later, is the resurrection 'in power'.

The person who weighs the consequences of these positions will probably see their practical bearing upon medical science. This is, however, by no means the proper place for displaying the proofs and discussing the consequences of this too generally unrecognized state of facts.

In pursuance of my habit, I was covertly observing Mr Jennings, with all my caution—I think he perceived it—and I saw plainly that he was as cautiously observing me. Lady Mary happening to address me by my name, as Dr Hesselius, I saw that he glanced at me more sharply, and then became thoughtful for a few minutes.

After this, as I conversed with a gentleman at the other end of the room, I saw him look at me more steadily, and with an interest which I thought I understood. I then saw him take an opportunity of chatting with Lady Mary, and was, as one always is, perfectly aware of being the subject of a distant inquiry and answer.

This tall clergyman approached me by-and-by: and in a little time we had got into conversation. When two people, who like reading, and know books and places, having travelled, wish to converse, it is very strange if they can't find topics. It was not accident that brought him near me, and led him into conversation. He knew German, and had read my *Essays on Metaphysical Medicine* which suggest more than they actually say.

This courteous man, gentle, shy, plainly a man of thought and reading, who moving and talking among us, was not altogether of us, and whom I already suspected of leading a life whose transactions and alarms were carefully concealed, with an impenetrable reserve from, not only the world, but his best-beloved friends—was cautiously weighing in his own mind the idea of taking a certain step with regard to me.

I penetrated his thoughts without his being aware of it, and was careful to say nothing which could betray to his sensitive vigilance my suspicions respecting his position, or my surmises about his plans respecting myself.

We chatted upon indifferent subjects for a time; but at last he said:

'I was very much interested by some papers of yours, Dr Hesselius, upon what you term Metaphysical Medicine—I read them in German, ten or twelve years ago—have they been translated?'

'No, I'm sure they have not—I should have heard. They would have asked my leave, I think.'

'I asked the publishers here, a few months ago, to get the book for me in the original German; but they tell me it is out of print.'

'So it is, and has been for some years; but it flatters me as an author to find that you have not forgotten my little book, although', I added, laughing, 'ten or twelve years is a considerable time to have managed without it; but I suppose you have been turning the subject over again in your mind, or something has happened lately to revive your interest in it.'

At this remark, accompanied by a glance of inquiry, a sudden embarrassment disturbed Mr Jennings, analogous to that which makes a young lady blush and look foolish. He dropped his eyes, and folded his hands together uneasily, and looked oddly, and you would have said, guiltily for a moment.

I helped him out of his awkwardness in the best way, by appearing not to observe it, and going straight on, I said: 'Those revivals of interest in a subject happen to me often; one book suggests another, and often sends me back a wild-goose chase over an interval of twenty years. But if you still care to possess a copy, I shall be only too happy to provide you; I have still got two or three by me—and if you allow me to present one I shall be very much honoured.'

'You are very good indeed,' he said, quite at his ease again, in a moment: 'I almost despaired—I don't know how to thank you.'

'Pray don't say a word; the thing is really so little worth that I am only ashamed of having offered it, and if you thank me any more I shall throw it into the fire in a fit of modesty.'

Mr Jennings laughed. He inquired where I was staying in London, and after a little more conversation on a variety of subjects, he took his departure.

CHAPTER II

THE DOCTOR QUESTIONS LADY MARY, AND
SHE ANSWERS

'I like your vicar* so much, Lady Mary,' said I, so soon as he was gone. 'He has read, travelled, and thought, and having also suffered, he ought to be an accomplished companion.'

'So he is, and, better still, he is a really good man,' said she. 'His advice is invaluable about my schools, and all my little undertakings at Dawlbridge,* and he's so painstaking, he takes so much trouble—you have no idea—wherever he thinks he can be of use: he's so good-natured and so sensible.'

'It is pleasant to hear so good an account of his neighbourly virtues. I can only testify to his being an agreeable and gentle companion, and in addition to what you have told me, I think I can tell you two or three things about him,' said I.

'Really!'

'Yes, to begin with, he's unmarried.'

'Yes, that's right—go on.'

'He has been writing, that is he *was*, but for two or three years perhaps, he has not gone on with his work, and the book was upon some rather abstract subject—perhaps theology.'

'Well, he was writing a book, as you say; I'm not quite sure what it was about, but only that it was nothing that I cared for, very likely you are right, and he certainly did stop—yes.'

'And although he only drank a little coffee here to-night, he likes tea, at least, did like it, extravagantly.'

'Yes, that's *quite* true.'

'He drank green tea,* a good deal, didn't he?' I pursued.

'Well, that's very odd! Green tea was a subject on which we used almost to quarrel.'

'But he has quite given that up,' said I.

'So he has.'

'And, now, one more fact. His mother or his father, did you know them?'

'Yes, both; his father is only ten years dead, and their place is near Dawlbridge. We knew them very well,' she answered.

'Well, either his mother or his father—I should rather think his father, saw a ghost,' said I.

'Well, you really are a conjurer, Dr Hesselius.'

'Conjurer or no, haven't I said right?' I answered merrily.

'You certainly have, and it *was* his father: he was a silent, whimsical man, and he used to bore my father about his dreams, and at last he told him a story about a ghost he had seen and talked with, and a very odd story it was. I remember it particularly, because I was so afraid of him. This story was long before he died—when I was quite a child—and his ways were so silent and moping, and he used to drop in, sometimes, in the dusk, when I was alone in the drawing-room, and I used to fancy there were ghosts about him.'

I smiled and nodded.

'And now having established my character as a conjurer I think I must say good-night,' said I.

'But how *did* you find it out?'

'By the planets of course, as the gipsies do,' I answered, and so, gaily, we said good-night.

Next morning I sent the little book he had been inquiring after, and a note to Mr Jennings, and on returning late that evening, I found that he had called, at my lodgings, and left his card. He asked whether I was at home, and asked at what hour he would be most likely to find me.

Does he intend opening his case, and consulting me 'profesionally', as they say? I hope so. I have already conceived a theory about him. It is supported by Lady Mary's answers to my parting questions. I should like much to ascertain from his own lips. But what can I do consistently with good breeding to invite a confession? Nothing. I rather think he meditates one. At all events, my dear Van L., I shan't make myself difficult of access; I mean to return his visit to-morrow. It will be only civil in return for his politeness, to ask to see him. Perhaps something may come of it. Whether much, little, or nothing, my dear Van L., you shall hear.

CHAPTER III

Well, I have called at Blank Street.

On inquiring at the door, the servant told me that Mr Jennings was engaged very particularly with a gentleman, a clergyman from Kenlis, his parish in the country. Intending to reserve my privilege and to call again, I merely intimated that I should try another time, and had turned to go, when the servant begged my pardon, and asked me, looking at me a little more attentively than well-bred persons of his order usually do, whether I was Dr Hesselius; and, on learning that I was, he said, 'Perhaps then, sir, you would allow me to mention it to Mr Jennings, for I am sure he wishes to see you.'

The servant returned in a moment, with a message from Mr Jennings, asking me to go into his study, which was in effect his back drawing-room, promising to be with me in a very few minutes.

This was really a study—almost a library. The room was lofty, with two tall slender windows, and rich dark curtains. It was much larger than I had expected, and stored with books on every side, from the floor to the ceiling. The upper carpet—for to my tread it felt that there were two or three—was a Turkey carpet.* My steps fell noiselessly. The book-cases standing out, placed the windows, particularly narrow ones, in deep recesses. The effect of the room was, although extremely comfortable, and even luxurious, decidedly gloomy, and aided by the silence, almost oppressive. Perhaps, however, I ought to have allowed something for association. My mind had connected peculiar ideas with Mr Jennings. I stepped into this perfectly silent room, of a very silent house, with a peculiar foreboding; and its darkness, and solemn clothing of books, for except where two narrow looking-glasses were set in the wall, they were everywhere, helped this sombre feeling.

While awaiting Mr Jennings's arrival, I amused myself by looking into some of the books with which his shelves were laden. Not among these, but immediately under them, with their backs upward, on the floor, I lighted upon a complete set of Swedenborg's Arcana Caelestia,* in the original Latin, a very fine folio set, bound in the natty livery which theology affects, pure vellum, namely, gold letters, and carmine edges. There were paper markers in several of these volumes. I raised and placed them, one after the other, upon the table, and opening where these papers were placed, I read in the solemn Latin phraseology, a series of sentences indicated by a pencilled line at the margin. Of these I copy here a few, translating them into English.

'When man's interior sight is opened, which is that of his spirit, then there appear the things of another life, which cannot possibly be made visible to the bodily sight.'

'By the internal sight it has been granted me to see things that are in the other life, more clearly than I see those that are in the world. From these considerations, it is evident that external vision exists from interior vision, and this from a vision still more interior, and so on.'*

'There are with every man at least two evil spirits.'*

'With wicked genii there is also a fluent speech, but harsh and grating. There is also among them a speech which is not fluent, wherein the dissent of the thoughts is perceived as something secretly creeping along within it.'

'The evil spirits associated with man are, indeed, from the hells, but when with man they are not then in hell, but are taken out thence. The place where they then are is in the midst between heaven and hell, and is called the world of spirits—when the evil spirits who are with man, are in that world, they are not in any infernal torment, but in every thought and affection of the man, and so, in all that the man himself enjoys. But when they are remitted into their hell, they return to the former state.'

'If evil spirits could perceive that they were associated with man, and yet that they were spirits separate from him, and if they could flow in into the things of his body, they would attempt by a thousand means to destroy him; for they hate man with a deadly hatred.'

'Knowing, therefore, that I was a man in the body, they were continually striving to destroy me, not as to the body only, but especially as to the soul; for to destroy any man or spirit is the very delight of the life of all who are in hell; but I have been continually protected by the Lord. Hence it appears how dangerous it is for man to be in a living consort with spirits, unless he be in the good of faith.'

'Nothing is more carefully guarded from the knowledge of associate spirits than their being thus conjoint with a man, for if they knew it they would speak to him, with the intention to destroy him.'

'The delight of hell is to do evil to man, and to hasten his eternal ruin.'*

A long note, written with a very sharp and fine pencil, in Mr Jennings's neat hand, at the foot of the page, caught my eye. Expecting his criticism upon the text, I read a word or two, and stopped, for it was something quite different, and began with these words, *Deus miseraeatur mei*—'May God compassionate me'. Thus warned of its private nature, I averted my eyes, and shut the book, replacing all the volumes as I had found them, except one which interested me, and in which, as men studious and solitary in their habits will do, I grew so absorbed as to take no cognisance of the outer world, nor to remember where I was.

I was reading some pages which refer to 'representatives' and 'correspondents', in the technical language of Swedenborg, and had arrived at a passage, the substance of which is, that evil spirits, when seen by other eyes than those of their infernal associates, present themselves, by 'correspondence', in the shape of the beast (fera) which represents their particular lust and life, in aspect direful and atrocious. This is a long passage, and particularizes a number of those bestial forms.*

I was running the head of my pencil-case along the line as I read it, and something caused me to raise my eyes.

Directly before me was one of the mirrors I have mentioned, in which I saw reflected the tall shape of my friend Mr Jennings leaning over my shoulder, and reading the page at which I was busy, and with a face so dark and wild that I should hardly have known him.

I turned and rose. He stood erect also, and with an effort laughed a little, saying:

'I came in and asked you how you did, but without succeeding in awaking you from your book; so I could not restrain my curiosity, and very impertinently, I'm afraid, peeped over your shoulder. This is not your first time of looking into those pages. You have looked into Swedenborg, no doubt, long ago?'

'O dear, yes! I owe Swedenborg a great deal; you will discover traces of him in the little book on Metaphysical Medicine, which you were so good as to remember.'

Although my friend affected a gaiety of manner, there was a slight flush in his face, and I could perceive that he was inwardly much perturbed.

'I'm scarcely yet qualified, I know so little of Swedenborg. I've only had them a fortnight,' he answered, 'and I think they are rather likely to make a solitary man nervous—that is, judging from the very little I have read—I don't say that they have made me so,' he laughed; 'and I'm so very much obliged for the book. I hope you got my note?'

I made all proper acknowledgments and modest disclaimers.

'I never read a book that I go with, so entirely, as that of yours,' he continued. 'I saw at once there is more in it than is quite unfolded. Do you know Dr Harley?'* he asked, rather abruptly.

In passing, the editor remarks that the physician here

named was one of the most eminent who had ever practised in England.

I did, having had letters to him, and had experienced from him great courtesy and considerable assistance during my visit to England.

'I think that man one of the very greatest fools I ever met in my life,' said Mr Jennings.

This was the first time I had ever heard him say a sharp thing of anybody, and such a term applied to so high a name a little startled me.

'Really! and in what way?' I asked.

'In his profession,' he answered.

I smiled.

'I mean this,' he said: 'he seems to me, one half, blind—I mean one half of all he looks at is dark—preternaturally bright and vivid all the rest; and the worst of it is, it seems *wilful*. I can't get him—I mean he won't—I've had some experience of him as a physician, but I look on him as, in that sense, no better than a paralytic mind, an intellect half dead, I'll tell you—I know I shall some time—all about it,' he said, with a little agitation. 'You stay some months longer in England. If I should be out of town during your stay for a little time, would you allow me to trouble you with a letter?'

'I should be only too happy,' I assured him.

'Very good of you. I am so utterly dissatisfied with Harley.'

'A little leaning to the materialistic school,' I said.

'A *mere* materialist,' he corrected me; 'you can't think how that sort of thing worries one who knows better. You won't tell any one—any of my friends you know—that I am hippish;* now, for instance, no one knows—not even Lady Mary—that I have seen Dr Harley, or any other doctor. So pray don't mention it; and, if I should have any threatening of an attack, you'll kindly let me write, or, should I be in town, have a talk with you.'

I was full of conjecture, and unconsciously I found I had fixed my eyes gravely on him, for he lowered his for a moment, and he said:

'I see you think I might as well tell you now, or else you are forming a conjecture; but you may as well give it up. If you were guessing all the rest of your life, you will never hit on it.'

He shook his head smiling, and over that wintry sunshine a black cloud suddenly came down, and he drew his breath in, through his teeth as men do in pain.

'Sorry, of course, to learn that you apprehend occasion to consult any of us; but, command me when and how you like, and I need not assure you that your confidence is sacred.'

He then talked of quite other things, and in a comparatively cheerful way and after a little time, I took my leave.

CHAPTER V

DR HESSELIUS IS SUMMONED TO RICHMOND

We parted cheerfully, but he was not cheerful, nor was I. There are certain expressions of that powerful organ of spirit— the human face—which, although I have seen them often, and possess a doctor's nerve, yet disturb me profoundly. One look of Mr Jennings haunted me. It had seized my imagination with so dismal a power that I changed my plans for the evening, and went to the opera, feeling that I wanted a change of ideas.

I heard nothing of or from him for two or three days, when a note in his hand reached me. It was cheerful, and full of hope. He said that he had been for some little time so much better—quite well, in fact—that he was going to make a little experiment, and run down for a month or so to his parish, to try whether a little work might not quite set him up. There was in it a fervent religious expression of gratitude for his restoration, as he now almost hoped he might call it.

A day or two later I saw Lady Mary, who repeated what his note had announced, and told me that he was actually in Warwickshire, having resumed his clerical duties at Kenlis; and she added, 'I begin to think that he is really perfectly well, and that there never was anything the matter, more than nerves and fancy; we are all nervous, but I fancy there is nothing like a little hard work for that kind of weakness, and he has made up his mind to try it. I should not be surprised if he did not come back for a year.'

Notwithstanding all this confidence, only two days later I had this note, dated from his house off Piccadilly:

'Dear Sir.—I have returned disappointed. If I should feel at all able to see you, I shall write to ask you kindly to call. At present I am too low, and, in fact, simply unable to say all I wish to say. Pray don't mention my name to my friends. I can see no one. By-and-by, please God, you shall hear from me. I mean to take a run into Shropshire, where some of my people* are. God bless you! May we, on my return, meet more happily than I can now write.'

About a week after this I saw Lady Mary at her own house, the last person, she said, left in town, and just on the wing for Brighton, for the London season* was quite over. She told me that she had heard from Mr Jennings's niece, Martha, in Shropshire. There was nothing to be gathered from her letter, more than that he was low and nervous. In those words, of which healthy people think so lightly, what a world of suffering is sometimes hidden!

Nearly five weeks passed without any further news of Mr Jennings. At the end of that time I received a note from him. He wrote:

'I have been in the country, and have had change of air, change of scene, change of faces, change of everything and in everything—but *myself*. I have made up my mind, so far as the most irresolute creature on each can do it, to tell my case fully to you. If your engagements will permit, pray come to me to-day, to-morrow, or the next day; but, pray defer as little as possible. You know not how much I need help. I have a quiet house at Richmond,* where I now am. Perhaps you can manage to come to dinner, or to luncheon, or even to tea. You shall have no trouble in finding me out. The servant at Blank Street, who takes this note, will have a carriage at your door at any hour you please; and I am always to be found. You will say that I ought not to be alone. I have tried everything. Come and see.'

I called up the servant, and decided on going out the same evening, which accordingly I did.

He would have been much better in a lodging-house, or hotel, I thought, as I drove up through a short double row of sombre elms to a very old-fashioned brick house, darkened by the foliage of these trees, which over-topped, and nearly surrounded it. It was a perverse choice, for nothing could be imagined more triste and silent. The house, I found, belonged to him. He had stayed for a day or two in town, and, finding it for some cause insupportable, had come out here, probably because being furnished and his own, he was relieved of the thought and delay of selection, by coming here.

The sun had already set, and the red reflected light of the western sky illuminated the scene with the peculiar effect with which we are all familiar. The hall seemed very dark, but, getting to the back drawing-room, whose windows command the west, I was again in the same dusky light.

I sat down, looking out upon the richly-wooded landscape that glowed in the grand and melancholy light which was every moment fading. The corners of the room were already dark; all was growing dim, and the gloom was insensibly toning my mind, already prepared for what was sinister. I was waiting alone for his arrival, which soon took place. The door communicating with the front room opened, and the tall figure of Mr Jennings, faintly seen in the ruddy twilight, came, with quiet stealthy steps, into the room.

We shook hands, and, taking a chair to the window, where there was still light enough to enable us to see each other's faces, he sat down beside me, and, placing his hand upon my arm, with scarcely word of preface began his narrative.

CHAPTER VI

HOW MR JENNINGS MET HIS COMPANION

The faint glow of the west, the pomp of the then lonely woods of Richmond, were before us, behind and about us the darkening room, and on the stony face of the sufferer—for the character of his face, though still gentle and sweet, was changed—rested that dim, odd glow which seems to descend and produce, where it touches, lights, sudden though faint, which are lost, almost without gradation, in darkness. The silence, too, was utter; not a distant wheel, or bark, or whistle from without; and within the depressing stillness of an invalid bachelor's house.

I guessed well the nature, though not even vaguely the particulars of the revelations I was about to receive, from the fixed face of suffering that so oddly flushed stood out, like a portrait of Schalken's,* before its background of darkness.

'It began', he said, 'on the 15th of October, three years and eleven weeks ago, and two days—I keep very accurate count, for every day is torment. If I leave anywhere a chasm in my narrative tell me.

'About four years ago I began a work, which had cost me very much thought and reading. It was upon the religious metaphysics of the ancients.'

'I know,' said I; 'the actual religion of educated and thinking paganism, quite apart from symbolic worship? A wide and very interesting field.'

'Yes; but not good for the mind—the Christian mind, I mean. Paganism is all bound together in essential unity, and, with evil sympathy, their religion involves their art, and both their manners, and the subject is a degrading fascination and the nemesis* sure. God forgive me!

'I wrote a great deal; I wrote late at night. I was always thinking on the subject, walking about, wherever I was, everywhere. It thoroughly infected me. You are to remember that all the material ideas connected with it were more or less of the beautiful, the subject itself delightfully interesting, and I, then, without a care.'

He sighed heavily.

'I believe that every one who sets about writing in earnest does his work, as a friend of mine phrased it, *on* something— tea, or coffee, or tobacco. I suppose there is a material waste that must be hourly supplied in such occupations, or that we should grow too abstracted, and the mind, as it were, pass out of the body, unless it were reminded often of the connection by actual sensation. At all events, I felt the want, and I supplied it. Tea was my companion—at first the ordinary black tea, made in the usual way, not too strong: but I drank a good deal, and increased its strength as I went on. I never experienced an uncomfortable symptom from it. I began to take a little green tea. I found the effect pleasanter, it cleared and intensified the power of thought so. I had come to take it frequently, but not stronger than one might take it for pleasure. I wrote a great deal out here, it was so quiet, and in this room. I used to sit up very late, and it became a habit with me to sip my tea—green tea—every now and then as my work proceeded. I had a little kettle on my table, that swung over a lamp, and made tea two or three times between eleven o'clock and two or three in the morning, my hours of going to bed. I used to go into town every day. I was not a monk, and, although I spent an hour or two in a library, hunting up authorities and looking out lights upon my theme, I was in no morbid state as far as I can judge. I met my friends pretty much as usual, and enjoyed their society, and, on the whole, existence had never been, I think, so pleasant before.

'I had met with a man who had some odd old books, German editions in medieval Latin, and I was only too happy to be permitted access to them. This obliging person's books were in the City,* a very out-of-the-way part of it. I had rather out-stayed my intended hour, and, on coming out, seeing no cab near, I was tempted to get into the omnibus which used to drive past this house. It was darker than this by the time the 'bus had reached an old house, you may have remarked, with four poplars at each side of the door, and there the last passenger but myself got out. We drove along rather faster. It was twilight now. I leaned back in my corner next the door ruminating pleasantly.

'The interior of the omnibus was nearly dark. I had observed in the corner opposite to me at the other side, and at the end next the horses, two small circular reflections, as it seemed to me of a reddish light. They were about two inches apart, and about the size of those small brass buttons that yachting men used to put upon their jackets. I began to speculate, as listless men will, upon this trifle, as it seemed. From what centre did that faint but deep red light come, and from what—glass beads, buttons, toy decorations—was it reflected? We were lumbering along gently, having nearly a mile still to go. I had not solved the puzzle, and it became in another minute more odd, for these two luminous points, with a sudden jerk, descended nearer the floor, keeping still their relative distance and horizontal position, and then, as suddenly, they rose to the level of the seat on which I was sitting, and I saw them no more.

'My curiosity was now really excited, and, before I had time to think, I saw again these two dull lamps, again together near the floor; again they disappeared, and again in their old corner I saw them.

'So, keeping my eyes upon them, I edged quietly up my own side, towards the end at which I still saw these tiny discs of red.

'There was very little light in the 'bus. It was nearly dark. I leaned forward to aid my endeavour to discover what these little circles really were. They shifted their position a little as I did so. I began now to perceive an outline of something black, and I soon saw with tolerable distinctness the outline of a small black monkey, pushing its face forward in mimicry to meet mine; those were its eyes, and I now dimly saw its teeth grinning at me.

'I drew back, not knowing whether it might not meditate a spring. I fancied that one of the passengers had forgot this ugly pet, and wishing to ascertain something of its temper, though not caring to trust my fingers to it, I poked my umbrella softly towards it. It remained immovable—up to it—

through it! For through it, and back and forward, it passed, without the slightest resistance.

'I can't, in the least, convey to you the kind of horror that I felt. When I had ascertained that the thing was an illusion, as I then supposed, there came a misgiving about myself and a terror that fascinated me in impotence to remove my gaze from the eyes of the brute for some moments. As I looked, it made a little skip back, quite into the corner, and I, in a panic, found myself at the door, having put my head out, drawing deep breaths of the outer air, and staring at the lights and trees we were passing, too glad to reassure myself of reality.

'I stopped the 'bus and got out. I perceived the man look oddly at me as I paid him. I daresay there was something unusual in my looks and manner, for I had never felt so strangely before.'

CHAPTER VII

THE JOURNEY: FIRST STAGE

'When the omnibus drove on, and I was alone upon the road, I looked carefully round to ascertain whether the monkey had followed me. To my indescribable relief I saw it nowhere. I can't describe easily what a shock I had received, and my sense of genuine gratitude on finding myself, as I supposed, quite rid of it.

'I had got out a little before we reached this house, two or three hundred steps. A brick wall runs along the footpath, and inside the wall is a hedge of yew or some dark evergreen of that kind, and within that again the row of fine trees which you may have remarked as you came.

'This brick wall is about as high as my shoulder, and happening to raise my eyes I saw the monkey, with that stooping gait, on all fours, walking or creeping, close beside me on top of the wall. I stopped looking at it with a feeling of loathing and horror. As I stopped so did it. It sat up on the wall with its long hands on its knees looking at me. There was not light enough to see it much more than in outline, nor was it dark enough to bring the peculiar light of its eyes into stronger relief. I still saw, however, that red foggy light plainly enough. It did not show its teeth, nor exhibit any sign of irritation, but seemed jaded and sulky, and was observing me steadily.

'I drew back into the middle of the road. It was an unconscious recoil, and there I stood, still looking at it. It did not move.

'With an instinctive determination to try something—anything, I turned about and walked briskly towards town with a skance* look, all the time, watching the movements of the beast. It crept swiftly along the wall, at exactly my pace.

'Where the wall ends, near the turn of the road, it came down and with a wiry spring or two brought itself close to my feet, and continued to keep up with me, as I quickened my pace. It was at my left side, so close to my leg that I felt every moment as if I should tread upon it.

'The road was quite deserted and silent, and it was darker every moment. I stopped dismayed and bewildered, turning as I did so, the other way—I mean, towards this house, away from which I had been walking. When I stood still, the monkey drew back to a distance of, I suppose, about five or six yards, and remained stationary, watching me.

'I had been more agitated than I have said. I had read, of course, as every one has, something about "spectral illusions", as you physicians term the phenomena of such cases. I considered my situation, and looked my misfortune in the face.

'These affections, I had read, are sometimes transitory and sometimes obstinate. I had read of cases in which the appearance, at first harmless, had, step by step, degenerated into something direful and insupportable, and ended by wearing its victim out. Still, as I stood there, but for my bestial companion, quite alone, I tried to comfort myself by repeating again and again the assurance, "the thing is purely disease, a well-known physical affection, as distinctly as small-pox or neuralgia. Doctors are all agreed on that, philosophy demonstrates it. I must not be a fool. I've been sitting up too late, and I daresay my digestion is quite wrong, and with God's help, I shall be all right, and this is but a symptom of nervous dyspepsia." Did I believe all this? Not one word of it, no more than any other miserable being ever did who is once seized and riveted in this satanic captivity. Against my convictions, I might say my knowledge, I was simply bullying myself into a false courage.

'I now walked homeward. I had only a few hundred yards to go. I had forced myself into a sort of resignation, but I had not got over the sickening shock and the flurry of the first certainty of my misfortune.

'I made up my mind to pass the night at home. The brute moved close beside me, and I fancied there was the sort of anxious drawing toward the house, which one sees in tired horses or dogs, sometimes as they come toward home.

'I was afraid to go into town, I was afraid of any one's seeing and recognizing me. I was conscious of an irrepressible agitation in my manner. Also, I was afraid of any violent change in my habits, such as going to a place of amusement, or walking from home in order to fatigue myself. At the hall door it waited till I mounted the steps, and when the door was opened entered with me.

'I drank no tea that night. I got cigars and some brandy-and-water. My idea was that I should act upon my material system, and by living for a while in sensation apart from thought, send myself forcibly, as it it were, into a new groove. I came up here to this drawing-room. I sat just here. The monkey then got upon a small table that then stood *there*. It looked dazed and languid. An irrepressible uneasiness as to its movements kept my eyes always upon it. Its eyes were half closed, but I could see them glow. It was looking steadily at me. In all situations, at all hours, it is awake and looking at me. That never changes.

'I shall not continue in detail my narrative of this particular night. I shall describe, rather, the phenomena of the first year, which never varied, essentially. I shall describe the monkey as it appeared in daylight. In the dark, as you shall presently hear, there are peculiarities. It is a small monkey, perfectly black. It had only one peculiarity—a character of malignity— unfathomable malignity. During the first year it looked sullen and sick. But this character of intense malice and vigilance was always underlying that surly languor. During all that time it acted as if on a plan of giving me as little trouble as was consistent with watching me. Its eyes were never off me. I have never lost sight of it, except in my sleep, light or dark, day or night, since it came here, excepting when it withdraws for some weeks at a time, unaccountably.

'In total dark it is visible as in daylight. I do not mean merely its eyes. It is *all* visible distinctly in a halo that resembles a glow of red embers, and which accompanies it in all its movements.

'When it leaves me for a time, it is always at night, in the dark, and in the same way. It grows at first uneasy, and then furious, and then advances towards me, grinning and shaking, its paws clenched, and, at the same time, there comes the appearance of fire in the grate. I never have any fire. I can't sleep in the room where there is any, and it draws nearer and nearer to the chimney, quivering, it seems, with rage, and when its fury rises to the highest pitch, it springs into the grate, and up the chimney, and I see it no more.

'When first this happened I thought I was released. I was a new man. A day passed—a night—and no return, and a blessed week—a week—another week. I was always on my knees, Dr Hesselius, always, thanking God and praying. A whole month passed of liberty, but on a sudden, it was with me again.'

CHAPTER VIII

THE SECOND STAGE

'It was with me, and the malice which before was torpid under a sullen exterior, was now active. It was perfectly unchanged in every other respect. This new energy was apparent in its activity and its looks, and soon in other ways.

'For a time, you will understand, the change was shown only in an increased vivacity, and an air of menace, as if it was always brooding over some atrocious plan. Its eyes, as before, were never off me.'

'Is it here now?' I asked.

'No,' he replied, 'it has been absent exactly a fortnight and a day—fifteen days. It has sometimes been away so long as nearly two months, once for three. Its absence always exceeds a fortnight, although it may be out by a single day. Fifteen days having past since I saw it last, it may return now at any moment.'

'Is its return', I asked, 'accompanied by any peculiar manifestation?'

'Nothing—no,' he said. 'It is simply with me again. On lifting my eyes from a book, or turning my head, I see it, as usual, looking at me, and then it remains, as before, for its appointed time. I have never told so much and so minutely before to any one.'

I perceived that he was agitated, and looking like death, and he repeatedly applied his handkerchief to his forehead; I suggested that he might be tired, and told him that I would call, with pleasure, in the morning, but he said:

'No, if you don't mind hearing it all now. I have got so far, and I should prefer making one effort of it. When I spoke to Dr Harley, I had nothing like so much to tell. You are a philosophic physician. You give spirit its proper rank. If this thing is real—'

He paused, looking at me with agitated inquiry.

'We can discuss it by-and-by, and very fully. I will give you all I think,' I answered, after an interval.

'Well—very well. If it is anything real, I say, it is prevailing, little by little, and drawing me more interiorly into hell. Optic nerves, he talked of. Ah! well—there are other nerves of communication. May God Almighty help me! You shall hear.

'Its power of action, I tell you, had increased. Its malice became, in a way aggressive. About two years ago, some questions that were pending between me and the bishop having been settled, I went down to my parish in Warwickshire, anxious to find occupation in my profession. I was not prepared for what happened, although I have since thought I might have apprehended something like it. The reason of my saying so, is this—'

He was beginning to speak with a great deal more effort and reluctance, and sighed often, and seemed at times nearly overcome. But at this time his manner was not agitated. It was more like that of a sinking patient, who has given himself up.

'Yes, but I will first tell you about Kenlis, my parish.

'It was with me when I left this place for Dawlbridge. It was my silent travelling companion, and it remained with me at the vicarage. When I entered on the discharge of my duties, another change took place. The thing exhibited an atrocious determination to thwart me. It was with me in the church—in the reading-desk—in the pulpit—within the communion rails. At last, it reached this extremity, that while I was reading to the congregation, it would spring upon the open book and squat there, so that I was unable to see the page. This happened more than once.

'I left Dawlbridge for a time. I placed myself in Dr Harley's hands. I did everything he told me. He gave my case a great deal of thought. It interested him, I think. He seemed successful. For nearly three months I was perfectly free from a return. I began to think I was safe. With his full assent I returned to Dawlbridge.

'I travelled in a chaise. I was in good spirits. I was more—I was happy and grateful. I was returning, as I thought delivered from a dreadful hallucination, to the scene of duties which I longed to enter upon. It was a beautiful sunny evening, everything looked serene and cheerful, and I was delighted. I remember looking out of the window to see the spire of my church at Kenlis among the trees, at the point where one has the earliest view of it. It is exactly where the little stream that bounds the parish passes under the road by a culvert, and where it emerges at the road-side, a stone with an old inscription is placed. As we passed this point, I drew my head in and sat down, and in the corner of the chaise was the monkey.

'For a moment I felt faint, and then quite wild with despair and horror. I called to the drive, and got out, and sat down at the road-side, and prayed to God silently for mercy. A despairing resignation supervened. My companion was with me as I re-entered the vicarage. The same persecution followed. After a short struggle I submitted, and soon I left the place.

'I told you', he said, 'that the beast has before this become in certain ways aggressive. I will explain a little. It seemed to be actuated by intense and increasing fury, whenever I said my prayers, or even meditated prayer. It amounted at last to a dreadful interruption. You will ask, how could a silent immaterial phantom effect that? It was thus, whenever I meditated praying; it was always before me, and nearer and nearer.

'It used to spring on a table, on the back of a chair, on the chimney-piece, and slowly to swing itself from side to side, looking at me all the time. There is in its motion an indefinable power to dissipate thought, and to contract one's attention to that monotony, till the ideas shrink, as it were, to a point, and at last to nothing—and unless I had started up, and shook off the catalepsy I have felt as if my mind were on the point of losing itself. There are other ways,' he sighed heavily; 'thus, for instance, while I pray with my eyes closed, it comes closer and closer, and I see it. I know it is not to be accounted for physically, but I do actually see it, though my lids are closed, and so it rocks my mind, as it were, and overpowers me, and I am obliged to rise from my knees. If you had ever yourself known this, you would be acquainted with desperation.'

CHAPTER IX

THE THIRD STAGE

'I see, Dr Hesselius, that you don't lose one word of my statement. I need not ask you to listen specially to what I am now going to tell you. They talk of the optic nerves, and of spectral illusions, as if the organ of sight was the only point assailable by the influences that have fastened upon me—I know better. For two years in my direful case that limitation prevailed. But as food is taken in softly at the lips, and then brought under the teeth, as the tip of the little finger caught in a mill crank will draw in the hand, and the arm, and the whole body, so the miserable mortal who has been once caught firmly by the end of the finest fibre of his nerve, is drawn in and in, by the enormous machinery of hell, until he is as I am. Yes, Doctor, as *I* am, for while I talk to you, and implore relief, I feel that my prayer is for the impossible, and my pleading with the inexorable.'

I endeavoured to calm his visibly increasing agitation, and told him that he must not despair.

While we talked the night had overtaken us. The filmy moonlight was wide over the scene which the window commanded, and I said:

'Perhaps you would prefer having candles. This light, you know, is odd. I should wish you, as much as possible, under your usual conditions while I make my diagnosis, shall I call it—otherwise I don't care.'

'All lights are the same to me,' he said: 'except when I read or write, I care not if night were perpetual. I am going to tell you what happened about a year ago. The thing began to speak to me.'

'Speak! How do you mean—speak as a man does, do you mean?'

'Yes; speak in words and consecutive sentences, with a perfect coherence and articulation; but there is a peculiarity. It is not like the tone of a human voice. It is not by my ears it reaches me—it comes like a singing through my head.

'This faculty, the power of speaking to me, will be my undoing. It won't let me pray, it interrupts me with dreadful blasphemies. I dare not go on, I could not. Oh! Doctor, can the skill, and thought, and prayers of man avail me nothing!'

'You must promise me, my dear sir, not to trouble yourself with unnecessarily exciting thoughts; confine yourself strictly to the narrative of *facts*; and recollect, above all, that even if the thing that infests you be as you seem to suppose, a reality with an actual independent life and will, yet it can have no power to hurt you, unless it be given from above: its access to

your senses depends mainly upon your physical condition—
this is, under God, your comfort and reliance: we are all alike
environed. It is only that in your case, the "*paries*",* the veil of
the flesh, the screen, is a little out of repair, and sights and
sounds are transmitted. We must enter on a new course, sir—
be encouraged. I'll give to-night to the careful consideration of
the whole case.'

'You are very good, sir; you think it worth trying, you don't
give me quite up; but, sir, you don't know, it is gaining such
an influence over me: it orders me about, it is such a tyrant,
and I'm growing so helpless. May God deliver me!'

'It orders you about—of course you mean by speech?'

'Yes, yes; it is always urging me to crimes, to injure others,
or myself. You see, Doctor, the situation is urgent, it is indeed.
When I was in Shropshire, a few weeks ago' (Mr Jennings was
speaking rapidly and trembling now, holding my arm with one
hand, and looking in my face), 'I went out one day with a
party of friends for a walk: my persecutor, I tell you, was with
me at the time. I lagged behind the rest: the country near the
Dee,* you know, is beautiful. Our path happened to lie near a
coal mine, and at the verge of the wood is a perpendicular
shaft, they say, a hundred and fifty feet deep. My niece had
remained behind with me—she knows, of course, nothing of
the nature of my sufferings. She knew, however, that I had
been ill, and was low, and she remained to prevent my being
quite alone. As we loitered slowly on together the brute that
accompanied me was urging me to throw myself down the
shaft. I tell you now—oh, sir, think of it!—the one consideration that saved me from that hideous death was the fear lest
the shock of witnessing the occurrence should be too much for
the poor girl. I asked her to go on and take her walk with her
friends, saying that I could go no further. She made excuses,
and the more I urged her the firmer she became. She looked
doubtful and frightened. I suppose there was something in my
looks or manner that alarmed her; but she would not go, and
that literally saved me. You had no idea, sir, that a living man
could be made so abject a slave of Satan,' he said, with a
ghastly groan and a shudder.

There was a pause here, and I said, 'You *were* preserved

nevertheless. It was the act of God. You are in his hands and in the power of no other being: be therefore confident for the future.'

CHAPTER X

HOME

I made him have candles lighted, and saw the room looking cheery and inhabited before I left him. I told him that he must regard his illness strictly as one dependent on physical, though *subtle* physical, causes. I told him that he had evidence of God's care and love in the deliverance which he had just described, and that I had perceived with pain that he seemed to regard its peculiar features as indicating that he had been delivered over to spiritual reprobation. Than such a conclusion nothing could be, I insisted, less warranted; and not only so, but more contrary to facts, as disclosed in his mysterious deliverance from that murderous influence during his Shropshire excursion. First, his niece had been retained by his side without his intending to keep her near him; and, secondly, there had been infused into his mind an irresistible repugnance to execute the dreadful suggestion in her presence.

As I reasoned this point with him, Mr Jennings wept. He seemed comforted. One promise I exacted, which was that should the monkey at any time return, I should be sent for immediately; and, repeating my assurance that I would give neither time nor thought to any other subject until I had thoroughly investigated his case, and that tomorrow he should hear the result, I took my leave.

Before getting into the carriage I told the servant that his master was far from well, and that he should make a point of frequently looking into his room.

My own arrangements I made with a view to being quite secure from interruption.

I merely called at my lodgings, and with a travelling-desk and carpet-bag, set off in a hackney-carriage for an inn about two miles out of town, called The Horns, a very quiet and comfortable house, with good thick walls. And there I resolved, without the possibility of intrusion or distraction, to devote some hours of the night, in my comfortable sitting-room, to Mr Jennings's case, and so much of the morning as it might require.

(There occurs here a careful note of Dr Hesselius' opinion upon the case and of the habits, dietary, and medicines which he prescribed. It is curious—some persons would say mystical. But on the whole I doubt whether it would sufficiently interest a reader of the kind I am likely to meet with, to warrant its being here reprinted. The whole letter was plainly written at the inn where he had hid himself for the occasion. The next letter is dated from his town lodgings.)

I left town for the inn where I slept last night at half-past nine, and did not arrive at my room in town until one o'clock this afternoon. I found a letter in Mr Jennings's hand upon my table. It had not come by post, and, on inquiry, I learned that Mr Jennings's servant had brought it, and on learning that I was not to return until to-day, and that no one could tell him my address, he seemed very uncomfortable, and said that his orders from his master were that he was not to return without an answer.

I opened the letter, and read:

'Dear Dr Hesselius. It is here. You had not been an hour gone when it returned. It is speaking. It knows all that has happened. It knows everything—it knows you and is frantic and atrocious. It reviles. I send you this. It knows every word I have written—I write. This I promised, and I therefore write, but I fear very confused, very incoherently. I am so interrupted, disturbed.

'Ever yours, sincerely, yours

'Robert Lynder Jennings.'

'When did this come?' I asked.

'About eleven last night: the man was here again, and has been here three times to-day. The last time is about an hour since.'

Thus answered, and with the notes I had made upon his

case in my pockets, I was in a few minutes driving towards Richmond, to see Mr Jennings.

I by no means, as you perceive, despaired of Mr Jennings's case. He had himself remembered and applied, though quite in a mistaken way, the principle which I lay down in my *Metaphysical Medicine*, and which governs all such cases. I was about to apply it in earnest. I was profoundly interested, and very anxious to see and examine him while the 'enemy' was actually present.

I drove up to the sombre house, and ran up the steps, and knocked. The door, in a little time, was opened by a tall woman in black silk. She looked ill, and as if she had been crying. She curtseyed, and heard my question, but she did not answer. She turned her face away, extending her hand towards two men who were coming down-stairs; and thus having, as it were, tacitly made me over to them, she passed through a side-door hastily and shut it.

The man who was nearest the hall, I at once accosted, but being now close to him, I was shocked to see that both his hands were covered with blood.

I drew back a little, and the man passing down-stairs merely said in a low tone, 'Here's the servant, sir.'

The servant had stopped on the stairs, confounded and dumb at seeing me. He was rubbing his hands in a handker-chief, and it was steeped in blood.

'Jones, what is it, what has happened?' I asked, while a sickening suspicion overpowered me.

The man asked me to come up to the lobby. I was beside him in a moment, and frowning and pallid, with contracted eyes, he told me the horror which I already half-guessed.

His master had made away with himself.

I went upstairs with him to the room—what I saw there I won't tell you. He had cut his throat with his razor. It was a frightful gash. The two men had laid him on the bed and composed his limbs. It had happened, as the immense pool of blood on the floor declared, at some distance between the bed and the window. There was carpet round his bed, and a carpet under his dressing-table, but none on the rest of the floor, for the man said he did not like a carpet in his bedroom. In this sombre, and now terrible room, one of the great elms that darkened the house was slowly moving the shadow of one of its great boughs upon this dreadful floor.

I beckoned to the servant and we went down-stairs together. I turned off the hall into an old-fashioned panelled room, and there standing, I heard all the servant had to tell. It was not a great deal.

'I concluded, sir, from your words, and looks, sir, as you left last night, that you thought my master seriously ill. I thought it might be that you were afraid of a fit, or something. So I attended very close to your directions. He sat up late, till past three o'clock. He was not writing or reading. He was talking a great deal to himself, but that was nothing unusual. At about that hour I assisted him to undress, and left him in his slippers and dressing-gown. I went back softly in about half an hour. He was in his bed, quite undressed, and a pair of candles lighted on the table beside his bed. He was leaning on his elbow and looking out at the other side of the bed when I came in. I asked him if he wanted anything, and he said no.

'I don't know whether it was what you said to me, sir, or something a little unusual about him, but I was uneasy, uncommon uneasy about him last night.

'In another half hour, or it might be a little more, I went up again. I did not hear him talking as before. I opened the door a little. The candles were both out, which was not usual. I had a bedroom candle, and I let the light in, a little bit, looking softly round. I saw him sitting in that chair beside the dressing-table with his clothes on again. He turned round and looked at me. I thought it strange he should get up and dress, and put out the candles to sit in the dark, that way. But I only asked him again if I could do anything for him. He said, no, rather sharp, I thought. I asked if I might light the candles, and he said, "Do as you like, Jones." So I lighted them, and I lingered about the room, and he said, "Tell me truth, Jones, why did you come again—you did not hear any one cursing?" "No, sir," I said, wondering what he could mean.

'"No," said he, after me, "of course, no"; and I said to him, "Wouldn't it be well, sir, you went to bed? It's just five o'clock"; and he said nothing but, "Very likely; good-night,

Jones." So I went, sir, but in less than an hour I came again. The door was fast, and he heard me, and called as I thought from the bed to know what I wanted, and he desired me not to disturb him again. I lay down and slept for a little. It must have been between six and seven when I went up again. The door was still fast, and he made no answer, so I did not like to disturb him, and thinking he was asleep, I left him till nine. It was his custom to ring when he wished me to come, and I had no particular hour for calling him. I tapped very gently, and getting no answer, I stayed away a good while, supposing he was getting some rest then. It was not till eleven o'clock I grew really uncomfortable about him—for at the latest he was never, that I could remember, later than half-past ten. I got no answer. I knocked and called, and still no answer. So not being able to force the door, I called Thomas from the stables, and together we forced it, and found him in the shocking way you saw.'

Jones had no more to tell. Poor Mr Jennings was very gentle, and very kind. All his people were fond of him. I could see that the servant was very much moved.

So, dejected and agitated, I passed from that terrible house, and its dark canopy of elms, and I hope I shall never see it more. While I write to you I feel like a man who has but half waked from a frightful and monotonous dream. My memory rejects the picture with incredulity and horror. Yet I know it is true. It is the story of the process of a poison, a poison which excites the reciprocal action of spirit and nerve, and paralyses the tissue that separates those cognate functions of the senses, the external and the interior. Thus we find strange bedfellows, and the mortal and immortal prematurely make acquaintance.

CONCLUSION

A WORD FOR THOSE WHO SUFFER

My dear Van L——, you have suffered from an affection similar to that which I have just described. You twice complained of a return of it.

Who, under God, cured you? Your humble servant, Martin Hesselius. Let me rather adopt the more emphasized piety of a certain good old French surgeon of three hundred years ago: 'I treated, and God cured you.'

Come, my friend, you are not to be hippish. Let me tell you a fact.

I have met with, and treated, as my book shows, fifty-seven cases of this kind of vision, which I term indifferently 'sublimated', 'precocious', and 'interior'.

There is another class of affections which are truly termed—though commonly confounded with those which I describe—spectral illusions. These latter I look upon as being no less simply curable than a cold in the head or a trifling dyspepsia.

It is those which rank in the first category that test our promptitude of thought. Fifty-seven such cases have I encountered, neither more nor less. And in how many of these have I failed? In no one single instance.

There is no one affliction of mortality more easily and certainly reducible, with a little patience, and a rational confidence in the physician. With these simple conditions, I look upon the cure as absolutely certain.

You are to remember that I had not even commenced to treat Mr Jennings' case. I have not any doubt that I should have cured him perfectly in eighteen months, or possibly it might have extended to two years. Some cases are very rapidly curable, others extremely tedious. Every intelligent physician who will give thought and diligence to the task, will effect a cure.

You know my tract on *The Cardinal Functions of the Brain*. I there, by the evidence of innumerable facts, prove, as I think, the high probability of a circulation arterial and venous in its mechanism, through the nerves. Of this system, thus considered, the brain is the heart. The fluid, which is propagated hence through one class of nerves, returns in an altered state through another, and the nature of that fluid is spiritual, though not immaterial, any more than, as I before remarked, light or electricity are so.

By various abuses, among which the habitual use of such agents as green tea is one, this fluid may be affected as to its quality, but it is more frequently disturbed as to equilibrium. This fluid being that which we have in common with spirits, a congestion found upon the masses of brain or nerve, connected with the interior sense, forms a surface unduly exposed, on which disembodied spirits may operate: communication is thus more or less effectually established. Between this brain circulation and the heart circulation there is an intimate sympathy. The seat, or rather the instrument of exterior vision, is the eye. The seat of interior vision is the nervous tissue and brain, immediately about and above the eyebrow. You remember how effectually I dissipated your pictures by the simple application of iced eau-de-cologne. Few cases, however, can be treated exactly alike with anything like rapid success. Cold acts powerfully as a repellant of the nervous fluid. Long enough continued it will even produce that permanent insensibility which we call numbness, and a little longer, muscular as well as sensational paralysis.

I have not, I repeat, the slightest doubt that I should have first dimmed and ultimately sealed that inner eye which Mr Jennings had inadvertently opened. The same senses are opened in delirium tremens, and entirely shut up again when the over-action of the cerebral heart, and the prodigious nervous congestions that attend it, are terminated by a decided change in the state of the body. It is by acting steadily upon the body, by a simple process, that this result is produced— and inevitably produced—I have never yet failed.

Poor Mr Jennings made away with himself. But that catastrophe was the result of a totally different malady, which, as it were, projected itself upon that disease which was established. His case was in the distinctive manner a complication, and the complaint under which he really succumbed, was hereditary suicidal mania. Poor Mr Jennings I cannot call a patient of mine, for I had not even begun to treat his case, and he had not yet given me, I am convinced, his full and unreserved confidence. If the patient do not array himself on the side of the disease, his cure is certain.

THE FAMILIAR

PROLOGUE

OUT of about two hundred and thirty cases, more or less nearly akin to that I have entitled 'Green Tea,' I select the following, which I call 'The Familiar'.

To this MS Doctor Hesselius, has, after his wont, attached some sheets of letter-paper, on which are written, in his hand nearly as compact as print, his own remarks upon the case. He says—

'In point of conscience, no more unexceptionable narrator, than the venerable Irish Clergyman who has given me this paper, on Mr Barton's case, could have been chosen. The statement is, however, medically imperfect. The report of an intelligent physician, who had marked its progress, and attended the patient, from its earlier stages to its close, would have supplied what is wanting to enable me to pronounce with confidence. I should have been acquainted with Mr Barton's probable hereditary predispositions; I should have known, possibly, by very early indications, something of a remoter origin of the disease than can now be ascertained.

'In a rough way, we may reduce all similar cases to three distinct classes. They are founded on the primary distinction between the subjective and the objective. Of those whose senses are alleged to be subject to supernatural impressions—some are simply visionaries, and propagate the illusions of which they complain, from diseased brain or nerves. Others are, unquestionably, infested by, as we term them, spiritual agencies, exterior to themselves. Others, again, owe their sufferings to a mixed condition. The interior sense, it is true, is opened; but it has been and continues open by the action of disease. This form of disease may, in one sense, be compared to the loss of the scarf-skin, and a consequent exposure of surfaces for whose excessive sensitiveness, nature has provided a muffling. The loss of this covering is attended by an habitual impassability, by influences against which we were intended to be guarded. But in the case of the brain, and the nerves immediately connected with its functions and its sensuous impressions, the cerebral circulation undergoes periodically that vibratory disturbance, which, I believe, I have satisfactorily examined and demonstrated, in my MS Essay, A. 17. This vibratory disturbance differs, as I there prove, essentially from the congestive disturbance, the phenomena of which are examined in A. 19. It is, when excessive, invariably accompanied by *illusions*.

'Had I seen Mr Barton, and examined him upon the points, in his case, which need elucidation, I should have without difficulty referred those phenomena to their proper disease. My diagnosis is now, necessarily, conjectural.'

Thus writes Doctor Hesselius; and adds a great deal which is of interest only to a scientific physician.

The Narrative of the Rev. Thomas Herbert, which furnishes all that is known of the case, will be found in the chapters that follow.

CHAPTER I

FOOT-STEPS

I was a young man at the time, and intimately acquainted with some of the actors in this strange tale; the impression which its incidents made on me, therefore, were deep, and lasting. I shall now endeavour, with precision, to relate them all, combining, of course, in the narrative, whatever I have learned from various sources, tending, however imperfectly, to illuminate the darkness which involves its progress and termination.

Somewhere about the year 1794, the younger brother of a certain baronet, whom I shall call Sir James Barton, returned to Dublin. He had served in the navy with some distinction, having commanded one of His Majesty's frigates during the greater part of the American war.* Captain Barton was apparently some two or three-and-forty years of age. He was an intelligent and agreeable companion when he pleased it, though generally reserved, and occasionally even moody.

In society, however, he deported himself as a man of the world, and a gentleman. He had not contracted any of the noisy brusqueness sometimes acquired at sea; on the contrary, his manners were remarkably easy, quiet, and even polished. He was in person about the middle size, and somewhat strongly formed—his countenance was marked with the lines of thought, and on the whole wore an expression of gravity and melancholy; being, however, as I have said, a man of perfect breeding, as well as of good family, and in affluent circumstances, he had, of course, ready access to the best society of Dublin, without the necessity of any other credentials.

In his personal habits Mr Barton was inexpensive. He occupied lodgings in one of the *then* fashionable streets in the south side of the town*—kept but one horse and one servant— and though a reputed free-thinker,* yet lived an orderly and moral life—indulging neither in gaming,* drinking, nor any other vicious pursuit—living very much to himself, without forming intimacies, or choosing any companions, and appearing to mix in gay society rather for the sake of its bustle and distraction, than for any opportunities it offered of interchanging thought or feeling with its votaries.

Barton was therefore pronounced a saving, prudent, unsocial sort of fellow, who bid fair to maintain his celibacy alike against stratagem and assault, and was likely to live to a good old age, die rich, and leave his money to an hospital.

It was now apparent, however, that the nature of Mr Barton's plans had been totally misconceived. A young lady, whom I shall call Miss Montague, was at this time introduced into the gay world, by her aunt, the Dowager Lady L——.* Miss Montague was decidedly pretty and accomplished, and having some natural cleverness, and a great deal of gaiety, became for a while a reigning toast.*

Her popularity, however, gained her, for a time, nothing more than that unsubstantial admiration which, however, pleasant as an incense to vanity, is by no means necessarily antecedent to matrimony—for, unhappily for the young lady in question, it was an understood thing, that beyond her personal attractions, she had no kind of earthly provision. Such being the state of affairs, it will readily be believed that no little surprise was consequent upon the appearance of Captain Barton as the avowed lover of the penniless Miss Montague.

His suit prospered, as might have been expected, and in a short time it was communicated by old Lady L— to each of her hundred-and-fifty particular friends in succession, that Captain Barton had actually tendered proposals of marriage, with her approbration, to her niece, Miss Montague, who had, moreover, accepted the offer of his hand, conditionally upon the consent of her father, who was then upon his homeward voyage from India, and expected in two or three weeks at the furthest.

About this consent there could be no doubt—the delay, therefore, was one merely of form—they were looked upon as absolutely engaged, and Lady L—, with a rigour of old-fashioned decorum with which her niece would, no doubt, gladly have dispensed, withdrew her thenceforward from all further participation in the gaieties of the town.

Captain Barton was a constant visitor, as well as a frequent guest at the house, and was permitted all the privileges of intimacy which a betrothed suitor is usually accorded. Such was the relation of parties, when the mysterious circumstances which darken this narrative first begun to unfold themselves.

Lady L— resided in a handsome mansion at the north side of Dublin, and Captain Barton's lodgings, as we have already said, were situated at the south. The distance intervening was considerable, and it was Captain Barton's habit generally to walk home without an attendant, as often as he passed the evening with the old lady and her fair charge.

His shortest way in such nocturnal walks, lay, for a considerable space, through a line of street which had as yet merely been laid out,* and little more than the foundations of the houses constructed.

One night, shortly after his engagement with Miss Montague had commenced, he happened to remain unusually late, in company with her and Lady L——. The conversation had turned upon the evidences of revelation,* which he had disputed with the callous scepticism of a confirmed infidel. What were called 'French principles', had in those days found their way a good deal into fashionable society, especially that portion of it which professed allegiance to Whiggism,* and neither the old lady nor her charge were so perfectly free from the taint, as to look upon Mr Barton's views as any serious objection to the proposed union.

The discussion had degenerated into one upon the supernatural and the marvellous, in which he had pursued precisely the same line of argument and ridicule. In all this, it is but truth to state, Captain Barton was guilty of no affectation—the doctrines upon which he insisted, were, in reality, but too truly the basis of his own fixed belief, if so it might be called; and perhaps not the least strange of the many strange circumstances connected with my narrative, was the fact, that the subject of the fearful influences I am about to describe, was himself, from the deliberate conviction of years, an utter disbeliever in what are usually termed preternatural agencies.

It was considerably past midnight when Mr Barton took his leave, and set out upon his solitary walk homeward. He had now reached the lonely road, with its unfinished dwarf walls tracing the foundations of the projected row of houses on either side—the moon was shining mistily, and its imperfect light made the road he trod but additionally dreary—that utter silence which has in it something indefinably exciting, reigned there, and made the sound of his steps, which alone broke it, unnaturally loud and distinct.

He had proceeded thus some way, when he, on a sudden, heard other footfalls, pattering at a measured pace, and, as it seemed, about two score steps behind him.

The suspicion of being dogged is at all times unpleasant; it is, however, especially so in a spot so lonely; and this suspicion became so strong in the mind of Captain Barton, that he abruptly turned about to confront his pursuer, but, though there was quite sufficient moonlight to disclose any object upon the road he had traversed, no form of any kind was visible there.

The steps he had heard could not have been the reverberation of his own, for he stamped his foot upon the ground, and walked briskly up and down, in the vain attempt to awake an echo; though by no means a fanciful person, therefore, he was at last fain to charge the sounds upon his imagination, and treat them as an illusion. Thus satisfying himself, he resumed his walk, and before he had proceeded a dozen paces, the mysterious footfall was again audible from behind, and this time, as if with the special design of showing that the sounds were not the responses of an echo—the steps sometimes slackened nearly to a halt, and sometimes hurried for six or eight strides to a run, and again abated to a walk.

Captain Barton, as before, turned suddenly round, and with the same result—no object was visible above the deserted level of the road. He walked back over the same ground, determined that, whatever might have been the cause of the sounds which had so disconcerted him, it should not escape his search—the endeavour, however, was unrewarded.

In spite of all his scepticism, he felt something like a superstitious fear stealing fast upon him, and with these unwonted and uncomfortable sensations, he once more turned and pursued his way. There was no repetition of these haunting sounds, until he had reached the point where he had last stopped to retrace his steps—here they were resumed— and with sudden starts of running, which threatened to bring the unseen pursuer up to the alarmed pedestrian.

Captain Barton arrested his course as formerly—the unaccountable nature of the occurrence filled him with vague and disagreeable sensations—and yielding to the excitement that was gaining upon him, he shouted sternly, 'Who goes there?' The sound of one's own voice, thus exerted, in utter solitude, and followed by total silence, has in it something unpleasantly dismaying, and he felt a degree of nervousness which, perhaps, from no cause had he ever known before.

To the very end of this solitary street the steps pursued him—and it required a strong effort of stubborn pride on his part, to resist the impulse that prompted him every moment to run for safety at the top of his speed. It was not until he had reached his lodging, and sate by his own fire-side, that he felt sufficiently reassured to rearrange and reconsider in his own mind the occurrences which had so discomposed him. So little a matter, after all, is sufficient to upset the pride of scepticism and vindicate the old simple laws of nature within us.

CHAPTER II

THE WATCHER

Mr Barton was next morning sitting at a late breakfast, reflecting upon the incidents of the previous night, with more of inquisitiveness than awe, so speedily do gloomy impressions upon the fancy disappear under the cheerful influence of day, when a letter just delivered by the postman was placed upon the table before him.

There was nothing remarkable in the address of this missive, except that it was written in a hand which he did not know— perhaps it was disguised—for the tall narrow characters were sloped backward; and with the self-inflicted suspense which we often see practised in such cases, he puzzled over the inscription for a full minute before he broke the seal. When he did so, he read the following words, written in the same hand:

'Mr Barton, late captain of the *Dolphin*, is warned of DANGER. He will do wisely to avoid——street—[here the locality of his last night's adventure was named]—if he walks there as usual he will meet with something unlucky—let him take warning, once for all, for he has reason to dread

'THE WATCHER.'

Captain Barton read and re-read this strange effusion; in every light and in every direction he turned it over and over; he examined the paper on which it was written, and scrutinized the hand-writing once more. Defeated here, he turned to the seal; it was nothing but a patch of wax, upon which the accidental impression of a thumb* was imperfectly visible.

There was not the slightest mark, or clue of any kind, to lead him to even a guess as to its possible origin. The writer's object seemed a friendly one, and yet he subscribed himself as one whom he had 'reason to dread'. Altogether the letter, its author, and its real purpose were to him an inexplicable puzzle, and one, moreover, unpleasantly suggestive, in his mind, of other associations connected with his last night's adventure.

In obedience to some feeling—perhaps of pride—Mr Barton did not communicate, even to his intended bride, the occurrences which I have just detailed. Trifling as they might appear, they had in reality most disagreeably affected his imagination, and he cared not to disclose, even to the young lady in question, what she might possibly look upon as evidences of weakness. The letter might very well be but a hoax, and the mysterious footfall but a delusion or a trick. But although he affected to treat the whole affair as unworthy of a thought, it yet haunted him pertinaciously, tormenting him with perplexing doubts, and depressing him with undefined apprehensions. Certain it is, that for a considerable time afterwards he carefully avoided the street indicated in the letter as the scene of danger.

It was not until about a week after the receipt of the letter which I have transcribed, that anything further occurred to remind Captain Barton of its contents, or to counteract the gradual disappearance from his mind of the disagreeable impressions then received.

He was returning one night, after the interval I have stated, from the theatre, which was then situated in Crow-street,* and having there seen Miss Montague and Lady L——into their carriage, he loitered for some time with two or three acquaintances.

With these, however, he parted close to the College,* and pursued his way alone. It was now fully one o'clock, and the streets were quite deserted. During the whole of his walk with the companions from whom he had just parted, he had been at times painfully aware of the sound of steps, as it seemed, dogging them on their way.

Once or twice he had looked back, in the uneasy anticipation that he was again about to experience the same mysterious annoyances which had so disconcerted him a week before, and earnestly hoping that he might *see* some form to account naturally for the sounds. But the street was deserted—no one was visible.

Proceeding now quite alone upon his homeward way, he grew really nervous and uncomfortable, as he became sensible, with increased distinctness, of the well-known and now absolutely dreaded sounds.

By the side of the dead wall which bounded the College Park,* the sounds followed, recommencing almost simultaneously with his own steps. The same unequal pace—sometimes slow, sometimes for a score yards or so, quickened almost to a run—was audible from behind him. Again and again he turned; quickly and stealthily he glanced over his shoulder—almost at every half-dozen steps; but no one was visible.

The irritation of this intangible and unseen pursuit became gradually all but intolerable; and when at last he reached his home, his nerves were strung to such a pitch of excitement that he could not rest, and did not attempt even to lie down until after the daylight had broken.

He was awakened by a knock at his chamber-door, and his servant entering, handed him several letters which had just been received by the penny post. One among them instantly arrested his attention—a single glance at the direction aroused him thoroughly. He at once recognized its character, and read as follows:

'You may as well think, Captain Barton, to escape from your own shadow as from me; do what you may, I will see you as often as I please, and you shall see me, for I do not want to hide myself, as you fancy. Do not let it trouble your rest, Captain Barton; for, with a *good conscience*, what need you fear from the eye of

'THE WATCHER.'

It is scarcely necessary to dwell upon the feelings that accompanied a perusal of this strange communication. Captain Barton was observed to be unusually absent and out of spirits for several days afterwards; but no one divined the cause.

Whatever he might think as to the phantom steps which

followed him, there could be no possible illusion about the letters he had received; and, to say the least, their immediate sequence upon the mysterious sounds which had haunted him, was an odd coincidence.

The whole circumstance was, in his own mind, vaguely and instinctively connected with certain passages in his past life, which, of all others, he hated to remember.

It happened, however, that in addition to his own approaching nuptials, Captain Barton had just then—fortunately, perhaps, for himself—some business of an engrossing kind connected with the adjustment of a large and long-litigated claim upon certain properties.

The hurry and excitement of business had its natural effect in gradually dispelling the gloom which had for a time occasionally oppressed him, and in a little while his spirits had entirely recovered their accustomed tone.

During all this time, however, he was, now and then, dismayed by indistinct and half-heard repetitions of the same annoyance, and that in lonely places, in the day-time as well as after nightfall. These renewals of the strange impressions from which he had suffered so much, were, however, desultory and faint, insomuch that often he really could not, to his own satisfaction, distinguish between them and the mere suggestions of an excited imagination.

One evening he walked down to the House of Commons with a Member, an acquaintance of his and mine.* This was one of the few occasions upon which I have been in company with Captain Barton. As we walked down together, I observed that he became absent and silent, and to a degree that seemed to argue the pressure of some urgent and absorbing anxiety.

I afterwards learned that during the whole of our walk, he had heard the well-known footsteps tracking him as we proceeded.

This, however, was the last time he suffered from this phase of the persecution, of which he was already the anxious victim. A new and a very different one was about to be presented.

CHAPTER III

AN ADVERTISEMENT

Of the new series of impressions which were afterwards gradually to work out his destiny, I that evening witnessed the first; and but for its relation to the train of events which followed, the incident would scarcely have been now remembered by me.

As we were walking in at the passage from College Green, a man, of whom I remember only that he was short in stature, looked like a foreigner, and wore a kind of fur travelling-cap, walked very rapidly, and as if under fierce excitement, directly towards us, muttering to himself fast and vehemently the while.

This odd-looking person walked straight toward Barton, who was foremost of the three, and halted, regarding him for a moment or two with a look of maniacal menace and fury; and then turning about as abruptly, he walked before us at the same agitated pace, and disappeared at a side passage. I do distinctly remember being a good deal shocked at the countenance and bearing of this man, which indeed irresistibly impressed me with an undefined sense of danger, such as I have never felt before or since from the presence of anything human; but these sensations were, on my part, far from amounting to anything so disconcerting as to flurry or excite me—I had seen only a singularly evil countenance, agitated, as it seemed, with the excitement of madness.

I was absolutely astonished, however, at the effect of this apparition upon Captain Barton. I knew him to be a man of proud courage and coolness in real danger—a circumstance which made his conduct upon this occasion the more conspicuously odd. He recoiled a step or two as the stranger advanced, and clutched my arm in silence, with what seemed to be a spasm of agony or terror! and then, as the figure disappeared, shoving me roughly back, he followed it for a few paces, stopped in great disorder, and sat down upon a form. I never beheld a countenance more ghastly and haggard.

'For God's sake, Barton, what is the matter?' said——, our companion, really alarmed at his appearance. 'You're not hurt, are you?—or unwell? What is it?'

'What did he say?—I did not hear it—what was it?' asked Barton, wholly disregarding the question.

'Nonsense,' said——, greatly surprised; 'who cares what the fellow said. You are unwell, Barton—decidedly unwell; let me call a coach.'

'Unwell! No—not unwell,' he said, evidently making an effort to recover his self-possession; 'but, to say the truth, I am fatigued—a little over-worked—and perhaps over anxious. You know I have been in Chancery,* and the winding up of a suit is always a nervous affair. I have felt uncomfortable all this evening; but I am better now. Come, come—shall we go on?'

'No, no. Take my advice, Barton, and go home; you really do need rest! you are looking quite ill. I really do insist on your allowing me to see you home,' replied his friend.

I seconded——'s advice, the more readily as it was obvious that Barton was not himself disinclined to be persuaded. He left us, declining our offered escort. I was not sufficiently intimate with——to discuss the scene we had both just witnessed. I was, however, convinced from his manner in the few common-place comments and regrets we exchanged, that he was just as little satisfied as I with the extempore plea of illness with which he had accounted for the strange exhibition, and that we were both agreed in suspecting some lurking mystery in the matter.

I called next day at Barton's lodgings, to enquire for him, and learned from the servant that he had not left his room since his return the night before; but that he was not seriously indisposed, and hoped to be out in a few days. That evening he sent for Dr R——,* then in large and fashionable practice in Dublin, and their interview was, it is said, an odd one.

He entered into a detail of his own symptoms in an abstracted and desultory way, which seemed to argue a strange want of interest in his own cure, and, at all events, made it manifest that there was some topic engaging his mind of more engrossing importance than his present ailment. He complained of occasional palpitations and headache.

Doctor R—— asked him among other questions, whether there was any irritating circumstance or anxiety then occupying his thoughts. This he denied quickly and almost peevishly; and the physician thereupon declared his opinion, that there was nothing amiss except some slight derangement of the digestion, for which he accordingly wrote a prescription, and was about to withdraw, when Mr Barton, with the air of a man who recollects a topic which had nearly escaped him, recalled him.

'I beg your pardon, Doctor, but I really almost forgot; will you permit me to ask you two or three medical questions— rather odd ones, perhaps, but as a wager depends upon their solution, you will, I hope, excuse my unreasonableness.'

The physician readily undertook to satisfy the inquirer.

Barton seemed to have some difficulty about opening the proposed interrogatories, for he was silent for a minute, then walked to his book-case, and returned as he had gone; at last he sat down, and said—

'You'll think them very childish questions, but I can't recover my wager without a decision; so I must put them. I want to know first about lock-jaw.* If a man actually has had that complaint, and appears to have died of it—so much so, that a physician of average skill pronounces him actually dead—may he, after all, recover?'

The physician smiled, and shook his head.

'But—but a blunder may be made,' resumed Barton. 'Suppose an ignorant pretender to medical skill; may *he* be so deceived by any stage of the complaint, as to mistake what is only a part of the progress of the disease, for death itself?'

'No one who had ever seen death', answered he, 'could mistake it in a case of lock-jaw.'

Barton mused for a few minutes. 'I am going to ask you a question, perhaps, still more childish; but first, tell me, are the regulations of foreign hospitals, such as that of, let us say, Naples,* very lax and bungling? May not all kinds of blunders and slips occur in their entries of names, and so forth?'

Doctor R——professed his incompetence to answer that query.

'Well, then, Doctor, here is the last of my questions. You will, probably, laugh at it; but it must out, nevertheless. Is there any disease, in all the range of human maladies, which would have the effect of perceptibly contracting the stature, and the whole frame—causing the man to shrink in all his proportions, and yet to preserve his exact resemblance to himself in every particular—with the one exception, his height and bulk; *any* disease, mark—no matter how rare—how little believed in, generally—which could possibly result in producing such an effect?'

The physician replied with a smile, and a very decided negative.

'Tell me, then,' said Barton, abruptly, 'if a man be in reasonable fear of assault from a lunatic who is at large, can he not procure a warrant for his arrest and detention?'

'Really that is more a lawyer's question than one in my way,' replied Dr R——:

'but I believe, on applying to a magistrate, such a course would be directed.'

The physician then took his leave; but, just as he reached the hall-door, remembered that he had left his cane upstairs, and returned. His reappearance was awkward, for a piece of paper, which he recognized as his own prescription, was slowly burning upon the fire, and Barton sitting close by with an expression of settled gloom and dismay.

Doctor R——had too much tact to observe what presented itself; but he had seen quite enough to assure him that the mind, and not the body, of Captain Barton was in reality the seat of suffering.

A few days afterwards, the following advertisement appeared in the Dublin newspapers.

'If Sylvester Yelland, formerly a foremast-man* on board his Majesty's frigate *Dolphin,* or his nearest of kin, will apply to Mr Hubert Smith, attorney, at his office, Dame Street,* he or they may hear of something greatly to his or their advantage. Admission may be had at any hour up to twelve o'clock at night, should parties desire to avoid observation; and the strictest secresy, as to all communications intended to be confidential, shall be honourably observed.'

The *Dolphin,* as I have mentioned, was the vessel which Captain Barton had commanded; and this circumstance, connected with the extraordinary exertions made by the circulation of hand-bills, &c., as well as by repeated advertisements, to secure for this strange notice the utmost possible publicity, suggested to Dr R——the idea that Captain Barton's extreme uneasiness was somehow connected with the individual to whom the advertisment was addressed, and he himself the author of it.

This, however, it is needless to add, was no more than a conjecture. No information whatsoever, as to the real purpose of the advertisement was divulged by the agent, nor yet any hint as to who his employer might be.

CHAPTER IV

HE TALKS WITH A CLERGYMAN

Mr Barton, although he had latterly begun to earn for himself the character of an hypochondriac, was yet very far from deserving it. Though by no means lively, he had yet, naturally, what are termed 'even spirits', and was not subject to undue depressions.

He soon, therefore, began to return to his former habits; and one of the earliest symptoms of this healthier tone of spirits was, his appearing at a grand dinner of the Freemasons, of which worthy fraternity he was himself a brother. Barton, who had been at first gloomy and abstracted, drank much more freely than was his wont—possibly with the purpose of dispelling his own secret anxieties—and under the influence of good wine, and pleasant company, became gradually (unlike himself) talkative, and even noisy.

It was under this unwonted excitement that he left his

company at about half-past ten o'clock; and, as conviviality is a strong incentive to gallantry, it occurred to him to proceed forthwith to Lady L——'s and pass the remainder of the evening with her and his destined bride.

Accordingly, he was soon at——street, and chatting gaily with the ladies. It is not to be supposed that Captain Barton had exceeded the limits which propriety prescribes to good fellowship—he had merely taken enough wine to raise his spirits, without, however, in the least degree unsteadying his mind, or affecting his manners.

With this undue elevation of spirits had supervened an entire oblivion or contempt of those undefined apprehensions which had for so long weighed upon his mind, and to a certain extent estranged him from society; but as the night wore away, and his artificial gaiety began to flag, these painful feelings gradually intruded themselves again, and he grew abstracted and anxious as heretofore.

He took his leave at length, with an unpleasant foreboding of some coming mischief, and with a mind haunted with a thousand mysterious apprehensions, such as, even while he acutely felt their pressure, he, nevertheless, inwardly strove, or affected to contemn.

It was this proud defiance of what he regarded as his own weakness, which prompted him upon the present occasion to that course which brought about the adventure I am now about to relate.

Mr Barton might have easily called a coach, but he was conscious that his strong inclination to do so proceeded from no cause other than what he desperately persisted in representing to himself to be his own superstitious tremors.

He might also have returned home by a *route* different from that against which he had been warned by his mysterious correspondent; but for the same reason he dismissed this idea also, and with a dogged and half desperate resolution to force matters to a crisis of some kind, if there were any reality in the causes of his former suffering, and if not, satisfactorily to bring their delusiveness to the proof, he determined to follow precisely the course which he had trodden upon the night so painfully memorable in his own mind as that on which his strange persecution commenced.

Though, sooth to say, the pilot who for the first time steers his vessel under the muzzles of a hostile battery, never felt his resolution more severely tasked than did Captain Barton as he breathlessly pursued this solitary path—a path which, spite of every effort of scepticism and reason, he felt to be infested by some (as respected *him*) malignant being.

He pursued his way steadily and rapidly, scarcely breathing from intensity of suspense; he, however, was troubled by no renewal of the dreaded footsteps, and was beginning to feel a return of confidence, as more than three-fourths of the way being accomplished with impunity, he approached the long line of twinkling oil lamps which indicated the frequented streets.

This feeling of self-congratulation was, however, but momentary. The report of a musket at some hundred yards behind him, and the whistle of a bullet close to his head, disagreeably and startlingly dispelled it. His first impulse was to retrace his steps in pursuit of the assassin; but the road on either side was, as we have said, embarrassed by the foundations of a street, beyond which extended waste fields, full of rubbish and neglected lime and brick-kilns and all now as utterly silent as though no sound had ever disturbed their dark and unsightly solitude. The futility of, single-handed, attempting, under such circumstances, a search for the murderer, was apparent, especially as no sound, either of retreating steps or any other kind, was audible to direct his pursuit.

With the tumultuous sensations of one whose life has just been exposed to a murderous attempt, and whose escape has been the narrowest possible, Captain Barton turned again; and without, however, quickening his pace actually to a run, hurriedly pursued his way.

He had turned, as I have said, after a pause of a few seconds, and had just commenced his rapid retreat, when on a sudden he met the well-remembered little man in the fur cap. The encounter was but momentary. The figure was walking at the same exaggerated pace, and with the same strange air of

menace as before; and as it passed him, he thought he heard it
say, in a furious whisper, 'Still alive—still alive!'

The state of Mr Barton's spirits began now to work a
corresponding alteration in his health and looks, and to such a
degree that it was impossible that the change should escape
general remark.

For some reasons, known but to himself, he took no step
whatsoever to bring the attempt upon his life, which he had so
narrowly escaped, under the notice of the authorities; on the
contrary, he kept it jealously to himself; and it was not for
many weeks after the occurrence that he mentioned it, and
then in strict confidence, to a gentleman, whom the torments
of his mind at last compelled him to consult.

Spite of his blue devils,* however, poor Barton, having no
satisfactory reason to render to the public for any undue
remissness in the attentions exacted by the relation subsisting
between him and Miss Montague, was obliged to exert himself,
and present to the world a confident and cheerful bearing.

The true source of his sufferings, and every circumstance
connected with them, he guarded with a reserve so jealous,
that it seemed dictated by at least a suspicion that the origin
of his strange persecution was known to himself, and that it
was of a nature which, upon his own account, he could not or
dared not disclose.

The mind thus turned in upon itself, and constantly occupied with a haunting anxiety which it dared not reveal or
confide to any human breast, became daily more excited, and,
of course, more vividly impressible, by a system of attack
which operated through the nervous system; and in this state
he was destined to sustain, with increasing frequency, the
stealthy visitations of that apparition which from the first had
seemed to possess so terrible a hold upon his imagination.

*   *   *

It was about this time that Captain Barton called upon the
then celebrated preacher, Dr——,* with whom he had a slight
acquaintance, and an extraordinary conversation ensued.

The divine was seated in his chambers in College, surrounded with works upon his favourite pursuit, and deep in theology, when Barton was announced.

There was something at once embarrassed and excited in his manner, which, along with his wan and haggard countenance, impressed the student with the unpleasant consciousness that his visitor must have recently suffered terribly indeed, to account for an alteration so striking—almost shocking.

After the usual interchange of polite greeting, and a few common-place remarks, Captain Barton, who obviously perceived the surprise which his visit had excited, and which Doctor——was unable wholly to conceal, interrupted a brief pause by remarking—

'This is a strange call, Doctor——, perhaps scarcely warranted by an acquaintance so slight as mine with you. I should not under ordinary circumstances have ventured to disturb you; but my visit is neither an idle nor impertinent intrusion. I am sure you will not so account it, when I tell you how afflicted I am.'

Doctor——interrupted him with assurances such as good breeding suggested, and Barton resumed—

'I am come to task your patience by asking your advice. When I say your patience, I might, indeed, say more; I might have said your humanity—your compassion; for I have been and am a great sufferer.'

'My dear sir,' replied the churchman, 'it will, indeed, afford me infinite gratification if I can give you comfort in any distress of mind; but—you know—'

'I know what you would say,' resumed Barton, quickly; 'I am an unbeliever, and, therefore, incapable of deriving help from religion; but don't take that for granted. At least you must not assume that, however unsettled my convictions may be, I do not feel a deep—a very deep—interest in the subject. Circumstances have lately forced it upon my attention, in such a way as to compel me to review the whole question in a more candid and teachable spirit, I believe, than I ever studied it in before.'

'Your difficulties, I take it for granted, refer to the evidences of revelation,' suggested the clergyman.

'Why—no—not altogether; in fact I am ashamed to say I

have not considered even my objections sufficiently to state them connectedly; but—but there is one subject on which I feel a peculiar interest.'

He paused again, and Doctor——pressed him to proceed.

'The fact is,' said Barton, 'whatever may be my uncertainty as to the authenticity of what we are taught to call revelation, of one fact I am deeply and horribly convinced, that there does exist beyond this a spiritual world—a system whose workings are generally in mercy hidden from us—a system which may be, and which is sometimes, partially and terribly revealed. I am sure—I *know*,' continued Barton, with increasing excitement, 'that there is a God—a dreadful God—and that retribution follows guilt, in ways the most mysterious and stupendous—by agencies the most inexplicable and terrific;—there is a spiritual system—great God, how I have been convinced!—a system malignant, and implacable, and omnipotent, under whose persecutions I am, and have been, suffering the torments of the damned!—yes, sir—yes—the fires and frenzy of hell!'

As Barton spoke, his agitation became so vehement that the Divine was shocked, and even alarmed. The wild and excited rapidity with which he spoke, and, above all, the indefinable horror, that stamped his features, afforded a contrast to his ordinary cool and unimpassioned self-possession striking and painful in the last degree.

CHAPTER V

MR BARTON STATES HIS CASE

'My dear sir,' said Doctor——, after a brief pause, 'I fear you have been very unhappy, indeed; but I venture to predict that the depression under which you labour will be found to originate in purely physical causes, and that with a change of air, and the aid of a few tonics, your spirits will return, and the tone of your mind be once more cheerful and tranquil as heretofore. There was, after all, more truth than we are quite willing to admit in the classic theories which assigned the undue predominance of any one affection of the mind, to the undue action or torpidity of one or other of our bodily organs. Believe me, that a little attention to diet, exercise, and the other essentials of health, under competent direction, will make you as much yourself as you can wish.'

'Doctor——,' said Barton, with something like a shudder, 'I *cannot* delude myself with such a hope. I have no hope to cling to but one, and that is, that by some other spiritual agency more potent than that which tortures me, *it* may be combated, and I delivered. If this may not be, I am lost—now and for ever lost.'

'But, Mr Barton, you must remember', urged his companion, 'that others have suffered as you have done, and—'

'No, no, no,' interrupted he, with irritability—'no, sir, I am not a credulous—far from a superstitious man. I have been, perhaps, too much the reverse—too sceptical, too slow of belief; but unless I were one whom no amount of evidence could convince, unless I were to contemn the repeated, the *perpetual* evidence of my own senses, I am now—now at last constrained to believe—I have no escape from the conviction—the overwhelming certainty—that I am haunted and dogged, go where I may, by—by a DEMON!'

There was a preternatural energy of horror in Barton's face, as, with its damp and deathlike lineaments turned towards his companion, he thus delievered himself.

'God help you, my poor friend,' said Dr——, much shocked, 'God help you; for, indeed, you *are* a sufferer, however your sufferings may have been caused.'

'Ay, ay, God help me,' echoed Barton, sternly; 'but *will* he help me—will he help me?'

'Pray to him—pray in an humble and trusting spirit,' said he.

'Pray, pray,' echoed he again; 'I can't pray—I could as easily move a mountain by an effort of my will. I have not belief enough to pray; there is something within me that will not pray. You prescribe impossibilities—literal impossibilities.'

'You will not find it so, if you will but try,' said Doctor——.

'Try! I *have* tried, and the attempt only fills me with confusion; and, sometimes, terror; I have tried in vain, and more than in vain. The awful, unutterable idea of eternity and infinity oppresses and maddens my brain whenever my mind approaches the contemplation of the Creator; I recoil from the effort scared. I tell you, Doctor——, if I am to be saved, it must be by other means. The idea of an eternal Creator is to me intolerable—my mind cannot support it.'

'Say, then, my dear sir,' urged he, 'say how you would have me serve you—what you would learn of me—what I can do or say to relieve you?'

'Listen to me first,' replied Captain Barton, with a subdued air, and an effort to suppress his excitement, 'listen to me while I detail the circumstances of the persecution under which my life has become all but intolerable—a persecution which has made me fear *death* and the world beyond the grave as much as I have grown to hate existence.'

Barton then proceeded to relate the circumstances which I have already detailed, and then continued:

'This has now become habitual—an accustomed thing. I do not mean the actual seeing him in the flesh—thank God, *that* at least is not permitted daily. Thank God, from the ineffable horrors of that visitation I have been mercifully allowed intervals of repose, though none of security; but from the consciousness that a malignant spirit is following and watching me wherever I go, I have never, for a single instant, a temporary respite. I am pursued with blasphemies, cries of despair and appalling hatred. I hear those dreadful sounds called after me as I turn the corners of the streets; they come in the night-time, while I sit in my chamber alone; they haunt me everywhere, charging me with hideous crimes, and—great God!—threatening me with coming vengeance and eternal misery. Hush! do you hear *that?*' he cried with a horrible smile of triumph; 'there—there, will that convince you?'

The clergyman felt a chill of horror steal over him, while, during the wail of a sudden gust of wind, he heard, or fancied he heard, the half articulate sounds of rage and derision mingling in the sough.

'Well, what do you think of *that?*' at length Barton cried, drawing a long breath through his teeth.

'I heard the wind,' said Doctor——. 'What should I think of it—what is there remarkable about it?'

'The prince of the powers of the air,'* muttered Barton, with a shudder.

'Tut, tut! my dear sir,' said the student, with an effort to reassure himself; for though it was broad day-light, there was nevertheless something disagreeably contagious in the nervous excitement under which his visitor so miserably suffered. 'You must not give way to those wild fancies; you must resist these impulses of the imagination.'

'Ay, ay; "resist the devil and he will flee from thee,"'* said Barton, in the same tone; 'but *how* resist him? ay, there it is—there is the rub. What—*what* am I to do? what *can* I do?'

'My dear sir, this *is* fancy,' said the man of folios; 'you are your own tormentor.'

'No, no, sir—fancy has no part in it,' answered Barton, somewhat sternly. 'Fancy! was it that made *you*, as well as me, hear, but this moment, those accents of hell? Fancy, indeed! No, no.'

'But you have seen this person frequently,' said the ecclesiastic; 'why have you not accosted or secured him? Is it not a little precipitate, to say no more, to assume, as you have done, the existence of preternatural agency, when, after all, everything may be easily accountable, if only proper means were taken to sift the matter.'

'There are circumstances connected with this—this *appearance,*' said Barton, 'which it is needless to disclose, but which to *me* are proof of its horrible nature. I know that the being that follows me is not human—I say I *know* this; I could prove it to your own conviction.' He paused for a minute, and then added, 'And as to accosting it, I dare not, I could not; when I see it I am powerless; I stand in the gaze of death, in the triumphant presence of infernal power and malignity. My strength, and faculties, and memory, all forsake me. O God, I fear, sir, you know not what you speak of. Mercy, mercy; heaven have pity on me!'

He leaned his elbow on the table, and passed his hand

across his eyes, as if to exclude some image of horror, muttering the last words of the sentence he had just concluded, again and again.

'Doctor——,' he said, abruptly raising himself, and looking full upon the clergyman with an imploring eye, 'I know you will do for me whatever may be done. You know now fully the circumstances and the nature of my affliction. I tell you I cannot help myself; I cannot hope to escape; I am utterly passive. I conjure you, then, to weigh my case well, and if anything may be done for me by vicarious supplication—by the intercession of the good—or by any aid or influence whatsoever, I implore of you, I adjure you in the name of the Most High, give me the benefit of that influence—deliver me from the body of this death. Strive for me, pity me; I know you will; you cannot refuse this; it is the purpose and object of my visit. Send me away with some hope, however little, some faint hope of ultimate deliverance, and I will nerve myself to endure, from hour to hour, the hideous dream into which my existence has been transformed.'

Doctor——assured him that all he could do was to pray earnestly for him, and that so much he would not fail to do. They parted with a hurried and melancholy valediction. Barton hastened to the carriage that awaited him at the door, drew down the blinds, and drove away, while Doctor—— returned to his chamber, to ruminate at leisure upon the strange interview which had just interrupted his studies.

CHAPTER VI

SEEN AGAIN

It was not to be expected that Captain Barton's changed and eccentric habits should long escape remark and discussion. Various were the theories suggested to account for it. Some attributed the alteration to the pressure of secret pecuniary embarrassments; others to a repugnance to fulfil an engagement into which he was presumed to have too precipitately entered; and others, again, to the supposed incipiency of mental disease, which latter, indeed, was the most plausible, as well as the most generally received, of the hypotheses circulated in the gossip of the day.

From the very commencement of this change, at first so gradual in its advances, Miss Montague had of course been aware of it. The intimacy involved in their peculiar relation, as well as the near interest which it inspired afforded, in her case, a like opportunity and motive for the successful exercise of that keen and penetrating observation peculiar to her sex.

His visits became, at length, so interrupted, and his manner, while they lasted, so abstracted, strange, and agitated, that Lady L——, after hinting her anxiety and her suspicions more than once, at length distinctly stated her anxiety, and pressed for an explanation.

The explanation was given, and although its nature at first relieved the worst solicitudes of the old lady and her niece, yet the circumstances which attended it, and the really dreadful consequences which it obviously indicated, as regarded the spirits, and indeed the reason of the now wretched man who made the strange declaration, were enough, upon little reflection, to fill their minds with perturbation and alarm.

General Montague, the young lady's father, at length arrived. He had himself slightly known Barton, some ten or twelve years previously, and being aware of his fortune and connexions, was disposed to regard him as an unexceptionable and indeed a most desirable match for his daughter. He laughed at the story of Barton's supernatural visitations, and lost no time in calling upon his intended son-in-law.

'My dear Barton,' he continued, gaily, after a little conversation, 'my sister tells me that you are a victim to blue devils, in quite a new and original shape.'

Barton changed countenance, and sighed profoundly.

'Come, come; I protest this will never do,' continued the General; 'you are more like a man on his way to the gallows than to the altar. These devils have made quite a saint of you.'

Barton made an effort to change the conversation.

'No, no, it won't do,' said his visitor laughing; 'I am resolved to say what I have to say upon this magnificent mock mystery of yours. You must not be angry, but really it is too bad to see you at your time of life, absolutely frightened into good behaviour, like a naughty child by a bugaboo, and as far as I can learn, a very contemptible one. Seriously, I have been a good deal annoyed at what they tell me; but at the same time thoroughly convinced that there is nothing in the matter that may not be cleared up, with a little attention and management, within a week at furthest.'

'Ah, General, you do not know—' he began.

'Yes, but I do know quite enough to warrant my confidence,' interrupted the soldier, 'don't I know that all your annoyance proceeds from the occasional appearance of a certain little man in a cap and great-coat, with a red vest and a bad face, who follows you about, and pops upon you at corners of lanes, and throws you into ague fits. Now, my dear fellow, I'll make it my business to *catch* this mischievous little mountebank, and either beat him to a jelly with my own hands, or have him whipped through the town, at the cart's-tail,* before a month passes.'

'If *you* knew what *I* knew,' said Barton, with gloomy agitation, 'you would speak very differently. Don't imagine that I am so weak as to assume, without proof the most overwhelming, the conclusion to which I have been forced— the proofs are here, locked up here.' As he spoke he tapped upon his breast, and with an anxious sigh continued to walk up and down the room.

'Well, well, Barton,' said his visitor, 'I'll wager a rump and a dozen* I collar the ghost, and convince even you before many days are over.'

He was running on in the same strain when he was suddenly arrested, and not a little shocked, by observing Barton, who had approached the window, stagger slowly back, like one who had received a stunning blow; his arm extended toward the street—his face and his very lips white as ashes—while he muttered, 'There—by heaven!—there—there!'

General Montague started mechanically to his feet, and from the window of the drawing-room, saw a figure corresponding, as well as his hurry would permit him to discern, with the description of the person whose appearance so persistently disturbed the repose of his friend.

The figure was just turning from the rails of the area upon which it had been leaning, and, without waiting to see more, the old gentleman snatched his cane and hat, and rushed down the stairs and into the street, in the furious hope of securing the person, and punishing the audacity of the mysterious stranger.

He looked round him, but in vain, for any trace of the person he had himself distinctly seen. He ran breathlessly to the nearest corner, expecting to see from thence the retiring figure, but no such form was visible. Back and forward, from crossing to crossing, he ran, at fault,* and it was not until the curious gaze and laughing countenances of the passers-by reminded him of the absurdity of his pursuit, that he checked his hurried pace, lowered his walking cane from the menacing altitude which he had mechanically given it, adjusted his hat, and walked composedly back again, inwardly vexed and flurried. He found Barton pale and trembling in every joint; they both remained silent, though under emotions very different. At last Barton whispered, 'You saw it?'

'*It!*—him—some one—you mean—to be sure I did,' replied Montague, testily. 'But where is the good or the harm of seeing him? The fellow runs like a lamp-lighter.* I wanted to *catch* him, but he had stolen away before I could reach the hall-door. However, it is no great matter; next time, I dare say, I'll do better; and egad, if I once come within reach of him, I'll introduce his shoulders to the weight of my cane.'

Notwithstanding General Montague's undertakings and exhortations, however, Barton continued to suffer from the self-same unexplained cause; go how, when, or where he would, he was still constantly dogged or confronted by the being who had established over him so horrible an influence.

Nowhere and at no time was he secure against the odious appearance which haunted him with such diabolic perseverance.

His depression, misery, and excitement became more settled and alarming every day, and the mental agonies that ceaselessly preyed upon him began at last so sensibly to affect his health, that Lady L—— and General Montague succeeded, without, indeed, much difficulty, in persuading him to try a

short tour on the Continent, in the hope that an entire change
of scene would, at all events, have the effect of breaking
through the influences of local association, which the more
sceptical of his friends assumed to be by no means inoperative
in suggesting and perpetuating what they conceived to be a
mere form of nervous illusion.

General Montague indeed was persuaded that the figure
which haunted his intended son-in-law was by no means the
creation of his imagination, but, on the contrary, a substantial
form of flesh and blood, animated by a resolution, perhaps
with some murderous object in perspective, to watch and
follow the unfortunate gentleman.

Even this hypothesis was not a very pleasant one; yet it was
plain that if Barton could ever be convinced that there was
nothing preternatural in the phenomenon which he had hitherto regarded in that light, the affair would lose all its terrors
in his eyes, and wholly cease to exercise upon his health and
spirits the baleful influence which it had hitherto done. He
therefore reasoned, that if the annoyance were actually escaped
by mere locomotion and change of scene, it obviously could
not have originated in any supernatural agency.

CHAPTER VII

FLIGHT

Yielding to their persuasions, Barton left Dublin for England,
accompanied by General Montague. They posted rapidly to
London, and thence to Dover, whence they took the packet*
with a fair wind for Calais. The General's confidence in the
result of the expedition on Barton's spirits had risen day by
day, since their departure from the shores of Ireland; for to the
inexpressible relief and delight of the latter, he had not since
then, so much as even once fancied a repetition of those
impressions which had, when at home, drawn him gradually
down to the very depths of despair.

This exemption from what he had begun to regard as the

inevitable condition of his existence, and the sense of security which began to pervade his mind, were inexpressibly delightful; and in the exultation of what he considered his deliverance, he indulged in a thousand happy anticipations for a future into which so lately he had hardly dared to look; and in short, both he and his companion secretly congratulated themselves upon the termination of that persecution which had been to its immediate victim a source of such unspeakable agony.

It was a beautiful day, and a crowd of idlers stood upon the jetty to receive the packet, and enjoy the bustle of the new arrivals. Montague walked a few paces in advance of his friend, and as he made his way through the crowd, a little man touched his arm, and said to him, in a broad provincial *patois*—*

'Monsieur is walking too fast; he will lose his sick comrade in the throng, for, by my faith, the poor gentleman seems to be fainting.'

Montague turned quickly, and observed that Barton did indeed look deadly pale. He hastened to his side.

'My dear fellow, are you ill?' he asked anxiously.

The question was unheeded and twice repeated, ere Barton stammered—

'I saw him—by ——, I saw him!'

'*Him!*—the wretch—who—where now?—where is he?' cried Montague, looking around him.

'I saw him—but he is gone,' repeated Barton, faintly.

'But where—where? For God's sake speak,' urged Montague, vehemently.

'It is but this moment—*here,*' said he.

'But what did he look like—what had he on—what did he wear—quick, quick,' urged his excited companion, ready to dart among the crowd and collar the delinquent on the spot.

'He touched your arm—he spoke to you—he pointed to me. God be merciful to me, there is no escape,' said Barton, in the low, subdued tones of despair.

Montague had already bustled away in all the flurry of mingled hope and rage; but though the singular *personnel** of the stranger who had accosted him was vividly impressed upon his recollection, he failed to discover among the crowd even the slightest resemblance to him.

After a fruitless search, in which he enlisted the services of several of the bystanders, who aided all the more zealously, as they believed he had been robbed, he at length, out of breath and baffled, gave over the attempt.

'Ah, my friend, it won't do,' said Barton, with the faint voice and bewildered, ghastly look of one who had been stunned by some mortal shock; 'there is no use in contending; whatever it is, the dreadful association between me and it, is now established—I shall never escape—never!'

'Nonsense, nonsense, my dear Barton; don't talk so,' said Montague with something at once of irritation and dismay; 'you must not, I say; we'll jockey* the scoundrel yet; never mind, I say—never mind.'

It was, however, but labour lost to endeavour henceforward to inspire Barton with one ray of hope; he became desponding.

This intangible, and, as it seemed, utterly inadequate influence was fast destroying his energies of intellect, character, and health. His first object was now to return to Ireland, there, as he believed, and now almost hoped, speedily to die.

To Ireland accordingly he came and one of the first faces he saw upon the shore, was again that of his implacable and dreaded attendant. Barton seemed at last to have lost not only all enjoyment and every hope in existence, but all independence of will besides. He now submitted himself passively to the management of the friends most nearly interested in his welfare.

With the apathy of entire despair, he implicitly assented to whatever measures they suggested and advised; and as a last resource, it was determined to remove him to a house of Lady L——'s, in the neighbourhood of Clontarf,* where, with the advice of his medical attendant, who persisted in his opinion that the whole train of consequences resulted merely from some nervous derangement, it was resolved that he was to confine himself strictly to the house, and to make use only of those apartments which commanded a view of an enclosed yard, the gates of which were to be kept jealously locked.

Those precautions would certainly secure him against the

casual appearance of any living form that his excited imagination might possibly confound with the spectre which, as it was contended, his fancy recognized in every figure that bore even a distant or general resemblance to the peculiarities with which his fancy had at first invested it.

A month or six weeks' absolute seclusion under these conditions, it was hoped, might, by interrupting the series of these terrible impressions, gradually dispel the predisposing apprehensions, and the associations which had confirmed the supposed disease, and rendered recovery hopeless.

Cheerful society and that of his friends was to be constantly supplied, and on the whole, very sanguine expectations were indulged in, that under the treatment thus detailed, the obstinate hypochondria of the patient might at length give way.

Accompanied, therefore, by Lady L——, General Montague and his daughter—his own affianced bride—poor Barton—himself never daring to cherish a hope of his ultimate emancipation from the horrors under which his life was literally wasting away—took possession of the apartments, whose situation protected him against the intrusions from which he shrank with such unutterable terror.

After a little time, a steady persistence in this system began to manifest its results, in a very marked though gradual improvement, alike in the health and spirits of the invalid. Not, indeed, that anything at all approaching complete recovery was yet discernible. On the contrary, to those who had not seen him since the commencement of his strange sufferings, such an alteration would have been apparent as might well have shocked them.

The improvement, however, such as it was, was welcomed with gratitude and delight, especially by the young lady, whom her attachment to him, as well as her now singularly painful position, consequent on his protracted illness, rendered an object scarcely one degree less to be commiserated than himself.

A week passed—a fortnight—a month—and yet there had been no recurrence of the hated visitation. The treatment had, so far forth, been followed by complete success. The chain of

associations was broken. The constant pressure upon the
overtasked spirits had been removed, and, under these comparatively favourable circumstances, the sense of social com-
munity with the world about him, and something of human
interest, if not of enjoyment, began to reanimate him.

It was about this time that Lady L—— who, like most old
ladies of the day, was deep in family receipts,* and a great
pretender to medical science, dispatched her own maid to the
kitchen garden, with a list of herbs, which were there to be
carefully culled, and brought back to her housekeeper for the
purpose stated. The handmaiden, however, returned with her
task scarce half completed, and a good deal flurried and
alarmed. Her mode of accounting for her precipitate retreat
and evident agitation was odd, and, to the old lady, startling.

CHAPTER VIII

SOFTENED

It appeared that she had repaired to the kitchen garden,
pursuant to her mistress's directions, and had there begun to
make the specified election among the rank and neglected
herbs which crowded one corner of the enclosure, and while
engaged in this pleasant labour, she carelessly sang a fragment
of an old song, as she said, 'to keep herself company'. She was,
however, interrupted by an ill-natured laugh; and, looking up,
she saw through the old thorn hedge, which surrounded the
garden, a singularly ill-looking little man, whose countenance
wore the stamp of menace and malignity, standing close to
her, at the other side of the hawthorn screen.

She described herself as utterly unable to move or speak,
while he charged her with a message for Captain Barton; the
substance of which she distinctly remembered to have been to
the effect, that he, Captain Barton, must come abroad as
usual, and show himself to his friends, out of doors, or else
prepare for a visit in his own chamber.

On concluding this brief message, the stranger had, with a

threatening air, got down into the outer ditch, and, seizing the hawthorn stems in his hands, seemed on the point of climbing through the fence—a feat which might have been accomplished without much difficulty.

Without, of course, awaiting this result, the girl—throwing down her treasures of thyme and rosemary—had turned and run, with the swiftness of terror, to the house. Lady L—— commanded her, on pain of instant dismissal, to observe an absolute silence respecting all that passed of the incident which related to Captain Barton; and, at the same time, directed instant search to be made by her men, in the garden and the fields adjacent. This measure, however, was as usual, unsuccessful, and, filled with undefinable misgivings, Lady L—— communicated the incident to her brother. The story, however, until long afterwards, went no further, and, of course, it was jealously guarded from Barton, who continued to amend, though slowly.

Barton now began to walk occasionally in the court-yard which I have mentioned, and which being enclosed by a high wall, commanded no view beyond its own extent. Here he, therefore, considered himself perfectly secure: and, but for a careless violation of orders by one of the grooms, he might have enjoyed, at least for some time longer, his much-prized immunity. Opening upon the public road, this yard was entered by a wooden gate, with a wicket in it, and was further defended by an iron gate upon the outside. Strict orders had been given to keep both carefully locked; but, spite of these, it had happened that one day, as Barton was slowly pacing this narrow enclosure, in his accustomed walk, and reaching the further extremity, was turning to retrace his steps, he saw the boarded wicket ajar, and the face of his tormentor immovably looking at him through the iron bars. For a few seconds he stood riveted to the earth—breathless and bloodless—in the fascination of that dreaded gaze, and then fell helplessly insensible, upon the pavement.

There he was found a few minutes afterwards, and conveyed to his room—the apartment which he was never afterwards to leave alive. Henceforward a marked and unaccountable change was observable in the tone of his mind. Captain Barton was now no longer the excited and despairing man he had been before; a strange alteration had passed upon him—an unearthly tranquillity reigned in his mind—it was the anticipated stillness of the grave.

'Montague, my friend, this struggle is nearly ended now,' he said, tranquilly, but with a look of fixed and fearful awe. 'I have, at last, some comfort from that world of spirits, from which my punishment has come. I now know that my sufferings will soon be over.'

Montague pressed him to speak on.

'Yes,' said he, in a softened voice, 'my punishment is nearly ended. From sorrow, perhaps I shall never, in time or eternity, escape; but my *agony* is almost over. Comfort has been revealed to me, and what remains of my allotted struggle I will bear with submission—even with hope.'

'I am glad to hear you speak so tranquilly, my dear Barton,' said Montague; 'peace and cheer of mind are all you need to make you what you were.'

'No, no—I never can be that,' said he mournfully. 'I am no longer fit for life. I am soon to die. I am to see *him* but once again, and then all is ended.'

'He said so, then?' suggested Montague.

'*He?*—No, no: good tidings could scarcely come through him; and these were good and welcome; and they came so solemnly and sweetly—with unutterable love and melancholy, such as I could not—without saying more than is needful, or fitting, of other long-past scenes and persons—fully explain to you.'

As Barton said this he shed tears.

'Come, come,' said Montague, mistaking the source of his emotions, 'you must not give way. What is it, after all, but a pack of dreams and nonsense; or, at worst, the practices of a scheming rascal that enjoys his power of playing upon your nerves, and loves to exert it—a sneaking vagabond that owes you a grudge, and pays it off this way, not daring to try a more manly one.'

'A grudge, indeed, he owes me—you say rightly,' said Barton, with a sudden shudder; 'a grudge as you call it. Oh, my God! when the justice of Heaven permits the Evil one to carry out a scheme of vengeance—when its execution is committed to the lost and terrible victim of sin, who owes his own ruin to the man, the very man, whom he is commissioned to pursue—then, indeed, the torments and terrors of hell are anticipated on earth. But heaven has dealt mercifully with me—hope has opened to me at last; and if death could come without the dreadful sight I am doomed to see, I would gladly close my eyes this moment upon the world. But though death is welcome, I shrink with an agony you cannot understand— an actual frenzy of terror—from the last encounter with that— that DEMON, who has drawn me thus to the verge of the chasm, and who is himself to plunge me down. I am to see him again—once more—but under circumstances unutterably more terrific than ever.'

As Barton thus spoke, he trembled so violently that Montague was really alarmed at the extremity of his sudden agitation, and hastened to lead him back to the topic which had before seemed to exert so tranquillizing an effect upon his mind.

'It was not a dream,' he said, after a time; 'I was in a different state—I felt differently and strangely; and yet it was all as real, as clear, and vivid, as what I now see and hear—it was a reality.'

'And what *did* you see and hear?' urged his companion.

'When I wakened from the swoon I fell into on seeing *him*,' said Barton, continuing as if he had not heard the question, 'it was slowly, very slowly—I was lying by the margin of a broad lake, with misty hills all round, and a soft, melancholy, rose-coloured light illuminated it all. It was unusually sad and lonely, and yet more beautiful than any earthly scene. My head was leaning on the lap of a girl, and she was singing a song, that told, I know not how—whether by words or harmonies—of all my life—all that is past, and all that is still to come; and with the song the old feelings that I thought had perished within me came back, and tears flowed from my eyes—partly for the song and its mysterious beauty, and partly for the unearthly sweetness of her voice; and yet I knew the voice—oh! how well; and I was spell-bound as I listened and looked at the solitary scene, without stirring, almost without breathing—and, alas! alas! without turning my eyes toward the face that I knew was near me, so sweetly powerful was the enchantment that held me. And so, slowly, the song and scene grew fainter, and fainter, to my senses, till all was dark and still again. And then I awoke to this world, as you saw, comforted, for I knew that I was forgiven much.' Barton wept again long and bitterly.

From this time, as we have said, the prevailing tone of his mind was one of profound and tranquil melancholy. This, however, was not without its interruptions. He was thoroughly impressed with the conviction that he was to experience another and a final visitation, transcending in horror all he had before experienced. From this anticipated and unknown agony, he often shrank in such paroxysms of abject terror and distraction, as filled the whole household with dismay and superstitious panic. Even those among them who affected to discredit the theory of preternatural agency, were often in their secret souls visited during the silence of night with qualms and apprehensions, which they would not have readily confessed; and none of them attempted to dissuade Barton from the resolution on which he now systematically acted, of shutting himself up in his own apartment. The window-blinds of this room were kept jealously down; and his own man was seldom out of his presence, day or night, his bed being placed in the same chamber.

This man was an attached and respectable servant; and his duties, in addition to those ordinarily imposed upon valets, but which Barton's independent habits generally dispensed with, were to attend carefully to the simple precautions by means of which his master hoped to exclude the dreaded intrusion of the 'Watcher'. And, in addition to attending to those arrangements, which amounted merely to guarding against the possibility of his master's being, through any unscreened window or open door, exposed to the dreaded influence, the valet was never to suffer him to be alone—total solitude, even for a minute, had become to him now almost as intolerable as the idea of going abroad into the public ways— it was an instinctive anticipation of what was coming.

CHAPTER IX

REQUIESCAT*

It is needless to say, that under these circumstances, no steps were taken toward the fulfilment of that engagement into which he had entered. There was quite disparity enough in point of years, and indeed of habits, between the young lady and Captain Barton, to have precluded anything like a very vehement or romantic attachment on her part. Though grieved and anxious, therefore, she was very far from being heart-broken.*

Miss Montague, however, devoted much of her time to the patient but fruitless attempt to cheer the unhappy invalid. She read for him, and conversed with him; but it was apparent that whatever exertions he made, the endeavour to escape from the one ever waking fear that preyed upon him, was utterly and miserably unavailing.

Young ladies are much given to the cultivation of pets; and among those who shared the favour of Miss Montague was a fine old owl, which the gardener, who caught him napping among the ivy of a ruined stable, had dutifully presented to that young lady.

The caprice which regulates such preferences was mani-fested in the extravagant favour with which this grim and ill-favoured bird was at once distinguished by his mistress; and, trifling as this whimsical circumstance may seem, I am forced to mention it, inasmuch as it is connected, oddly enough, with the concluding scene of the story.

Barton, so far from sharing in this liking for the new favourite, regarded it from the first with an antipathy as violent as it was utterly unaccountable. Its very vicinity was unsupportable to him. He seemed to hate and dread it with a vehemence absolutely laughable, and which, to those who have never witnessed the exhibition of antipathies of this kind, would seem all but incredible.

With these few words of preliminary explanation, I shall proceed to state the particulars of the last scene in this strange series of incidents. It was almost two o'clock one winter's night, and Barton was, as usual at that hour, in his bed; the servant we have mentioned occupied a smaller bed in the same room, and a light was burning. The man was on a sudden aroused by his master, who said—

'I can't get it out of my head that that accursed bird has got out somehow, and is lurking in some corner of the room. I have been dreaming about him. Get up, Smith, and look about; search for him. Such hateful dreams!'

The servant rose, and examined the chamber, and while engaged in so doing, he heard the well-known sound, more like a long-drawn gasp than a hiss, with which these birds from their secret haunts affright the quiet of the night.

This ghostly indication of its proximity—for the sound proceeded from the passage upon which Barton's chamber-door opened—determined the search of the servant, who, opening the door, proceeded a step or two forward for the purpose of driving the bird away. He had however, hardly entered the lobby, when the door behind him slowly swung to under the impulse, as it seemed, of some gentle current of air; but as immediately over the door there was a kind of window, intended in the day time to aid in lighting the passage, and through which at present the rays of the candle were issuing, the valet could see quite enough for his purpose.

As he advanced he heard his master—who, lying in a well-curtained bed, had not, as it seemed, perceived his exit from the room—call him by name, and direct him to place the candle on the table by his bed. The servant, who was now some way in the long passage, and not liking to raise his voice for the purpose of replying, lest he should startle the sleeping inmates of the house, began to walk hurriedly and softly back again, when, to his amazement, he heard a voice in the interior of the chamber answering calmly, and actually saw, through the window which overtopped the door, that the light was slowly shifting, as if carried across the room in answer to his master's call. Palsied by a feeling akin to terror, yet not unmingled with curiosity, he stood breathless and listening at the threshold, unable to summon resolution to push open the door and enter. Then came a rustling of the curtains, and a

sound like that of one who in a low voice hushes a child to
rest, in the midst of which he heard Barton say, in a tone of
stifled horror—'Oh, God—oh, my God!' and repeat the same
exclamation several times. Then ensued a silence, which again
was broken by the same strange soothing sound; and at last
there burst forth, in one swelling peal, a yell of agony so
appalling and hideous, that, under some impulse of ungovern-
able horror, the man rushed to the door, and with his whole
strength strove to force it open. Whether it was that, in his
agitation, he had himself but imperfectly turned the handle, or
that the door was really secured upon the inside, he failed to
effect an entrance; and as he tugged and pushed, yell after yell
rang louder and wilder through the chamber, accompanied all
the while by the same hushed sounds. Actually freezing with
terror, and scarce knowing what he did, the man turned and
ran down the passage, wringing his hands in the extremity of
horror and irresolution. At the stair-head he was encountered
by General Montague, scared and eager, and just as they met
the fearful sounds had ceased.

'What is it? Who—where is your master?' said Montague
with the incoherence of extreme agitation. 'Has anything—for
God's sake is anything wrong?'

'Lord have mercy on us, it's all over,' said the man staring
wildly towards his master's chamber. 'He's dead, sir, I'm sure
he's dead.'

Without waiting for inquiry or explanation, Montague,
closely followed by the servant, hurried to the chamber-door,
turned the handle, and pushed it open. As the door yielded to
his pressure, the ill-omened bird of which the servant had been
in search, uttering its spectral warning, started suddenly from
the far side of the bed, and flying through the door-way close
over their heads, and extinguishing, in his passage, the candle
which Montague carried, crashed through the skylight that
overlooked the lobby, and sailed away into the darkness of the
outer space.

'There it is, God bless us,' whispered the man, after a
breathless pause.

'Curse that bird,' muttered the General, startled by the

suddenness of the apparition, and unable to conceal his discomposure.

'The candle is moved,' said the man, after another breathless pause, pointing to the candle that still burned in the room; 'see, they put it by the bed.'

'Draw the curtains, fellow, and don't stand gaping there,' whispered Montague, sternly.

The man hesitated.

'Hold this, then,' said Montague, impatiently thrusting the candlestick into the servant's hand, and himself advancing to the bed-side, he drew the curtains apart. The light of the candle, which was still burning at the bedside, fell upon a figure huddled together, and half upright, at the head of the bed. It seemed as though it had shrunk back as far as the solid panelling would allow, and the hands were still clutched in the bed-clothes.

'Barton, Barton, *Barton!*' cried the General, with a strange mixture of awe and vehemence. He took the candle, and held it so that it shone full upon the face. The features were fixed, stern, and white; the jaw was fallen; and the sightless eyes, still open, gazed vacantly forward toward the front of the bed. 'God Almighty! he's dead,' muttered the General, as he looked upon this fearful spectacle. They both continued to gaze upon it in silence for a minute or more.

'And cold, too,' whispered Montague, withdrawing his hand from that of the dead man.

'And see, see—may I never have life, sir,' added the man, after another pause, with a shudder, 'but there was something else on the bed with him. Look there—look there—see that, sir.'

As the man thus spoke, he pointed to a deep indenture, as if caused by a heavy pressure, near the foot of the bed.

Montague was silent.

'Come, sir, come away, for God's sake,' whispered the man, drawing close up to him, and holding fast by his arm, while he glanced fearfully round; 'what good can be done here now— come away, for God's sake!'

At this moment they heard the steps of more than one approaching, and Montague, hastily desiring the servant to arrest their progress, endeavoured to loose the rigid gripe with which the fingers of the dead man were clutched in the bed-clothes, and drew, as well as he was able, the awful figure into a reclining posture; then closing the curtains carefully upon it, he hastened himself to meet those persons that were approaching.

* * *

It is needless to follow the personages so slightly connected with this narrative, into the events of their after life; it is enough to say, that no clue to the solution of these mysterious occurrences was ever after discovered; and so long an interval having now passed since the event which I have just described concluded this strange history, it is scarcely to be expected that time can throw any new lights upon its dark and inexplicable outline. Until the secrets of the earth shall be no longer hidden, therefore, these transactions must remain shrouded in their original obscurity.

The only occurrence in Captain Barton's former life to which reference was ever made, as having any possible connexion with the sufferings with which his existence closed, and which he himself seemed to regard as working out a retribution for some grievous sin of his past life, was a circumstance which was not for several years after his death brought to light. The nature of this disclosure was painful to his relatives, and discreditable to his memory.

It appeared that some six years before Captain Barton's final return to Dublin, he had formed, in the town of Ply-mouth,* a guilty attachment, the object of which was the daughter of one of the ship's crew under his command. The father had visited the frailty of his unhappy child with extreme harshness, and even brutality, and it was said that she had died heart-broken. Presuming upon Barton's implication in her guilt, this man had conducted himself toward him with marked insolence, and Barton retaliated this, and what he resented with still more exasperated bitterness—his treatment of the unfortunate girl—by a systematic exercise of those terrible and arbitrary severities which the regulations of the navy placed at the command of those who are responsible for its discipline. The man had at length made his escape, while the vessel was in port at Naples, but died, as it was said, in an hospital in that town, of the wounds inflicted in one of his recent and sanguinary punishments.

Whether these circumstances in reality bear, or not, upon the occurrences of Barton's after-life, it is, of course, impossible to say. It seems, however, more than probable that they were at least, in his own mind, closely associated with them. But however the truth may be, as to the origin and motives of this mysterious persecution, there can be no doubt that, with respect to the agencies by which it was accomplished, absolute and impenetrable mystery is like to prevail until the day of doom.

Postscript by the editor

The preceding narrative is given in the *ipsissima verba** of the good old clergyman, under whose hand it was delivered to Doctor Hesselius. Notwithstanding the occasional stiffness and redundancy of his sentences, I thought it better to reserve to myself the power of assuring the reader, that in handing to the printer, the MS of a statement so marvellous, the Editor has not altered one letter of the original text. [*Ed. Papers of Dr Hesselius*.]

MR JUSTICE HARBOTTLE

PROLOGUE

ON this case, Doctor Hesselius has inscribed nothing more than the words, 'Harman's Report', and a simple reference to his own extraordinary Essay on 'the Interior Sense, and the Conditions of the opening thereof'.

The reference is to Vol. I. Section 317, Note Z^a. The note to which reference is thus made, simply says: 'There are two accounts of the remarkable case of the Honourable Mr Justice Harbottle, one furnished to me by Mrs Trimmer of Tunbridge Wells (June, 1805); the other at a much later date, by Anthony Harman, Esq. I much prefer the former; in the first place, because it is minute and detailed, and written, it seems to me, with more caution and knowledge; and in the next, because the letters from Doctor Hedstone, which are embodied in it, furnish matter of the highest value to a right apprehension of the nature of the case. It was one of the best declared cases of an opening of the interior sense, which I have met with. It was affected, too, by the phenomenon, which occurs so frequently as to indicate a law of these eccentric conditions; that is to say, it exhibited, what I may term, the contagious character of this sort of intrusion of the spirit-world upon the proper domain of matter. So soon as the spirit-action has established itself in the case of one patient, its developed energy begins to radiate, more or less effectually, upon others. The interior vision of the child was opened; as was, also, that of its mother, Mrs Pyneweck; and both the interior vision and hearing of the scullery-maid, were opened on the same occasion. After-appearances are the result of the law explained in Vol. II. Section 17 to 49. The common centre of association, simultaneously recalled, unites, or re-unites, as the case may be, for a period measured, as we see, in Section 37. The *maximum* will extend to days, the *minimum* is little more than a second. We see the operation of this principle perfectly displayed, in certain cases of lunacy, of epilepsy, of catalepsy, and of mania, of a peculiar and painful character, though unattended by incapacity of business.'

The memorandum of the case of Judge Harbottle, which was written by Mrs Trimmer of Tunbridge Wells, which Doctor Hesselius thought the better of the two, I have been unable to discover among his papers. I found in his escritoire a note to the effect that he had lent the Report of Judge Harbottle's case written by Mrs Trimmer, to Doctor F. Heyne. To that learned and able gentleman accordingly I wrote, and received from him, in his reply, which was full of alarms and regrets on account of the uncertain safety of that 'valuable MS,' a line written long since by Doctor Hesselius, which completely exonerated him, inasmuch as it acknowledged the safe return of the papers. The Narrative of Mr Harman, is, therefore, the only one available for this collection. The late Dr Hesselius, in another passage of the note that I have cited, says, 'As to the facts (non-medical) of the case, the narrative of Mr Harman exactly tallies with that furnished by Mrs Trimmer.' The strictly scientific view of the case would scarcely interest the popular reader; and, possibly, for the purposes of this selection, I should, even had I both papers to choose between, have preferred that of Mr Harman, which is given, in full, in the following pages.

CHAPTER I

THE JUDGE'S HOUSE

Thirty years ago, an elderly man, to whom I paid quarterly a small annuity charged on some property of mine, came on the quarter-day* to receive it. He was a dry, sad, quiet man, who had known better days, and had always maintained an unexceptionable character. No better authority could be imagined for a ghost story.

He told me one, though with a manifest reluctance; he was drawn into the narration by his choosing to explain what I should not have remarked, that he had called two days earlier than that week after the strict day of payment, which he had usually allowed to elapse. His reason was a sudden determination to change his lodgings, and the consequent necessity of paying his rent a little before it was due.

He lodged in a dark street in Westminster,* in a spacious old house, very warm, being wainscoted* from top to bottom, and furnished with no undue abundance of windows, and those fitted with thick sashes and small panes.

This house was, as the bills upon the windows testified, offered to be sold or let. But no one seemed to care to look at it.

A thin matron, in rusty black silk, very taciturn, with large, steady, alarmed eyes, that seemed to look in your face, to read what you might have seen in the dark rooms and passages through which you had passed, was in charge of it, with a solitary 'maid-of-all-work' under her command. My poor friend had taken lodgings in this house, on account of their extraordinary cheapness. He had occupied them for nearly a year without the slightest disturbance, and was the only tenant, under rent, in the house. He had two rooms; a sitting-room, and a bedroom with a closet opening from it, in which he kept his books and papers locked up. He had gone to his bed, having also locked the outer door. Unable to sleep, he had lighted a candle, and after having read for a time, had laid the book beside him. He heard the old clock at the stairhead strike one; and very shortly after, to his alarm, he saw the closet-door, which he thought he had locked, open stealthily, and a slight dark man, particularly sinister, and somewhere about fifty, dressed in mourning of a very antique fashion, such a suit as we see in Hogarth*, entered the room on tip-toe. He was followed by an elder man, stout, and blotched with scurvy, and whose features, fixed as a corpse's, were stamped with dreadful force with a character of sensuality and villainy.*

This old man wore a flowered-silk dressing-gown and ruffles, and he remarked a gold ring on his finger, and on his head a cap of velvet, such as, in the days of perukes,* gentlemen wore in undress.

This direful old man carried in his ringed and ruffled hand a coil of rope; and these two figures crossed the floor diagonally, passing the foot of his bed, from the closet-door at the farther end of the room, at the left, near the window, to the door opening upon the lobby, close to the bed's head, at his right.

He did not attempt to describe his sensations as these figures passed so near him. He merely said, that so far from sleeping in that room again, no consideration the world could offer would induce him so much as to enter it again alone, even in the daylight. He found both doors, that of the closet, and that of the room opening upon the lobby, in the morning fast locked, as he had left them before going to bed.

In answer to a question of mine, he said that neither appeared the least conscious of his presence. They did not seem to glide, but walked as living men do, but without any sound, and he felt a vibration on the floor as they crossed it. He so obviously suffered from speaking about the apparitions, that I asked him no more questions.

There were in his description, however, certain coincidences so very singular, as to induce me, by that very post, to write to a friend much my senior, then living in a remote part of England, for the information which I knew he could give me. He had himself more than once pointed out that old house to my attention, and told me, though very briefly, the strange story which I now asked him to give me in greater detail.

His answer satisfied me; and the following pages convey its substance.

Your letter (he wrote) tells me you desire some particulars about the closing years of the life of Mr Justice Harbottle, one of the judges of the Court of Common Pleas.* You refer, of course, to the extraordinary occurrences that made that period of his life long after a theme for 'winter tales'* and metaphysical speculation. I happen to know perhaps more than any other man living of those mysterious particulars.

The old family mansion, when I revisited London, more than thirty years ago, I examined for the last time. During the years that have passed since then, I hear that improvement, with its preliminary demolitions, has been doing wonders for

the quarter of Westminster in which it stood. If I were quite
certain that the house had been taken down, I should have no
difficulty about naming the street in which it stood. As what I
have to tell, however, is not likely to improve its letting value,*
and as I should not care to get into trouble, I prefer being
silent on that particular point.

How old the house was, I can't tell. People said it was built
by Roger Harbottle, a Turkey merchant, in the reign of King
James I.* I am not a good opinion upon such questions; but
having been in it, though in its forlorn and deserted state, I
can tell you in a general way what it was like. It was built of
dark-red brick, and the door and windows were faced with
stone that had turned yellow by time. It receded some feet
from the line of the other houses in the street; and it had a
florid and fanciful rail of iron about the broad steps that
invited your ascent to the hall-door, in which were fixed, under
a file of lamps, among scrolls and twisted leaves, two immense
'extinguishers', like the conical caps of fairies, into which, in
old times, the footmen used to thrust their flambeaux when
their chairs* or coaches had set down their great people in the
hall or at the steps, as the case might be. That hall is panelled
up to the ceiling, and has a large fire-place. Two or three
stately old rooms open from it at each side. The windows of
these are tall, with many small panes. Passing through the
arch at the back of the hall, you come upon the wide and
heavy well-staircase.* There is a back staircase also. The
mansion is large, and has not as much light, by any means, in
proportion to its extent, as modern houses enjoy. When I saw
it, it had long been untenanted, and had the gloomy reputation
beside of a haunted house. Cobwebs floated from the ceilings
or spanned the corners of the cornices, and dust lay thick over
everything. The windows were stained with the dust and rain
of fifty years, and darkness had thus grown darker.

When I made it my first visit, it was in company with my
father, when I was still a boy, in the year 1808. I was about
twelve years old, and my imagination impressible, as it always
is at that age. I looked about me with great awe. I was here in
the very centre and scene of those occurrences which I had

heard recounted at the fireside at home, with so delightful a horror.

My father was an old bachelor of nearly sixty when he married. He had, when a child, seen Judge Harbottle on the bench in his robes and wig a dozen times at least before his death, which took place in 1748, and his appearance made a powerful and unpleasant impression, not only on his imagination, but on his nerves.

The Judge was at that time a man of some sixty-seven years. He had a great mulberry-coloured face, a big, carbuncled nose, fierce eyes, and a grim and brutal mouth. My father, who was young at the time, thought it the most formidable face he had ever seen; for there were evidences of intellectual power in the formation and lines of the forehead. His voice was loud and harsh, and gave effect to the sarcasm which was his habitual weapon on the bench.

This old gentleman had the reputation of being about the wickedest man in England. Even on the bench he now and then showed his scorn of opinion. He had carried cases his own way, it was said, in spite of counsel, authorities, and even of juries, by a sort of cajolery, violence, and bamboozling, that somehow confused and overpowered resistance. He had never actually committed himself; he was too cunning to do that. He had the character of being, however, a dangerous and unscrupulous judge; but his character did not trouble him. The associates he chose for his hours of relaxation cared as little as he did about it.

CHAPTER II

MR PETERS

One night during the session of 1746* this old Judge went down in his chair to wait in one of the rooms of the House of Lords for the result of a division in which he and his order* were interested.

This over, he was about to return to his house close by, in

his chair; but the night had become so soft and fine that he changed his mind, sent it home empty, and with two footmen, each with a flambeau, set out on foot in preference. Gout had made him rather a slow pedestrian. It took him some time to get through the two or three streets he had to pass before reaching his house.

In one of those narrow streets of tall houses, perfectly silent at that hour, he overtook, slowly as he was walking, a very singular-looking old gentleman.

He had a bottle-green coat on, with a cape to it, and large stone buttons, a broad-leafed low-crowned hat, from under which a big powdered wig escaped; he stooped very much, and supported his bending knees with the aid of a crutch-handled cane, and so shuffled and tottered along painfully.

'I ask your pardon, sir,' said this old man in a very quavering voice, as the burly Judge came up with him, and he extended his hand feebly towards his arm.

Mr Justice Harbottle saw that the man was by no means poorly dressed, and his manner that of a gentleman.

The Judge stopped short, and said, in his harsh peremptory tones, 'Well, sir, how can I serve you?'

'Can you direct me to Judge Harbottle's house? I have some intelligence of the very last importance to communicate to him.'

'Can you tell it before witnesses?' asked the Judge.

'By no means; it must reach *his* ear only,' quavered the old man earnestly.

'If that be so, sir, you have only to accompany me a few steps farther to reach my house, and obtain a private audience; for I am Judge Harbottle.'

With this invitation the infirm gentleman in the white wig complied very readily; and in another minute the stranger stood in what was then termed the front parlour of the Judge's house, *tête-à-tête* with that shrewd and dangerous functionary.

He had to sit down, being very much exhausted, and unable for a little time to speak; and then he had a fit of coughing, and after that a fit of gasping; and thus two or three minutes passed, during which the Judge dropped his roquelaure* on an arm-chair, and threw his cocked-hat over that.

The venerable pedestrian in the white wig quickly recovered his voice. With closed doors they remained together for some time.

There were guests waiting in the drawing-rooms, and the sound of men's voices laughing, and then of a female voice singing to a harpsichord, were heard distinctly in the hall over the stairs; for old Judge Harbottle had arranged one of his dubious jollifications, such as might well make the hair of godly men's heads stand upright, for that night.

This old gentleman in the powdered white wig, that rested on his stooped shoulders, must have had something to say that interested the Judge very much; for he would not have parted on easy terms with the ten minutes and upwards which that conference filched from the sort of revelry. in which he most delighted, and in which he was the roaring king, and in some sort the tyrant also, of his company.

The footman who showed the aged gentleman out observed that the Judge's mulberry-coloured face, pimples and all, were bleached to a dingy yellow, and there was the abstraction of agitated thought in his manner, as he bid the stranger goodnight. The servant saw that the conversation had been of serious import, and that the Judge was frightened.

Instead of stumping upstairs forthwith to his scandalous hilarities, his profane company, and his great china bowl of punch—the identical bowl from which a bygone Bishop of London, good easy man, had baptized this Judge's grandfather, now clinking round the rim with silver ladles, and hung with scrolls of lemon-peel—instead, I say, of stumping and clambering up the great staircase to the cavern of his Circean enchantment,* he stood with his big nose flattened against the window-pane, watching the progress of the feeble old man, who clung stiffly to the iron rail as he got down, step by step, to the pavement.

The hall-door had hardly closed, when the old Judge was in the hall bawling hasty orders, with such stimulating expletives as old colonels under excitement sometimes indulge in now-a-days,* with a stamp or two of his big foot, and a waving of his clenched fist in the air. He commanded the footman to overtake the old gentleman in the white wig, to offer him his protection on his way home, and in no case to show his face again without having ascertained where he lodged, and who he was, and all about him.

'By—, sirrah! if you fail me in this, you doff my livery* tonight!'

Forth bounced the stalwart footman, with his heavy cane under his arm, and skipped down the steps, and looked up and down the street after the singular figure, so easy to recognize.

What were his adventures I shall not tell you just now.

The old man, in the conference to which he had been admitted in that stately panelled room, had just told the Judge a very strange story. He might be himself a conspirator; he might possibly be crazed; or possibly his whole story was straight and true.

The aged gentleman in the bottle-green coat, on finding himself alone with Mr Justice Harbottle, had become agitated. He said,

'There is, perhaps you are not aware, my lord, a prisoner in Shrewsbury jail, charged with having forged a bill of exchange for a hundred and twenty pounds, and his name is Lewis Pyneweck, a grocer of that town.'

'Is there?' said the Judge, who knew well that there was.

'Yes, my lord,' says the old man.

'Then you had better say nothing to affect his case. If you do, by—— I'll commit you; for I'm to try it,' says the Judge, with his terrible look and tone.

'I am not going to do anything of the kind, my lord; of him or his case I know nothing, and care nothing. But a fact has come to my knowledge which it behoves you to well consider.'

'And what may that fact be?' inquired the Judge; 'I'm in haste, sir, and beg you will use dispatch.'

'It has come to my knowledge, my lord, that a secret tribunal is in process of formation, the object of which is to take cognisance of the conduct of the judges; and first, of *your* conduct, my lord: it is a wicked conspiracy.'

'Who are of it?' demands the Judge.

'I know not a single name as yet. I know but the fact, my lord; it is most certainly true.'

'I'll have you before the Privy Council* sir,' says the Judge.

'That is what I most desire; but not for a day or two, my lord.'

'And why so?'

'I have not as yet a single name, as I told your lordship; but I expect to have a list of the most forward men in it, and some other papers connected with the plot, in two or three days.'

'You said one or two just now.'

'About that time, my lord.'

'Is this a Jacobite plot?'*

'In the main I think it is, my lord.'

'Why, then, it is political. I have tried no State prisoners,* nor am like to try any such. How, then, doth it concern me?'

'From what I can gather, my lord, there are those in it who desire private revenges upon certain judges.'

'What do they call their cabal?'

'The High Court of Appeal, my lord.'

'Who are you sir? What is your name?'

'Hugh Peters, my lord.'

'That should be a Whig name?'*

'It is, my lord.'

'Where do you lodge, Mr Peters?'

'In Thames-street, my lord, over against the sign of the Three Kings.'*

'Three Kings? Take care one be not too many for you, Mr Peters! How come you, an honest Whig, as you say, to be privy to a Jacobite plot? Answer me that.'

'My lord, a person in whom I take an interest has been seduced to take a part in it; and being frightened at the unexpected wickedness of their plans, he is resolved to become an informer for the Crown.'

'He resolves like a wise man, sir. What does he say of the persons? Who are in the plot? Doth he know them?'

'Only two, my lord; but he will be introduced to the club in a few days, and he will then have a list, and more exact information of their plans, and above all of their oaths, and their hours and places of meeting, with which he wishes to be acquainted before they can have any suspicions of his intentions. And being so informed, to whom, think you, my lord, had he best go then?'

'To the king's attorney-general* straight. But you say this concerns me, sir, in particular? How about this prisoner, Lewis Pyneweck? Is he one of them?'

'I can't tell, my lord; but for some reason, it is thought your lordship will be well advised if you try him not. For if you do, it is feared 'twill shorten your days.'

'So far as I can learn, Mr Peters, this business smells pretty strong of blood and treason. The king's attorney-general will know how to deal with it. When shall I see you again, sir?'

'If you give me leave, my lord, either before your lordship's court sits, or after it rises, to-morrow. I should like to come and tell your lordship what has passed.'

'Do so, Mr Peters, at nine o'clock to-morrow morning. And see you play me no trick, sir, in this matter; if you do, by——, sir, I'll lay you by the heels.'

'You need fear no trick from me, my lord; had I not wished to serve you, and acquit my own conscience, I never would have come all this way to talk with your lordship.'

'I'm willing to believe you, Mr Peters; I'm willing to believe you, sir.'

And upon this they parted.

'He has either painted his face, or he is consumedly sick,' thought the old Judge.

The light had shone more effectually upon his features as he turned to leave the room with a low bow, and they looked, he fancied, unnaturally chalky.

'D—— him!' said the judge ungraciously, as he began to scale the stairs: 'he has half-spoiled my supper.'

But if he had, no one but the Judge himself perceived it, and the evidence was all, as any one might perceive, the other way.

In the meantime, the footman dispatched in pursuit of Mr Peters speedily overtook that feeble gentleman. The old man stopped when he heard the sound of pursuing steps, but any alarms that may have crossed his mind seemed to disappear on his recognizing the livery. He very gratefully accepted the proferred assistance, and placed his tremulous arm within the servant's for support. They had not gone far, however, when the old man stopped suddenly, saying,

'Dear me! As I live, I have dropped it. You heard it fall. My eyes, I fear, won't serve me, and I'm unable to stoop low enough; but if *you* will look, you shall have half the find. It is a guinea;* I carried it in my glove.'

The street was silent and deserted. The footman had hardly descended to what he termed his 'hunkers', and begun to search the pavement about the spot which the old man indicated, when Mr Peters, who seemed very much exhausted, and breathed with difficulty, struck him a violent blow, from above, over the back of the head with a heavy instrument, and then another; and leaving him bleeding and senseless in the gutter, ran like a lamplighter* down a lane to the right, and was gone.

When, an hour later, the watchman* brought the man in livery home, still stupid and covered with blood, Judge Harbottle cursed his servant roundly, swore he was drunk, threatened him with an indictment for taking bribes to betray his master, and cheered him with a perspective of the broad street leading from the Old Bailey to Tyburn, the cart's tail, and the hangman's lash.*

Notwithstanding this demonstration, the Judge was pleased. It was a disguised 'affidavit man', or footpad,* no doubt, who had been employed to frighten him. The trick had fallen through.

A 'court of appeal', such as the false Hugh Peters had indicated, with assassination for its sanction, would be an uncomfortable institution for a 'hanging judge' like the Honourable Justice Harbottle. That sarcastic and ferocious administrator of the criminal code of England, at that time a rather pharisaical,* bloody, and heinous system of justice, had reasons of his own for choosing to try that very Lewis Pyneweck, on whose behalf this audacious trick was devised. Try him he would. No man living should take that morsel out of his mouth.

Of Lewis Pyneweck of course, so far as the outer world could see, he knew nothing. He would try him after his fashion, without fear, favour, or affection.

But did he not remember a certain thin man, dressed in mourning, in whose house, in Shrewsbury, the Judge's lodgings used to be, until a scandal of his ill-treating his wife came suddenly to light? A grocer with a demure look, a soft step, and a lean face as dark as mahogany, with a nose sharp and long, standing ever so little awry, and a pair of dark steady brown eyes under thinly-traced black brows—a man whose thin lips wore always a faint unpleasant smile.

Had not that scoundrel an account to settle with the Judge? had he not been troublesome lately? and was not his name Lewis Pyneweck, some time grocer in Shrewsbury, and now prisoner in the jail of that town?

The reader may take it, if he pleases, as a sign that Judge Harbottle was a good Christian, that he suffered nothing ever from remorse. That was undoubtedly true. He had nevertheless done his grocer, forger, what you will, some five or six years before, a grievous wrong; but it was not that, but a possible scandal, and possible complications, that troubled the learned Judge now.

Did he not, as a lawyer, know, that to bring a man from his shop to the dock, the chances must be at least ninety-nine out of a hundred that he is guilty.

A weak man like his learnéd brother Withershins was not a judge to keep the high-roads safe, and make crime tremble. Old Judge Harbottle was the man to make the evil-disposed quiver, and to refresh the world with showers of wicked blood, and thus save the innocent, to the refrain of the ancient saw he loved to quote:

> Foolish pity
> Ruins a city.

In hanging that fellow he could not be wrong. The eye of a man accustomed to look upon the dock could not fail to read 'villain' written sharp and clear in his plotting face. Of course he would try him, and no one else should.

A saucy-looking woman, still handsome, in a mob-cap gay with blue ribbons, in a saque* of flowered silk, with lace and rings on, much too fine for the Judge's housekeeper, which nevertheless she was, peeped into his study next morning, and, seeing the Judge alone, stepped in.

'Here's another letter from him, come by the post this morning. Can't you do nothing for him?' she said wheedlingly, with her arm over his neck, and her delicate finger and thumb fiddling with the lobe of his purple ear.

'I'll try,' said Judge Harbottle, not raising his eyes from the paper he was reading.

'I knew you'd do what I asked you,' she said.

The Judge clapt his gouty claw over his heart, and made her an ironical bow.

'What', she asked, 'will you do?'

'Hang him,' said the Judge with a chuckle.

'You don't mean to; no, you don't, my little man,' said she, surveying herself in a mirror on the wall.

'I'm d——d but I think you're falling in love with your husband at last!' said Judge Harbottle.

'I'm blest but I think you're growing jealous of him,' replied the lady with a laugh. 'But no; he was always a bad one to me; I've done with him long ago.'

'And he with you, by George! When he took your fortune and your spoons and your ear-rings, he had all he wanted of you. He drove you from his house; and when he discovered you had made yourself comfortable, and found a good situation, he'd have taken your guineas and your silver and your ear-rings over again, and then allowed you half-a-dozen years more to make a new harvest for his mill. You don't wish him good; if you say you do, you lie.'

She laughed a wicked saucy laugh, and gave the terrible Rhadamanthus* a playful tap on the chops.

'He wants me to send him money to fee a counsellor,' she said, while her eyes wandered over the pictures on the wall, and back again to the looking-glass; and certainly she did not look as if his jeopardy troubled her very much.

'Confound his impudence, the *scoundrel*!' thundered the old Judge, throwing himself back in his chair, as he used to do *in furore** on the bench, and the lines of his mouth looked brutal, and his eyes ready to leap from their sockets. 'If you answer his letter from my house to please yourself, you'll write your next from somebody else's to please me. You understand, my pretty witch, I'll not be pestered. Come, no pouting; whimpering won't do. You don't care a brass farthing for the villain, body or soul. You came here but to make a row. You are one of Mother Carey's chickens;* and where you come, the storm is up. Get you gone, baggage! get you *gone*!' he repeated with a stamp; for a knock at the hall-door made her instantaneous disappearance indispensable.

I need hardly say that the venerable Hugh Peters did not appear again. The Judge never mentioned him. But oddly enough, considering how he laughed to scorn the weak invention which he had blown into dust at the very first puff, his white-wigged visitor and the conference in the dark front parlour was often in his memory.

His shrewd eye told him that allowing for change of tints and such disguises as the playhouse affords every night, the features of this false old man, who had turned out too hard for his tall footman, were identical with those of Lewis Pyneweck.

Judge Harbottle made his registrar call upon the crown solicitor,* and tell him that there was a man in town who bore a wonderful resemblance to a prisoner in Shrewsbury jail named Lewis Pyneweck, and to make inquiry through the post forthwith whether any one was personating Pyneweck in prison, and whether he had thus or otherwise made his escape.

The prisoner was safe, however, and no question as to his identity.

CHAPTER IV

INTERRUPTION IN COURT

In due time Judge Harbottle went circuit;* and in due time the judges were in Shrewsbury. News travelled slowly in those days, and newspapers, like the wagons and stage-coaches, took matters easily. Mrs Pyneweck, in the Judge's house, with a diminished household—the greater part of the Judge's servants having gone with him, for he had given up riding circuit, and travelled in his coach in state—kept house rather solitarily at home.

In spite of quarrels, in spite of mutual injuries—some of them, inflicted by herself, enormous—in spite of a married life of spited bickerings—a life of which there seemed no love or liking or forbearance, for years—now that Pyneweck stood in near danger of death, something like remorse came suddenly upon her. She knew that in Shrewsbury were transacting the scenes which were to determine his fate. She knew she did not love him; but she could not have supposed, even a fortnight before, that the hour of suspense could have affected her so powerfully.

She knew the day on which the trial was expected to take place. She could not get it out of her head for a minute; she felt faint as it drew towards evening.

Two or three days passed; and then she knew that the trial must be over by this time. There were floods between London and Shrewsbury, and news was long delayed. She wished the floods would last for ever. It was dreadful waiting to hear; dreadful to know that the event was over, and that she could not hear till self-willed rivers subsided; dreadful to know that they must subside and the news come at last.

She had some vague trust in the Judge's good-nature, and much in the resources of chance and accident. She had contrived to send the money he wanted. He would not be without legal advice and energetic and skilled support.

At last the news did come—a long arrear all in a gush: a letter from a female friend in Shrewsbury; a return of the

sentences, sent up for the Judge; and most important, because
most easily got at, being told with great aplomb and brevity,
the long-deferred intelligence of the Shrewsbury Assizes* in
the *Morning Advertiser*. Like an impatient reader of a novel, who
reads the last page first, she read with dizzy eyes the list of the
executions.

Two were respited, seven were hanged; and in that capital
catalogue was this line:

'Lewis Pyneweck—forgery.'

She had to read it half-a-dozen times over before she was
sure she understood it. Here was the paragraph:

'*Sentence, Death*—7.

'Executed accordingly, on Friday the 13th instant, to wit:

'Thomas Primer, *alias* Duck—highway robbery.

'Flora Guy—stealing to the value of 11s. 6d.

'Arthur Pounden—burglary.

'Matilda Mummery—riot.

'Lewis Pyneweck—forgery, bill of exchange.'

And when she reached this, she read it over and over, feeling
very cold and sick.

This buxom housekeeper was known in the house as Mrs
Carwell—Carwell being her maiden name—which she had
resumed.

No one in the house except its master knew her history. Her
introduction had been managed craftily. No one suspected
that it had been concerted between her and the old reprobate
in scarlet and ermine.*

Flora Carwell ran up the stairs now, and snatched her little
girl, hardly seven years of age, whom she met on the lobby,
hurriedly up in her arms, and carried her into her bedroom,
without well knowing what she was doing, and sat down,
placing the child before her. She was not able to speak. She
held the child before her, and looked in the little girl's
wondering face, and burst into tears of horror.

She thought the Judge could have saved him. I daresay he
could. For a time she was furious with him; and hugged and
kissed her bewildered little girl, who returned her gaze with
large round eyes.

That little girl had lost her father, and knew nothing of the matter. She had been always told that her father was dead long ago.

A woman, coarse, uneducated, vain, and violent, does not reason, or even feel, very distinctly; but in these tears of consternation were mingling a self-upbraiding. She felt afraid of that little child.

But Mrs Carwell was a person who lived not upon sentiment, but upon beef and pudding; she consoled herself with punch; she did not trouble herself long even with resentments; she was a gross and material person, and could not mourn over the irrevocable for more than a limited number of hours, even if she would.

Judge Harbottle was soon in London again. Except the gout, this savage old epicurean* never knew a day's sickness. He laughed and coaxed and bullied away the young woman's faint upbraidings, and in a little time Lewis Pyneweck troubled her no more; and the Judge secretly chuckled over the perfectly fair removal of a bore, who might have grown little by little into something very like a tyrant.

It was the lot of the Judge whose adventures I am now recounting to try criminal cases at the Old Bailey shortly after his return. He had commenced his charge to the jury in a case of forgery, and was, after his wont, thundering dead against the prisoner, with many a hard aggravation and cynical gibe, when suddenly all died away in silence, and, instead of looking at the jury, the eloquent Judge was gaping at some person in the body of the court.

Among the persons of small importance who stand and listen at the sides was one tall enough to show with a little prominence; a slight mean figure, dressed in seedy black, lean and dark of visage. He had just handed a letter to the crier,* before he caught the Judge's eye.

That Judge descried, to his amazement, the features of Lewis Pyneweck. He had the usual faint thin-lipped smile; and with his blue chin raised in air, and as it seemed quite unconscious of the distinguished notice he had attracted,* he was stretching his low cravat with his crooked fingers, while he slowly turned his head from side to side—a process which enabled the Judge to see distinctly a stripe of swollen blue round his neck, which indicated, he thought, the grip of the rope.

This man, with a few others, had got a footing on a step, from which he could better see the court. He now stepped down, and the Judge lost sight of him.

His lordship signed energetically with his hand in the direction in which this man had vanished. He turned to the tipstaff.* His first effort to speak ended in a gasp. He cleared his throat, and told the astounded official to arrest that man who had interrupted the court.

'He's but this moment gone down *there*. Bring him in custody before me, within ten minutes' time, or I'll strip your gown from your shoulders and fine the sheriff!'* he thundered, while his eyes flashed round the court in search of the functionary.

Attorneys, counsellors, idle spectators, gazed in the direction in which Mr Justice Harbottle had shaken his gnarled old hand. They compared notes. Not one had seen any one making a disturbance. They asked one another if the Judge was losing his head.

Nothing came of the search. His lordship concluded his charge a great deal more tamely; and when the jury retired, he stared round the court with a wandering mind, and looked as if he would not have given sixpence to see the prisoner hanged.

CHAPTER V

CALEB SEARCHER

The Judge had received the letter; had he known from whom it came, he would no doubt have read it instantaneously. As it was he simply read the direction:

To the Honourable
The Lord Justice
Elijah Harbottle,

*One of his Majesty's Justices of
the Honourable Court of Common Pleas.*

It remained forgotten in his pocket till he reached home.

When he pulled out that and others from the capacious pocket of his coat, it had its turn, as he sat in his library in his thick silk dressing-gown; and then he found its contents to be a closely-written letter, in a clerk's hand, and an enclosure in 'secretary hand,' as I believe the angular scrivinary* of law-writings in those days was termed, engrossed on a bit of parchment about the size of this page. The letter said:

'Mr Justice Harbottle,—My Lord,

'I am ordered by the High Court of Appeal to acquaint your lordship, in order to your better preparing yourself for your trial, that a true bill hath been sent down, and the indictment lieth against your lordship for the murder of one Lewis Pyneweck of Shrewsbury, citizen, wrongfully executed for the forgery of a bill of exchange, on the —th day of—— last, by reason of the wilful perversion of the evidence, and the undue pressure put upon the jury, together with the illegal admission of evidence by your lordship, well knowing the same to be illegal, by all which the promoter of the prosecution of the said indictment, before the High Court of Appeal, hath lost his life.

'And the trial of the said indictment, I am farther ordered to acquaint your lordship, is fixed for the 10th day of—— next ensuing, by the right honourable the Lord Chief-Justice Twofold, of the court aforesaid, to wit, the High Court of Appeal, on which day it will most certainly take place. And I am farther to acquaint your lordship, to prevent any surprise or miscarriage, that your case stands first for the said day, and that the said High Court of Appeal sits day and night, and never rises; and herewith, by order of the said court, I furnish your lordship with a copy (extract) of the record in this case, except of the indictment, whereof, notwithstanding, the substance and effect is supplied to your lordship in this Notice. And farther I am to inform you, that in case the jury then to try your lordship should find you guilty, the right honourable the Lord Chief-Justice will, in passing sentence of death upon

you, fix the day of execution for the 10th day of——, being one
calendar month from the day of your trial.'

It was signed by

'Caleb Searcher,

'Officer of the Crown Solicitor in the

'Kingdom of Life and Death.'

The Judge glanced through the parchment.

''Sblood!* Do they think a man like me is to be bamboozled
by their buffoonery?'

The Judge's coarse features were wrung into one of his
sneers; but he was pale. Possibly, after all, there was a
conspiracy on foot. It was queer. Did they mean to pistol him
in his carriage? or did they only aim at frightening him?

Judge Harbottle had more than enough of animal courage.
He was not afraid of highwaymen, and he had fought more
than his share of duels, being a foul-mouthed advocate while
he held briefs at the bar.* No one questioned his fighting
qualities. But with respect to this particular case of Pyneweck,
he lived in a house of glass. Was there not his pretty, dark-
eyed, over-dressed housekeeper, Mrs Flora Carwell? Very easy
for people who knew Shrewsbury to identify Mrs Pyneweck, if
once put upon the scent; and had he not stormed and worked
hard in that case? Had he not made it hard sailing for the
prisoner? Did he not know very well what the bar thought of
it? It would be the worst scandal that ever blasted judge.

So much there was intimidating in the matter, but nothing
more. The Judge was a little bit gloomy for a day or two after,
and more testy with every one than usual.

He locked up the papers; and about a week after he asked
his housekeeper, one day, in the library:

'Had your husband never a brother?'

Mrs Carwell squalled on this sudden introduction of the
funereal topic, and cried exemplary 'piggins full',* as the
Judge used pleasantly to say. But he was in no mood for
trifling now, and he said sternly:

'Come, madam! this wearies me. Do it another time; and
give me an answer to my question.' So she did.

Pyneweck had no brother living. He once had one; but he died in Jamaica.

'How do you know he is dead?' asked the Judge.

'Because he told me so.'

'Not the dead man?'

'Pyneweck told me so.'

'Is that all?' sneered the Judge.

He pondered this matter; and time went on. The Judge was growing a little morose, and less enjoying. The subject struck nearer to his thoughts than he fancied it could have done. But so it is with most undivulged vexations, and there was no one to whom he could tell this one.

It was now the ninth; and Mr Justice Harbottle was glad. He knew nothing would come of it. Still it bothered him; and to-morrow would see it well over.

[What of the paper I have cited? No one saw it during his life; no one, after his death. He spoke of it to Dr Hedstone; and what purported to be 'a copy', in the old Judge's hand-writing, was found. The original was nowhere. Was it a copy of an illusion, incident to brain disease? Such is my belief.]*

CHAPTER VI

ARRESTED

Judge Harbottle went this night to the play at Drury Lane.* He was one of those old fellows who care nothing for late hours, and occasional knocking about in pursuit of plesaure. He had appointed with two cronies of Lincoln's Inn* to come home in his coach with him to sup after the play.

They were not in his box, but were to meet him near the entrance, and to get into his carriage there; and Mr Justice Harbottle, who hated waiting, was looking a little impatiently from the window.

The Judge yawned.

He told the footman to watch for Counsellor Thavies* and Counsellor Beller, who were coming; and, with another yawn, he laid his cocked-hat on his knees, closed his eyes, leaned back in his corner, wrapped his mantle closer about him, and began to think of pretty Mrs Abington.*

And being a man who could sleep like a sailor, at a moment's notice, he was thinking of taking a nap. Those fellows had no business to keep a judge waiting.

He heard their voices now. Those rake-hell counsellors were laughing, and bantering, and sparring after their wont. The carriage swayed and jerked, as one got in, and then again as the other followed. The door clapped, and the coach was now jogging and rumbling over the pavement. The Judge was a little bit sulky. He did not care to sit up and open his eyes. Let them suppose he was asleep. He heard them laugh with more malice than good-humour, he thought, as they observed it. He would give them a d——d hard knock or two when they got to his door, and till then he would counterfeit his nap.

The clocks were chiming twelve. Beller and Thavies were silent as tombstones. They were generally loquacious and merry rascals.

The Judge suddenly felt himself roughly seized and thrust from his corner into the middle of the seat, and opening his eyes, instantly he found himself between his two companions.

Before he could blurt out the oath that was at his lips, he saw that they were two strangers—evil-looking fellows, each with a pistol in his hand, and dressed like Bow Street officers.*

The Judge clutched at the check-string.* The coach pulled up. He stared about him. They were not among houses; but through the windows, under a broad moonlight, he saw a black moor stretching lifelessly from right to left, with rotting trees, pointing fantastic branches in the air, standing here and there in groups, as if they held up their arms and twigs like fingers, in horrible glee at the Judge's coming.

A footman came to the window. He knew his long face and sunken eyes. He knew it was Dingly Chuff, fifteen years ago a footman in his service, whom he had turned off at a moment's notice, in a burst of jealousy, and indicted for a missing spoon. The man had died in prison of the jail-fever.

The Judge drew back in utter amazement. His armed

companions signed mutely; and they were again gliding over this unknown moor.

The bloated and gouty old man, in his horror, considered the question of resistance. But his athletic days were long over. This moor was a desert. There was no help to be had. He was in the hands of strange servants, even if his recognition turned out to be a delusion, and they were under the command of his captors. There was nothing for it but submission, for the present.

Suddenly the coach was brought nearly to a standstill, so that the prisoner saw an ominous sight from the window.

It was a gigantic gallows beside the road; it stood three-sided, and from each of its three broad beams at top depended in chains some eight or ten bodies, from several of which the cere-clothes had dropped away, leaving the skeletons swinging lightly by their chains.* A tall ladder reached to the summit of the structure, and on the peat beneath lay bones.

On top of the dark transverse beam facing the road, from which, as from the other two completing the triangle of death, dangled a row of these unfortunates in chains, a hangman, with a pipe in his mouth, much as we see him in the famous print of the 'Idle Apprentice,'* though here his perch was ever so much higher, was reclining at his ease and listlessly shying bones, from a little heap at his elbow, at the skeletons that hung round, bringing down now a rib or two, now a hand, now half a leg. A long-sighted man could have discerned that he was a dark fellow, lean; and from continually looking down on the earth from the elevation over which, in another sense, he always hung, his nose, his lips, his chin were pendulous and loose, and drawn down into a monstrous grotesque.

This fellow took his pipe from his mouth on seeing the coach, stood up, and cut some solemn capers high on his beam, and shook a new rope in the air, crying with a voice high and distant as the caw of a raven hovering over a gibbet, 'A rope for Judge Harbottle!'

The coach was now driving on at its old swift pace.

So high a gallows as that, the Judge had never, even in his most hilarious moments, dreamed of. He thought he must be raving. And the dead footman! He shook his ears and strained his eyelids; but if he was dreaming, he was unable to awake himself.

There was no good in threatening these scoundrels. A *brutum fulmen** might bring a real one on his head.

Any submission to get out of their hands; and then heaven and earth he would move to unearth and hunt them down.

Suddenly they drove round a corner of a vast white building, and under a *porte-cochère*.*

CHAPTER VII

CHIEF JUSTICE TWOFOLD

The Judge found himself in a corridor lighted with dingy oil-lamps, the walls of bare stone; it looked like a passage in a prison. His guards placed him in the hands of other people. Here and there he saw bony and gigantic soldiers passing to and fro, with muskets over their shoulders. They looked straight before them, grinding their teeth, in bleak fury, with no noise but the clank of their shoes.* He saw these by glimpses round corners, and at the ends of passages, but he did not actually pass them by.

And now, passing under a narrow doorway, he found himself in the dock, confronting a judge in his scarlet robes, in a large court-house. There was nothing to elevate this temple of Themis* above its vulgar kind elsewhere. Dingy enough it looked, in spite of candles lighted in decent abundance. A case had just closed, and the last juror's back was seen escaping through the door in the wall of the jury-box. There were some dozen barristers, some fiddling with pen and ink, others buried in briefs, some beckoning, with the plumes of their pens,* to their attorneys, of whom there were no lack; there were clerks toing and froing, and the officers of the court, and the registrar, who was handing up a paper to the judge; and the tipstaff, who was presenting a note at the end of his wand to a king's counsel* over the heads of the crowd between. If this was the High Court of Appeal, which never rose day or night, it might account for the pale and jaded aspect of everybody in it. An air of indescribable gloom hung upon the pallid features of all the people here; no one ever smiled; all looked more or less secretly suffering.

'The King against Elijah Harbottle!' shouted the officer.

'Is the appellant Lewis Pyneweck in court?' asked Chief-Justice Twofold, in a voice of thunder, that shook the wood-work of the court, and boomed down the corridors.*

Up stood Pyneweck from his place at the table.

'Arraign the prisoner!' roared the Chief; and Judge Harbottle felt the panels of the dock round him, and the floor, and the rails quiver in the vibrations of that tremendous voice.

The prisoner, *in limine*,* objected to this pretended court, as being a sham, and non-existent in point of law; and then, that, even if it were a court constituted by law (the Judge was growing dazed), it had not and could not have any jurisdiction to try him for his conduct on the bench.

Whereupon the Chief-Justice laughed suddenly, and every one in court, turning round upon the prisoner, laughed also, till the laugh grew and roared all round like a deafening acclamation;* he saw nothing but glittering eyes and teeth, a universal stare and grin; but though all the voices laughed, not a single face of all those that concentrated their gaze upon him looked like a laughing face. The mirth subsided as suddenly as it began.

The indictment was read. Judge Harbottle actually pleaded! He pleaded 'Not guilty'. A jury were sworn. The trial proceeded. Judge Harbottle was bewildered. This could not be real. He must be either mad, or *going* mad, he thought.

One thing could not fail to strike even him. This Chief-Justice Twofold, who was knocking him about at every turn with sneer and gibe, and roaring him down with his tremendous voice, was a dilated effigy of himself; an image of Mr Justice Harbottle, at least double his size, and with all his fierce colouring, and his ferocity of eye and visage, enhanced awfully.*

Nothing the prisoner could argue, cite, or state was permitted to retard for a moment the march of the case towards its catastrophe.

The Chief-Justice seemed to feel his power over the jury, and to exult and riot in the display of it. He glared at them, he nodded to them; he seemed to have established an understanding with them. The lights were faint in that part of the court. The jurors were mere shadows, sitting in rows; the prisoner could see a dozen pair of white eyes shining, coldly,* out of the darkness; and whenever the judge in his charge, which was contemptuously brief, nodded and grinned and gibed, the prisoner could see, in the obscurity, by the dip of all these rows of eyes together, that the jury nodded in acquiescence.

And now the charge was over, the huge Chief-Justice leaned back panting and gloating on the prisoner. Every one in the court turned about, and gazed with steadfast hatred on the man in the dock. From the jury-box where the twelve sworn brethren were whispering together, a sound in the general stillness like a prolonged 'hiss-s-s!' was heard; and then, in answer to the challenge of the officer, 'How say you, gentlemen of the jury, guilty or not guilty?' came in a melancholy voice the finding, 'Guilty'.

The place seemed to the eyes of the prisoner to grow gradually darker and darker, till he could discern nothing distinctly but the lumen of the eyes* that were turned upon him from every bench and side and corner and gallery of the building. The prisoner doubtless thought that he had quite enough to say, and conclusive, why sentence of death should not be pronounced upon him; but the Lord Chief-Justice puffed it contemptuously away, like so much smoke, and proceeded to pass sentence of death upon the prisoner, having named the 10th of the ensuing month for his execution.

Before he had recovered the stun of this ominous farce, in obedience to the mandate, 'Remove the prisoner', he was led from the dock. The lamps seemed all to have gone out, and there were stoves and charcoal-fires here and there, that threw a faint crimson light on the walls of the corridors through which he passed. The stones that composed them looked now enormous, cracked and unhewn.

He came into a vaulted smithy, where two men, naked to the waist, with heads like bulls, round shoulders, and the arms of giants, were welding red-hot chains together with hammers that pelted like thunderbolts.

They looked on the prisoner with fierce red eyes, and rested on their hammers for a minute; and said the elder to his companion, 'Take out Elijah Harbottle's gyves';* and with a pincers he plucked the end which lay dazzling in the fire from the furnace.

'One end locks,' said he, taking the cool end of the iron in one hand, while with the grip of a vice he seized the leg of the Judge, and locked the ring round his ankle. 'The other', he said with a grin, 'is welded.'

The iron band that was to form the ring for the other leg lay still red-hot upon the stone floor, with brilliant sparks sporting up and down its surface.

His companion, in his gigantic hands seized the old Judge's other leg, and pressed his foot immovably to the stone floor; while his senior in a twinkling, with a masterly application of pincers and hammer, sped the glowing bar round his ankle so tight that the skin and sinews smoked and bubbled again, and old Judge Harbottle uttered a yell that seemed to chill the very stones, and make the iron chains quiver on the wall.

Chains, vaults, smiths, and smithy all vanished in a moment; but the pain continued. Mr Justice Harbottle was suffering torture all round the ankle on which the infernal smiths had just been operating.

His friends Thavies and Beller were startled by the Judge's roar in the midst of their elegant trifling about a marriage *à-la-mode* case* which was going on. The Judge was in panic as well as pain. The street-lamps and the light of his own hall-door restored him.

'I'm very bad,' growled he between his set teeth; 'my foot's blazing. Who was he that hurt my foot? 'Tis the gout—'tis the gout!' he said, awaking completely. 'How many hours have we been coming from the playhouse? 'Sblood, what has happened on the way? I've slept half the night?'

There had been no hitch or delay, and they had driven home at a good pace.

The Judge, however, was in gout; he was feverish too; and the attack, though very short, was sharp; and when, in about a fortnight, it subsided, his ferocious joviality did not return. He could not get this dream, as he chose to call it, out of his head.

CHAPTER VIII

SOMEBODY HAS GOT INTO THE HOUSE

People remarked that the Judge was in the vapours. His doctor said he should go for a fortnight to Buxton.*

Whenever the Judge fell into a brown study, he was always conning over the terms of the sentence pronounced upon him in his vision—'in one calendar month from the date of this day'; and then the usual form, 'and you shall be hanged by the neck till you are dead', &c. 'That will be the 10th—I'm not much in the way of being hanged. I know what stuff dreams are,* and I laugh at them; but this is continually in my thoughts, as if it forecast misfortune of some sort. I wish the day my dream gave me were passed and over. I wish I were well purged of my gout. I wish I were as I used to be. 'Tis nothing but vapours, nothing but a maggot.*' The copy of the* parchment and letter which had announced his trial with many a snort and sneer he would read over and over again, and the scenery and people of his dream would rise about him in places the most unlikely, and steal him in a moment from all that surrounded him into a world of shadows.

The Judge had lost his iron energy and banter. He was growing taciturn and morose. The Bar remarked the change, as well they might. His friends thought him ill. The doctor said he was troubled with hypochondria, and that his gout was still lurking in his system, and ordered him to that ancient haunt of crutches and chalk-stones,* Buxton.

The Judge's spirits were very low; he was frightened about himself; and he described to his housekeeper, having sent for her to his study to drink a dish of tea, his strange dream in his drive home from Drury Lane playhouse. He was sinking into the state of nervous dejection in which men lose their faith in orthodox advice, and in despair consult quacks, astrologers, and nursery storytellers. Could such a dream mean that he was to have a fit, and so die on the 10th? She did not think so. On the contrary, it was certain some good luck must happen on that day.

The Judge kindled; and for the first time these many days, he looked for a minute or two like himself, and he tapped her on the cheek with the hand that was not in flannel.

'Odsbud! odsheart!* you dear rogue! I had forgot. There is young Tom—yellow Tom, my nephew, you know, lies sick at Harrogate; why shouldn't he go that day as well as another, and if he does, I get an estate by it? Why, lookee, I asked Doctor Hedstone yesterday if I was like to take a fit any time, and he laughed, and swore I was the last man in town to go off that way.'

The Judge sent most of his servants down to Buxton to make his lodgings and all things comfortable for him. He was to follow in a day or two.

It was now the 9th; and the next day well over, he might laugh at his visions and auguries.

On the evening of the 9th, Doctor Hedstone's footman knocked at the Judge's door. The doctor ran up the dusky stairs to the drawing-room. It was a March evening, near the hour of sunset, with an east wind whistling sharply through the chimney-stacks. A wood fire blazed cheerily on the hearth. And Judge Harbottle, in what was then called a brigadier-wig, with his red roquelaure on, helped the glowing effect of the darkened chamber, which looked red all over like a room on fire.

The Judge had his feet on a stool, and his huge grim purple face confronted the fire, and seemed to pant and swell, as the blaze alternately spread upward and collapsed. He had fallen again among his blue devils,* and was thinking of retiring from the Bench, and of fifty other gloomy things.

But the doctor, who was an energetic son of Aesculapius,* would listen to no croaking, told the Judge he was full of gout, and in his present condition no judge even of his own case, but promised him leave to pronounce on all those melancholy questions a fortnight later.

In the meantime the Judge must be very careful. He was over-charged with gout, and he must not provoke an attack, till the waters of Buxton should do that office for him, in their own salutary way.*

The doctor did not think him perhaps quite so well as he pretended, for he told him he wanted rest, and would be better if he went forthwith to his bed.

Mr Gerningham, his valet, assisted him, and gave him his drops; and the Judge told him to wait in his bedroom till he should go to sleep.

Three persons that night had specially odd stories to tell.

The housekeeper had got rid of the trouble of amusing her little girl at this anxious time by giving her leave to run about the sitting-rooms and look at the pictures and china, on the usual condition of touching nothing. It was not until the last gleam of sunset had for some time faded, and the twilight had so deepened that she could no longer discern the colours on the china figures on the chimneypiece or in the cabinets, that the child returned to the housekeeper's room to find her mother.

To her she related, after some prattle about the china, and the pictures, and the Judge's two grand wigs in the dressing-room off the library, an adventure of an extraordinary kind.

In the hall was placed, as was customary in those times, the sedan-chair which the master of the house occasionally used, covered with stamped leather, and studded with gilt nails, and with its red silk blinds down. In this case, the doors of this old-fashioned conveyance were locked, the windows up, and, as I said, the blinds down, but not so closely that the curious child could not peep underneath one of them, and see into the interior.

A parting beam from the setting sun, admitted through the window of a back room, shot obliquely through the open door, and lighting on the chair, shone with a dull transparency through the crimson blind.

To her surprise, the child saw in the shadow a thin man dressed in black seated in it; he had sharp dark features; his nose, she fancied, a little awry, and his brown eyes were looking straight before him; his hand was on his thigh, and he stirred no more than the waxen figure she had seen at Southwark fair.*

A child is so often lectured for asking questions and on the propriety of silence, and the superior wisdom of its elders, that it accepts most things at last in good faith; and the little girl acquiesced respectfully in the occupation of the chair by this mahogany-faced person as being all right and proper.

It was not until she asked her mother who this man was, and observed her scared face as she questioned her more minutely upon the appearance of the stranger, that she began to understand that she had seen something unaccountable.

Mrs Carwell took the key of the chair from its nail over the footman's shelf, and led the child by the hand up to the hall, having a lighted candle in her other hand. She stopped at a distance from the chair, and placed the candlestick in the child's hand.*

'Peep in, Margery, again, and try if there's anything there,' she whispered; 'hold the candle near the blind so as to throw its light through the curtain.'

The child peeped, this time with a very solemn face, and intimated at once that he was gone.

'Look again, and be sure,' urged her mother.

The little girl was quite certain; and Mrs Carwell, with her mob-cap of lace and cherry-coloured ribbons, and her dark brown hair, not yet powdered, over a very pale face, unlocked the door, looked in, and beheld emptiness.

'All a mistake, child, you see.'

'*There*, ma'am! see there! He's gone round the corner,' said the child.

'Where?' said Mrs Carwell, stepping backward a step.

'Into that room.'

'Tut, child! 'twas the shadow,' cried Mrs Carwell angrily, because she was frightened. 'I moved the candle.' But she clutched one of the poles of the chair, which leant against the wall in the corner, and pounded the floor furiously with one end of it, being afraid to pass the open door the child had pointed to.

The cook and two kitchen-maids came running upstairs, not knowing what to make of this unwonted alarm.

They all searched the room; but it was still and empty, and no sign of any one's having been there.

Some people may suppose that the direction given to her thoughts by this odd little incident will account for a very strange illusion which Mrs Carwell herself experienced about two hours later.

CHAPTER IX

THE JUDGE LEAVES HIS HOUSE

Mrs Flora Carwell was going up the great staircase with a posset* for the Judge in a china bowl, on a little silver tray.

Across the top of the well-staircase there runs a massive oak rail; and, raising her eyes accidentally, she saw an extremely odd-looking stranger, slim and long, leaning carelessly over with a pipe between his finger and thumb. Nose, lips, and chin seemed all to droop downward into extraordinary length, as he leant his odd peering face over the banister. In his other hand he held a coil of rope, one end of which escaped from under his elbow and hung over the rail.

Mrs Carwell, who had no suspicion at the moment, that he was not a real person, and fancied that he was some one employed in cording the Judge's* luggage, called to know what he was doing there.

Instead of answering, he turned about, and walked across the lobby, at about the same leisurely pace at which she was ascending, and entered a room, into which she followed him. It was an uncarpeted and unfurnished chamber. An open trunk lay upon the floor empty, and beside it the coil of rope; but except herself there was no one in the room.

Mrs Carwell was very much frightened, and now concluded that the child must have seen the same ghost that had just appeared to her. Perhaps, when she was able to think it over, it was a relief to believe so; for the face, figure, and dress described by the child were awfully like Pyneweck; and this certainly was not he.

Very much scared and very hysterical, Mrs Carwell ran down to her room, afraid to look over her shoulder, and got some companions about her, and wept, and talked, and drank more than one cordial, and talked and wept again, and so on, until, in those early days, it was ten o'clock, and time to go to bed.

A scullery-maid remained up finishing some of her scouring and 'scalding' for some time after the other servants—who, as I said, were few in number—that night had got to their beds. This was a low-browed, broad-faced, intrepid wench with black hair, who did not 'vally* a ghost not a button', and treated the housekeeper's hysterics with measureless scorn.

The old house was quiet, now. It was near twelve o'clock, no sounds were audible except the muffled wailing of the wintry winds, piping high among the roofs and chimneys, or rumbling at intervals, in under gusts, through the narrow channels of the street.

The spacious solitudes of the kitchen level were awfully dark, and this sceptical kitchen-wench was the only person now up and about, in the house. She hummed tunes to herself, for a time; and then stopped and listened; and then resumed her work again. At last, she was destined to be more terrified than even was the housekeeper.*

There was a back-kitchen in this house, and from this she heard, as if coming from below its foundations, a sound like heavy strokes,* that seemed to shake the earth beneath her feet. Sometimes a dozen in sequence, at regular intervals; sometimes fewer. She walked out softly into the passage,* and was surprised to see a dusky glow issuing from this room, as if from a charcoal fire.

The room seemed thick with smoke.*

Looking in, she very dimly beheld a monstrous figure, over a furnace, beating with a mighty hammer the rings and rivets of a chain.*

The strokes, swift and heavy as they looked, sounded hollow and distant. The man stopped, and pointed to something on the floor, that, through the smoky haze, looked, she thought, like a dead body. She remarked no more; but the servants in the room close by, startled from their sleep by a hideous scream, found her in a swoon on the flags, close to the door, where she had just witnessed this ghastly vision.

Startled by the girl's incoherent asseverations that she had seen the Judge's corpse on the floor, two servants having first searched the lower part of the house,* went rather frightened up-stairs to inquire whether their master was well. They found him, not in his bed, but in his room. He had a table with candles burning at his bedside, and was getting on his clothes again; and he swore and cursed at them roundly in his old style, telling them that he had business, and that he would discharge on the spot any scoundrel who should dare to disturb him again.

So the invalid was left to his quietude.

In the morning it was rumoured here and there in the street that the Judge was dead. A servant was sent from the house three doors away, by Counsellor Traverse, to inquire at Judge Harbottle's hall-door.

The servant who opened it was pale and reserved, and would only say that the Judge was ill. He had had a dangerous accident; Doctor Hedstone had been with him at seven o'clock in the morning.

There were averted looks, short answers, pale and frowning faces, and all the usual signs that there was a secret that sat heavily upon their minds, and the time for disclosing which had not yet come. That time would arrive when the coroner had arrived, and the mortal scandal that had befallen the house could be no longer hidden. For that morning Mr Justice Harbottle had been found hanging by the neck from the banister at the top of the great staircase, and quite dead.

There was not the smallest sign of any struggle or resistance. There had not been heard a cry or any other noise in the slightest degree indicative of violence. There was medical evidence to show that, in his atrabilious state,* it was quite on the cards that he might have made away with himself. The jury found accordingly that it was a case of suicide. But to those who were acquainted with the strange story which Judge Harbottle had related to at least two persons, the fact that the

catastrophe occurred on the morning of the 10th March
seemed a startling coincidence.

A few days after, the pomp of a great funeral attended him
to the grave; and so, in the language of Scripture, 'the rich
man died, and was buried.'*

THE ROOM IN THE DRAGON VOLANT

PROLOGUE

THE curious case which I am about to place before you, is referred to, very pointedly, and more than once, in the extraordinary Essay upon the drugs of the Dark and the Middle Ages, from the pen of Doctor Hesselius.

This Essay he entitles *Mortis Imago*, and he, therein, discusses the *Vinum letiferum*, the *Beatifica*, the *Somnus Angelorum*, the *Hypnus Sagarum*, the *Aqua Thessaliae**, and about twenty other infusions and distillations, well known to the sages of eight hundred years ago, and two of which are still, he alleges, known to the fraternity of thieves, and, among them, as police-office inquiries sometimes disclose to this day, in practical use.

The Essay, *Mortis Imago*, will occupy as nearly as I can, at present, calculate, two volumes, the ninth and tenth, of the collected papers of Doctor Martin Hesselius.

This Essay, I may remark, in conclusion, is very curiously enriched by citations, in great abundance, from medieval verse and prose romance, some of the most valuable of which, strange to say, are Egyptian.

I have selected this particular statement from among many cases equally striking, but hardly, I think, so effective as mere narratives. In this irregular form of publication, it is simply as a story that I present it.

CHAPTER I

ON THE ROAD

In the eventful year, 1815, I was exactly three-and-twenty, and had just succeeded to a very large sum in consols,* and other securities. The first fall of Napoleon had thrown the continent open to English excursionists, anxious, let us suppose, to improve their minds by foreign travel; and I—the slight check of the 'hundred days' removed by the genius of Wellington, on the field of Waterloo*—was now added to the philosophic throng.

I was posting up to Paris from Bruxelles, following, I presume, the route that the allied army had pursued but a few weeks before—more carriages than you could believe were pursuing the same line. You could not look back or forward, without seeing into far perspective the clouds of dust which marked the line of the long series of vehicles. We were, perpetually, passing relays of return-horses, on their way, jaded and dusty, to the inns from which they had been taken. They were arduous times for those patient public servants. The whole world seemed posting up to Paris.

I ought to have noted it more particularly, but my head was so full of Paris and the future, that I passed the intervening scenery with little patience and less attention; I think, however, that it was about four miles to the frontier side* of a rather picturesque little town, the name of which, as of many more important places through which I posted in my hurried journey, I forget, and about two hours before sunset, that we came up with a carriage in distress.

It was not quite an upset. But the two leaders* were lying flat. The booted postillions had got down, and two servants who seemed very much at sea in such matters, were by way of assisting them. A pretty little bonnet and head were popped out of the window of the carriage in distress. Its *tournure*,* and that of the shoulders that also appeared for a moment, was captivating: I resolved to play the part of a good Samaritan; stopped my chaise, jumped out, and with my servant lent a very willing hand in the emergency. Alas! the lady with the pretty bonnet wore a very thick, black veil. I could see nothing but the pattern of the Bruxelles lace, as she drew back.

A lean old gentleman, almost at the same time, stuck his head out of the window. An invalid he seemed, for although the day was hot, he wore a black muffler which came up to his ears and nose, quite covering the lower part of his face, an arrangement which he disturbed by pulling it down for a moment, and poured forth a torrent of French thanks, as he uncovered his black wig, and gesticulated with grateful animation.

One of my very few accomplishments besides boxing, which was cultivated by all Englishmen at that time, was French; and I replied, I hope and believe, grammatically. Many bows being exchanged, the old gentleman's head went in again, and the demure, pretty little bonnet once more appeared.

The lady must have heard me speak to my servant, for she framed her little speech in such pretty, broken English, and in a voice so sweet, that I more than ever cursed the black veil that baulked my romantic curiosity.

The arms that were emblazoned on the panel were peculiar; I remember especially, one device, it was the figure of a stork, painted in carmine, upon what the heralds call a 'field or'. The bird was standing upon one leg, and in the other claw held a stone. This is, I believe, the emblem of vigilance. Its oddity struck me, and remained impressed upon my memory. There were supporters* besides, but I forget what they were.

The courtly manners of these people, the style of their servants, the elegance of their travelling carriage, and the supporters to their arms, satisfied me that they were noble.

The lady, you may be sure, was not the less interesting on that account. What a fascination a title exercises upon the imagination! I do not mean on that of snobs or moral flunkies. Superiority of rank is a powerful and genuine influence in love. The idea of superior refinement is associated with it. The careless notice of the squire tells more upon the heart of the pretty milkmaid, than years of honest Dobbin's* manly devotion, and so on and up. It is an unjust world!

But in this case there was something more. I was conscious of being good-looking. I really believe I was; and there could be no mistake about my being nearly six feet high. Why need this lady have thanked me? Had not her husband, for such I assumed him to be, thanked me quite enough, and for both? I was instinctively aware that the lady was looking on me with no unwilling eyes; and, through her veil, I felt the power of her gaze.

She was now rolling away, with a train of dust behind her

wheels, in the golden sunlight, and a wise young gentleman followed her with ardent eyes, and sighed profoundly as the distance increased.

I told the postillions on no account to pass the carriage, but to keep it steadily in view, and to pull up at whatever posting-house it should stop at. We were soon in the little town, and the carriage we followed drew up at the Belle Etoile, a comfortable old inn. They got out of the carriage and entered the house.

At a leisurely pace we followed. I got down, and mounted the steps listlessly, like a man quite apathetic and careless.

Audacious as I was, I did not care to inquire in what room I should find them. I peeped into the apartment to my right, and then into that on my left. *My* people were not there.

I ascended the stairs. A drawing-room door stood open. I entered with the most innocent air in the world. It was a spacious room, and, beside myself, contained but one living figure—a very pretty and lady-like one. There was the very bonnet with which I had fallen in love. The lady stood with her back toward me. I could not tell whether the envious veil* was raised; she was reading a letter.

I stood for a minute in fixed attention, gazing upon her, in the vague hope that she might turn about, and give me an opportunity of seeing her features. She did not; but with a step or two she placed herself before a little cabriole-table,* which stood against the wall, from which rose a tall mirror, in a tarnished frame.

I might, indeed, have mistaken it for a picture; for it now reflected a half-length portrait of a singularly beautiful woman.

She was looking down upon a letter which she held in her slender fingers, and in which she seemed absorbed.

The face was oval, melancholy, sweet. It had in it, nevertheless, a faint and undefinably sensual quality also. Nothing could exceed the delicacy of its features, or the brilliancy of its tints. The eyes, indeed, were lowered, so that I could not see their colour; nothing but their long lashes, and delicate eyebrows. She continued reading. She must have been deeply interested; I never saw a living form so motionless—I gazed on a tinted statue.

Being at that time blessed with long and keen vision, I saw this beautiful face with perfect distinctness. I saw even the blue veins that traced their wanderings on the whiteness of her full throat.

I ought to have retreated as noiselessly as I came in, before my presence was detected. But I was too much interested to move from the spot, for a few moments longer; and while they were passing, she raised her eyes. Those eyes were large, and of that hue which modern poets term 'violet'.

These splendid melancholy eyes were turned upon me from the glass, with a haughty stare, and hastily the lady lowered her black veil, and turned about.

I fancied that she hoped I had not seen her. I was watching every look and movement, the minutest, with an attention as intense as if an ordeal involving my life depended on them.

CHAPTER II

THE INN-YARD OF THE BELLE ETOILE

The face was, indeed, one to fall in love with at first sight. Those sentiments that take such sudden possession of young men were now dominating my curiosity. My audacity faltered before her; and I felt that my presence in this room was probably an impertinence. This point she quickly settled, for the same very sweet voice I had heard before, now said coldly, and this time in French, 'Monsieur cannot be aware that this apartment is not public.'

I bowed very low, faltered some apologies, and backed to the door.

I suppose I looked penitent and embarrassed. I certainly felt so; for the lady said, by way it seemed of softening matters, 'I am happy, however, to have an opportunity of again thanking Monsieur for the assistance, so prompt and effectual, which he had the goodness to render us to-day.'

It was more the altered tone in which it was spoken, than the speech itself that encouraged me. It was also true that she need not have recognized me; and even if she had, she certainly was not obliged to thank me over again.

All this was indescribably flattering, and all the more so that it followed so quickly on her slight reproof.

The tone in which she spoke had become low and timid, and I observed that she turned her head quickly towards a second door of the room. I fancied that the gentleman in the black wig, a jealous husband, perhaps, might reappear through it. Almost at the same moment, a voice at once reedy and nasal, was heard snarling some directions to a servant, and evidently approaching. It was the voice that had thanked me so profusely, from the carriage windows, about an hour before.

'Monsieur will have the goodness to retire,' said the lady, in a tone that resembled entreaty, at the same time gently waving her hand toward the door through which I had entered. Bowing again very low, I stepped back, and closed the door.

I ran down the stairs, very much elated. I saw the host of the Belle Etoile which, as I said, was the sign and designation of my inn.

I described the apartment I had just quitted, said I liked it, and asked whether I could have it.

He was extremely troubled, but that apartment and two adjoining rooms were engaged—

'By whom?'

'People of distinction.'

'But who are they? They must have names, or titles.'

'Undoubtedly, Monsieur, but such a stream is rolling into Paris, that we have ceased to inquire the names or titles of our guests—we designate them simply by the rooms they occupy.'

'What stay do they make?'

'Even that, Monsieur, I cannot answer. It does not interest us. Our rooms, while this continues, can never be, for a moment, disengaged.'

'I should have liked those rooms so much! Is one of them a sleeping apartment?'

'Yes, sir, and Monsieur will observe that people do not usually engage bed-rooms, unless they mean to stay the night.'

'Well, I can, I suppose, have some rooms, any, I don't care in what part of the house?'

'Certainly, Monsieur can have two apartments. They are the last at present disengaged.'

I took them instantly.

It was plain these people meant to make a stay here; at least they would not go till morning. I began to feel that I was all but engaged in an adventure.

I took possession of my rooms, and looked out of the window, which I found commanded the inn-yard. Many horses were being liberated from the traces, hot and weary, and others fresh from the stables, being put to. A great many vehicles—some private carriages, others, like mine, of that public class, which is equivalent to our old English post-chaise, were standing on the pavement, waiting their turn for relays. Fussy servants were toing and froing, and idle ones lounging or laughing, and the scene, on the whole, was animated and amusing.

Among these objects, I thought I recognized the travelling carriage, and one of the servants of the 'persons of distinction' about whom I was, just then, so profoundly interested.

I therefore ran down the stairs, made my way to the back door; and so, behold me, in a moment, upon the uneven pavement, among all these sights and sounds which in such a place attend upon a period of extraordinary crush and traffic.

By this time the sun was near its setting, and threw its golden beams on the red brick chimneys of the offices, and made the two barrels, that figured as pigeon-houses, on the tops of poles, look as if they were on fire. Everything in this light becomes picturesque; and things interest us which, in the sober grey of morning, are dull enough.

After a little search, I lighted upon the very carriage, of which I was in quest. A servant was locking one of the doors, for it was made with the security of lock and key. I paused near, looking at the panel of the door.

'A very pretty device that red stork!' I observed, pointing to the shield on the door, 'and no doubt indicates a distinguished family?'

The servant looked at me, for a moment, as he placed the little key in his pocket, and said with a slightly sarcastic bow and smile, 'Monsieur is at liberty to conjecture.'

Nothing daunted, I forthwith administered the laxative which, on occasion, acts so happily upon the tongue—I mean a 'tip'.

The servant looked at the Napoleon* in his hand, and then, in my face, with a sincere expression of surprise.

'Monsieur is very generous!'

'Not worth mentioning—who are the lady and gentleman who came here, in this carriage, and whom, you may remember, I and my servant assisted to-day in an emergency, when their horses had come to the ground?'

'They are the Count, and the young lady we call the Countess—but I know not, she may be his daughter.'

'Can you tell me where they live?'

'Upon my honour, Monsieur, I am unable—I know not.'

'Not know where your master lives! Surely you know something more about him than his name?'

'Nothing worth relating, Monsieur; in fact, I was hired in Bruxelles, on the very day they started. Monsieur Picard, my fellow-servant, Monsieur the Comte's gentleman, he has been years in his service and knows everything; but he never speaks except to communicate an order. From him I have learned nothing. We are going to Paris, however, and there I shall speedily pick up all about them. At present I am as ignorant of all that as Monsieur himself.'

'And where is Monsieur Picard?'

'He has gone to the cutler's to get his razors set.* But I do not think he will tell anything.'

This was a poor harvest for my golden sowing. The man, I think, spoke truth, and would honestly have betrayed the secrets of the family, if he had possessed any. I took my leave politely; and mounting the stairs again, I found myself once more in my room.

Forthwith I summoned my servant. Though I had brought him with me from England, he was a native of France—a useful fellow, sharp, bustling, and, of course, quite familiar with the ways and tricks of his countrymen.

'St Clair, shut the door; and come here. I can't rest till I have made out something about those people of rank who have got the apartments under mine. Here are fifteen francs; make out the servants we assisted today; have them to a *petit souper*,* and come back and tell me their entire history. I have, this moment, seen one of them who knows nothing, and has communicated it. The other, whose name I forget, is the unknown nobleman's valet, and knows everything. Him you must pump. It is, of course, the venerable peer, and not the young lady who accompanies him, that interests me—you understand? Begone! fly! and return with all the details I sigh for, and every circumstance that can possibly interest me.'

It was a commission which admirably suited the tastes and spirits of my worthy St Clair, to whom, you will have observed, I had accustomed myself to talk with the peculiar familiarity which the old French comedy establishes between master and valet.*

I am sure he laughed at me in secret; but nothing could be more polite and deferential.

With several wise looks, nods and shrugs, he withdrew; and looking down from my window, I saw him, with incredible quickness, enter the yard, where I soon lost sight of him among the carriages.

CHAPTER III

DEATH AND LOVE TOGETHER MATED

When the day drags, when a man is solitary, and in a fever of impatience and suspense; when the minute-hand of his watch travels as slowly as the hour-hand used to do, and the hour-hand has lost all appreciable motion; when he yawns, and beats the devil's tattoo,* and flattens his handsome nose against the window, and whistles tunes he hates, and, in short, does not know what to do with himself, it is deeply to be regretted that he cannot make a solemn dinner of three courses more than once in a day. The laws of matter, to which we are slaves, deny us that resource.

But in the times I speak of, supper was still a substantial meal, and its hour was approaching. This was consolatory.

Three-quarters of an hour, however, still interposed. How was I to dispose of that interval?

I had two or three idle books, it is true, as travelling companions; but there are many moods in which one cannot read. My novel lay with my rug* and walking-stick on the sofa, and I did not care if the heroine and the hero were both drowned together in the water-barrel that I saw in the inn-yard under my window.

I took a turn or two up and down my room, and sighed, looking at myself in the glass, adjusted my great white 'choker', folded and tied after Brummel,* the immortal 'Beau', put on a buff waistcoat and my blue swallow-tailed coat with gilt buttons; I deluged my pocket handkerchief with Eau-de-Cologne (we had not then the variety of bouquets with which the genius of perfumery has since blessed us); I arranged my hair, on which I piqued myself, and which I loved to groom in those days. That dark-brown *chevelure*,* with a natural curl, is now represented by a few dozen perfectly white hairs, and its place—a smooth, bald, pink head—knows it no more. But let us forget these mortifications. It was then rich, thick, and dark-brown. I was making a very careful toilet. I took my unexceptionable hat from its case, and placed it lightly on my wise head, as nearly as memory and practice enabled me to do so, at that very slight inclination which the immortal person I have mentioned was wont to give to his. A pair of light French gloves and a rather club-like knotted walking-stick, such as just then came into vogue, for a year or two again in England, in the phraseology of Sir Walter Scott's romances,* 'completed my equipment'.

All this attention to effect, preparatory to a mere lounge in the yard, or on the steps of the Belle Etoile, was a simple act of devotion to the wonderful eyes which I had that evening beheld for the first time, and never, never could forget! In plain terms, it was all done in the vague, very vague hope that those eyes might behold the unexceptionable get-up of a melancholy slave, and retain the image, not altogether without secret approbation.

As I completed my preparations the light failed me; the last level streak of sunlight disappeared, and a fading twilight only remained. I sighed in unison with the pensive hour, and threw open the window, intending to look out for a moment before going downstairs. I perceived instantly that the window underneath mine was also open, for I heard two voices in conversation, although I could not distinguish what they were saying.

The male voice was peculiar; it was, as I told you, reedy and nasal. I knew it, of course, instantly. The answering voice spoke in those sweet tones which I recognized only too easily. The dialogue was only for a minute; the repulsive male voice laughed, I fancied, with a kind of devilish satire, and retired from the window, so that I almost ceased to hear it.

The other voice remained nearer the window, but not so near as at first.

It was not an altercation; there was evidently nothing the least exciting in the colloquy. What would I not have given that it had been a quarrel—a violent one—and I the redresser of wrongs, and the defender of insulted beauty! Alas! so far as I could pronounce upon the character of the tones I heard, they might be as tranquil a pair as any in existence. In a moment more the lady began to sing an odd little *chanson*. I need not remind you how much farther the voice is heard *singing* than speaking. I could distinguish the words. The voice was of that exquisitely sweet kind which is called, I believe, a semi-contralto; it had something pathetic, and something, I fancied, a little mocking in its tones. I venture a clumsy, but adequate translation of the words:

> 'Death and Love, together mated,
>   Watch and wait in ambuscade;
> At early morn, or else belated,
>   They meet and mark the man or maid.

> 'Burning sigh, or breath that freezes,
>   Numbs or maddens man or maid;
> Death or Love the victim seizes,
>   Breathing from their ambuscade.'

'Enough, Madame!' said the old voice, with sudden severity. 'We do not desire, I believe, to amuse the grooms and hostlers in the yard with our music.'

The lady's voice laughed gaily.

'You desire to quarrel, Madame!' And the old man, I presume, shut down the window. Down it went, at all events, with a rattle that might easily have broken the glass.

Of all thin partitions, glass is the most effectual excluder of sound. I heard no more, not even the subdued hum of the colloquy.

What a charming voice this Countess had! How it melted, swelled, and trembled! How it moved, and even agitated me! What a pity that a hoarse old jackdaw should have power to crow down such a Philomel!* 'Alas! what a life it is!' I moralized, wisely. 'That beautiful Countess, with the patience of an angel and the beauty of a Venus and the accomplishments of all the Muses, a slave! She knows perfectly who occupies the apartments over hers; she heard me raise my window. One may conjecture pretty well for whom that music was intended—ay, old gentleman, and for whom you suspected it to be intended.'

In a very agreeable flutter I left my room, and descending the stairs, passed the Count's door very much at my leisure. There was just a chance that the beautiful songstress might emerge. I dropped my stick on the lobby, near their door, and you may be sure it took me some little time to pick it up! Fortune, nevertheless, did not favour me. I could not stay on the lobby all night picking up my stick, so I went down to the hall.

I consulted the clock, and found that there remained but a quarter of an hour to the moment of supper.

Every one was roughing it now, every inn in confusion; people might do at such a juncture what they never did before. Was it just possible that, for once, the Count and Countess would take their chairs at the table-d'hôte?*

CHAPTER IV

MONSIEUR DROQVILLE

Full of this exciting hope, I sauntered out, upon the steps of the Belle Etoile. It was now night, and a pleasant moonlight over everything. I had entered more into my romance since my arrival, and the poetic light heightened the sentiment. What a drama, if she turned out to be the Count's daughter, and in love with me! What a delightful—*tragedy*, if she turned out to be the Count's wife!

In this luxurious mood, I was accosted by a tall and very elegantly-made gentleman, who appeared to be about fifty. His air was courtly and graceful, and there was in his whole manner and appearance something so distinguished, that it was impossible not to suspect him of being a person of rank.

He had been standing upon the steps, looking out, like me, upon the moonlight effects that transformed, as it were, the objects and buildings in the little street. He accosted me, I say, with the politeness, at once easy and lofty, of a French nobleman of the old school. He asked me if I were not Mr Beckett? I assented; and he immediately introduced himself as the Marquis d'Harmonville (this information he gave me in a low tone), and asked leave to present me with a letter from Lord R——, who knew my father slightly, and had once done me, also, a trifling kindness.

This English peer, I may mention, stood very high in the political world, and was named as the most probable successor to the distinguished post of English Minister at Paris.

I received it with a low bow, and read:

'My Dear Beckett,
'I beg to introduce my very dear friend, the Marquis d'Harmonville, who will explain to you the nature of the services it may be in your power to render him and us.'

He went on to speak of the Marquis as a man whose great wealth, whose intimate relations with the old families, and whose legitimate influence with the court rendered him the fittest possible person for those friendly offices which, at the desire of his own sovereign, and of our government, he has so obligingly undertaken.

It added a great deal to my perplexity, when I read, further—

'By-the-by, Walton was here yesterday, and told me that your seat was likely to be attacked;* something, he says, is unquestionably going on at Domwell. You know there is an awkwardness in my meddling ever so cautiously. But I advise, if it is not very officious, your making Haxton look after it, and report immediately. I fear it is serious. I ought to have mentioned that, for reasons that you will see, when you have talked with him for five minutes, the Marquis—with the concurrence of all our friends—drops his title, for a few weeks, and is at present plain Monsieur Droqville.

'I am this moment going to town, and can say no more.

'Yours faithfully,

    'R——.'

I was utterly puzzled. I could scarcely boast of Lord ——'s acquaintance. I knew no one named Haxton, and, except my hatter, no one called Walton; and this peer wrote as if we were intimate friends! I looked at the back of the letter, and the mystery was solved. And now, to my consternation—for I was plain Richard Beckett—I read—

*'To George Stanhope Beckett, Esq., M.P.'**

I looked with consternation in the face of the Marquis.

'What apology can I offer to Monsieur the Mar—to Monsieur Droqville? It is true my name is Beckett—it is true I am known, though very slightly, to Lord R——; but the letter was not intended for me. My name is Richard Beckett—this is to Mr Stanhope Beckett, the member for Shillingsworth. What can I say, or do, in this unfortunate situation? I can only give you my honour as a gentleman, that, for me, the letter, which I now return, shall remain as unviolated a secret as before I opened it. I am so shocked and grieved that such a mistake should have occurred!'

I dare say my honest vexation and good faith were pretty

legibly written in my countenance; for the look of gloomy embarrassment which had for a moment settled on the face of the Marquis, brightened; he smiled, kindly, and extended his hand.

'I have not the least doubt that Monsieur Beckett will respect my little secret. As a mistake was destined to occur, I have reason to thank my good stars that it should have been with a gentleman of honour. Monsieur Beckett will permit me, I hope, to place his name among those of my friends?'

I thanked the Marquis very much for his kind expressions. He went on to say—

'If, Monsieur, I can persuade you to visit me at Claironville, in Normandy, where I hope to see, on the 15th August, a great many friends, whose acquaintance it might interest you to make, I shall be too happy.'

I thanked him, of course, very gratefully for his hospitality. He continued:

'I cannot, for the present, see my friends, for reasons which you may surmise, at my house in Paris. But Monsieur will be so good as to let me know the hotel he means to stay at in Paris; and he will find that although the Marquis d'Harmonville is not in town, that Monsieur Droqville will not lose sight of him.'

With many acknowledgements I gave him the information he desired.

'And in the meantime,' he continued, 'if you think of any way in which Monsieur Droqville can be of use to you, our communication shall not be interrupted, and I shall so manage matters that you can easily let me know.'

I was very much flattered. The Marquis had, as we say, taken a fancy to me. Such likings at first sight often ripen into lasting friendships. To be sure it was just possible that the Marquis might think it prudent to keep the involuntary depository of a political secret, even so vague a one, in good humour.

Very graciously the Marquis took his leave, going up the stairs of the Belle Etoile.

I remained upon the steps, for a minute lost in speculation upon this new theme of interest. But the wonderful eyes, the thrilling voice, the exquisite figure of the beautiful lady who had taken possession of my imagination, quickly reasserted their influence. I was again gazing at the sympathetic moon, and descending the steps, I loitered along the pavements among strange objects, and houses that were antique and picturesque, in a dreamy state, thinking.

In a little while, I turned into the inn-yard again. There had come a lull. Instead of the noisy place it was, an hour or two before, the yard was perfectly still and empty, except for the carriages that stood here and there. Perhaps there was a servants' table-d'hôte just then. I was rather pleased to find solitude; and undisturbed I found out my lady-love's carriage, in the moonlight. I mused, I walked round it; I was as utterly foolish and maudlin as very young men, in my situation, usually are. The blinds were down, the doors, I suppose, locked. The brilliant moonlight revealed everything, and cast sharp, black shadows of wheel, and bar, and spring, on the pavement. I stood before the escutcheon painted on the door, which I had examined in the daylight. I wondered how often her eyes had rested on the same object. I pondered in a charming dream. A harsh, loud voice, over my shoulder, said suddenly,

'A red stork—good! The stork is a bird of prey; it is vigilant, greedy, and catches gudgeons.* Red, too!—blood red! Ha! ha! the symbol is appropriate.'

I had turned about, and beheld the palest face I ever saw. It was broad, ugly, and malignant. The figure was that of a French officer, in undress,* and was six feet high. Across the nose and eyebrow there was a deep scar, which made the repulsive face grimmer.

The officer elevated his chin and his eyebrows, with a scoffing chuckle, and said,—'I have shot a stork, with a rifle bullet, when he thought himself safe in the clouds, for mere sport!' (He shrugged, and laughed malignantly.) 'See, Monsieur; when a man like me—a man of energy, you understand, a man with all his wits about him, a man who has made the tour of Europe under canvas, and, *parbleu!** often without it— resolves to discover a secret, expose a crime, catch a thief, spit a robber on the point of his sword, it is odd if he does not succeed. Ha! ha! ha! Adieu, Monsieur!'

He turned with an angry whisk on his heel, and swaggered with long strides out of the gate.

CHAPTER V

SUPPER AT THE BELLE ETOILE

The French army were in a rather savage temper, just then. The English, especially, had but scant courtesy to expect at their hands. It was plain, however, that the cadaverous gentleman who had just apostrophized the heraldry of the Count's carriage, with such mysterious acrimony, had not intended any of his malevolence for me. He was stung by some old recollection, and had marched off, seething with fury.

I had received one of those unacknowledged shocks which startle us, when fancying ourselves perfectly alone, we discover on a sudden, that our antics have been watched by a spectator, almost at our elbow. In this case, the effect was enhanced by the extreme repulsiveness of the face, and, I may add, its proximity, for, as I think, it almost touched mine. The enigmatical harangue of this person, so full of hatred and implied denunciation, was still in my ears. Here at all events was new matter for the industrious fancy of a lover to work upon.

It was time now to go to the table-d'hôte. Who could tell what lights the gossip of the supper-table might throw upon the subject that interested me so powerfully!

I stepped into the room, my eyes searching the little assembly, about thirty people, for the persons who specially interested me.

It was not easy to induce people, so hurried and overworked as those of the Belle Etoile just now, to send meals up to one's private apartments, in the midst of this unparalleled confusion; and, therefore, many people who did not like it, might find

themselves reduced to the alternative of supping at the table-
d'hôte, or starving.

The Count was not there, nor his beautiful companion; but
the Marquis d'Harmonville, whom I hardly expected to see in
so public a place, signed, with a significant smile, to a vacant
chair beside himself. I secured it, and he seemed pleased, and
almost immediately entered into conversation with me.

'This is, probably, your first visit to France?' he said.

I told him it was, and he said:

'You must not think me very curious and impertinent; but
Paris is about the most dangerous capital a high-spirited and
generous young gentleman could visit without a Mentor. If
you have not an experienced friend as a companion during
your visit—' He paused.

I told him I was not so provided, but that I had my wits
about me; that I had seen a good deal of life in England, and
that, I fancied, human nature was pretty much the same in all
parts of the world. The Marquis shook his head, smiling.

'You will find very marked differences, notwithstanding,' he
said. 'Peculiarities of intellect and peculiarities of character,
undoubtedly, do pervade different nations; and this results,
among the criminal classes, in a style of villainy no less
peculiar. In Paris, the class who live by their wits, is three or
four times as great as in London; and they live much better;
some of them even splendidly. They are more ingenious than
the London rogues; they have more animation, and invention,
and the dramatic faculty, in which your countrymen are
deficient, is everywhere. These invaluable attributes place
them upon a totally different level. They can affect the
manners and enjoy the luxuries of people of distinction. They
live, many of them, by play.'*

'So do many of our London rogues.'

'Yes, but in a totally different way. They are the *habitués** of
certain gaming-tables, billiard-rooms, and other places,
including your races, where high play goes on; and by superior
knowledge of chances, by masking their play, by means of
confederates, by means of bribery, and other artifices, varying
with the subject of their imposture, they rob the unwary. But
here it is more elaborately done, and with a really exquisite

finesse. There are people whose manners, style, conversation, are unexceptionable, living in handsome houses in the best situations, with everything about them in the most refined taste, and exquisitely luxurious, who impose even upon the Parisian bourgeois,* who believe them to be, in good faith, people of rank and fashion, because their habits are expensive and refined, and their houses are frequented by foreigners of distinction, and, to a degree, by foolish young Frenchmen of rank. At all these houses play goes on. The ostensible host and hostess seldom join in it; they provide it simply to plunder their guests, by means of their accomplices, and thus wealthy strangers are inveigled and robbed.'

'But I have heard of a young Englishman, a son of Lord Rooksbury, who broke two Parisian gaming-tables only last year.'

'I see,' he said laughing, 'you are come here to do likewise. I, myself, at about your age, undertook the same spirited enterprise. I raised no less a sum than five hundred thousand francs to begin with; I expected to carry all before me by the simple expedient of going on doubling my stakes. I had heard of it, and I fancied that the sharpers, who kept the table, knew nothing of the matter. I found, however, that they not only knew all about it, but had provided against the possibility of any such experiments; and I was pulled up before I had well begun, by a rule which forbids the doubling of an original stake more than four times, consecutively.'

'And is that rule in force still?' I inquired, chap-fallen.

He laughed and shrugged, 'Of course it is, my young friend. People who live by an art, always understand it better than an amateur. I see you had formed the same plan, and no doubt came provided.'

I confessed I had prepared for conquest upon a still grander scale. I had arrived with a purse of thirty thousand pounds sterling.

'Any acquaintance of my very dear friend, Lord R——, interests me; and, besides my regard for him, I am charmed with you; so you will pardon all my, perhaps, too officious questions and advice.'

I thanked him most earnestly for his valuable counsel, and

begged that he would have the goodness to give me all the advice in his power.

'Then if you take my advice,' said he, 'you will leave your money in the bank where it lies. Never risk a Napoleon in a gaming-house. The night I went to break the bank, I lost between seven and eight thousand pounds sterling of your English money; and my next adventure, I had obtained an introduction to one of those elegant gaming-houses which affect to be the private mansions of persons of distinction, and was saved from ruin by a gentleman, whom, ever since, I have regarded with increasing respect and friendship. It oddly happens he is in this house at this moment. I recognized his servant, and made him a visit in his apartments here, and found him the same brave, kind, honourable man I always knew him. But that he is living so entirely out of the world, now, I should have made a point of introducing you. Fifteen years ago he would have been the man of all others to consult. The gentleman I speak of is the Comte de St Alyre. He represents a very old family. He is the very soul of honour, and the most sensible man in the world, except in one particular.'

'And that particular?' I hesitated. I was now deeply interested.

'Is that he has married a charming creature, at least five-and-forty years younger than himself, and is, of course, although I believe absolutely without cause, horribly jealous.'

'And the lady?'

'The Countess is, I believe, in every way worthy of so good a man,' he answered, a little drily.

'I think I heard her sing this evening.'

'Yes, I daresay; she is very accomplished.' After a few moments' silence he continued.

'I must not lose sight of you, for I should be sorry, when next you meet my friend Lord R——, that you had to tell him you had been pigeoned* in Paris. A rich Englishman as you are, with so large a sum at his Paris bankers, young, gay, generous, a thousand ghouls and harpies will be contending who shall be first to seize and devour you.'

At this moment I received something like a jerk from the

elbow of the gentleman at my right. It was an accidental jog, as he turned in his seat.

'On the honour of a soldier, there is no man's flesh in this company heals so fast as mine.'

The tone in which this was spoken was harsh and stentorian, and almost made me bounce. I looked round and recognized the officer, whose large white face had half-scared me in the inn-yard, wiping his mouth furiously, and then with a gulp of Mâcon,* he went on—

'*No* one! It's not blood; it is ichor!* it's miracle! Set aside stature, thew, bone, and muscle—set aside courage, and by all the angels of death I'd fight a lion naked and dash his teeth down his jaws with my fist, and flog him to death with his own tail! Set aside, I say, all those attributes, which I am allowed to possess, and I am worth six men in any campaign, for that one quality of healing as I do—rip me up; punch me through, tear me to tatters with bomb-shells, and nature has me whole again, as your tailor would fine-draw* an old-coat. *Parbleu!* gentlemen, if you saw me naked, you would laugh? Look at my hand, a sabre-cut across the palm, to the bone, to save my head, taken up with three stitches, and five days afterwards I was playing ball with an English general, a prisoner in Madrid, against the wall of the convent of the Santa Maria de la Castita! At Arcola,* by the great devil himself! that was an action. Every man there, gentlemen, swallowed as much smoke in five minutes as would smother you all, in this room! I received, at the same moment, two musket balls in the thighs, a grape shot through the calf of my leg, a lance through my left shoulder, a piece of a shrapnel in the left deltoid, a bayonet through the cartilage of my right ribs, a sabre-cut that carried away a pound of flesh from my chest, and the better part of a congreve rocket* on my forehead. Pretty well, ha, ha! and all while you'd say *bah*! and in eight days and a half I was making a forced march, without shoes, and only one gaiter, the life and soul of my company, and as sound as a roach!'

'Bravo! Bravissimo! Per Bacco! un gallant uomo!'* exclaimed, in a martial ecstacy, a fat little Italian, who manufactured toothpicks and wicker cradles on the island of Notre Dame;

'your exploits shall resound through Europe! and the history of those wars should be written in your blood!'

'Never mind! a trifle!' exclaimed the soldier. 'At Ligny,* the other day, where we smashed the Prussians into ten hundred thousand milliards of atoms, a bit of a shell cut me across the leg and opened an artery. It was spouting as high as the chimney, and in half a minute I had lost enough to fill a pitcher. I must have expired in another minute, if I had not whipped off my sash like a flash of lightning, tied it round my leg above the wound, whipped a bayonet out of the back of a dead Prussian, and passing it under, made a tourniquet of it with a couple of twists, and so stayed the hemorrhage, and saved my life. But, *sacré bleu!** gentlemen, I lost so much blood, I have been as pale as the bottom of a plate ever since. No matter. A trifle. Blood well spent, gentlemen.' He applied himself now to his bottle of *vin ordinaire.**

The Marquis had closed his eyes, and looked resigned and disgusted, while all this was going on.

'*Garçon,*'* said the officer, for the first time, speaking in a low tone over the back of his chair to the waiter; 'who came in that travelling carriage, dark yellow and black, that stands in the middle of the yard, with arms and supporters emblazoned on the door, and a red stork, as red as my facings?'*

The waiter could not say.

The eye of the eccentric officer, who had suddenly grown grim and serious, and seemed to have abandoned the general conversation to other people, lighted, as it were, accidentally, on me.

'Pardon me, Monsieur,' he said. 'Did I not see you examining the panel of that carriage at the same time that I did so, this evening? Can you tell me who arrived in it?'

'I rather think the Count and Countess de St Alyre.'

'And are they here, in the Belle Etoile?' he asked.

'They have got apartments up-stairs,' I answered.

He started up, and half-pushed his chair from the table. He quickly sat down again, and I could hear him *sacré*-ing and muttering to himself, and grinning and scowling. I could not tell whether he was alarmed or furious.

I turned to say a word or two to the Marquis, but he was

gone. Several other people had dropped out also, and the supper party soon broke up.

Two or three substantial pieces of wood smouldered on the hearth, for the night had turned out chilly. I sat down by the fire in a great arm-chair, of carved oak, with a marvellously high back, that looked as old as the days of Henry IV.*

'*Garçon*,' said I, 'do you happen to know who that officer is?'

'That is Colonel Gaillarde, Monsieur.'

'Has he been often here?'

'Once before, Monsieur, for a week; it is a year since.'

'He is the palest man I ever saw.'

'That is true, Monsieur; he has been often taken for a *revenant*.'*

'Can you give me a bottle of really good Burgundy?'

'The best in France, Monsieur.'

'Place it, and a glass by my side, on this table, if you please. I may sit here for half an hour?'

'Certainly, Monsieur.'

I was very comfortable, the wine excellent, and my thoughts glowing and serene. 'Beautiful Countess! Beautiful Countess! shall we ever be better acquainted.'

CHAPTER VI

THE NAKED SWORD

A man who has been posting all day long, and changing the air he breathes every half hour, who is well-pleased with himself, and has nothing on earth to trouble him, and who sits alone by a fire in a comfortable chair after having eaten a hearty supper, may be pardoned if he takes an accidental nap.

I had filled my fourth glass when I fell asleep. My head, I daresay, hung uncomfortably; and it is admitted, that a variety of French dishes is not the most favourable precursor to pleasant dreams.

I had a dream as I took mine ease in mine inn on this occasion. I fancied myself in a huge cathedral, without light, except from four tapers that stood at the corners of a raised platform hung with black, on which lay, draped also in black, what seemed to me the dead body of the Countess de St Alyre. The place seemed empty, it was cold, and I could see only (in the halo of the candles) a little way round.

The little I saw bore the character of Gothic gloom, and helped my fancy to shape and furnish the black void that yawned all round me. I heard a sound like the slow tread of two persons walking up the flagged aisle. A faint echo told of the vastness of the place. An awful sense of expectation was upon me, and I was horribly frightened when the body that lay on the catafalque* said (without stirring), in a whisper that froze me, 'They come to place me in the grave alive; save me.'

I found that I could neither speak nor move. I was horribly frightened.

The two people who approached now emerged from the darkness. One, the Count de St Alyre, glided to the head of the figure and placed his long thin hands under it. The white-faced Colonel, with the scar across his face, and a look of infernal triumph, placed his hands under her feet, and they began to raise her.

With an indescribable effort I broke the spell that bound me, and started to my feet with a gasp.

I was wide awake, but the broad, wicked face of Colonel Gaillarde was staring, white as death, at me, from the other side of the hearth. 'Where is she?' I shuddered.

'That depends on who she is, Monsieur,' replied the Colonel, curtly.

'Good heavens!' I gasped, looking about me.

The Colonel, who was eyeing me sarcastically, had had his *demi-tasse* of *café noir*,* and now drank his *tasse*, diffusing a pleasant perfume of brandy.

'I fell asleep and was dreaming,' I said, lest any strong language, founded on the *rôle* he played in my dream, should have escaped me. 'I did not know for some moments where I was.'

'You are the young gentleman who has the apartments over

the Count and Countess de St Alyre?' he said, winking one eye, close in meditation, and glaring at me with the other.

'I believe so—yes,' I answered.

'Well, younker, take care you have not worse dreams than that some night,' he said, enigmatically, and wagged his head with a chuckle. 'Worse dreams,' he repeated.

'What does Monsieur the Colonel mean?' I inquired.

'I am trying to find that out myself,' said the Colonel; 'and I think I shall. When *I* get the first inch of the thread fast between my finger and thumb, it goes hard but I follow it up, bit by bit, little by little, tracing it this way and that, and up and down, and round about, until the whole clue is wound up on my thumb, and the end, and its secret, fast in my fingers. Ingenious! Crafty as five foxes! wide awake as a weazel! *Parbleu*! if I had descended to that occupation I should have made my fortune as a spy. Good wine here?' he glanced interrogatively at my bottle.

'Very good,' said I, 'Will Monsieur the Colonel try a glass?'

He took the largest he could find, and filled it, raised it with a bow, and drank it slowly. 'Ah! ah! Bah! That is not it,' he exclaimed, with some disgust, filling it again. 'You ought to have told *me* to order your Burgundy, and they would not have brought you that stuff.'

I got away from this man as soon as I civilly could, and, putting on my hat, I walked out with no other company than my sturdy walking stick. I visited the inn-yard, and looked up to the windows of the Countess's apartments. They were closed, however, and I had not even the unsubstantial consolation of contemplating the light in which that beautiful lady was at the moment writing or reading, or sitting and thinking of—any one you please.

I bore this serious privation as well as I could, and took a little saunter through the town. I shan't bore you with moonlight effects, nor with the maunderings of a man who has fallen in love at first sight with a beautiful face. My ramble, it is enough to say, occupied about half-an-hour, and, returning by a slight *détour*, I found myself in a little square, with about two high gabled houses on each side, and a rude stone statue, worn by centuries of rain, on a pedestal in the centre of the pavement. Looking at this statue was a slight and rather tall man, whom I instantly recognized as the Marquis d'Harmonville: he knew me almost as quickly. He walked a step towards me, shrugged and laughed:

'You are surprised to find Monsieur Droqville staring at that old stone figure by moonlight. Anything to pass the time. You, I see, suffer from *ennui*,* as I do. These little provincial towns! Heavens! what an effort it is to live in them! If I could regret having formed in early life a friendship that does me honour, I think its condemning me to a sojourn in such a place would make me do so. You go on towards Paris, I suppose, in the morning?'

'I have ordered horses.'

'As for me I await a letter, or an arrival, either would emancipate me; but I can't say how soon either event will happen.'

'Can I be of any use in this matter?' I began.

'None, Monsieur, I thank you a thousand times. No, this is a piece in which every *rôle* is already cast. I am but an amateur, and induced, solely by friendship, to take a part.'

So he talked on, for a time, as we walked slowly toward the Belle Etoile, and then came a silence, which I broke by asking him if he knew anything of Colonel Gaillarde.

'Oh! yes, to be sure. He is a little mad; he has had some bad injuries of the head. He used to plague the people in the War Office to death. He has always some delusion. They contrived some employment for him—not regimental, of course—but in this campaign Napoleon, who could spare nobody, placed him in command of a regiment. He was always a desperate fighter, and such men were more than ever needed.'

There is, or was, a second inn, in this town, called l'Ecu de France. At its door the Marquis stopped, bade me a mysterious good-night, and disappeared.

As I walked slowly toward my inn, I met, in the shadow of a row of poplars, the *garçon* who had brought me my Burgundy a little time ago. I was thinking of Colonel Gaillarde, and I stopped the little waiter as he passed me.

'You said, I think, that Colonel Gaillarde was at the Belle Etoile for a week at one time.'

'Yes, Monsieur.'

'Is he perfectly in his right mind?'

The waiter stared. 'Perfectly, Monsieur.'

'Has he been suspected at any time of being out of his mind?'

'Never, Monsieur; he is a little noisy, but a very shrewd man.'

'What is a fellow to think?' I muttered, as I walked on.

I was soon within sight of the lights of the Belle Etoile. A carriage, with four horses, stood in the moonlight at the door, and a furious altercation was going on in the hall, in which the yell of Colonel Gaillarde out-topped all other sounds.

Most young men like, at least, to witness a row. But, intuitively, I felt that this would interest me in a very special manner. I had only fifty yards to run, when I found myself in the hall of the old inn. The principal actor in this strange drama was, indeed, the Colonel, who stood facing the old Count de St Alyre, who, in his travelling costume, with his black silk scarf covering the lower part of his face, confronted him; he had evidently been intercepted in an endeavour to reach his carriage. A little in the rear of the Count stood the Countess, also in travelling costume, with her thick black veil down, and holding in her delicate fingers a white rose. You can't conceive a more diabolical effigy of hate and fury than the Colonel; the knotted veins stood out on his forehead, his eyes were leaping from their sockets, he was grinding his teeth, and froth was on his lips. His sword was drawn, in his hand, he accompanied his yelling denunciations with stamps upon the floor and flourishes of his weapon in the air.

The host of the Belle Etoile was talking to the Colonel in soothing terms utterly thrown away. Two waiters, pale with fear, stared uselessly from behind. The Colonel screamed, and thundered, and whirled his sword. 'I was not sure of your red birds of prey; I could not believe you would have the audacity to travel on high roads, and to stop at honest inns, and lie under the same roof with honest men. You! *you!* both—vampires, wolves, ghouls. Summon the *gendarmes*, I say. By St Peter and all the devils, if either of you try to get out of that door I'll take your heads off.'

For a moment I had stood aghast. Here was a situation! I walked up to the lady; she laid her hand wildly upon my arm. 'Oh! Monsieur,' she whispered, in great agitation, 'that dreadful madman! What are we to do? He won't let us pass; he will kill my husband.'

'Fear nothing, Madame,' I answered, with romantic devotion, and stepping between the Count and Gaillarde, as he shrieked his invective, 'Hold your tongue, and clear the way, you ruffian, you bully, you coward!' I roared.

A faint cry escaped the lady, which more than repaid the risk I ran, as the sword of the frantic soldier, after a moment's astonished pause, flashed in the air to cut me down.

CHAPTER VII

THE WHITE ROSE

I was too quick for Colonel Gaillarde. As he raised his sword, reckless of all consequences but my condign punishment,* and quite resolved to cleave me to the teeth, I struck him across the side of his head, with my heavy stick; and while he staggered back, I struck him another blow, nearly in the same place, that felled him to the floor, where he lay as if dead.

I did not care one of his own regimental buttons, whether he was dead or not; I was, at that moment, carried away by such a tumult of delightful and diabolical emotions!

I broke his sword under my foot, and flung the pieces across the street. The old Count de St Alyre skipped nimbly without looking to the right or left, or thanking anybody, over the floor, out of the door, down the steps, and into his carriage. Instantly I was at the side of the beautiful Countess, thus left to shift for herself; I offered her my arm, which she took, and I led her to her carriage. She entered, and I shut the door. All this without a word.

I was about to ask if there were any commands with which she would honour me—my hand was laid upon the lower edge of the window, which was open.

The lady's hand was laid upon mine timidly and excitedly. Her lips almost touched my cheek as she whispered hurriedly.

'I may never see you more, and, oh! that I could forget you. Go—farewell—for God's sake, go!'

I pressed her hand for a moment. She withdrew it, but tremblingly pressed into mine the rose which she had held in her fingers during the agitating scene she had just passed through.

All this took place while the Count was commanding, entreating, cursing his servants, tipsy, and out of the way during the crisis, my conscience afterwards insinuated, by my clever contrivance. They now mounted to their places with the agility of alarm. The postillions' whips cracked, the horses scrambled into a trot, and away rolled the carriage, with its precious freightage, along the quaint main street, in the moonlight, toward Paris.

I stood on the pavement, till it was quite lost to eye and ear in the distance.

With a deep sigh, I then turned, my white rose folded in my handkerchief—the little parting *gage*—the

'Favour secret, sweet, and precious;'

which no mortal eye but hers and mine had seen conveyed to me.

The care of the host of the Belle Etoile, and his assistants, had raised the wounded hero of a hundred fights partly against the wall, and propped him at each side with portmanteaus and pillows, and poured a glass of brandy, which was duly placed to his account, into his big mouth, where, for the first time, such a Godsend remained unswallowed.

A bald-headed little military surgeon of sixty, with spectacles, who had cut off eighty-seven legs and arms to his own share, after the battle of Eylau,* having retired with his sword and his saw, his laurels and his sticking-plaster to this, his native town, was called in, and rather thought the gallant Colonel's skull was fractured, at all events there was concussion of the seat of thought, and quite enough work for his remarkable self-healing powers, to occupy him for a fortnight.

I began to grow a little uneasy. A disagreeable surprise, if my excursion, in which I was to break banks and hearts, and, as you see, heads, should end upon the gallows or the guillotine. I was not clear, in those times of political oscillation, which was the established apparatus.

The Colonel was conveyed, snorting apoplectically to his room.

I saw my host in the apartment in which we had supped. Wherever you employ a force of any sort, to carry a point of real importance, reject all nice calculations of economy. Better to be a thousand per cent over the mark, than the smallest fraction of a unit under it. I instinctively felt this.

I ordered a bottle of my landlord's very best wine; made him partake with me, in the proportion of two glasses to one; and then told him that he must not decline a trifling *souvenir* from a guest who had been so charmed with all he had seen of the renowned Belle Etoile. Thus saying, I placed five-and thirty Napoleons in his hand. At touch of which his countenance, by no means encouraging before, grew sunny, his manners thawed, and it was plain, as he dropped the coins hastily into his pocket, that benevolent relations had been established between us.

I immediately placed the Colonel's broken head upon the *tapis.** We both agreed that if I had not given him that rather smart tap of my walking-cane, he would have beheaded half the inmates of the Belle Etoile. There was not a waiter in the house who would not verify that statement on oath.

The reader may suppose that I had other motives, beside the desire to escape the tedious inquisition of the law, for desiring to recommence my journey to Paris with the least possible delay. Judge what was my horror then to learn, that for love or money, horses were nowhere to be had that night. The last pair in the town had been obtained from the Ecu de France, by a gentleman who dined and supped at the Belle Etoile, and was obliged to proceed to Paris that night.

Who was the gentleman? Had he actually gone? Could he possibly be induced to wait till morning?

The gentleman was now upstairs getting his things together, and his name was Monsieur Droqville.

I ran upstairs. I found my servant St Clair in my room. At

sight of him, for a moment, my thoughts were turned into a different channel.

'Well, St Clair, tell me this moment who the lady is?' I demanded.

'The lady is the daughter or wife, it matters not which, of the Count de St Alyre—the old gentleman who was so near being sliced like a cucumber to-night, I am informed, by the sword of the general whom Monsieur, by a turn of fortune, has put to bed of an apoplexy.'

'Hold your tongue, fool! The man's beastly drunk—he's sulking—he could talk if he liked—who cares? Pack up my things. Which are Monsieur Droqville's apartments?'

He knew, of course; he always knew everything.

Half an hour later Monsieur Droqville and I were travelling towards Paris, in my carriage, and with his horses. I ventured to ask the Marquis d'Harmonville, in a little while, whether the lady, who accompanied the Count, was certainly the Countess. 'Has he not a daughter?'

'Yes: I believe a very beautiful and charming young lady—I cannot say—it may have been she, his daughter by an earlier marriage. I saw only the Count himself to-day.'

The Marquis was growing a little sleepy and, in a little while, he actually fell asleep in his corner. I dozed and nodded; but the Marquis slept like a top. He awoke only for a minute or two at the next posting-house, where he had fortunately secured horses by sending on his man, he told me.

'You will excuse my being so dull a companion,' he said, 'but till to-night I have had but two hours' sleep, for more than sixty hours. I shall have a cup of coffee here; I have had my nap. Permit me to recommend you to do likewise. Their coffee is really excellent.' He ordered two cups of *café noir*, and waited, with his head from the window. 'We will keep the cups,' he said, as he received them from the waiter, 'and the tray. Thank you.'

There was a little delay as he paid for these things; and then he took in the little tray, and handed me a cup of coffee.

I declined the tray; so he placed it on his own knees, to act as a miniature table.

'I can't endure being waited for and hurried,' he said, 'I like to sip my coffee at leisure.'

I agreed. It really *was* the very perfection of coffee.

'I, like Monsieur le Marquis, have slept very little for the last two or three nights; and find it difficult to keep awake. This coffee will do wonders for me; it refreshes one so.'

Before we had half done, the carriage was again in motion.

For a time our coffee made us chatty, and our conversation was animated.

The Marquis was extremely good-natured, as well as clever, and gave me a brilliant and amusing account of Parisian life, schemes, and dangers, all put so as to furnish me with practical warnings of the most valuable kind.

In spite of the amusing and curious stories which the Marquis related, with so much point and colour, I felt myself again becoming gradually drowsy and dreamy.

Perceiving this, no doubt, the Marquis good-naturedly suffered our conversation to subside into silence. The window next him was open. He threw his cup out of it; and did the same kind office for mine, and finally the little tray flew after, and I heard it clank on the road; a valuable waif, no doubt, for some early wayfarer in wooden shoes.*

I leaned back in my corner; I had my beloved *souvenir*—my white rose—close to my heart, folded, now, in white paper. It inspired all manner of romantic dreams. I began to grow more and more sleepy. But actual slumber did not come. I was still viewing, with my half-closed eyes, from my corner, diagonally, the interior of the carriage.

I wished for sleep; but the barrier between waking and sleeping seemed absolutely insurmountable; and instead, I entered into a state of novel and indescribable indolence.

The Marquis lifted his dispatch-box from the floor, placed it on his knees, unlocked it, and took out what proved to be a lamp, which he hung with two hooks, attached to it, to the window opposite to him. He lighted it with a match, put on his spectacles, and taking out a bundle of letters, began to read them carefully.

We were making way very slowly. My impatience had hitherto employed four horses from stage to stage. We were in this emergency, only too happy to have secured two. But the difference in pace was depressing.

I grew tired of the monotony of seeing the spectacled Marquis reading, folding, and docketing, letter after letter. I wished to shut out the image which wearied me, but something prevented my being able to shut my eyes. I tried again and again; but, positively, I had lost the power of closing them.

I would have rubbed my eyes, but I could not stir my hand, my will no longer acted on my body—I found that I could not move one joint, or muscle, no more than I could, by an effort of my will, have turned the carriage about.

Up to this I had experienced no sense of horror. Whatever it was, simple night-mare was not the cause. I was awfully frightened! Was I in a fit?

It was horrible to see my good-natured companion pursue his occupation so serenely, when he might have dissipated my horrors by a single shake.

I made a stupendous exertion to call out but in vain; I repeated the effort again and again, with no result.

My companion now tied up his letters, and looked out of the window, humming an air from an opera. He drew back his head, and said, turning to me—

'Yes, I see the lights; we shall be there in two or three minutes.'

He looked more closely at me, and with a kind smile, and a little shrug, he said, 'Poor child! how fatigued he must have been—how profoundly he sleeps! when the carriage stops he will waken.'

He then replaced his letters in the dispatch-box, locked it, put his spectacles in his pocket, and again looked out of the window.

We had entered a little town. I suppose it was past two o'clock by this time. The carriage drew up, I saw an inn-door open, and a light issuing from it.

'Here we are!' said my companion, turning gaily to me. But I did not awake.

'Yes, how tired he must have been!' he exclaimed, after he had waited for an answer.

My servant was at the carriage door, and opened it.

'Your master sleeps soundly, he is so fatigued! It would be cruel to disturb him. You and I will go in, while they change the horses, and take some refreshment, and choose something that Monsieur Beckett will like to take in the carriage, for when he awakes by-and-by, he will, I am sure, be hungry.'

He trimmed his lamp, poured in some oil; and taking care not to disturb me, with another kind smile, and another word or caution to my servant, he got out, and I heard him talking to St Clair, as they entered the inn-door, and I was left in my corner, in the carriage, in the same state.

CHAPTER VIII

A THREE MINUTES' VISIT

I have suffered extreme and protracted bodily pain, at different periods of my life, but anything like that misery, thank God, I never endured before or since. I earnestly hope it may not resemble any type of death, to which we are liable. I was, indeed, a spirit in prison; and unspeakable was my dumb and unmoving agony.

The power of thought remained clear and active. Dull terror filled my mind. How would this end? Was it actual death?

You will understand that my faculty of observing was unimpaired. I could hear and see anything as distinctly as ever I did in my life. It was simply that my will had, as it were, lost its hold of my body.

I told you that the Marquis d'Harmonville had not extinguished his carriage lamp on going into this village inn. I was listening intently, longing for his return, which might result, by some lucky accident, in awaking me from my catalepsy.

Without any sound of steps approaching, to announce an arrival, the carriage-door suddenly opened, and a total stranger got in silently, and shut the door.

The lamp gave about as strong a light as a wax-candle, so I could see the intruder perfectly. He was a young man, with a dark grey, loose surtout, made with a sort of hood, which was pulled over his head. I thought, as he moved, that I saw the gold band of military undress cap under it; and I certainly saw the lace and buttons of a uniform, on the cuffs of the coat that were visible under the wide sleeves of his outside wrapper.

This young man had thick moustaches, and an imperial,* and I observed that he had a red scar running upward from his lip across his cheek.

He entered, shut the door softly, and sat down beside me. It was all done in a moment; leaning toward me, and shading his eyes with his gloved hand, he examined my face closely, for a few seconds.

This man had come as noiselessly as a ghost; and everything he did was accomplished with the rapidity and decision, that indicated a well defined and pre-arranged plan. His designs were evidently sinister. I thought he was going to rob, and, perhaps, murder me. I lay, nevertheless, like a corpse under his hands. He inserted his hand in my breast pocket, from which he took my precious white rose and all the letters it contained, among which was a paper of some consequence to me.

My letters he glanced at. They were plainly not what he wanted. My precious rose, too, he laid aside with them. It was evidently about the paper I have mentioned, that he was concerned; for the moment he opened it, he began with a pencil, in a small pocket-book, to make rapid notes of its contents.

This man seemed to glide through his work with a noiseless and cool celerity which argued, I thought, the training of the police-department.

He re-arranged the papers, possibly in the very order in which he had found them, replaced them in my breast-pocket, and was gone.

His visit, I think, did not quite last three minutes. Very soon after his disappearance, I heard the voice of the Marquis once more. He got in, and I saw him look at me, and smile, half envying me, I fancied, my sound repose. If he had but known all!

He resumed his reading and docketing, by the light of the little lamp which had just subserved the purposes of a spy.

We were now out of the town, pursuing our journey at the same moderate pace. We had left the scene of my police visit, as I should have termed it, now two leagues behind us, when I suddenly felt a strange throbbing in one ear, and a sensation as if air passed through it into my throat. It seemed as if a bubble of air, formed deep in my ear, swelled, and burst there. The indescribable tension of my brain seemed all at once to give way; there was an odd humming in my head, and a sort of vibration through every nerve of my body, such as I have experienced in a limb that has been, in popular phraseology, asleep. I uttered a cry and half rose from my seat, and then fell back trembling, and with a sense of mortal faintness.

The Marquis stared at me, took my hand, and earnestly asked if I was ill. I could answer only with a deep groan.

Gradually the process of restoration was completed; and I was able, though very faintly, to tell him how very ill I had been; and then to describe the violation of my letters, during the time of his absence from the carriage.

'Good heaven!' he exclaimed, 'the miscreant did not get at my dispatch-box?'

I satisfied him, so far as I had observed, on that point. He placed the box on the seat beside him, and opened and examined its contents very minutely.

'Yes, undisturbed; all safe, thank heaven!' he murmured. 'There are half-a-dozen letters here, that I would not have some people read, for a great deal.'

He now asked with a very kind anxiety all about the illness I complained of. When he had heard me, he said—

'A friend of mine once had an attack as like yours as possible. It was on board ship, and followed a state of high excitement. He was a brave man like you; and was called on to exert both his strength and his courage suddenly. An hour or two after, fatigue overpowered him, and he appeared to fall into a sound sleep. He really sank into a state which he afterwards described so, that I think it must have been precisely the same affection as yours.'

'I am happy to think that my attack was not unique. Did he ever experience a return of it.'

'I knew him for years after, and never heard of any such

thing. What strikes me is a parallel in the predisposing causes of each attack. Your unexpected, and gallant hand-to-hand encounter, at such desperate odds, with an experienced swordsman, like that insane colonel of dragoons, your fatigue, and, finally, your composing yourself, as my other friend did, to sleep.'

'I wish,', he resumed, 'one could make out who that *coquin** was, who examined your letters. It is not worth turning back, however, because we should learn nothing. Those people always manage so adroitly. I am satisfied, however, that he must have been an agent of the police. A rogue of any other kind would have robbed you.'

I talked very little, being ill and exhausted, but the Marquis talked on agreeably.

'We grow so intimate,' said he, at last, 'that I must remind you that I am not, for the present, the Marquis d'Harmonville, but only Monsieur Droqville; nevertheless, when we get to Paris, although I cannot see you often, I may be of use. I shall ask you to name to me the hotel at which you mean to put up; because the Marquis being, as you are aware, on his travels, the Hôtel* d'Harmonville is, for the present, tenanted only by two or three old servants, who must not even see Monsieur Droqville. That gentleman will, nevertheless, contrive to get you access to the box of Monsieur le Marquis, at the Opera; as well, possibly, as to other places more difficult; and so soon as the diplomatic office of the Marquis d'Harmonville is ended, and he at liberty to declare himself, he will not excuse his friend, Monsieur Beckett, from fulfilling his promise to visit him this autumn at the Château d'Harmonville.'

You may be sure I thanked the Marquis.

The nearer we got to Paris, the more I valued his protection. The countenance of a great man on the spot, just then, taking so kind an interest in the stranger whom he had, as it were, blundered upon, might make my visit ever so many degrees more delightful than I had anticipated.

Nothing could be more gracious than the manner and looks of the Marquis; and, as I still thanked him, the carriage suddenly stopped in front of the place where a relay of horses awaited us, and where, as it turned out, we were to part.

CHAPTER IX

GOSSIP AND COUNSEL

My eventful journey was over, at last. I sat in my hotel window looking out upon brilliant Paris, which had, in a moment, recovered all its gaiety, and more than its accustomed bustle. Every one has read of the kind of excitement that followed the catastrophe of Napoleon, and the second restoration of the Bourbons.* I need not, therefore, even if, at this distance, I could, recall and decribe my experiences and impressions of the peculiar aspect of Paris, in those strange times. It was, to be sure, my first visit. But, often as I have seen it since, I don't think I ever saw that delightful capital in a state, pleasurably, so excited and exciting.

I had been two days in Paris, and had seen all sorts of sights, and experienced none of that rudeness and insolence of which others complained, from the exasperated officers of the defeated French army.

I must say this, also. My romance had taken complete possession of me; and the chance of seeing the object of my dream, gave a secret and delightful interest to my rambles and drives in the streets and environs, and my visits to the galleries and other sights of the metropolis.

I had neither seen nor heard of Count or Countess, nor had the Marquis d'Harmonville made any sign. I had quite recovered from the strange indisposition under which I had suffered during my night journey.

It was now evening, and I was beginning to fear that my patrician acquaintance had quite forgotten me, when the waiter presented me the card of 'Monsieur Droqville'; and, with no small elation and hurry, I desired him to show the gentleman up.

In came the Marquis d'Harmonville, kind and gracious as ever.

'I am a night-bird at present,' said he, so soon as we had exchanged the little speeches which are usual. 'I keep in the shade, during the daytime, and even now I hardly ventured to

come in a close carriage. The friends for whom I have
undertaken a rather critical service, have so ordained it. They
think all is lost, if I am known to be in Paris. First let me
present you with these orders for my box. I am so vexed that I
cannot command it oftener during the next fortnight; during
my absence, I had directed my secretary to give it for any
night to the first of my friends who might apply, and the result
is, that I find next to nothing left at my disposal.'

I thanked him very much.

'And now, a word, in my office of Mentor. You have not
come here, of course, without introductions?'

I produced half-a-dozen letters, the addresses of which he
looked at.

'Don't mind these letters,' he said. 'I will introduce you. I
will take you myself from house to house. One friend at your
side is worth many letters. Make no intimacies, no acquaintances, until then. You young men like best to exhaust the
public amusements of a great city, before embarrassing yourself with the engagements of society. Go to all these. It will
occupy you, day and night, for at least three weeks. When this
is over, I shall be at liberty, and will myself introduce you to
the brilliant but comparatively quiet routine of society. Place
yourself in my hands; and in Paris remember, when once in
society, you are always there.'

I thanked him very much, and promised to follow his
counsels implicitly.

He seemed pleased, and said—

'I shall now tell you some of the places you ought to go to.
Take your map, and write letters or numbers upon the points
I will indicate, and we will make out a little list. All the places
that I shall mention to you are worth seeing.'

In this methodical way, and with a great deal of amusing
and scandalous anecdote, he furnished me with a catalogue
and a guide, which, to a seeker of novelty and pleasure, was
invaluable.

'In a fortnight, perhaps in a week,' he said, 'I shall be at
leisure to be of real use to you. In the meantime, be on your
guard. You must not play; you will be robbed if you do.
Remember, you are surrounded, here, by plausible swindler

and villains of all kinds, who subsist by devouring strangers.
Trust no one but those you know.'

I thanked him again, and promised to profit by his advice.
But my heart was too full of the beautiful lady of the Belle
Etoile, to allow our interview to close without an effort to learn
something about her. I therefore asked for the Count and
Countess de St Alyre, whom I had had the good fortune to
extricate from an extremely unpleasant row in the hall of the
inn.

Alas! he had not seen them since. He did not know where
they were staying. They had a fine old house only a few leagues
from Paris; but he thought it probable that they would remain,
for a few days at least, in the city, as preparations would, no
doubt, be necessary, after so long an absence, for their
reception at home.

'How long have they been away?'

'About eight months, I think.'

'They are poor, I think you said?'

'What *you* would consider poor. But, Monsieur, the Count
has an income which affords them the comforts, and even the
elegancies of life, living as they do, in a very quiet and retired
way, in this cheap country.'

'Then they are very happy.'

'One would say they *ought* to be happy.'

'And what prevents?'

'He is jealous.'

'But his wife—she gives him no cause?'

'I am afraid she does.'

'How, Monsieur?'

'I always thought she was a little too—a *great deal* too—'

'Too *what*, Monsieur?'

'Too handsome. But although she has remarkably fine eyes,
exquisite features, and the most delicate complexion in the
world, I believe that she is a woman of probity. You have
never seen her?'

'There was a lady, muffled up in a cloak, with a very thick
veil on, the other night, in the hall of the Belle Etoile, when I
broke that fellow's head who was bullying the old Count. But
her veil was so thick I could not see a feature through it.' My

answer was diplomatic, you observe. 'She may have been the Count's daughter. Do they quarrel?'

'Who, he and his wife?'

'Yes.'

'A little.'

'Oh! and what do they quarrel about?'

'It is a long story; about the lady's diamonds. They are valuable—they are worth, La Perelleuse says, about a million of francs. The Count wishes them sold and turned into revenue, which he offers to settle as she pleases. The Countess, whose they are, resists, and for a reason which, I rather think, she can't disclose to him.'

'And pray what is that?' I asked, my curiosity a good deal piqued.

'She is thinking, I conjecture, how well she will look in them when she marries her second husband.'

'Oh?—yes, to be sure. But the Count de St Alyre is a good man?'

'Admirable, and extremely intelligent.'

'I should wish so much to be presented to the Count: you tell me he's so—'

'So agreeably married. But they are living quite out of the world. He takes her now and then to the Opera, or to a public entertainment; but that is all.'

'And he must remember so much of the old *régime*, and so many of the scenes of the revolution!'

'Yes, the very man for a philosopher, like you! And he falls asleep after dinner; and his wife don't. But, seriously, he has retired from the gay and the great world, and has grown apathetic; and so has his wife; and nothing seems to interest her now, not even—her husband!'

The Marquis stood up to take his leave.

'Don't risk your money,' said he. 'You will soon have an opportunity of laying out some of it to great advantage. Several collections of really good pictures, belonging to persons who have mixed themselves up in this Bonapartist restoration, must come within a few weeks to the hammer. You can do wonders when these sales commence. There will be startling bargains! Reserve yourself for them. I shall let you know all

about it. By-the-by,' he said, stopping short as he approached
the door, 'I was so near forgetting. There is to be, next week,
the very thing you would enjoy so much, because you see so
little of it in England—I mean a *bal masqué* conducted, it is
said, with more than usual splendour. It takes place at
Versailles—all the world will be there; there is such a rush for
cards!* But I think I may promise you one. Good-night!
Adieu!'

CHAPTER X

THE BLACK VEIL

Speaking the language fluently and with unlimited money,
there was nothing to prevent my enjoying all that was enjoy-
able in the French capital. You may easily suppose how two
days were passed. At the end of that time, and at about the
same hour, Monsieur Droqville called again.

Courtly, good-natured, gay, as usual, he told me that the
masquerade ball was fixed for the next Wednesday, and that
he had applied for a card for me.

How awfully unlucky. I was so afraid I should not be able
to go.

He stared at me for a moment with a suspicious and
menacing look which I did not understand, in silence, and
then inquired, rather sharply.

'And will Monsieur Beckett be good enough to say, why
not?'

I was a little surprised, but answered the simple truth: I
had made an engagement for that evening with two or three
English friends, and did not see how I could.

'Just so! You English, wherever you are, always look out for
your English boors, your beer and "*bifstek*";* and when you
come here, instead of trying to learn something of the people
you visit, and pretend to study, you are guzzling, and swearing,
and smoking with one another, and no wiser or more polished

at the end of your travels than if you had been all the time
carousing in a booth at Greenwich.'*

He laughed sarcastically, and looked as if he could have
poisoned me.

'There it is,' said he, throwing the card on the table. 'Take
it or leave it, just as you please. I suppose I shall have my
trouble for my pains; but it is not usual when a man, such as
I, takes trouble, asks a favour, and secures a privilege for an
acquaintance, to treat him so.'

This was astonishingly impertinent!

I was shocked, offended, penitent. I had possibly committed
unwittingly a breach of good-breeding, according to French
ideas, which almost justified the brusque severity of the
Marquis's undignified rebuke.

In a confusion, therefore, of many feelings, I hastened to
make my apologies, and to propitiate the chance friend who
had showed me so much disinterested kindness.

I told him that I would, at any cost, break through the
engagement in which I had unluckily entangled myself; that I
had spoken with too little reflection, and that I certainly had
not thanked him at all in proportion to his kindness and to my
real estimate of it.

'Pray say not a word more; my vexation was entirely on
your account; and I expressed it, I am only too conscious, in
terms a great deal too strong, which, I am sure, your good
nature will pardon. Those who know me a little better are
aware that I sometimes say a good deal more than I intend;
and am always sorry when I do. Monsieur Beckett will forget
that his old friend, Monsieur Droqville, has lost his temper in
his cause, for a moment, and—we are as good friends as
before.'

He smiled like the Monsieur Droqville of the Belle Etoile,
and extended his hand, which I took very respectfully and
cordially.

Our momentary quarrel had left us only better friends.

The Marquis then told me I had better secure a bed in some
hotel at Versailles, as a rush would be made to take them; and
advised my going down next morning for the purpose.

I ordered horses accordingly for eleven o'clock; and, after a little more conversation, the Marquis d'Harmonville bid me good-night, and ran down the stairs with his handkerchief to his mouth and nose, and, as I saw from my window, jumped into his close carriage again and drove away.

Next day I was at Versailles. As I approached the door of the Hôtel de France, it was plain that I was not a moment too soon, if, indeed, I were not already too late.

A crowd of carriages were drawn up about the entrance, so that I had no chance of approaching except by dismounting and pushing my way among the horses. The hall was full of servants and gentlemen screaming to the proprietor, who, in a state of polite distraction, was assuring them, one and all, that there was not a room or a closet disengaged in his entire house.

I slipped out again, leaving the hall to those who were shouting, expostulating, wheedling, in the delusion that the host might, if he pleased, manage something for them. I jumped into my carriage and drove, at my horses' best pace, to the Hôtel du Reservoir. The blockade about this door was as complete as the other. The result was the same. It was very provoking, but what was to be done? My postillion had, a little officiously, while I was in the hall talking with the hotel authorities, got his horses, bit by bit, as other carriages moved away, to the very steps of the inn door.

This arrangement was very convenient so far as getting in again was concerned. But, this accomplished, how were we to get on? There were carriages in front, and carriages behind, and no less than four rows of carriages, of all sorts, outside.

I had at this time remarkably long and clear sight, and if I had been impatient before, guess what my feelings were when I saw an open carriage pass along the narrow strip of roadway left open at the other side, a barouche in which I was certain I recognized the veiled Countess and her husband. This carriage had been brought to a walk by a cart which occupied the whole breadth of the narrow way, and was moving with the customary tardiness of such vehicles.

I should have done more wisely if I had jumped down on the *trottoir*,* and run round the block of carriages in front of the barouche. But, unfortunately, I was more of a Murat than a Moltke, and preferred a direct charge upon my object to relying on *tactique*.* I dashed across the back seat to a carriage which was next mine, I don't know how; tumbled through a sort of gig, in which an old gentleman and a dog were dozing; stepped with an incoherent apology over the side of an open carriage, in which were four gentlemen engaged in a hot dispute; tripped at the far side in getting out, and fell flat across the backs of a pair of horses, who instantly began plunging and threw me head foremost in the dust.

To those who observed my reckless charge without being in the secret of my object I must have appeared demented. Fortunately, the interesting barouche had passed before the catastrophe, and covered as I was with dust, and my hat blocked, you may be sure I did not care to present myself before the object of my Quixotic devotion.

I stood for a while amid a storm of *sacré*-ing, tempered disagreeably with laughter; and in the midst of these, while endeavouring to beat the dust from my clothes with my handkerchief, I heard a voice with which I was acquainted call, 'Monsieur Beckett'.

I looked and saw the Marquis peeping from a carriage-window. It was a welcome sight. In a moment I was at his carriage side.

'You may as well leave Versailles,' he said; 'you have learned, no doubt, that there is not a bed to hire in either of the hotels; and I can add that there is not a room to let in the whole town. But I have managed something for you that will answer just as well. Tell your servant to follow us, and get in here and sit beside me.'

Fortunately an opening in the closely-packed carriages had just occurred, and mine was approaching.

I directed the servant to follow us; and the Marquis having said a word to his driver, we were immediately in motion.

'I will bring you to a comfortable place, the very existence of which is known to but few Parisians, where, knowing how things were here, I secured a room for you. It is only a mile away, and an old comfortable inn, called Le Dragon Volant. It was fortunate for you that my tiresome business called me to this place so early.'

I think we had driven about a mile-and-a-half to the further side of the palace when we found ourselves upon a narrow old road, with the woods of Versailles on one side, and much older trees, of a size seldom seen in France, on the other.

We pulled up before an antique and solid inn, built of Caen stone,* in a fashion richer and more florid than was ever usual in such houses, and which indicated that it was originally designed for the private mansion of some person of wealth, and probably, as the wall bore many carved shields and supporters, of distinction also. A kind of porch, less ancient than the rest, projected hospitably with a wide and florid arch, over which, cut in high relief in stone, and painted and gilded, was the sign of the inn. This was the Flying Dragon,* with wings of brilliant red and gold, expanded, and its tail, pale green and gold, twisted and knotted into ever so many rings, and ending in a burnished point barbed like the dart of death.

'I shan't go in—but you will find it a comfortable place; at all events better than nothing. I would go in with you, but my incognito forbids. You will, I daresay, be all the better pleased to learn that the inn is haunted—I should have been, in my young days, I know. But don't allude to that awful fact in hearing of your host, for I believe it is a sore subject. Adieu. If you want to enjoy yourself at the ball take my advice, and go in a domino.* I think I shall look in; and certainly, if I do, in the same costume. How shall we recognize one another? Let me see, something held in the fingers—a flower won't do, so many people will have flowers. Suppose you get a red cross a couple of inches long—you're an Englishman*—stitched or pinned on the breast of your domino, and I a white one? Yes, that will do very well; and whatever room you go into keep near the door till we meet. I shall look for you at all the doors I pass; and you, in the same way, for me; and we *must* find each other soon. So that is understood. I can't enjoy a thing of that kind with any but a young person; a man of my age requires the contagion of young spirits and the companionship of some one who enjoys everything spontaneously. Farewell, we meet to-night.'

By this time I was standing *on* the road; I shut the carriage-door; bid him good-bye; and away he drove.

CHAPTER XI

THE DRAGON VOLANT

I took one look about me. The building was picturesque; the trees made it more so. The antique and sequestered character of the scene, contrasted strangely with the glare and bustle of the Parisian life, to which my eye and ear had become accustomed.

Then I examined the gorgeous old sign for a minute or two. Next I surveyed the exterior of the house more carefully. It was large and solid, and squared more with my ideas of an ancient English hostelry, such as the Canterbury pilgrims might have put up at, than a French house of entertainment. Except, indeed, for a round turret, that rose at the left flank of the house, and terminated in the extinguisher-shaped roof that suggests a French château.

I entered and announced myself as Monsieur Beckett, for whom a room had been taken. I was received with all the consideration due to an English milord,* with, of course, an unfathomable purse.

My host conducted me to my apartment. It was a large room, a little sombre, panelled with dark wainscoting, and furnished in a stately and sombre style, long out of date. There was a wide hearth, and a heavy mantelpiece, carved with shields, in which I might, had I been curious enough, have discovered a correspondence with the heraldry on the outer walls. There was something interesting, melancholy, and even depressing in all this. I went to the stone-shafted window, and looked out upon a small park, with a thick wood, forming the background of a château, which presented a cluster of such conical-topped turrets as I have just now mentioned.

The wood and château were melancholy objects. They showed signs of neglect, and almost of decay; and the gloom of fallen grandeur, and a certain air of desertion hung oppressively over the scene.

I asked my host the name of the château.

'That, Monsieur, is the Château de la Carque,'* he answered.

'It is a pity it is so neglected,' I observed. 'I should say, perhaps, a pity that its proprietor is not more wealthy?'

'Perhaps so, Monsieur.'

'*Perhaps?*'—I repeated, and looked at him. 'Then I suppose he is not very popular.'

'Neither one thing nor the other, Monsieur,' he answered; 'I meant only that we could not tell what use he might make of riches.'

'And who is he?' I inquired.

'The Count de St Alyre.'

'Oh! The Count! You are quite sure?' I asked, very eagerly.

It was now the innkeeper's turn to look at me.

'*Quite* sure, Monsieur, the Count de St Alyre.'

'Do you see much of him in this part of the world?'

'Not a great deal, Monsieur; he is often absent for a considerable time.'

'And is he poor?' I inquired.

'I pay rent to him for this house. It is not much; but I find he cannot wait long for it,' he replied, smiling satirically.

'From what I have heard, however, I should think he cannot be very poor?' I continued.

'They say, Monsieur, he plays. I know not. He certainly is not rich. About seven months ago, a relation of his died in a distant place. His body was sent to the Count's house here, and by him buried in Père la Chaise,* as the poor gentleman had desired. The Count was in profound affliction; although he got a handsome legacy, they say, by that death. But money never seems to do him good for any time.'

'He is old, I believe?'

'Old? we call him the "Wandering Jew,"* except, indeed, that he has not always the five *sous*ived in his pocket. Yet, Monsieur, his courage does not fail him. He has taken a young and handsome wife.'

'And, she?' I urged—

'Is the Countess de St Alyre.'

'Yes; but I fancy we may say something more? She has attributes?'

'Three, Monsieur, three, at least most amiable.'

'Ah! And what are they?'

'Youth, beauty, and—diamonds.'

I laughed. The sly old gentleman was foiling my curiosity.

'I see, my friend,' said I, 'you are reluctant—'

'To quarrel with the Count,' he concluded. 'True. You see, Monsieur, he could vex me in two or three ways; so could I him. But, on the whole, it is better each to mind his business, and to maintain peaceful relations; you understand.'

It was, therefore, no use trying, at least for the present. Perhaps he had nothing to relate. Should I think differently, by-and-by, I could try the effect of a few Napoleons. Possibly he meant to extract them.

The host of the Dragon Volant was an elderly man, thin, bronzed, intelligent, and with an air of decision, perfectly military. I learned afterwards that he had served under Napoleon in his early Italian campaigns.

'One question, I think you may answer,' I said, 'without risking a quarrel. Is the Count at home?'

'He has many homes, I conjecture,' said the host evasively. 'But—but I think I may say, Monsieur, that he is, I believe, at present staying at the Château de la Carque.'

I looked out of the window, more interested than ever, across the undulating grounds to the château, with its gloomy background of foliage.

'I saw him to-day, in his carriage at Versailles,' I said.

'Very natural.'

'Then his carriage and horses and servants are at the château?'

'The carriage he puts up here, Monsieur, and the servants are hired for the occasion. There is but one who sleeps at the château. Such a life must be terrifying for Madame the Countess,' he replied.

'The old screw!' I thought. 'By this torture, he hopes to extract her diamonds. What a life! What fiends to contend with—jealousy and extortion!'

The knight having made his speech to himself, cast his eyes once more upon the enchanter's castle, and heaved a gentle sigh—a sigh of longing, of resolution, and of love.

What a fool I was! and yet, in the sight of angels, are we any wiser as we grow older? It seems to me, only, that our illusions change as we go on; but, still, we are madmen all the same.

'Well, St Clair,' said I, as my servant entered, and began to arrange my things. 'You have got a bed?'

'In the cock-loft, Monsieur, among the spiders and, *par ma foi*! the cats and the owls. But we agree very well. *Vive la bagatelle*!'*

'I had no idea it was so full.'

'Chiefly the servants, Monsieur, of those persons who were fortunate enough to get apartments at Versailles.'

'And what do you think of the Dragon Volant?'

'The Dragon Volant! Monsieur; the old fiery dragon! The devil himself, if all is true! On the faith of a Christian, Monsieur, they say that diabolical miracles have taken place in this house.'

'What do you mean? *Revenants*'

'Not at all, sir; I wish it was no worse. *Revenants*? No! People who have *never* returned—who vanished, before the eyes of half-a-dozen men, all looking at them.'

'What do you mean, St Clair? Let us hear the story, or miracle, or whatever it is.'

'It is only this, Monsieur, that an ex-master-of-the-horse of the late king, who lost his head*—Monsieur will have the goodness to recollect, in the revolution—being permitted by the Emperor to return to France, lived here in this hotel, for a month, and at the end of that time vanished, visibly, as I told you, before the faces of half-a-dozen credible witnesses! The other was a Russian nobleman, six feet high and upwards, who, standing in the centre of the room, downstairs, describing to seven gentlemen of unquestionable veracity, the last moments of Peter the Great, and having a glass of *eau de vie** in his left hand, and his *tasse de café*, nearly finished, in his right, in like manner vanished. His boots were found on the floor where he had been standing; and the gentleman at his right, found, to his astonishment, his cup of coffee in his fingers, and the gentleman at his left, his glass of *eau de vie*—'

'Which he swallowed in his confusion,' I suggested.

'Which was preserved for three years among the curious articles of this house, and was broken by the *curé** while conversing with Mademoiselle Fidone in the housekeeper's room; but of the Russian nobleman himself, nothing more was ever seen or heard! *Parbleu*! when *we* go out of the Dragon Volant, I hope it may be by the door. I heard all this, Monsieur, from the postillion who drove us.'

'Then it *must* be true!' said I, jocularly: but I was beginning to feel the gloom of the view, and of the chamber in which I stood; there had stolen over me, I know not how, a presentiment of evil; and my joke was with an effort, and my spirit flagged.

CHAPTER XII

THE MAGICIAN

No more brilliant spectacle than this masked ball could be imagined. Among other *salons* and galleries, thrown open, was the enormous perspective of the 'Grande Galerie des Glaces',* lighted up on that occasion with no less than four thousand wax candles, reflected and repeated by all the mirrors, so that the effect was almost dazzling. The grand suite of *salons* was thronged with masques, in every conceivable costume. There was not a single room deserted. Every place was animated with music, voices, brilliant colours, flashing jewels, the hilarity of extemporized comedy, and all the spirited incidents of a cleverly sustained masquerade. I had never seen before anything, in the least, comparable to this magnificent *fête*.* I moved along, indolently, in my domino and mask, loitering, now and then, to enjoy a clever dialogue, a farcical song, or an amusing monologue, but, at the same time, keeping my eyes about me, lest my friend in the black domino, with the little white cross on his breast, should pass me by.

I had delayed and looked about me, specially, at every door I passed, as the Marquis and I had agreed; but he had not yet appeared.

While I was thus employed, in the very luxury of lazy

amusement, I saw a gilded sedan chair, or, rather, a Chinese palanquin, exhibiting the fantastic exuberance of 'Celestial'* decoration, borne forward on gilded poles by four richly-dressed Chinese; one with a wand in his hand marched in front, and another behind; and a slight and solemn man, with a long black beard, a tall fez, such as a dervish* is represented as wearing, walked close to its side. A strangely-embroidered robe fell over his shoulders, covered with hieroglyphic symbols; the embroidery was in black and gold, upon a variegated ground of brilliant colours. The robe was bound about his waist with a broad belt of gold, with cabalistic devices* traced on it, in dark red and black; red stockings, and shoes embroidered with gold, and pointed and curved upward at the toes, in Oriental fashion, appeared below the skirt of the robe. The man's face was dark, fixed, and solemn, and his eyebrows black, and enormously heavy—he carried a singular-looking book under his arm, a wand of polished black wood in his other hand, and walked with his chin sunk on his breast, and his eyes fixed upon the floor. The man in front waved his wand right and left to clear the way for the advancing palanquin, the curtains of which were closed; and there was something so singular, strange, and solemn about the whole thing, that I felt at once interested.

I was very well pleased when I saw the bearers set down their burthen within a few yards of the spot on which I stood.

The bearers and the men with the gilded wands forthwith clapped their hands, and in silence danced round the palanquin a curious and half frantic dance, which was yet, as to figures and postures, perfectly methodical. This was soon accompanied by a clapping of hands and a ha-ha-ing, rhythmically delivered.

While the dance was going on a hand was lightly laid on my arm, and, looking round, a black domino with a white cross stood beside me.

'I am so glad I have found you,' said the Marquis; 'and at this moment. This is the best group in the rooms. *You* must speak to the wizard. About an hour ago I lighted upon them, in another *salon*, and consulted the oracle, by putting questions. I never was more amazed. Although his answers were a little disguised it was soon perfectly plain that he knew every detail about the business, which no one on earth had heard of but myself, and two or three other men, about the most cautious persons in France. I shall never forget that shock. I saw other people who consulted him, evidently as much surprised, and more frightened than I. I came with the Count St Alyre and the Countess.'

He nodded toward a thin figure, also in a domino. It was the Count.

'Come,' he said to me, 'I'll introduce you.'

I followed, you may suppose, readily enough.

The Marquis presented me, with a very prettily-turned allusion to my fortunate intervention in his favour at the Belle Etoile; and the Count overwhelmed me with polite speeches, and ended by saying, what pleased me better still:

'The Countess is near us, in the next *salon* but one, chatting with her old friend the Duchesse d'Argensaque;* I shall go for her in a few minutes; and when I bring her here, she shall make your acquaintance; and thank you, also, for your assistance, rendered with so much courage when we were so very disagreeably interrupted.'

'You must, positively, speak with the magician,' said the Marquis to the Count de St Alyre, 'you will be so much amused. *I* did so; and, I assure you, I could not have anticipated such answers! I don't know what to believe.'

'Really! Then, by all means, let us try,' he replied.

We three approached, together, the side of the palanquin, at which the black-bearded magician stood.

A young man, in a Spanish dress, who, with a friend at his side, had just conferred with the conjurer, was saying, as he passed us by:

'Ingenious mystification! Who is that in the palanquin. He seems to know everybody!'

The Count, in his mask and domino, moved along, stiffly, with us, toward the palanquin. A clear circle was maintained by the Chinese attendants, and the spectators crowded round in a ring.

One of these men—he who with a gilded wand had preceded

the procession—advanced, extending his empty hand, palm upward.

'Money?' inquired the Count.

'Gold,' replied the usher.

The Count placed a piece of money in his hand; and I and the Marquis were each called on in turn to do likewise as we entered the circle. We paid accordingly.

The conjuror stood beside the palanquin, its silk curtain in his hand; his chin sunk, with its long, jet-black beard, on his chest; the outer hand grasping the black wand, on which he leaned; his eyes were lowered, as before, to the ground; his face looked absolutely lifeless. Indeed, I never saw face or figure so moveless, except in death.

The first question the Count put, was—

'Am I married, or unmarried?'

The conjuror drew back the curtain quickly, and placed his ear toward a richly-dressed Chinese, who sat in the litter; withdrew his head, and closed the curtain again; and then answered—

'Yes.'

The same preliminary was observed each time, so that the man with the black wand presented himself, not as a prophet, but as a medium; and answered, as it seemed, in the words of a greater than himself.

Two or three questions followed, the answers to which seemed to amuse the Marquis very much; but the point of which I could not see, for I knew next to nothing of the Count's peculiarities and adventures.

'Does my wife love me?' asked he playfully.

'As well as you deserve.'

'Whom do I love best in the world?'

'Self.'

'Oh! That I fancy is pretty much the case with every one. But, putting myself out of the question, do I love anything on earth better than my wife?'

'Her diamonds.'

'Oh!' said the Count.

The Marquis, I could see, laughed.

'Is it true,' said the Count, changing the conversation peremptorily, 'that there has been a battle in Naples?'

'No; in France.'

'Indeed,' said the Count, satirically, with a glance round. 'And may I inquire between what powers, and on what particular quarrel?'

'Between the Count and Countess de St Alyre, and about a document they subscribed on the 25th July, 1811.'

The Marquis afterwards told me that this was the date of their marriage settlement.

The Count stood stock-still for a minute or so; and one could fancy that they saw his face flushing through his mask.

Nobody, but we two, knew that the inquirer was the Count de St Alyre.

I thought he was puzzled to find a subject for his next question; and, perhaps, repented having entangled himself in such a colloquy. If so, he was relieved; for the Marquis, touching his arm, whispered—

'Look to your right, and see who is coming.'

I looked in the direction indicated by the Marquis, and I saw a gaunt figure stalking toward us. It was not a masque. The face was broad, scarred, and white. In a word, it was the ugly face of Colonel Gaillarde, who, in the costume of a corporal of the Imperial Guard,* with his left arm so adjusted as to look like a stump, leaving the lower part of the coat-sleeve empty, and pinned up to the breast. There were strips of very real sticking-plaster across his eyebrow and temple, where my stick had left its mark, to score, hereafter, among the more honourable scars of war.

CHAPTER XIII

THE ORACLE TELLS ME WONDERS

I forgot for a moment how impervious my mask and domino were to the hard stare of the old campaigner, and was preparing for an animated scuffle. It was only for a moment, of course; but the Count cautiously drew a little back as the gasconading corporal, in blue uniform, white vest, and white gaiters—for my friend Gaillarde was as loud and swaggering in his assumed character as in his real one of a colonel of dragoons—drew near. He had already twice all but got himself turned out of doors for vaunting the exploits of Napoleon le Grand, in terrific mock-heroics, and had very nearly come to hand-grips with a Prussian hussar.* In fact, he would have been involved in several sanguinary rows already, had not his discretion reminded him that the object of his coming there at all, namely, to arrange a meeting with an affluent widow, on whom he believed he had made a tender impression, would not have been promoted by his premature removal from the festive scene, of which he was an ornament, in charge of a couple of gendarmes.

'Money! Gold! Bah! What money can a wounded soldier like your humble servant have amassed, with but his sword-hand left, which, being necessarily occupied, places not a finger at his command with which to scrape together the spoils of a routed enemy?'

'No gold from him,' said the magician. 'His scars frank him.'

'Bravo, Monsieur le prophète! Bravissimo! Here I am. Shall I begin, *mon sorcier*,* without further loss of time, to question you?'

Without waiting for an answer, he commenced, in stentorian tones.

After half-a-dozen questions and answers, he asked—

'Whom do I pursue at present?'

'Two persons.'

'Ha! Two? Well, who are they?'

'An Englishman, whom, if you catch, he will kill you; and a French widow, whom if you find, she will spit in your face.'

'Monsieur le magicien calls a spade a spade, and knows that his cloth protects him. No matter! Why do I pursue them?'

'The widow has inflicted a wound on your heart, and the Englishman a wound on your head. They are each separately too strong for you; take care your pursuit does not unite them.'

'Bah! How could that be?'

'The Englishman protects ladies. He has got that fact into your head. The widow, if she sees, will marry him. It takes some time, she will reflect, to become a colonel, and the Englishman is unquestionably young.'

'I will cut his cock's-comb for him,' he ejaculated with an oath and a grin; and in a softer tone he asked, 'Where is she?'

'Near enough to be offended if you fail.'

'So she ought, by my faith. You are right, Monsieur le prophète! A hundred thousand thanks! Farewell!' And staring about him, and stretching his lank neck as high as he could, he strode away with his scars, and white waistcoat and gaiters, and his bearskin shako.*

I had been trying to see the person who sat in the palanquin. I had only once an opportunity of a tolerably steady peep. What I saw was singular. The oracle was dressed, as I have said, very richly, in the Chinese fashion. He was a figure altogether on a larger scale than the interpreter, who stood outside. The features seemed to me large and heavy, and the head was carried with a downward inclination! the eyes were closed, and the chin rested on the breast of his embroidered pelisse.* The face seemed fixed, and the very image of apathy. Its character and *pose* seemed an exaggerated repetition of the immobility of the figure who communicated with the noisy outer world. This face looked blood-red; but that was caused, I concluded, by the light entering through the red silk curtains. All this struck me almost at a glance; I had not many seconds in which to make my observation. The ground was now clear, and the Marquis said, 'Go forward, my friend.'

I did so. When I reached the magician, as we called the man with the black wand, I glanced over my shoulder to see whether the Count was near.

No, he was some yards behind; and he and the Marquis, whose curiosity seemed to be, by this time, satisfied, were now conversing generally upon some subject of course quite different.

I was relieved, for the sage seemed to blurt out secrets in an unexpected way; and some of mine might not have amused the Count.

I thought for a moment. I wished to test the prophet. A Church-of-England man was a *rara avis** in Paris.

'What is my religion?' I asked.

'A beautiful heresy,' answered the oracle instantly.

'A heresy?—and pray how is it named?'

'Love.'

'Oh! Then I suppose I am a polytheist, and love a great many?'

'One.'

'But, seriously,' I asked, intending to turn the course of our colloquy a litle out of an embarrassing channel, 'have I ever learned any words of devotion by heart?'

'Yes.'

'Can you repeat them?'

'Approach.'

I did, and lowered my ear.

The man with the black wand closed the curtains, and whispered, slowly and distinctly, these words, which, I need scarcely tell you, I instantly recognized:

I may never see you more; and, oh! that I could forget you! go— farewell—for God's sake, go!

I started as I heard them. They were, you know, the last words whispered to me by the Countess.

Good Heaven! How miraculous! Words heard, most assuredly, by no ear on earth but my own and the lady's who uttered them, till now!

I looked at the impassive face of the spokesman with the wand. There was no trace of meaning, or even of a consciousness that the words he had uttered could possibly interest me.

'What do I most long for?' I asked, scarcely knowing what I said.

'Paradise.'

'And what prevents my reaching it?'

'A black veil.'

Stronger and stronger! The answers seemed to me to indicate the minutest acquaintance with every detail of my little romance, of which not even the Marquis knew anything!

And I, the questioner, masked and robed so that my own brother could not have known me!

'You said I loved some one. Am I loved in return?' I asked.

'Try.'

I was speaking lower than before, and stood near the dark man with the beard, to prevent the necessity of his speaking in a loud key.

'Does any one love me?' I repeated.

'Secretly,' was the answer.

'Much or little?' I inquired.

'Too well.'

'How long will that love last?'

'Till the rose casts its leaves.'

'The rose—another allusion!'

'Then—darkness!' I sighed. 'But till then I live in light.'

'The light of violet eyes.'

Love, if not a religion, as the oracle had just pronounced it, is, at least, a superstition. How it exalts the imagination! How it enervates the reason! How credulous it makes us!

All this which, in the case of another, I should have laughed at, most powerfully affected me in my own. It inflamed my ardour, and half crazed my brain, and even influenced my conduct.

The spokesman of this wonderful trick—if trick it were— now waved me backward with his wand, and as I withdrew, my eyes still fixed upon the group, by this time encircled with an aura of mystery in my fancy, backing toward the ring of spectators, I saw him raise his hand suddenly, with a gesture of command, as a signal to the usher who carried the golden wand in front.

The usher struck his wand on the ground, and, in a shrill voice, proclaimed; 'The great Confu* is silent for an hour.'

Instantly the bearers pulled down a sort of blind of bamboo, which descended with a sharp clatter, and secured it at the bottom; and then the man in the tall fez, with the black beard and wand, began a sort of dervish dance. In this the men with the gold wands joined, and finally, in an outer ring, the bearers, the palanquin being the centre of the circles described by these solemn dancers, whose pace, little by little, quickened, whose gestures grew sudden, strange, frantic, as the motion became swifter and swifter, until at length the whirl became so rapid that the dancers seemed to fly by with the speed of a mill-wheel, and amid a general clapping of hands, and universal wonder, these strange performers mingled with the crowd, and the exhibition, for the time at least, ended.

The Marquis d'Harmonville was standing not far away, looking on the ground, as one could judge by his attitude and musing. I approached, and he said:

'The Count has just gone away to look for his wife. It is a pity she was not here to consult the prophet; it would have been amusing, I daresay, to see how the Count bore it. Suppose we follow him. I have asked him to introduce you.'

With a beating heart, I accompanied the Marquis d'Harmonville.

CHAPTER XIV

MADEMOISELLE DE LA VALLIÈRE

We wandered through the salons, the Marquis and I. It was no easy matter to find a friend in rooms so crowded.

'Stay here,' said the Marquis, 'I have thought of a way of finding him. Besides, his jealousy may have warned him that there is no particular advantage to be gained by presenting you to his wife, I had better go and reason with him; as you seem to wish an introduction so very much.'

This occurred in the room that is now called the 'Salon d'Apollon'.* The paintings remained in my memory, and my adventure of that evening was destined to occur there.

I sat down upon a sofa; and looked about me. Three or four persons beside myself were seated on this roomy piece of gilded furniture. They were chatting all very gaily; all—except the person who sat next me, and she was a lady. Hardly two feet interposed between us. The lady sat apparently in a reverie. Nothing could be more graceful. She wore the costume perpetuated in Collignan's full-length portrait of Mademoiselle de la

Vallière.* It is, as you know, not only rich, but elegant. Her hair was powdered, but one could perceive that it was naturally a dark brown. One pretty little foot appeared, and could anything be more exquisite than her hand?

It was extremely provoking that this lady wore her mask, and did not, as many did, hold it for a time in her hand.

I was convinced that she was pretty. Availing myself of the privilege of a masquerade, a microcosm in which it is impossible, except by voice and allusion, to distinguish friend from foe, I spoke—

'It is not easy, Mademoiselle, to deceive me,' I began.

'So much the better for Monsieur,' answered the mask, quietly.

'I mean', I said, determined to tell my fib, 'that beauty is a gift more difficult to conceal than Mademoiselle supposes.'

'Yet Monsieur has succeeded very well,' she said in the same sweet and careless tones.

'I see the costume of this, the beautiful Mademoiselle de la Vallière, upon a form that surpasses her own; I raise my eyes, and I behold a mask, and yet I recognize the lady; beauty is like that precious stone in the "Arabian Nights",* which emits, no matter how concealed, a light that betrays it.'

'I know the story,' said the young lady. 'The light betrayed it, not in the sun, but in darkness. Is there so little light in these rooms, Monsieur, that a poor glowworm can show so brightly. I thought we were in a luminous atmosphere, wherever a certain countess moved?'

Here was an awkward speech! How was I to answer? This lady might be, as they say some ladies are, a lover of mischief, or an intimate of the Countess de St Alyre. Cautiously, therefore, I inquired,

'What countess?'

'If you know me, you must know that she is my dearest friend. Is she not beautiful?'

'How can I answer, there are so many countesses.'

'Every one who knows me, knows who my best beloved friend is. You don't know me?'

'That is cruel. I can scarcely believe I am mistaken.'

'With whom were you walking, just now?' she asked.

'A gentleman, a friend,' I answered.

'I saw him, of course, a friend; but I think I know him, and should like to be certain. Is he not a certain marquis?'

Here was another question that was extremely awkward.

'There are so many people here, and one may walk, at one time, with one, and at another with a different one, that—'

'That an unscrupulous person has no difficulty in evading a simple question like mine. Know then, once for all, that nothing disgusts a person of spirit so much as suspicion. You, Monsieur are a gentleman of discretion. I shall respect you accordingly.'

'Mademoiselle would despise me, were I to violate a confidence.'

'But you don't deceive me. You imitate your friend's diplomacy. I hate diplomacy. It means fraud and cowardice. Don't you think I know him. The gentleman with the cross of white ribbon on his breast. I know the Marquis d'Harmonville perfectly. You see to what good purpose your ingenuity has been expended.'

'To that conjecture I can answer neither yes nor no.'

'You need not. But what was your motive in mortifying a lady?'

'Is is the last thing on earth I should do.'

'You affected to know me, and you don't; through caprice or listlessness or curiosity you wished to converse, not with a lady, but with a costume. You admired, and you pretend to mistake me for another. But who is quite perfect? Is truth any longer to be found on earth?'

'Mademoiselle has formed a mistaken opinion of me.'

'And you also of me; you find me less foolish than you supposed. I know perfectly whom you intend amusing with compliments and melancholy declamation, and whom, with that amiable purpose, you have been seeking.'

'Tell me whom you mean,' I entreated.

'Upon one condition.'

'What is that?'

'That you will confess if I name the lady.'

'You describe my object unfairly.' I objected. 'I can't admit that I proposed speaking to any lady in the tone you describe.'

'Well, I shan't insist on that; only if I name the lady, you will promise to admit that I am right.'

'*Must* I promise?'

'Certainly not, there is no compulsion, but your promise is the only condition on which I will speak to you again.'

I hesitated for a moment; but how could she possibly tell? The Countess would scarcely have admitted this little romance to any one; and the mask in the La Vallière costume could not possibly know who the masked domino beside her was.

'I consent,' I said, 'I promise.'

'You must promise on the honour of a gentleman.'

'Well, I do; on the honour of a gentleman.'

'Then this lady is the Countess de St Alyre.' I was unspeakably surprised; I was disconcerted; but I remembered my promise and said—

'The Countess de St Alyre *is*, unquestionably, the lady to whom I hoped for an introduction to-night; but I beg to assure you also on the honour of a gentleman, that she has not the faintest imaginable suspicion that I was seeking such an honour, nor, in all probability, does she remember that such a person as I exists. I had the honour to render her and the Count a trifling service, too trifling, I fear, to have earned more than an hour's recollection.'

'The world is not so ungrateful as you suppose; or if it be, there are, nevertheless, a few hearts that redeem it. I can answer for the Countess de St Alyre, she never forgets a kindness. She does not show all she feels; for she is unhappy, and cannot.'

'Unhappy! I feared, indeed, that might be. But for all the rest that you are good enough to suppose, it is but a flattering dream.'

'I told you that I am the Countess's friend, and being so I must know something of her character; also, there are confidences between us, and I may know more than you think, of those trifling services of which you suppose the recollection is so transitory.'

I was becoming more and more interested. I was as wicked as other young men, and the heinousness of such a pursuit was as nothing, now that self-love and all the passions that mingle in such a romance, were roused. The image of the beautiful Countess had now again quite superseded the pretty counterpart of La Vallière, who was before me. I would have given a great deal to hear, in solemn earnest, that she did remember the champion who, for her sake, had thrown himself before the sabre of an enraged dragoon, with only a cudgel in his hand, and conquered.

'You say the Countess is unhappy,' said I. 'What causes her unhappiness?'

'Many things. Her husband is old, jealous, and tyrannical. Is not that enough? Even when relieved from his society, she is lonely.'

'But you are her friend?' I suggested.

'And you think one friend enough?' she answered; 'she has one alone, to whom she can open her heart.'

'Is there room for another friend?'

'Try.'

'How can I find a way?'

'She will aid you.'

'How?'

She answered by a question. 'Have you secured rooms in either of the hotels of Versailles?'

'No, I could not. I am lodged in the Dragon Volant, which stands at the verge of the grounds of the Château de la Carque.'

'That is better still. I need not ask if you have courage for an adventure. I need not ask if you are a man of honour. A lady may trust herself to you, and fear nothing. There are few men to whom the interview, such as I shall arrange, could be granted with safety. You shall meet her at two o'clock this morning in the park of the Château de la Carque. What room do you occupy in the Dragon Volant?'

I was amazed at the audacity and decision of this girl. Was she, as we say in England, hoaxing me?

'I can describe that accurately,' said I. 'As I look from the rear of the house, in which my apartment is, I am at the extreme right, next the angle; and one pair of stairs up, from the hall.'

'Very well; you must have observed, if you looked into the

park, two or three clumps of chestnut and lime-trees, growing so close together as to form a small grove. You must return to your hotel, change your dress, and, preserving a scrupulous secrecy, as to why or where you go, leave the Dragon Volant, and climb the park-wall, unseen; you will easily recognize the grove I have mentioned; there you will meet the Countess, who will grant you an audience of a few minutes, who will expect the most scrupulous reserve on your part, and who will explain to you, in a few words, a great deal which *I* could not so well tell you here.'

I cannot describe the feeling with which I heard these words. I was astounded. Doubt succeeded. I could not believe these agitating words.

'Mademoiselle will believe that if I only dared assure myself that so great a happiness and honour were really intended for me, my gratitude would be as lasting as my life. But how dare I believe that Mademoiselle does not speak, rather from her own sympathy or goodness, than from a certainty that the Countess de St Alyre would concede so great an honour?'

'Monsieur believes either that I am not, as I pretend to be, in the secret which he hitherto supposed to be shared by no one but the Countess and himself, or else that I am cruelly mystifying him. That I am in her confidence, I swear by all that is dear in a whispered farewell. By the last companion of this flower!' and she took for a moment in her fingers the nodding head of a white rosebud that was nestled in her bouquet. 'By my own good star, and hers—or shall I call it our "*belle étoile*?" Have I said enough?'

'Enough?' I repeated, 'more than enough—a thousand thanks.'

'And being thus in her confidence, I am clearly her friend; and being a friend would it be friendly to use her dear name so; and all for sake of practising a vulgar trick upon you—a stranger?'

'Mademoiselle will forgive me. Remember how very precious is the hope of seeing, and speaking to the Countess. Is it wonderful, then, that I should falter in my belief? You have convinced me, however, and will forgive my hesitation.'

'You will be at the place I have described, then, at two o'clock?'

'Assuredly,' I answered.

'And Monsieur, I know, will not fail, through fear. No, he need not assure me; his courage is already proved.'

'No danger, in such a case, will be unwelcome to me.'

'Had you not better go now, Monsieur, and rejoin your friend?'

'I promised to wait here for my friend's return. The Count de St Alyre said that he intended to introduce me to the Countess.'

'And Monsieur is so simple as to believe him?'

'Why should I not?'

'Because he is jealous and cunning. You will see. He will never introduce you to his wife. He will come here and say he cannot find her, and promise another time.'

'I think I see him approaching, with my friend. No—there is no lady with him.'

'I told you so. You will wait a long time for that happiness, if it is never to reach you except through his hands. In the meantime, you had better not let him see you so near me. He will suspect that we have been talking of his wife; and that will whet his jealousy and his vigilance.'

I thanked my unknown friend in the mask, and withdrawing a few steps, came, by a little 'circumbendibus',* upon the flank of the Count.

I smiled under my mask, as he assured me that the Duchesse de la Roqueme had changed her place, and taken the Countess with her; but he hoped, at some very early time, to have an opportunity of enabling her to make my acquaintance.

I avoided the Marquis d'Harmonville, who was following the Count. I was afraid he might propose accompanying me home, and had no wish to be forced to make an explanation.

I lost myself quickly, therefore, in the crowd, and moved, as rapidly as it would allow me, toward the Galerie des Glaces, which lay in the direction opposite to that in which I saw the Count and my friend the Marquis moving.

CHAPTER XVI

STRANGE STORY OF THE DRAGON VOLANT

These *fêtes* were earlier in those days, and in France, than our modern balls are in London. I consulted my watch. It was a little past twelve.

It was a still and sultry night; the magnificent suite of rooms, vast as some of them were, could not be kept at a temperature less than oppressive, especially to people with masks on. In some places the crowd was inconvenient, and the profusion of lights added to the heat. I removed my mask, therefore, as I saw some other people do, who were as careless of mystery as I. I had hardly done so, and began to breathe more comfortably, when I heard a friendly English voice call me by my name. It was Tom Whistlewick, of the—th Dragoons. He had unmasked, with a very flushed face, as I did. He was one of those Waterloo heroes, new from the mint of glory, whom, as a body, all the world, except France, revered; and the only thing I knew against him, was a habit of allaying his thirst, which was excessive, at balls, *fêtes*, musical parties, and all gatherings, where it was to be had, with champagne; and, as he introduced me to his friend, Monsieur Carmaignac, I observed that he spoke a little thick. Monsieur Carmaignac was little, lean, and as straight as a ramrod. He was bald, took snuff, and wore spectacles; and, as I soon learned, held an official position.

Tom was facetious, sly, and rather difficult to understand, in his present pleasant mood. He was elevating his eyebrows and screwing his lips oddly, and fanning himself vaguely with his mask.

After some agreeable conversation, I was glad to observe that he preferred silence, and was satisfied with the *rôle* of listener, as I and Monsieur Carmaignac chatted; and he seated himself, with extraordinary caution and indecision, upon a bench, beside us, and seemed very soon to find a difficulty in keeping his eyes open.

'I heard you mention', said the French gentleman, 'that you

had engaged an apartment in the Dragon Volant, about half a league from this. When I was in a different police department, about four years ago, two very strange cases were connected with that house. One was of a wealthy *émigré*, permitted to return to France, by the Em—by Napoleon.* He vanished. The other—equally strange—was the case of a Russian of rank and wealth. He disappeared just as mysteriously.'

'My servant', I said, 'gave me a confused account of some occurrences, and, as well as I recollect he described the same persons—I mean a returned French nobleman, and a Russian gentleman. But he made the whole story so marvellous—I mean in the supernatural sense—that, I confess, I did not believe a word of it.'

'No, there was nothing supernatural; but a great deal inexplicable,' said the French gentleman. 'Of course there may be theories; but the thing was never explained, nor, so far as I know, was a ray of light ever thrown upon it.'

'Pray let me hear the story,' I said. 'I think I have a claim, as it affects my quarters. You don't suspect the people of the house?'

'Oh! It has changed hands since then. But there seemed to be a fatality about a particular room.'

'Could you describe that room?'

'Certainly. It is a spacious, panelled bed-room, up one pair of stairs, in the back of the house, and at the extreme right, as you look from its windows.'

'Ho! Really? Why, then, I have got the very room!' I said, beginning to be more interested—perhaps the least bit in the world, disagreeably. 'Did the people die, or were they actually spirited away?'

'No, they did not die—they disappeared very oddly. I'll tell you the particulars—I happen to know them exactly, because I made an official visit, on the first occasion, to the house, to collect evidence; and although I did not go down there, upon the second, the papers came before me, and I dictated the official letter dispatched to the relations of the people who had disappeared; they had applied to the government to investigate the affair. We had letters from the same relations more than two years later, from which we learned that the missing men had never turned up.'

He took a pinch of snuff, and looked steadily at me.

'Never! I shall relate all that happened, so far as we could discover. The French noble, who was the Chevalier Chateau Blassemare, unlike most *émigrés*, had taken the matter in time, sold a large portion of his property before the revolution had proceeded so far as to render that next to impossible, and retired with a large sum. He brought with him about half a million of francs, the greater part of which he invested in the French funds; a much larger sum remained in Austrian land and securities. You will observe then that this gentleman was rich, and there was no allegation of his having lost money, or being, in any way, embarrassed. You see?'

I assented.

'This gentleman's habits were not expensive in proportion to his means. He had suitable lodgings in Paris; and for a time, society, the theatres, and other reasonable amusements, engrossed him. He did not play. He was a middle-aged man, affecting youth, with the vanities which are usual in such persons; but, for the rest, he was a gentle and polite person, who disturbed nobody—a person, you see, not likely to provoke an enmity.'

'Certainly not,' I agreed.

'Early in the summer of 1811, he got an order permitting him to copy a picture in one of these *salons*, and came down here, to Versailles, for the purpose. His work was getting on slowly. After a time he left his hotel, here, and went, by way of change, to the Dragon Volant: there he took, by special choice, the bed-room which has fallen to you by chance. From this time, it appeared, he painted little; and seldom visited his apartments in Paris. One night he saw the host of the Dragon Volant, and told him that he was going into Paris, to remain for a day or two, on very particular business; that his servant would accompany him, but that he would retain his apartments at the Dragon Volant, and return in a few days. He left some clothes there, but packed a portmanteau, took his dressing-case, and the rest, and, with his servant behind his carriage, drove into Paris. You observe all this, Monsieur?'

'Most attentively,' I answered.

'Well, Monsieur, as soon as they were approaching his lodgings, he stopped the carriage on a sudden, told his servant that he had changed his mind; that he would sleep elsewhere that night, that he had very particular business in the north of France, not far from Rouen, that he would set out before daylight on his journey, and return in a fortnight. He called a *fiacre*,* took in his hand a leather bag which, the servant said, was just large enough to hold a few shirts and a coat, but that it was enormously heavy, as he could testify, for he held it in his hand, while his master took out his purse to count thirty-six Napoleons, for which the servant was to account when he should return. He then sent him on, in the carriage; and he, with the bag I have mentioned, got into the *fiacre*. Up to that, you see, the narrative is quite clear.'

'Perfectly,' I agreed.

'Now comes the mystery,' said Monsieur Carmaignac. 'After that, the Count Château Blassemare* was never more seen, so far as we can make out, by acquaintance or friend. We learned that the day before the Count's stockbroker had, by his direction, sold all his stock in the French funds, and handed him the cash it realized. The reason he gave him for this measure tallied with what he said to his servant. He told him that he was going to the north of France to settle some claims, and did not know exactly how much might be required. The bag, which had puzzled the servant by its weight, contained, no doubt, a large sum in gold. Will Monsieur try my snuff?'

He politely tendered his open snuff-box, of which I partook, experimentally.

'A reward was offered,' he continued, 'when the inquiry was instituted, for any information tending to throw a light upon the mystery, which might be afforded by the driver of the *fiacre* "employed on the night of" (so-and-so), "at about the hour of half-past ten, by a gentleman, with a black-leather travelling-bag in his hand, who descended from a private carriage, and gave his servant some money, which he counted twice over." About a hundred-and-fifty drivers applied, but not one of them was the right man. We did, however, elicit a curious and unexpected piece of evidence in quite another quarter. What a racket that plaguey harlequin* makes with his sword!'

'Intolerable!' I chimed in.

The harlequin was soon gone, and he resumed.

'The evidence I speak of, came from a boy, about twelve years old, who knew the appearance of the Count perfectly, having been often employed by him as a messenger. He stated that about half-past twelve o'clock, on the same night—upon which you are to observe, there was a brilliant moon—he was sent, his mother having been suddenly taken ill, for the *sage femme** who lived within a stone's throw of the Dragon Volant. His father's house, from which he started, was a mile away, or more, from that inn, in order to reach which he had to pass round the park of the Château de la Carque, at the site most remote from the point to which he was going. It passes the old churchyard of St Aubin, which is separated from the road only by a very low fence, and two or three enormous old trees. The boy was a little nervous as he approached this ancient cemetery; and, under the bright moonlight, he saw a man whom he distinctly recognized as the Count, whom they designated by a soubriquet which means 'the man of smiles'. He was looking rueful enough now, and was seated on the side of a tombstone, on which he had laid a pistol, while he was ramming home the charge of another.

'The boy got cautiously by, on tiptoe, with his eyes all the time on the Count Chateau Blassemare, or the man he mistook for him; his dress was not what he usually wore, but the witness swore that he could not be mistaken as to his identity. He said his face looked grave and stern; but though he did not smile, it was the same face he knew so well. Nothing would make him swerve from that. If that were he, it was the last time he was seen. He has never been heard of since. Nothing could be heard of him in the neighbourhood of Rouen. There has been no evidence of his death; and there is no sign that he is living.'

'That certainly is a most singular case,' I replied; and was about to ask a question or two, when Tom Whistlewick who, without my observing it, had been taking a ramble, returned, a great deal more awake, and a great deal less tipsy.

'I say, Carmaignac, it is getting late, and I must go; I really must, for the reason I told you—and, Beckett, we must soon meet again.'

'I regret very much, Monsieur, my not being able at present to relate to you the other case, that of another tenant of the very same room—a case more mysterious and sinister than the last—and which occurred in the autumn of the same year.'

'Will you both do a very good-natured thing, and come and dine with me at the Dragon Volant to-morrow?'

So, as we pursued our way along the Galerie des Glaces, I extracted their promise.

'By Jove!' said Whistlewick, when this was done; 'look at that pagoda, or sedan chair, or whatever it is, just where those fellows set it down, and not one of them near it! I can't imagine how they tell fortunes so devilish well. Jack Nuffles—I met him here to-night—says they are gipsies—where are they, I wonder? I'll go over and have a peep at the prophet.'

I saw him plucking at the blinds, which were constructed something on the principle of Venetian blinds; the red curtains were inside; but they did not yield, and he could only peep under one that did not come quite down.

When he rejoined us, he related: 'I could scarcely see the old fellow, it's so dark. He is covered with gold and red, and has an embroidered hat on like a mandarin's;* he's fast alseep; and, by jove, he smells like a polecat! It's worth going over only to have it to say. Fiew! pooh! oh! it *is* a perfume. Faugh!'

Not caring to accept this tempting invitation, we got along slowly toward the door. I bid them good-night, reminding them of their promise. And so found my way at last to my carriage; and was soon rolling slowly toward the Dragon Volant, on the loneliest of roads, under old trees, and the soft moonlight.

What a number of things had happened within the last two hours! what a variety of strange and vivid pictures were crowded together in that brief space! What an adventure was before me!

The silent, moonlighted, solitary road, how it contrasted with the many-eddied whirl of pleasure from whose roar and music, lights, diamonds and colours, I had just extricated myself.

The sight of lonely Nature at such an hour, acts like a sudden sedative. The madness and guilt of my pursuit struck me with momentary compunction and horror. I wished I had never entered the labyrinth which was leading me, I knew not whither. It was too late to think of that now; but the bitter was already stealing into my cup; and vague anticipations lay, for a few minutes, heavy on my heart. It would not have taken much to make me disclose my unmanly state of mind to my lively friend, Alfred Ogle, nor even to the milder ridicule of the agreeable Tom Whistlewick.

CHAPTER XVI

THE PARK OF THE CHATEAU DE LA CARQUE

There was no danger of the Dragon Volant's closing its doors on that occasion till three or four in the morning. There were quartered there many servants of great people, whose masters would not leave the ball till the last moment, and who could not return to their corners in the Dragon Volant, till their last services had been rendered.

I knew, therefore, I should have ample time for my mysterious excursion without exciting curiosity by being shut out.

And now we pulled up under the canopy of boughs, before the sign of the Dragon Volant, and the light that shone from its hall-door.

I dismissed my carriage, ran up the broad staircase, mask in hand, with my domino fluttering about me, and entered the large bed-room. The black wainscoting and stately furniture, with the dark curtains of the very tall bed, made the night there more sombre.

An oblique patch of moonlight was thrown upon the floor from the window to which I hastened. I looked out upon the landscape slumbering in those silvery beams. There stood the outline of the Château de la Carque, its chimneys, and many turrets with their extinguisher-shaped roofs black against the soft grey sky. There, also, more in the foreground, about midway between the window where I stood, and the château, but a little to the left, I traced the tufted masses of the grove which the lady in the mask had appointed as the trysting-place, where I and the beautiful Countess were to meet that night.

I took 'the bearings' of this gloomy bit of wood, whose foliage glimmered softly at top in the light of the moon.

You may guess with what a strange interest and swelling of the heart I gazed on the unknown scene of my coming adventure.

But time was flying, and the hour already near. I threw my robe upon a sofa; I groped out a pair of boots, which I substituted for those thin heelless shoes, in those days called 'pumps', without which a gentleman could not attend an evening party. I put on my hat, and lastly, I took a pair of loaded pistols which I had been advised were satisfactory companions in the then unsettled state of French society: swarms of disbanded soldiers, some of them alleged to be desperate characters, being everywhere to be met with. These preparations made, I confess I took a looking-glass to the window to see how I looked in the moonlight; and being satisfied, I replaced it, and ran downstairs.

In the hall I called for my servant.

'St Clair,' said I; 'I mean to take a little moonlight ramble, only ten minutes or so. You must not go to bed until I return. If the night is very beautiful, I may possibly extend my ramble a little.'

So down the steps I lounged, looking first over my right, and then over my left shoulder, like a man uncertain which direction to take, and I sauntered up the road, gazing now at the moon, and now at the thin white clouds in the opposite direction, whistling, all the time, an air which I had picked up at one of the theatres.

When I had got a couple of hundred yards away from the Dragon Volant, my minstrelsy totally ceased; and I turned about, and glanced sharply down the road that looked as white as hoar-frost under the moon, and saw the gable of the old inn, and a window, partly concealed by the foliage, with a dusky light shining from it.

No sound of footstep was stirring; no sign of human figure in sight. I consulted my watch, which the light was sufficiently strong to enable me to do. It now wanted but eight minutes of the appointed hour. A thick mantle of ivy at this point covered the wall and rose in a clustering head at top.

It afforded me facilities for scaling the wall, and a partial screen for my operations, if any eye should chance to be looking that way. And now it was done. I was in the park of the Château de la Carque, as nefarious a poacher as ever trespassed on the grounds of unsuspicious lord!

Before me rose the appointed grove, which looked as black as a clump of gigantic hearse-plumes.* It seemed to tower higher and higher at every step; and cast a broader and blacker shadow toward my feet. On I marched, and was glad when I plunged into the shadow which concealed me. Now I was among the grand old lime and chestnut trees—my heart beat fast with expectation.

This grove opened, a little, near the middle; and in the space thus cleared, there stood with a surrounding flight of steps, a small Greek temple or shrine, with a statue in the centre. It was built of white marble with fluted Corinthian columns, and the crevices were tufted with grass; moss had shown itself on pedestal and cornice, and signs of long neglect and decay were apparent in its discoloured and weather-worn marble. A few feet in front of the steps a fountain, fed from the great ponds at the other side of the château, was making a constant tinkle and plashing in a wide marble basin, and the jet of water glimmered like a shower of diamonds in the broken moonlight. The very neglect and half-ruinous state of all this made it only the prettier, as well as sadder. I was too intently watching for the arrival of the lady, in the direction of the château, to study these things; but the half-noted effect of them was romantic, and suggested somehow the grotto and the fountain, and the apparition of Egeria.*

As I watched a voice spoke to me, a little behind my left shoulder. I turned, almost with a start, and the masque, in the costume of Mademoiselle de la Vallière, stood there.

'The Countess will be here presently,' she said. The lady stood upon the open space, and the moonlight fell unbroken upon her. Nothing could be more becoming; her figure looked more graceful and elegant than ever. 'In the meantime I shall tell you some peculiarities of her situation. She is unhappy; miserable in an ill-sorted marriage, with a jealous tyrant who now would constrain her to sell her diamonds, which are—'

'Worth thirty thousand pounds sterling. I heard all that from a friend. Can I aid the Countess in her unequal struggle? Say but how, and the greater the danger or the sacrifice, the happier will it make me. *Can* I aid her?'

'If you despise a danger—which, yet, is not a danger; if you despise, as she does, the tyrannical canons of the world; and, if you are chivalrous enough to devote yourself to a lady's cause, with no reward but her poor gratitude; if you can do these things you can aid her, and earn a foremost place, not in her gratitude only, but in her friendship.'

At those words the lady in the mask turned away, and seemed to weep.

I vowed myself the willing slave of the Countess. 'But', I added, 'you told me she would soon be here.'

'That is, if nothing unforeseen should happen; but with the eye of the Count de St Alyre in the house, and open, it is seldom safe to stir.'

'Does she wish to see me?' I asked, with a tender hesitation.

'First, say have you really thought of *her*, more than once, since the adventure of the Belle Etoile.'

'She never leaves my thoughts; day and night her beautiful eyes haunt me; her sweet voice is always in my ear.'

'Mine is said to resemble hers,' said the mask.

'So it does,' I answered. 'But it is only a resemblance.'

'Oh! then mine is better?'

'Pardon me, Mademoiselle, I did not say *that*. Yours is a sweet voice, but I fancy a little higher.'

'A little shriller, you would say,' answered the de la Vallière, I fancied a good deal vexed.

'No, not shriller: your voice is not shrill, it is beautifully sweet; but not so pathetically sweet as her.'

'That is prejudice, Monsieur; it is not true.'

I bowed; I could not contradict a lady.

'I see, Monsieur, you laugh at me; you think me vain, because I claim in some points to be equal to the Countess de St Alyre. I challenge you to say, my hand, at least, is less beautiful than hers.' As she thus spoke, she drew her glove off, and extended her hand, back upward, in the moonlight.

The lady seemed really nettled. It was undignified and irritating; for in this uninteresting competition the precious moments were flying, and my interview leading apparently to nothing.

'You will admit, then, that my hand is as beautiful as hers?'

'I cannot admit it, Mademoiselle,' said I, with the honesty, of irritation. 'I will not enter into comparisons, but the Countess de St Alyre is, in all respects, the most beautiful lady I ever beheld.'

The masque laughed coldly, and then, more and more softly, said, with a sigh, 'I will prove all I say.' And as she spoke she removed the mask: and the Countess de St Alyre, smiling, confused, bashful, more beautiful than ever, stood before me!

'Good IIeavens!' I exclaimed. 'How monstrously stupid I have been. And it was to Madame la Comtesse that I spoke for so long in the *salon!*' I gazed on her in silence. And with a low sweet laugh of good nature she extended her hand. I took it, and carried it to my lips.

'No, you must not do that,' she said, quietly, 'we are not old enough friends yet. I find, although you were mistaken, that you do remember the Countess of the Belle Etoile, and that you are a champion true and fearless. Had you yielded to the claims just now pressed upon you by the rivalry of Mademoiselle de la Vallière, in her mask, the Countess de St Alyre should never have trusted or seen you more. I now am sure that you are true, as well as brave. You now know that I have not forgotten you; and, also, that if you would risk your life for me, I, too, would brave some danger, rather than lose my friend for ever. I have but a few moments more. Will you come here again to-morrow night, at a quarter past eleven? I will be here at that moment; you must exercise the most scrupulous care to prevent suspicion that you have come here, Monsieur. *You owe that to me.*'

She spoke these last words with the most solemn entreaty.

I vowed again and again, that I would die rather than permit the least rashness to endanger the secret which made all the interest and value of my life.

She was looking, I thought, more and more beautiful every moment. My enthusiasm expanded in proportion.

'You must come to-morrow night by a different route,' she said; 'and if you come again, we can change it once more. At the other side of the château there is a little churchyard, with a ruined chapel. The neighbours are afraid to pass it by night. The road is deserted there, and a stile opens a way into these grounds. Cross it and you can find a covert of thickets, to within fifty steps of this spot.'

I promised, of course, to observe her instructions implicitly.

'I have lived for more than a year in an agony of irresolution. I have decided at last. I have lived a melancholy life; a lonelier life than is passed in the cloister. I have had no one to confide in; no one to advise me; no one to save me from the horrors of my existence. I have found a brave and prompt friend at last. Shall I ever forget the heroic tableau of the hall of the Belle Etoile? Have you—have you really kept the rose I gave you, as we parted? Yes—you swear it. You need not; I trust you. Richard, how often have I in solitude repeated your name, learned from my servant. Richard, my hero! Oh! Richard! Oh, my king!* I love you.'

I would have folded her to my heart—thrown myself at her feet. But this beautiful and—shall I say it—inconsistent woman repelled me.

'No, we must not waste our moments in extravagances. Understand my case. There is no such thing as indifference in the married state. Not to love one's husband', she continued, 'is to hate him. The Count, ridiculous in all else, is formidable in his jealousy. In mercy, then, to me, observe caution. Affect to all you speak to, the most complete ignorance of all the people in the Château de la Carque; and, if any one in your presence mentions the Count or Countess de St Alyre, be sure you say you never saw either. I shall have more to say to you to-morrow night. I have reasons that I cannot now explain, for all I do, and all I postpone. Farewell. Go! Leave me.'

She waved me back, peremptorily. I echoed her 'farewell', and obeyed.

This interview had not lasted, I think, more than ten minutes. I scaled the park-wall again, and reached the Dragon Volant before its doors were closed.

I lay awake in my bed, in a fever of elation. I saw, till the dawn broke, and chased the vision, the beautiful Countess de St Alyre, always in the dark, before me.

CHAPTER XVII

THE TENANT OF THE PALANQUIN

The Marquis called on me next day. My late breakfast was still upon the table.

He had come, he said, to ask a favour. An accident had happened to his carriage in the crowd on leaving the ball, and he begged if I were going into Paris, a seat in mine—I was going in, and was extremely glad of his company. He came with me to my hotel; we went up to my rooms. I was surprised to see a man seated in an easy chair, with his back towards us, reading a newspaper. He rose. It was the Count de St Alyre, his gold spectacles on his nose; his black wig, in oily curls, lying close to his narrow head, and showing, like carved ebony over a repulsive visage of boxwood. His black muffler had been pulled down. His right arm was in a sling. I don't know whether there was anything unusual in his countenance that day, or whether it was but the effect of prejudice arising from all I had heard in my mysterious interview in his park, but I thought his countenance was more strikingly forbidding than I had seen it before.

I was not callous enough in the ways of sin to meet this man, injured at least in intent, thus suddenly, without a momentary disturbance.

He smiled.

'I called, Monsieur Beckett, in the hope of finding you here,' he croaked, 'and I meditated, I fear, taking a great liberty, but my friend the Marquis d'Harmonville, on whom I have perhaps some claim, will perhaps give me the assistance I require so much.'

'With great pleasure,' said the Marquis, 'but not till after six o'clock. I must go this moment to a meeting of three or four people, whom I cannot disappoint, and I know, perfectly, we cannot break up earlier.'

'What am I to do?' exclaimed the Count, 'an hour would have done it all. Was ever *contre-temps** so unlucky!'

'I'll give you an hour, with pleasure,' said I.

'How very good of you, Monsieur, I hardly dare to hope it. The business, for so gay and charming a man as Monsieur Beckett, is a little *funeste**. Pray read this note which reached me this morning.'

It certainly was not cheerful. It was a note stating that the body of his, the Count's cousin, Monsieur de St Amand, who had died at his house, the Château Clery, had been, in accordance with his written directions, sent for burial at Père la Chaise,* and, with the permission of the Count de St Alyre, would reach his house (the Château de la Carque), at about ten o'clock on the night following, to be conveyed thence in a hearse, with any member of the family who might wish to attend the obsequies.

'I did not see the poor gentleman twice in my life,' said the Count, 'but this office, as he has no other kinsman, disagreeable as it is, I could scarcely decline, and so I want to attend at the office to have the book signed, and the order entered. But here is another misery. By ill luck, I have sprained my thumb, and can't sign my name for a week to come. However, one name answers as well as another. Yours as well as mine. And as you are so good as to come with me, all will go right.'

Away we drove. The Count gave me a memorandum of the Christian and surnames of the deceased, his age, the complaint he died of, and the usual particulars; also a note of the exact position in which a grave, the dimensions of which were described, of the ordinary simple kind, was to be dug, between two vaults belonging to the family of St Amand. The funeral, it was stated, would arrive at half-past one o'clock AM (the next night but one); and he handed me the money, with extra fees, for a burial by night. It was a good deal; and I asked him, as he entrusted the whole affair to me, in whose name I should take the receipt.

'Not in mine, my good friend. They wanted me to become an executor, which I, yesterday, wrote to decline; and I am informed that if the receipt were in my name it would constitute me an executor in the eye of the law, and fix me in that position. Take it, pray, if you have no objection, in your own name.'

This, accordingly, I did.

'You will see, by-and-by, why I am obliged to mention all these particulars.'

The Count, meanwhile, was leaning back in the carriage, with his black silk muffler up to his nose, and his hat shading his eyes, while he dozed in his corner; in which state I found him on my return.

Paris had lost its charm for me. I hurried through the little business I had to do, longed once more for my quiet room in the Dragon Volant, the melancholy woods of the Château de la Carque, and the tumultuous and thrilling influence of proximity to the object of my wild but wicked romance.

I was delayed some time by my stockbroker. I had a very large sum, as I told you, at my banker's, uninvested. I cared very little for a few days' interest—very little for the entire sum, compared with the image that occupied my thoughts, and beckoned me with a white arm, through the dark, toward the spreading lime-trees and chestnuts of the Château de la Carque. But I had fixed this day to meet him, and was relieved when he told me that I had better let it lie in my banker's hands for a few days longer, as the funds would certainly fall immediately. This accident, too, was not without its immediate bearing on my subsequent adventures.

When I reached the Dragon Volant, I found, in my sitting-room, a good deal to my chagrin, my two guests, whom I had quite forgotten. I inwardly cursed my own stupidity for having embarrassed myself with their agreeable society. It could not be helped now, however, and a word to the waiters put all things in train for dinner.

Tom Whistlewick was in great force; and he commenced almost immediately with a very odd story.

He told me that not only Versailles, but all Paris, was in a ferment, in consequence of a revolting, and all but sacrilegious, practical joke, played off on the night before.

The pagoda, as he persisted in calling the palanquin, had been left standing on the spot where we last saw it. Neither conjuror, nor usher, nor bearers had ever returned. When the ball closed, and the company at length retired, the servants who attended to put out the lights, and secure the doors, found it still there.

It was determined, however, to let it stand where it was until next morning, by which time, it was conjectured, its owners would send messengers to remove it.

None arrived. The servants were then ordered to take it away; and its extraordinary weight, for the first time, reminded them of its forgotten human occupant. Its door was forced; and, judge what was their disgust, when they discovered, not a living man, but a corpse! Three or four days must have passed since the death of the burly man in the Chinese tunic and painted cap. Some people thought it was a trick designed to insult the Allies,* in whose honour the ball was got up. Others were of opinion that it was nothing worse than a daring and cynical jocularity which, shocking as it was, might yet be forgiven to the high spirits and irrepressible buffoonery of youth. Others, again, fewer in number, and mystically given, insisted that the corpse was *bonâ fide* necessary to the exhibition, and that the disclosures and allusions which had astonished so many people were distinctly due to necromancy.*

'The matter, however, is now in the hands of the police,' observed Monsieur Carmaignac, 'and we are not the body we were two or three months ago, if the offenders against propriety and public feeling are not traced, and convicted, unless, indeed, they have been a great deal more cunning than such fools generally are.'

I was thinking within myself how utterly inexplicable was my colloquy with the conjuror, so cavalierly dismissed by

Monsieur Carmaignac as a 'fool'; and the more I thought the more marvellous it seemed.

'It certainly was an original joke, though not a very clear one,' said Whistlewick.

'Not even original,' said Carmaignac. 'Very nearly the same thing was done, a hundred years ago or more, at a state ball in Paris; and the rascals who played the trick were never found out.'*

In this Monsieur Carmaignac as I afterwards discovered, spoke truly; for, among my books of French anecdote and memoirs, the very incident is marked, by my own hand.

While we were thus talking, the waiter told us that dinner was served; and we withdrew accordingly; my guests more than making amends for my comparative taciturnity.

CHAPTER XVIII

THE CHURCH-YARD

Our dinner was really good, so were the wines; better, perhaps, at this out-of-the-way inn, than at some of the more pretentious hotels in Paris. The moral effect of a really good dinner is immense—we all felt it. The serenity and good nature that follow are more solid and comfortable than the tumultuous benevolences of Bacchus.*

My friends were happy, therefore, and very chatty; which latter relieved me of the trouble of talking, and prompted them to entertain me and one another incessantly with agreeable stories and conversation, of which, until suddenly a subject emerged, which interested me powerfully, I confess, so much were my thoughts engaged elsewhere, I heard next to nothing.

'Yes,' said Carmaignac, continuing a conversation which had escaped me, 'there was another case, beside that Russian nobleman, odder still. I remembered it this morning, but cannot recall the name. He was a tenant of the very same room. By-the-by, Monsieur, might it not be as well,' he added, turning to me, with a laugh, half joke whole earnest, as they say, 'if you were to get into another apartment, now that the house is no longer crowded? that is, if you mean to make any stay here.'

'A thousand thanks! no. I'm thinking of changing my hotel; and I can run into town so easily at night; and though I stay here, for this night, at least, I don't expect to vanish like those others. But you say there is another adventure, of the same kind, connected with the same room. Do let us hear it. But take some wine first.'

The story he told was curious.

'It happened,' said Carmaignac, 'as well as I recollect, before either of the other cases. A French gentleman—I wish I could remember his name—the son of a merchant, came to this inn (the Dragon Volant), and was put by the landlord into the same room of which we have been speaking. *Your* apartment, Monsieur. He was by no means young—past forty—and very far from good-looking. The people here said that he was the ugliest man, and the most good-natured, that ever lived. He played on the fiddle, sang, and wrote poetry. His habits were odd and desultory. He would sometimes sit all day in his room writing, singing, and fiddling, and go out at night for a walk. An eccentric man! He was by no means a millionaire, but he had a *modicum bonum,** you understand—a trifle more than half a million of francs. He consulted his stockbroker about investing this money in foreign stocks, and drew the entire sum from his banker. You now have the situation of affairs when the catastrophe occurred.'

'Pray fill your glass,' I said.

'Dutch courage,* Monsieur, to face the catastrophe!' said Whistlewick, filling his own.

'Now, that was the last that ever was heard of his money,' resumed Carmaignac. 'You shall hear about himself. The night after this financial operation, he was seized with a poetic frenzy; he sent for the then landlord of this house, and told him that he long meditated an epic, and meant to commence that night, and that he was on no account to be disturbed until nine o'clock in the morning. He had two pairs of wax candles, a little cold supper on a side-table, his desk open, paper enough upon it to contain the entire Henriade,* and a proportionate store of pens and ink.

Seated at this desk he was seen by the waiter who brought him a cup of coffee at nine o'clock, at which time the intruder said he was writing fast enough to set fire to the paper—that was his phrase; he did not look up, he appeared too much engrossed. But, when the waiter came back, half an hour afterwards, the door was locked; and the poet, from within, answered, that he must not be disturbed.

Away went the *garçon*; and next morning at nine o'clock knocked at his door, and receiving no answer, looked through the key-hole; the lights were still burning, the window-shutters were closed as he had left them; he renewed his knocking, knocked louder, no answer came. He reported this continued and alarming silence to the inn-keeper, who, finding that his guest had not left his key in the lock, succeeded in finding another that opened it. The candles were just giving up the ghost in their sockets, but there was light enough to ascertain that the tenant of the room was gone! The bed had not been disturbed; the window-shutter was barred. He must have let himself out, and, locking the door on the outside, put the key in his pocket, and so made his way out of the house. Here, however, was another difficulty, the Dragon Volant shut its doors and made all fast at twelve o'clock; after that hour no one could leave the house, except by obtaining the key and letting himself out, and of necessity leaving the door unsecured, or else by collusion and aid of some person in the house.

Now it happened that, some time after the doors were secured, at half-past twelve, a servant who had not been apprised of his order to be left undisturbed, seeing a light shine through the key-hole, knocked at the door to inquire whether the poet wanted anything. He was very little obliged to his disturber, and dismissed him with a renewed charge that he was not to be interrupted again during the night. This incident established the fact that he was in the house after the doors had been locked and barred. The inn-keeper himself kept the keys, and swore that he found them hung on the wall above his head, in his bed, in their usual place, in the morning; and that nobody could have taken them away without awakening him. That was all we could discover. The Count de St Alyre, to whom this house belongs, was very active and very much chagrined. But nothing was discovered.'

'And nothing heard since of the epic poet?' I asked.

'Nothing—not the slightest clue—he never turned up again. I suppose he is dead; if he is not, he must have got into some devilish bad scrape, of which we have heard nothing, that compelled him to abscond with all the secresy and expedition in his power. All that we know for certain is that, having occupied the room in which you sleep, he vanished, nobody ever knew how, and never was heard of since.'

'You have now mentioned three cases,' I said, 'and all from the same room.'

'Three. Yes, all equally unintelligible. When men are murdered, the great and immediate difficulty the assassins encounter is how to conceal the body. It is very hard to believe that three persons should have been consecutively murdered, in the same room, and their bodies so effectually disposed of that no trace of them was ever discovered.'

From this we passed to other topics, and the grave Monsieur Carmaignac amused us with a perfectly prodigious collection of scandalous anecdote, which his opportunities in the police department had enabled him to accumulate.

My guests happily had engagements in Paris, and left me about ten.

I went up to my room, and looked out upon the grounds of the Château de la Carque. The moonlight was broken by clouds, and the view of the park in this desultory light, acquired a melancholy and fantastic character.

The strange anecdotes recounted of the room in which I stood, by Monsieur Carmaignac, returned vaguely upon my mind, drowning in sudden shadows the gaiety of the more frivolous stories with which he had followed them. I looked round me on the room that lay in ominous gloom, with an almost disagreeable sensation. I took my pistols now with an undefined apprehension that they might be really needed before my return to-night. This feeling, be it understood, in no wise chilled my ardour. Never had my enthusiasm mounted higher. My adventure absorbed and carried me away; but it added a strange and stern excitement to the expedition.

I loitered for a time in my room. I had ascertained the exact point at which the little churchyard lay. It was about a mile away; I did not wish to reach it earlier than necessary.

I stole quietly out, and sauntered along the road to my left, and thence entered a narrower track, still to my left, which, skirting the park wall, and describing a circuitous route, all the way, under grand old trees, passes the ancient cemetery. That cemetery is embowered in trees, and occupies little more than half an acre of ground, to the left of the road, interposing between it and the park of the Château de la Carque.

Here, at this haunted spot, I paused and listened. The place was utterly silent. A thick cloud had darkened the moon, so that I could distinguish little more than the outlines of near objects, and that vaguely enough; and sometimes, as it were, floating in black fog, the white surface of a tombstone emerged.

Among the forms that met my eye against the iron-grey of the horizon, were some of those shrubs or trees that grow like our junipers, some six feet high, in form like a miniature poplar, with the darker foliage of the yew. I do not know the name of the plant, but I have often seen it in such funereal places.

Knowing that I was a little too early, I sat down upon the edge of a tombstone to wait, as, for aught I knew, the beautiful Countess might have wise reasons for not caring that I should enter the grounds of the château earlier than she had appointed. In the listless state induced by waiting, I sat there, with my eyes on the object straight before me, which chanced to be that faint black outline I have described. It was right before me, about half-a-dozen steps away.

The moon now began to escape from under the skirt of the cloud that had hid her face for so long; and, as the light gradually improved, the tree on which I had been lazily staring began to take a new shape. It was no longer a tree, but a man standing motionless. Brighter and brighter grew the moonlight, clearer and clearer the image became, and at last stood out perfectly distinctly. It was Colonel Gaillarde.

Luckily, he was not looking toward me. I could only see him

in profile; but there was no mistaking the white moustache, the *farouche** visage, and the gaunt six-foot stature. There he was, his shoulder toward me, listening and watching, plainly, for some signal or person expected, straight in front of him.

If he were, by chance, to turn his eyes in my direction, I knew that I must reckon upon an instantaneous renewal of the combat only commenced in the hall of the Belle Etoile. In any case, could malignant fortune have posted, at this place and hour, a more dangerous watcher? What ecstasy to him, by a single discovery, to hit me so hard, and blast the Countess de St Alyre, whom he seemed to hate.

He raised his arm; he whistled softly; I heard an answering whistle as low; and, to my relief, the Colonel advanced in the direction of this sound, widening the distance between us at every step; and immediately I heard talking, but in a low and cautious key.

I recognized, I thought, even so, the peculiar voice of Gaillarde.

I stole softly forward in the direction in which those sounds were audible. In doing so, I had, of course, to use the extremest caution.

I thought I saw a hat above a jagged piece of ruined wall, and then a second—yes, I saw two hats conversing; the voices came from under them. They moved off, not in the direction of the park, but of the road, and I lay along the grass, peeping over a grave, as a skirmisher might, observing the enemy. One after the other, the figures emerged full into view as they mounted the stile* at the road-side. The Colonel, who was last, stood on the wall for awhile, looking about him, and then jumped down on the road. I heard their steps and talk as they moved away together, with their backs toward me, in the direction which led them farther and farther from the Dragon Volant.

I waited until these sounds were quite lost in the distance before I entered the park. I followed the instructions I had received from the Countess de St Alyre, and made my way among brushwood and thickets to the point nearest the ruinous temple, and crossed the short intervening space of open ground rapidly.

I was now once more under the gigantic boughs of the old lime and chestnut trees; softly, and with a heart throbbing fast, I approached the little structure.

The moon was now shining steadily, pouring down its radiance on the soft foliage, and here and there mottling the verdure under my feet.

I reached the steps; I was among its worn marble shafts. She was not there, nor in the inner sanctuary, the arched windows of which were screened almost entirely by masses of ivy. The lady had not yet arrived.

CHAPTER XIX

THE KEY

I stood now upon the steps, watching and listening. In a minute or two I heard the crackle of withered sticks trod upon, and, looking in the direction, I saw a figure approaching among the trees, wrapped in a mantle.

I advanced eagerly. It was the Countess. She did not speak, but gave me her hand, and I led her to the scene of our last interview. She repressed the ardour of my impassioned greeting with a gentle but peremptory firmness. She removed her hood, shook back her beautiful hair, and, gazing on me with sad and glowing eyes, sighed deeply. Some awful thought seemed to weigh upon her.

'Richard, I must speak plainly. The crisis of my life has come. I am sure you would defend me. I think you pity me; perhaps you even love me.'

At these words I became eloquent, as young madmen in my plight do. She silenced me, however, with the same melancholy firmness.

'Listen, dear friend, and then say whether you can aid me. How madly I am trusting you; and yet my heart tells me how wisely! To meet you here as I do—what insanity it seems! How poorly you must think of me! But when you know all, you will judge me fairly. Without your aid I cannot accomplish my purpose. That purpose unaccomplished, I must die. I am chained to a man whom I despise—whom I abhor. I have resolved to fly. I have jewels, principally diamonds, for which I am offered thirty thousand pounds of your English money. They are my separate property by my marriage settlement; I will take them with me. You are a judge, no doubt, of jewels. I was counting mine when the hour came, and brought this in my hand to show you. Look.'

'It is magnificent!' I exclaimed, as a collar of diamonds twinkled and flashed in the moonlight, suspended from her pretty fingers. I thought, even at that tragic moment, that she prolonged the show, with a feminine delight in these brilliant toys.

'Yes,' she said, 'I shall part with them all. I will turn them into money, and break, for ever, the unnatural and wicked bonds that tied me, in the name of a sacrament, to a tyrant. A man young, handsome, generous, brave as you, can hardly be rich. Richard, you say you love me; you shall share all this with me. We will fly together to Switzerland; we will evade pursuit; my powerful friends will intervene and arrange a separation; and I shall, at length, be happy and reward my hero.'

You may suppose the style, florid and vehement, in which I poured forth my gratitude, vowed the devotion of my life, and placed myself absolutely at her disposal.

'To-morrow night,' she said, 'my husband will attend the remains of his cousin, Monsieur de St Amand, to Père la Chaise. The hearse, he says, will leave this at half-past nine. You must be here, where we stand, at nine o'clock.'

I promised punctual obedience.

'I will not meet you here; but you see a red light in the window of the tower at that angle of the château?'

I assented.

'I placed it there, that, to-morrow night, when it comes, you may recognize it. So soon as that rose-coloured light appears at that window, it will be a signal to you that the funeral has left the château, and that you may approach safely. Come, then, to that window; I will open it, and admit you. Five minutes after a travelling-carriage, with four horses, shall stand ready in the *porte-cochère*.* I will place my diamonds in your hands; and so soon as we enter the carriage, our flight commences. We shall have at least five hours' start; and with energy, stratagem, and resource, I fear nothing. Are you ready to undertake all this for my sake?'

Again I vowed myself her slave.

'My only difficulty,' she said, 'is how we shall quickly enough convert my diamonds into money; I dare not remove them while my husband is in the house.'

Here was the opportunity I wished for. I now told her that I had in my banker's hands no less a sum than thirty thousand pounds, with which, in the shape of gold and notes, I should come furnished, and thus the risk and loss of disposing of her diamonds in too much haste would be avoided.

'Good heaven!' she exclaimed, with a kind of disappointment. 'You are rich, then? and I have lost the felicity of making my generous friend more happy. Be it so! since so it must be. Let us contribute, each, in equal shares, to our common fund. Bring you, your money; I, my jewels. There is a happiness to me even in mingling my resources with yours.'

On this there followed a romantic colloquy, all poetry and passion, such as I should, in vain, endeavour to reproduce.

Then came a very special instruction.

'I have come provided, too, with a key, the use of which I must explain.'

It was a double key—a long, slender stem, with a key at each end—one about the size which opens an ordinary room door; the other, as small, almost, as the key of a dressing-case.

'You cannot employ too much caution to-morrow night. An interruption would murder all my hopes. I have learned that you occupy the haunted room in the Dragon Volant. It is the very room I would have wished you in. I will tell you why— there is a story of a man, who, having shut himself up in that room one night, disappeared before morning. The truth is, he wanted, I believe, to escape from creditors; and the host of the Dragon Volant, at that time, being a rogue, aided him in absconding. My husband investigated the matter, and dis- covered how his escape was made. It was by means of this key. Here is a memorandum and a plan describing how they are to be applied. I have taken them from the Count's escritoire. And now, once more I must leave to your ingenuity how to mystify the people at the Dragon Volant. Be sure you try the keys first, to see that the locks turn freely. I will have my jewels ready. You, whatever we divide, had better bring your money, because it may be many months before you can revisit Paris, or disclose our place of residence to any one; and our passports—arrange all that; in what names, and whither, you please. And now, dear Richard' (she leaned her arm fondly on my shoulder, and looked with ineffable passion in my eyes, with her other hand clasped in mine), 'my very life is in your hands; I have staked all on your fidelity.'

As she spoke the last word, she, on a sudden, grew deadly pale, and gasped, 'Good God! who is here?'

At the same moment she receded through the door in the marble screen, close to which she stood, and behind which was a small roofless chamber, as small as the shrine, the window of which was darkened by a clustering mass of ivy so dense that hardly a gleam of light came through the leaves.

I stood upon the threshold which she had just crossed, looking in the direction in which she had thrown that one terrified glance. No wonder she was frightened. Quite close upon us, not twenty yards away, and approaching at a quick step, very distinctly lighted by the moon, Colonel Gaillarde and his companion were coming. The shadow of the cornice and a piece of wall were upon me. Unconscious of this, I was expecting the moment when, with one of his frantic yells, he should spring forward to assail me.

I made a step backward, drew one of my pistols from my pocket, and cocked it. It was obvious he had not seen me.

I stood, with my finger on the trigger, determined to shoot him dead if he should attempt to enter the place where the Countess was. It would, no doubt, have been a murder; but, in my mind, I had no question or qualm about it. When once we engage in secret and guilty practices we are nearer other and greater crimes than we at all suspect.

'There's the statue,' said the Colonel, in his brief discordant tones. 'That's the figure.'

'Alluded to in the stanzas?' inquired his companion.

'The very thing. We shall see more next time. Forward, Monsieur; let us march.'

And, much to my relief, the gallant Colonel turned on his heel, and marched through the trees, with his back toward the château, striding over the grass, as I quickly saw, to the park wall, which they crossed not far from the gables of the Dragon Volant.

I found the Countess trembling in no affected, but a very real terror. She would not hear of my accompanying her toward the château. But I told her that I would prevent the return of the mad Colonel; and upon that point, at least, that she need fear nothing. She quickly recovered, again bid me a fond and lingering good-night, and left me, gazing after her, with the key in my hand, and such a phantasmagoria floating in my brain as amounted very nearly to madness.

There was I, ready to brave all dangers, all right and reason, plunge into murder itself, on the first summons, and entangle myself in consequences inextricable and horrible (what cared I?) for a woman of whom I knew nothing, but that she was beautiful and reckless!

I have often thanked heaven for its mercy in conducting me through the labyrinths in which I had all but lost myself.

CHAPTER XX

A HIGH-CAULD CAP

I was now upon the road, within two or three hundred yards of the Dragon Volant. I had undertaken an adventure with a vengeance! And by way of prelude, there not improbably awaited me, at my inn, another encounter, perhaps, this time, not so lucky, with the grotesque sabreur.*

I was glad I had my pistols. I certainly was bound by no law to allow a ruffian to cut me down, unresisting.

Stooping boughs from the old park, gigantic poplars on the other side, and the moonlight over all, made the narrow road to the inn-door picturesque.

I could not think very clearly just now; events were succeeding one another so rapidly, and I, involved in the action of a drama so extravagant and guilty, hardly knew myself or believed my own story, as I slowly paced towards the still open door of the Flying Dragon.

No sign of the Colonel, visible or audible, was there. In the hall I inquired. No gentleman had arrived at the inn for the last half hour. I looked into the public room. It was deserted. The clock struck twelve and I heard the servant barring the great door. I took my candle. The lights in this rural hostelry were by this time out, and the house had the air of one that had settled to slumber for many hours. The cold moonlight streamed in at the window on the landing, as I ascended the broad staircase; and I paused for a moment to look over the wooded grounds to the turreted château, to me, so full of interest. I bethought me, however, that prying eyes might read a meaning in this midnight gazing, and possibly the Count himself might, in his jealous mood, surmise a signal in this unwonted light in the stair-window of the Dragon Volant.

On opening my room door, with a little start, I met an extremely old woman with the longest face I ever saw; she had what used to be termed, a high-cauld cap,* on, the white border of which contrasted with her brown and yellow skin, and made her wrinkled face more ugly. She raised her curved shoulders, and looked up in my face, with eyes unnaturally black and bright.

'I have lighted a little wood, Monsieur, because the night is chill.'

I thanked her, but she did not go. She stood with her candle in her tremulous fingers.

'Excuse an old woman, Monsieur,' she said; 'but what on earth can a young English *milord*, with all Paris at his feet, find to amuse him in the Dragon Volant?'

Had I been at the age of fairy tales, and in daily intercourse with the delightful Countess d'Aulnois, I should have seen in this withered apparition, the *genius loci*,* the malignant fairy, at the stamp of whose foot, the ill-fated tenants of this very room had, from time to time, vanished. I was past that, however; but the old woman's dark eyes were fixed on mine, with a steady meaning that plainly told me that my secret was known. I was embarrassed and alarmed; I never thought of asking her what business that was of hers.

'These old eyes saw you in the park of the château to-night.'

'*I!*' I began, with all the scornful surprise I could affect.

'It avails nothing, Monsieur; I know why you stay here; and I tell you to begone. Leave this house to-morrow morning, and never come again.'

She lifted her disengaged hand, as she looked at me with intense horror in her eyes.

'There is nothing on earth—I don't know what you mean,' I answered; 'and why should you care about me?'

'I don't care about you, Monsieur—I care about the honour of an ancient family, whom I served in their happier days, when to be noble, was to be honoured. But my words are thrown away, Monsieur; you are insolent. I will keep my secret, and you, yours; that is all. You will soon find it hard enough to divulge it.'

The old woman went slowly from the room and shut the door, before I had made up my mind to say anything. I was standing where she had left me, nearly five minutes later. The jealousy of Monsieur the Count, I assumed, appears to this old creature about the most terrible thing in creation. Whatever contempt I might entertain for the dangers which this old lady so darkly intimated, it was by no means pleasant, you may suppose, that a secret so dangerous should be so much as suspected by a stranger, and that stranger a partisan of the Count de St Alyre.

Ought I not, at all risks, to apprise the Countess, who had trusted me so generously, or, as she said herself, so madly, of the fact that our secret was, at least, suspected by another? But was there not greater danger in attempting to communicate? What did the beldame* mean by saying, 'Keep your secret, and I'll keep mine?'

I had a thousand distracting questions before me. My progress seemed like a journey through the Spessart,* where at every step some new goblin or monster starts from the ground or steps from behind a tree.

Peremptorily I dismissed these harassing and frightful

doubts. I secured my door, sat myself down at my table, and with a candle at each side, placed before me the piece of vellum which contained the drawings and notes on which I was to rely for full instructions as to how to use the key.

When I had studied this for awhile, I made my investiga-tion. The angle of the room at the right side of the window was cut off by an oblique turn in the wainscot. I examined this carefully, and, on pressure, a small bit of the frame of the woodwork slid aside, and disclosed a keyhole. On removing my finger, it shot back to its place again, with a spring. So far I had interpreted my instructions successfully. A similar search, next the door, and directly under this, was rewarded by a like discovery. The small end of the key fitted this, as it had the upper keyhole; and now, with two or three hard jerks at the key, a door in the panel opened, showing a strip of the bare wall, and a narrow, arched doorway, piercing the thick-ness of the wall; and within which I saw a screw-staircase of stone.

Candle in hand I stepped in. I do not know whether the quality of air, long undisturbed, is peculiar; to me it has always seemed so, and the damp smell of the old masonry hung in this atmosphere. My candle faintly lighted the bare stone wall that enclosed the stair, the foot of which I could not see. Down I went, and a few turns brought me to the stone floor. Here was another door, of the simple, old, oak kind, deep sunk in the thickness of the wall. The large end of the key fitted this. The lock was stiff; I set the candle down upon the stair, and applied both hands; it turned with difficulty, and as it revolved, uttered a shriek that alarmed me for my secret.

For some minutes I did not move. In a little time, however, I took courage, and opened the door. The night-air floating in, puffed out the candle. There was a thicket of holly and underwood, as dense as a jungle, close about the door. I should have been in pitch-darkness, were it not that through the topmost leaves, there twinkled, here and there, a glimmer of moonshine.

Softly, lest any one should have opened his window, at the sound of the rusty bolt, I struggled through this, till I gained a view of the open grounds. Here I found that the brushwood spread a good way up the park, uniting with the wood that approached the little temple I have described.

A general could not have chosen a more effectually-covered approach from the Dragon Volant to the trysting-place where hitherto I had conferred with the idol of my lawless adoration.

Looking back upon the old inn, I discovered that the stair I descended, was enclosed in one of those slender turrets that decorate such buildings. It was placed at that angle which corresponded with the part of the panelling of my room indicated in the plan I had been studying.

Thoroughly satisfied with my experiment, I made my way back to the door, with some little difficulty, re-mounted to my room, locked my secret door again; kissed the mysterious key that her hand had pressed that night, and placed it under my pillow, upon which, very soon after, my giddy head was laid, not, for some time, to sleep soundly.

CHAPTER XXI

I SEE THREE MEN IN A MIRROR

I awoke very early next morning, and was too excited to sleep again. As soon as I could, without exciting remark, I saw my host. I told him that I was going into town that night, and thence to——, where I had to see some people on business, and requested him to mention my being there to any friend who might call. That I expected to be back in about a week, and that in the meantime my servant, St Clair, would keep the key of my room, and look after my things.

Having prepared this mystification for my landlord, I drove into Paris, and there transacted the financial part of the affair. The problem was to reduce my balance, nearly thirty thousand pounds, to a shape in which it would be not only easily portable, but available, wherever I might go, without involving correspondence, or any other incident which would disclose my place of residence, for the time being. All these points were as nearly provided for as they could be. I need not trouble you about my arrangements for passports. It is enough to say that the point I selected for our flight was, in the spirit of romance, one of the most beautiful and sequestered nooks in Switzerland.

Luggage, I should start with none. The first considerable town we reached next morning, would supply an extemporized wardrobe. It was now two o'clock; *only* two! How on earth was I to dispose of the remainder of the day?

I had not yet seen the cathedral of Notre Dame; and thither I drove. I spent an hour or more there; and then to the Conciergerie, the Palais de Justice, and the beautiful Sainte Chapelle.* Still there remained some time to get rid of, and I strolled into the narrow streets adjoining the cathedral. I recollect seeing, in one of them, an old house with a mural inscription stating that it had been the residence of Canon Fulbert, the uncle of Abelard's Eloise.* I don't know whether these curious old streets, in which I observed fragments of ancient Gothic churches fitted up as warehouses, are still extant. I lighted, among other dingy and eccentric shops, upon one that seemed that of a broker of all sorts of old decorations, armour, china, furniture. I entered the shop; it was dark, dusty, and low. The proprietor was busy scouring a piece of inlaid armour, and allowed me to poke about his shop, and examine the curious things accumulated there, just as I pleased. Gradually I made my way to the farther end of it, where there was but one window with many panes, each with a bull's-eye* in it, and in the dirtiest possible state. When I reached this window, I turned about, and in a recess, standing at right angles with the side wall of the shop, was a large mirror in an old-fashioned dingy frame. Reflected in this I saw, what in old houses I have heard termed an 'alcove', in which, among lumber, and various dusty articles hanging on the wall, there stood a table, at which three persons were seated, as it seemed to me, in earnest conversation. Two of these persons I instantly recognized; one was Colonel Gaillarde, the other was the Marquis d'Harmonville. The third, who was fiddling with a pen, was a lean, pale man, pitted with the small-pox, with lank black hair, and about as mean-looking a person as I had ever seen in my life. The Marquis looked up, and his glance was instantaneously followed by his two companions. For a moment I hesitated what to do. But it was plain that I was not recognized, as indeed I could hardly have been, the light from the window being behind me, and the portion of the shop immediately before me, being very dark indeed.

Perceiving this, I had presence of mind to affect being entirely engrossed by the objects before me, and strolled slowly down the shop again. I paused for a moment to hear whether I was followed, and was relieved when I heard no step. You may be sure I did not waste more time in that shop, where I had just made a discovery so curious and so unexpected.

It was no business of mine to inquire what brought Colonel Gaillarde and the Marquis together, in so shabby, and even dirty a place, or who the mean person, biting the feather end of his pen, might be. Such employments as the Marquis had accepted sometimes make strange bed-fellows.

I was glad to get away, and just as the sun set, I had reached the steps of the Dragon Volant, and dismissed the vehicle in which I arrived, carrying in my hand a strong box, of marvellously small dimensions considering all it contained, strapped in a leather cover, which disguised its real character.

When I got to my room, I summoned St Clair. I told him nearly the same story, I had already told my host. I gave him fifty pounds, with orders to expend whatever was necessary on himself, and in payment for my rooms till my return. I then ate a slight and hasty dinner. My eyes were often upon the solemn old clock over the chimney-piece, which was my sole accomplice in keeping tryst in this iniquitous venture. The sky favoured my design, and darkened all things with a sea of clouds.

The innkeeper met me in the hall, to ask whether I should want a vehicle to Paris? I was prepared for this question, and instantly answered that I meant to walk to Versailles, and take a carriage there. I called St Clair.

'Go', said I, 'and drink a bottle of wine with your friends. I shall call you if I should want anything; in the meantime, here is the key of my room; I shall be writing some notes, so don't allow any one to disturb me, for at least half an hour. At the end of that time you will probably find that I have left this for Versailles; and should you not find me in the room, you may take that for granted; and you take charge of everything, and lock the door, you understand?'

St Clair took his leave, wishing me all happiness and no doubt promising himself some little amusement with my money. With my candle in my hand, I hastened upstairs. It wanted now but five minutes to the appointed time. I do not think there is anything of the coward in my nature; but I confess, as the crisis approached, I felt something of the suspense and awe of a soldier going into action. Would I have receded? Not for all this earth could offer.

I bolted my door, put on my great coat, and placed my pistols, one in each pocket. I now applied my key to the secret locks; drew the wainscot-door a little open, took my strong box under my arm, extinguished my candle, unbolted my door, listened at it for a few moments to be sure that no one was approaching, and then crossed the floor of my room swiftly, entered the secret door, and closed the spring lock after me. I was upon the screw-stair in total darkness, the key in my fingers. Thus far the undertaking was successful.

CHAPTER XXII

RAPTURE

Down the screw-stair I went in utter darkness; and having reached the stone floor, I discerned the door and groped out the key-hole. With more caution, and less noise than upon the night before, I opened the door, and stepped out into the thick brushwood. It was almost as dark in this jungle.

Having secured the door, I slowly pushed my way through the bushes, which soon became less dense. Then, with more ease, but still under thick cover, I pursued in the track of the wood, keeping near its edge.

At length, in the darkened air, about fifty yards away, the shafts of the marble temple rose like phantoms before me, seen through the trunks of the old trees. Everything favoured my enterprise. I had effectually mystified my servant and the people of the Dragon Volant, and so dark was the night, that even had I alarmed the suspicions of all the tenants of the inn, I might safely defy their united curiosity, though posted at every window of the house.

Through the trunks, over the roots of the old trees, I reached the appointed place of observation. I laid my treasure, in its leathern case, in the embrasure, and leaning my arms upon it, looked steadily in the direction of the château. The outline of the building was scarcely discernible, blending dimly, as it did, with the sky. No light in any window was visible. I was plainly to wait; but for how long?

Leaning on my box of treasure, gazing toward the massive shadow that represented the château, in the midst of my ardent and elated longings, there came upon me an odd thought, which you will think might well have struck me long before. It seemed on a sudden, as it came, that the darkness deepened, and a chill stole into the air around me.

Suppose I were to disappear finally, like those other men whose stories I had listened to! Had I not been at all the pains that mortal could, to obliterate every trace of my real proceedings, and to mislead every one to whom I spoke as to the direction in which I had gone?

This icy, snake-like thought stole through my mind, and was gone.

It was with me the full-blooded season of youth, conscious strength, rashness, passion, pursuit, the adventure! Here were a pair of double-barrelled pistols, four lives in my hands? What could possibly happen? The Count—except for the sake of my dulcinea,* what was it to me whether the old coward whom I had seen, in an ague of terror before the brawling Colonel, interposed or not? I was assuming the worst that could happen. But with an ally so clever and courageous as my beautiful Countess, could any such misadventure befall? Bah! I laughed at all such fancies.

As I thus communed with myself, the signal light sprang up. The rose-coloured light, *couleur de rose*, emblem of sanguine hope, and the dawn of a happy day.

Clear, soft, and steady, glowed the light from the window. The stone shafts showed black against it. Murmuring words of passionate love as I gazed upon the signal, I grasped my strong box under my arm, and with rapid strides approached the Château de la Carque. No sign of light or life, no human voice, no tread of foot, no bark of dog, indicated a chance of interruption. A blind was down; and as I came close to the tall window, I found that half-a-dozen steps led up to it, and that a large lattice, answering for a door, lay open.

A shadow from within fell upon the blind; it was drawn aside, and as I ascended the steps, a soft voice murmured— 'Richard, dearest Richard, come, oh! come! how I have longed for this moment!'

Never did she look so beautiful. My love rose to passionate enthusiasm. I only wished there were some real danger in the adventure worthy of such a creature. When the first tumultuous greeting was over, she made me sit beside her on a sofa. There we talked for a minute or two. She told me that the Count had gone, and was by that time more than a mile on his way, with the funeral, to Père la Chaise. Here were her diamonds. She exhibited, hastily, an open casket containing a profusion of the largest brilliants.

'What is this?' she asked.

'A box containing money to the amount of thirty thousand pounds,' I answered.

'What! all that money?' she exclaimed.

'Every *sou*.'

'Was it not unnecessary to bring so much, seeing all these,' she said, touching her diamonds. 'It would have been kind of you, to allow me to provide for both for a time, at least. It would have made me happier even than I am.'

'Dearest, generous angel!' Such was my extravagant declamation. 'You forget that it may be necessary, for a long time to observe silence as to where we are, and impossible to communicate safely with any one.'

'You have then here this great sum—are you certain; have you counted it?'

'Yes, certainly; I received it to-day,' I answered, perhaps

showing a little surprise in my face. 'I counted it, of course, on drawing it from my bankers.'

'It makes me feel a little nervous, travelling with so much money; but these jewels make as great a danger; *that* can add but little to it. Place them side by side; you shall take off your great coat when we are ready to go, and with it manage to conceal these boxes. I should not like the drivers to suspect that we are conveying such a treasure. I must ask you now to close the curtains of that window, and bar the shutters.'

I had hardly done this when a knock was heard at the room-door.

'I know who this is,' she said, in a whisper to me.

I saw that she was not alarmed. She went softly to the door, and a whispered conversation for a minute followed.

'My trusty maid, who is coming with us. She says we cannot safely go sooner than ten minutes. She is bringing some coffee to the next room.'

She opened the door and looked in.

'I must tell her not to take too much luggage. She is so odd! Don't follow—stay where you are—it is better that she should not see you.'

She left the room with a gesture of caution.

A change had come over the manner of this beautiful woman. For the last few minutes a shadow had been stealing over her, an air of abstraction, a look bordering on suspicion. Why was she pale? Why had there come that dark look in her eyes? Why had her very voice become changed? Had anything gone suddenly wrong? Did some danger threaten?

This doubt, however, speedily quieted itself. If there had been anything of the kind, she would, of course, have told me. It was only natural that, as the crisis approached, she should become more and more nervous. She did not return quite so soon as I had expected. To a man in my situation absolute quietude is next to impossible. I moved restlessly about the room. It was a small one. There was a door at the other end. I opened it, rashly enough. I listened, it was perfectly silent. I was in an excited, eager state, and every faculty engrossed about what was coming, and in so far detached from the immediate present. I can't account, in any other way, for my having done so many foolish things that night, for I was, naturally, by no means deficient in cunning. About the most stupid of those was, that instead of immediately closing that door, which I never ought to have opened, I actually took a candle and walked into the room.

There I made, quite unexpectedly, a rather startling discovery.

CHAPTER XXIII

A CUP OF COFFEE

The room was carpetless. On the floor was a quantity of shavings, and some score of bricks. Beyond these, on a narrow table, lay an object, which I could hardly believe I saw aright.

I approached and drew from it a sheet which had very slightly disguised its shape. There was no mistake about it. It was a coffin; and on the lid was a plate, with the inscription in French:

PIERRE DE LA ROCHE ST AMAND
AGÉ DE XXIII ANS.

I drew back with a double shock. So, then, the funeral after all had not yet left! Here lay the body. I had been deceived. This, no doubt, accounted for the embarrassment so manifest in the Countess's manner. She would have done more wisely had she told me the true state of the case.

I drew back from this melancholy room, and closed the door. Her distrust of me was the worst rashness she could have committed. There is nothing more dangerous than misapplied caution. In entire ignorance of the fact I had entered the room, and there I might have lighted upon some of the very persons it was our special anxiety that I should avoid.

These reflections were interrupted, almost as soon as begun, by the return of the Countess de St Alyre. I saw at a glance that she detected in my face some evidence of what had happened, for she threw a hasty look towards the door.

'Have you seen anything—anything to disturb you, dear Richard? Have you been out of this room?'

I answered promptly, 'Yes,' and told her frankly what had happened.

'Well, I did not like to make you more uneasy than necessary. Besides, it is disgusting and horrible. The body *is* there; but the Count had departed a quarter of an hour before I lighted the coloured lamp, and prepared to receive you. The body did not arrive till eight or ten minutes after he had set out. He was afraid lest the people at Père la Chaise should suppose that the funeral was postponed. He knew that the remains of poor Pierre would certainly reach this to-night although an unexpected delay had occurred; and there are reasons why he wishes the funeral completed before to-morrow. The hearse with the body must leave this in ten minutes. So soon as it is gone, we shall be free to set out upon our wild and happy journey. The horses are to the carriage in the *porte-cochère*. As for this *funeste* horror (she shuddered very prettily), let us think of it no more.'

She bolted the door of communication, and when she turned, it was with such a pretty penitence in her face and attitude, that I was ready to throw myself at her feet.

'It is the last time', she said, in a sweet sad little pleading, 'I shall ever practise a deception on my brave and beautiful Richard—my hero? Am I forgiven?'

Here was another scene of passionate effusion, and lovers' raptures and declamations, but only murmured, lest the ears of listeners should be busy.

At length, on a sudden, she raised her hand, as if to prevent my stirring, her eyes fixed on me, and her ear toward the door of the room in which the coffin was placed, and remained breathless in that attitude for a few moments. Then, with a little nod towards me, she moved on tip-toe to the door, and listened, extending her hand backward as if to warn me against advancing; and after a little time, she returned, still on tip-toe, and whispered to me, 'They are removing the coffin—come with me.'

I accompanied her into the room from which her maid, as she told me, had spoken to her. Coffee and some old china cups, which appeared to me quite beautiful, stood on a silver tray; and some liqueur glasses, with a flask, which turned out to be noyeau,* on a salver beside it.

'I shall attend you. I'm to be your servant here; I am to have my own way; I shall not think myself forgiven by my darling if he refuses to indulge me in anything.'

She filled a cup with coffee, and handed it to me with her left hand, her right arm she fondly passed over my shoulder, and with her fingers through my curls caressingly, she whispered, 'Take this, I shall take some just now.'

It was excellent; and when I had done she handed me the liqueur, which I also drank.

'Come back, dearest, to the next room,' she said. 'By this time those terrible people must have gone away, and we shall be safer there, for the present, than here.'

'You shall direct, and I obey; you shall command me, not only now, but always, and in all things, my beautiful queen!' I murmured.

My heroics were unconsciously, I daresay, founded upon my ideal of the French school of lovemaking. I am, even now, ashamed as I recall the bombast to which I treated the Countess de St Alyre.

'There, you shall have another miniature glass—a fairy glass—of noyeau,' she said, gaily. In this volatile creature, the funereal gloom of the moment before, and the suspense of an adventure on which all her future was staked, disappeared in a moment. She ran and returned with another tiny glass, which, with an eloquent or tender little speech, I placed to my lips and sipped.

I kissed her hand, I kissed her lips, I gazed in her beautiful eyes, and kissed her again unresisting.

'You call me Richard, by what name am I to call my beautiful divinity?' I asked.

'You call me Eugenie, it is my name. Let us be quite real; that is, if you love as entirely as I do.'

'Eugenie!' I exclaimed, and broke into a new rapture upon the name.

It ended by my telling her how impatient I was to set out upon our journey; and, as I spoke, suddenly an odd sensation overcame me. It was not in the slightest degree like faintness. I can find no phrase to describe it, but a sudden constraint of the brain; it was as if the membrane in which it lies, if there be such a thing, contracted, and became inflexible.

'Dear Richard! what is the matter?' she exclaimed, with terror in her looks. 'Good Heavens! are you ill? I conjure you, sit down; sit in this chair.' She almost forced me into one; I was in no condition to offer the least resistance. I recognized but too truly the sensations that supervened. I was lying back in the chair in which I sat without the power, by this time, of uttering a syllable, of closing my eyelids, of moving my eyes, of stirring a muscle. I had in a few seconds glided into precisely the state in which I had passed so many appalling hours when approaching Paris, in my night-drive with the Marquis d'Harmonville.

Great and loud was the lady's agony. She seemed to have lost all sense of fear. She called me by my name, shook me by the shoulder, raised my arm and let it fall, all the time imploring of me, in distracting sentences, to make the slightest sign of life, and vowing that if I did not, she would make away with herself.

These ejaculations, after a minute or two, suddenly subsided. The lady was perfectly silent and cool. In a very business-like way she took a candle and stood before me, pale indeed, very pale, but with an expression only of intense scrutiny with a dash of horror in it. She moved the candle before my eyes slowly, evidently watching the effect. She then set it down, and rang a hand-bell two or three times sharply. She placed the two cases (I mean hers containing the jewels and my strong box) side by side on the table; and I saw her carefully lock the door that gave access to the room in which I had just now sipped my coffee.

CHAPTER XXIV

HOPE

She had scarcely set down my heavy box, which she seemed to have considerable difficulty in raising on the table, when the door of the room in which I had seen the coffin, opened, and a sinister and unexpected apparition entered.

It was the Count de St Alyre, who had been, as I have told you, reported to me to be, for some considerable time, on his way to Père la Chaise. He stood before me for a moment, with the frame of the doorway and a background of darkness enclosing him, like a portrait. His slight, mean figure was draped in the deepest mourning. He had a pair of black gloves in his hand, and his hat with crape* round it.

When he was not speaking his face showed signs of agitation; his mouth was puckering and working. He looked damnably wicked and frightened.

'Well, my dear Eugenie? Well, child—eh? Well, it all goes admirably?'

'Yes,' she answered, in a low, hard tone. 'But you and Planard should not have left that door open.'

This she said sternly. 'He went in there and looked about wherever he liked; it was fortunate he did not move aside the lid of the coffin.'

'Planard should have seen to that,' said the Count, sharply. '*Ma foi!** I can't be everywhere!' He advanced half-a-dozen short quick steps into the room toward me, and placed his glasses to his eyes.

'Monsieur Beckett,' he cried sharply, two or three times, 'Hi! don't you know me?'

He approached and peered more closely in my face; raised my hand and shook it, calling me again, then let it drop, and said—'It has set in admirably, my pretty *mignonne*.* When did it commence?'

The Countess came and stood beside him, and looked at me steadily for some seconds.

You can't conceive the effect of the silent gaze of those two pairs of evil eyes.

The lady glanced to where, I recollected, the mantel-piece stood, and upon it a clock, the regular click of which I sharply heard.

'Four—five—six minutes and a half,' she said slowly, in a cold hard way.

'Brava! Bravissima! my beautiful queen! my little Venus! my Joan of Arc! my heroine! my paragon of women!'

He was gloating on me with an odious curiosity, smiling, as he groped backward with his thin brown fingers to find the lady's hand; but she, not (I dare say) caring for his caresses, drew back a little.

'Come, *ma chère,** let us count these things. What is it? Pocket-book? Or—or—*what?*'

'It is *that!*' said the lady, pointing with a look of disgust to the box, which lay in its leather case on the table.

'Oh! Let us see—let us count—let us see,' he said, as he was unbuckling the straps with his tremulous fingers. 'We must count them—we must see to it. I have pencil and pocket-book—but—where's the key? See this cursed lock! My——! What is it? Where's the key?'

He was standing before the Countess, shuffling his feet, with his hands extended and all his fingers quivering.

'I have not got it; how could I? It is in his pocket, of course,' said the lady.

In another instant the fingers of the old miscreant were in my pockets: he plucked out everything they contained, and some keys among the rest.

I lay in precisely the state in which I had been during my drive with the Marquis to Paris. This wretch I knew was about to rob me. The whole drama, and the Countess's *rôle* in it, I could not yet comprehend. I could not be sure—so much more presence of mind and histrionic resource have women than fall to the lot of our clumsy sex—whether the return of the Count was not, in truth, a surprise to her; and this scrutiny of the contents of my strong box, an extempore undertaking of the Count's. But it was clearing more and more every moment:

and I was destined, very soon, to comprehend minutely my appalling situation.

I had not the power of turning my eyes this way or that, the smallest fraction of a hair's breadth. But let any one, placed as I was at the end of a room, ascertain for himself by experiment how wide is the field of sight, without the slightest alteration in the line of vision, he will find that it takes in the entire breadth of a large room, and that up to a very short distance before him; and imperfectly, by a refraction, I believe, in the eye itself, to a point very near indeed. Next to nothing that passed in the room, therefore, was hidden from me.

The old man had, by this time, found the key. The leather case was open. The box cramped round with iron, was next unlocked. He turned out its contents upon the table.

'Rouleaux* of a hundred Napoleons each. One, two, three. Yes, quick. Write down a thousand Napoleons. One, two; yes, right. Another thousand, *write!*' And so, on and on till gold was rapidly counted. Then came the notes.

'Ten thousand francs. *Write*. Ten thousand francs again: is it written? Another ten thousand francs: is it down? Smaller notes would have been better. They should have been smaller. These are horribly embarrassing. Bolt that door again; Planard would become unreasonable if he knew the amount. Why did you not tell him to get it in smaller notes? No matter now—go on—it can't be helped—*write*—another ten thousand francs—another—another.' And so on, till my treasure was counted out, before my face, while I saw and heard all that passed with the sharpest distinctness, and my mental perceptions were horribly vivid. But in all other respects I was dead.

He had replaced in the box every note and rouleau as he counted it, and now having ascertained the sum total, he locked it, replaced it, very methodically, in its cover, opened a buffet in the wainscoting, and, having placed the Countess's jewel-case and my strong box in it, he locked it; and immediately on completing these arrangements he began to complain, with fresh acrimony and maledictions, of Planard's delay.

He unbolted the door, looked in the dark room beyond, and listened. He closed the door again, and returned. The old man was in a fever of suspense.

'I have kept ten thousand francs for Planard,' said the Count, touching his waistcoat pocket.

'Will that satisfy him?' asked the lady.

'Why—curse him!' screamed the Count. 'Has he no conscience? I'll swear to him it's half the entire thing.'

He and the lady again came and looked at me anxiously for awhile, in silence; and then the old Count began to grumble again about Planard, and to compare his watch with the clock. The lady seemed less impatient; she sat no longer looking at me, but across the room, so that her profile was toward me—and strangely changed, dark and witch-like it looked. My last hope died as I beheld that jaded face from which the mask had dropped. I was certain that they intended to crown their robbery by murder. Why did they not dispatch me at once? What object could there be in postponing the catastrophe which would expedite their own safety. I cannot recall, even to myself, adequately the horrors unutterable that I underwent. You must suppose a real night-mare—I mean a nightmare in which the objects and the danger are real, and the spell of corporeal death appears to be protractable at the pleasure of the persons who preside at your unearthly torments. I could have no doubt as to the cause of the state in which I was.

In this agony, to which I could not give the slightest expression, I saw the door of the room where the coffin had been, open slowly, and the Marquis d'Harmonville entered the room.

CHAPTER XXV

DESPAIR

A moment's hope, hope violent and fluctuating, hope that was nearly torture, and then came a dialogue, and with it the terrors of despair.

'Thank heaven, Planard, you have come at last,' said the Count, taking him, with both hands, by the arm and clinging to it, and drawing him toward me. 'See, look at him. It has all gone sweetly, sweetly, sweetly up to this. Shall I hold the candle for you?'

My friend d'Harmonville, Planard, whatever he was, came to me, pulling off his gloves, which he popped into his pocket.

'The candle, a little this way,' he said, and stooping over me he looked earnestly in my face. He touched my forehead, drew his hand across it, and then looked in my eyes for a time.

'Well, doctor, what do you think?' whispered the Count.

'How much did you give him?' said the Marquis, thus suddenly stunted down to a doctor.

'Seventy drops,' said the lady.

'In the hot coffee?'

'Yes; sixty in a hot cup of coffee and ten in the liqueur.'

Her voice, low and hard, seemed to me to tremble a little. It takes a long course of guilt to subjugate nature completely, and prevent those exterior signs of agitation that outlive all good.

The doctor, however, was treating me as coolly as he might a subject which he was about to place on the dissecting-table for a lecture.

He looked into my eyes again for awhile, took my wrist, and applied his fingers to the pulse.

'That action suspended,' he said to himself.

Then again he placed something that, for the moment I saw it, looked like a piece of gold-beater's leaf,* to my lips, holding his head so far that his own breathing could not affect it.

'Yes,' he said in soliloquy, very low.

Then he plucked my shirt-breast open and applied the stethoscope,* shifted it from point to point, listened with his ear to its end, as if for a very far off sound, raised his head, and said, in like manner, softly to himself, 'All appreciable action of the lungs has subsided.'

Then turning from the sound, as I conjectured, he said:

'Seventy drops, allowing ten for waste, ought to hold him fast for six hours and a-half—that is ample. The experiment I tried in the carriage was only thirty drops, and showed a highly sensitive brain. It would not do to kill him, you know. You are certain you did not exceed *seventy*?'

'Perfectly,' said the lady.

'If he were to die the evaporation would be arrested, and foreign matter, some of it poisonous, would be found in the stomach, don't you see? If you are doubtful, it would be well to use the stomach-pump.'

'Dearest Eugenie, be frank, be frank, do be frank,' urged the Count.

'I am *not* doubtful, I am *certain*,' she answered.

'How long ago, exactly? I told you to observe the time.'

'I did; the minute-hand was exactly there, under the point of that Cupid's foot.'

'It will last, then, probably for seven hours. He will recover then; the evaporation will be complete, and not one particle of the fluid will remain in the stomach.'

It was reassuring, at all events, to hear that there was no intention to murder me. No one who has not tried it knows the terror of the approach of death, when the mind is clear, the instincts of life unimpaired, and no excitement to disturb the appreciation of that entirely new horror.

The nature and purpose of this tenderness was very, very peculiar, and as yet I had not a suspicion of it.

'You leave France, I suppose?' said the ex-Marquis.

'Yes, certainly, to-morrow,' answered the Count.

'And where do you mean to go?'

'That I have not yet settled,' he answered quickly.

'You won't tell a friend, eh?'

'I can't till I know. This has turned out an unprofitable affair.'

'We shall settle that by-and-by.'

'It is time we should get him lying down, eh?' said the Count, indicating me with one finger.

'Yes, we must proceed rapidly now. Are his night-shirt and night-cap—you understand—here?'

'All ready,' said the Count.

'Now, Madame,' said the doctor, turning to the lady, and making her, in spite of the emergency, a bow, 'it is time you should retire.'

The lady passed into the room, in which I had taken my cup of treacherous coffee, and I saw her no more.

The Count took a candle, and passed through the door at the further end of the room, returning with a roll of linen in his hand. He bolted first one door, then the other.

They now, in silence, proceeded to undress me rapidly. They were not many minutes in accomplishing this.

What the doctor had termed my night-shirt, a long garment which reached below my feet, was now on, and a cap, that resembled a female nightcap more than anything I had ever seen upon a male head, was fitted upon mine, and tied under my chin.

And now, I thought, I shall be laid in a bed, to recover how I can, and, in the meantime, the conspirators will have escaped with their booty, and pursuit be in vain.

This was my best hope at the time; but it was soon clear that their plans were very different.

The Count and Planard now went, together, into the room that lay straight before me. I heard them talking low, and a sound of shuffling feet; then a long rumble; it suddenly stopped; it recommenced; it continued; side by side they came in at the door, their backs toward me. They were dragging something along the floor that made a continued boom and rumble, but they interposed between me and it, so that I could not see it until they had dragged it almost beside me; and then, merciful heaven! I saw it plainly enough. It was the coffin I had seen in the next room. It lay now flat on the floor, its edge against the chair in which I sat. Planard removed the lid. The coffin was empty.

CHAPTER XXVI

CATASTROPHE

'Those seem to be good horses, and we change on the way,' said Planard. 'You give the men a Napoleon or two; we must do it within three hours and a quarter. Now, come; I'll lift him, upright, so as to place his feet in their proper berth, and you must keep them together, and draw the white shirt well down over them.'

In another moment I was placed, as he described, sustained in Planard's arms, standing at the foot of the coffin, and so lowered backward, gradually, till I lay my length in it. Then the man, whom he called Planard, stretched my arms by my sides, and carefully arranged the frills at my breast, and the folds of the shroud, and after that, taking his stand at the foot of the coffin, made a survey which seemed to satisfy him.

The Count, who was very methodical, took my clothes, which had just been removed, folded them rapidly together and locked them up, as I afterwards heard, in one of the three presses which opened by doors in the panel.

I now understood their frightful plan. This coffin had been prepared for *me*; the funeral of St Amand was a sham to mislead inquiry; I had myself given the order at Père la Chaise, signed it, and paid the fees for the interment of the fictitious Pierre de St Amand, whose place I was to take, to lie in his coffin, with his name on the plate above my breast, and with a ton of clay packed down upon me; to waken from this catalepsy,* after I had been for hours in the grave, there to perish by a death the most horrible that imagination can conceive.

If, hereafter, by any caprice of curiosity or suspicion, the coffin should be exhumed, and the body it enclosed examined, no chemistry could detect a trace of poison, nor the most cautious examination the slightest mark of violence.

I had myself been at the utmost pains to mystify inquiry, should my disappearance excite surmises, and had even written to my few correspondents in England to tell them that they were not to look for a letter from me for three weeks at least.

In the moment of my guilty elation death had caught me, and there was no escape. I tried to pray to God in my unearthly panic, but only thoughts of terror, judgment, and eternal anguish, crossed the distraction of my immediate doom.

I must not try to recall what is indeed indescribable—the multiform horrors of my own thoughts. I will relate, simply, what befell, every detail of which remains sharp in my memory as if cut in steel.

'The undertaker's men are in the hall,' said the Count.

'They must not come till this is fixed,' answered Planard. 'Be good enough to take hold of the lower part while I take this end.' I was not left long to conjecture what was coming, for in a few seconds more something slid across, a few inches above my face, and entirely excluded the light, and muffled sound, so that nothing that was not very distinct reached my ears henceforward; but very distinctly came the working of a turnscrew, and the crunching home of screws in succession. Than these vulgar sounds, no doom spoken in thunder could have been more tremendous.

The rest I must relate, not as it then reached my ears, which was too imperfectly and interruptedly to supply a connected narrative, but as it was afterwards told me by other people.

The coffin-lid being screwed down, the two gentlemen arranged the room, and adjusted the coffin so that it lay perfectly straight along the boards, the Count being specially anxious that there should be no appearance of hurry or disorder in the room, which might have suggested remark and conjecture.

When this was done, Doctor Planard said he would go to the hall to summon the men who were to carry the coffin out and place it in the hearse. The Count pulled on his black gloves, and held his white handkerchief in his hand, a very impressive chief-mourner. He stood a little behind the head of the coffin, awaiting the arrival of the persons who accompanied Planard, and whose fast steps he soon heard approaching.

Planard came first. He entered the room through the apartment in which the coffin had been originally placed. His manner was changed; there was something of a swagger in it.

'Monsieur le Comte,' he said, as he strode through the door, followed by half-a-dozen persons. 'I am sorry to have to announce to you a most unseasonable interruption. Here is Monsieur Carmaignac, a gentleman holding an office in the police department, who says he has information to the effect that large quantities of smuggled English and other goods have been distributed in this neighbourhood, and that a portion of them is concealed in your house. I have ventured to assure him, of my own knowledge, that nothing can be more false than that information, and that you would be only too happy to throw open for his inspection, at a moment's notice, every room, closet, and cupboard in your house.'

'Most assuredly,' exclaimed the Count, with a stout voice, but a very white face. 'Thank you, my good friend, for having anticipated me. I will place my house and keys at his disposal, for the purpose of his scrutiny, so soon as he is good enough to inform me, of what specific contraband goods he comes in search.'

'The Count de St Alyre will pardon me,' answered Carmaignac, a little dryly. 'I am forbidden by my instructions to make that disclosure; and that I *am* instructed to make a general search, this warrant will sufficiently apprise Monsieur le Comte.'

'Monsieur Carmaignac, may I hope', interposed Planard, 'that you will permit the Count de St Alyre to attend the funeral of his kinsman, who lies here, as you see—' (he pointed to the plate upon the coffin)—'and to convey whom to Père la Chaise, a hearse waits at this moment at the door.'

'That, I regret to say, I cannot permit. My instructions are precise; but the delay, I trust, will be but trifling. Monsieur le Comte will not suppose for a moment that I suspect him; but we have a duty to perform, and I must act as if I did. When I am ordered to search, I search; things are sometimes hid in such *bizarre* places. I can't say, for instance, what that coffin may contain.'

'The body of my kinsman, Monsieur Pierre de St Amand,' answered the Count, loftily.

'Oh! then you've seen him?'

'Seen him? Often, too often!' The Count was evidently a good deal moved.

'I mean the body.'

The Count stole a quick glance at Planard.

'N—no, Monsieur—that is, I mean only for a moment.' Another quick glance at Planard.

'But quite long enough, I fancy, to recognize him?' insinuated that gentleman.

'Of course—of course; instantly—perfectly. What! Pierre de St Amand? Not know him at a glance? No, no, poor fellow, I know him too well for that.'

'The things I am in search of', said Monsieur Carmaignac, 'would fit in a narrow compass—servants are so ingenious sometimes. Let us raise the lid.'

'Pardon me, Monsieur,' said the Count, peremptorily, advancing to the side of the coffin, and extending his arm across it. 'I cannot permit that indignity—that desecration.'

'There shall be none, sir,—simply the raising of the lid; you shall remain in the room. If it should prove as we all hope, you shall have the pleasure of one other look, really the last, upon your beloved kinsman.'

'But, sir, I can't.'

'But, Monsieur, I must.'

'But, besides, the thing, the turnscrew, broke when the last screw was turned; and I give you my sacred honour there is nothing but the body in this coffin.'

'Of course Monsieur le Comte believes all that; but he does not know so well as I the legerdemain* in use among servants, who are accustomed to smuggling. Here, Philippe, you must take off the lid of that coffin.'

The Count protested; but Philippe—a man with a bald head, and a smirched face, looking like a working blacksmith—placed on the floor a leather bag of tools, from which, having looked at the coffin, and picked with his nail at the screwheads, he selected a turnscrew, and, with a few deft twirls at each of the screws, they stood up like little rows of mushrooms, and the lid was raised. I saw the light, of which I thought I had seen my last, once more; but the axis of vision remained fixed. As I was reduced to the cataleptic state in a position nearly perpendicular,* I continued looking straight before me, and thus my gaze was now fixed upon the ceiling. I saw the face of Carmaignac leaning over me with a curious frown. It seemed to me that there was no recognition in his eyes. Oh, heaven! that I could have uttered were it but one cry! I saw the dark, mean mask of the little Count staring down at me from the other side; the face of the pseudo-marquis also peering at me, but not so full in the line of vision; there were other faces also.

'I see, I see,' said Carmaignac, withdrawing. 'Nothing of the kind there.'

'You will be good enough to direct your man to re-adjust the lid of the coffin, and to fix the screws,' said the Count, taking courage; 'and—and—really the funeral *must* proceed. It is not fair to the people who have but moderate fees for night-work, to keep them hour after hour beyond the time.'

'Count de St Alyre, you shall go in a very few minutes. I will direct, just now, all about the coffin.'

The Count looked toward the door, and there saw a gendarme; and two or three more grave and stalwart specimens of the same force were also in the room. The Count was very uncomfortably excited; it was growing insupportable.

'As this gentleman makes a difficulty about my attending the obsequies of my kinsman, I will ask you, Planard, to accompany the funeral in my stead.'

'In a few minutes,' answered the incorrigible Carmaignac. 'I must first trouble you for the key that opens that press.'

He pointed direct at the press, in which the clothes had just been locked up.

'I —I have no objection,' said the Count—'none, of course; only they have not been used for an age. I'll direct some one to look for the key.'

'If you have not got it about you, it is quite unnecessary. Philippe, try your skeleton-keys with that press. I want it opened. Whose clothes are these?' inquired Carmaignac when, the press having been opened, he took out the suit that had been placed there scarcely two minutes since.

'I can't say,' answered the Count. 'I know nothing of the contents of that press. A roguish servant, named Lablais, whom I dismissed about a year ago, had the key. I have not seen it open for ten years or more. The clothes are probably his.'

'Here are visiting cards, see, and here a marked pocket-handkerchief—"R.B." upon it. He must have stolen them from a person named Beckett—R. Beckett. "Mr Beckett, Berkley Square,"* the card says; and, my faith! here's a watch and a bunch of seals; one of them with the initials "R.B." upon it. That servant, Lablais, must have been a consummate rogue!'

'So he was; you are right, sir.'

'It strikes me that he possibly stole these clothes,' continued Carmaignac, 'from the man in the coffin, who, in that case, would be Monsieur Beckett, and not Monsieur de St Amand. For, wonderful to relate, Monsieur, the watch is still going! That man in the coffin, I believe, is not dead, but simply drugged. And for having robbed and intended to murder him, I arrest you, Nicolas de la Marque, Count de St Alyre.'

In another moment the old villain was a prisoner. I heard his discordant voice break quaveringly into sudden vehemence and volubility; now croaking—now shrieking, as he oscillated between protests, threats, and impious appeals to the God who will 'judge the secrets of men!'* And thus lying and raving, he was removed from the room, and placed in the same coach with his beautiful and abandoned accomplice, already arrested; and, with two *gendarmes* sitting beside them, they were immediately driving at a rapid pace towards the Conciergerie.

There were now added to the general chorus two voices, very different in quality; one was that of the gasconading* Colonel Gaillarde, who had with difficulty been kept in the background up to this; the other was that of my jolly friend Whistlewick, who had come to identify me.

I shall tell you, just now, how this project against my property and life, so ingenious and monstrous, was exploded. I must first say a word about myself. I was placed in a hot bath, under the direction of Planard, as consummate a villain as any of the gang, but now thoroughly in the interests of the prosecution. Thence I was laid in a warm bed, the window of the room being open. These simple measures restored me in about three hours; I should otherwise, probably, have continued under the spell for nearly seven.

The practices of these nefarious conspirators had been carried on with consummate skill and secrecy. Their dupes were led, as I was, to be themselves auxiliary to the mystery which made their own destruction both safe and certain.

A search was, of course, instituted. Graves were opened in

Père la Chaise. The bodies exhumed had lain there too long, and were too much decomposed to be recognized. One only was identified. The notice for the burial, in this particular case, had been signed, the order given, and the fees paid, by Gabriel Gaillarde, who was known to the official clerk, who had to transact with him this little funereal business. The very trick, that had been arranged for me, had been successfully practised in his case. The person for whom the grave had been ordered, was purely fictitious; and Gabriel Gaillarde himself filled the coffin, on the cover of which that false name was inscribed as well as upon a tomb-stone over the grave. Possibly, the same honour, under my pseudonym, may have been intended for me.

The identification was curious. This Gabriel Gaillarde had had a bad fall from a run-away horse, about five years before his mysterious disappearance. He had lost an eye and some teeth, in this accident, besides sustaining a fracture of the right leg, immediately above the ankle. He had kept the injuries to his face as profound a secret as he could. The result was, that the glass eye which had done duty for the one he had lost, remained in the socket, slightly displaced, of course, but recognizable by the 'artist' who had supplied it.

More pointedly recognizable were the teeth, peculiar in workmanship, which one of the ablest dentists in Paris had himself adapted to the chasms, the cast of which, owing to peculiarities in the accident, he happened to have preserved. This cast precisely fitted the gold plate found in the mouth of the skull. The mark, also, above the ankle, in the bone, where it had re-united, corresponded exactly with the place where the fracture had knit in the limb of Gabriel Gaillarde.

The Colonel, his younger brother, had been furious about the disappearance of Gabriel, and still more so about that of his money, which he had long regarded as his proper keepsake, whenever death should remove his brother from the vexations of living. He had suspected for a long time, for certain adroitly discovered reasons, that the Count de St Alyre and the beautiful lady, his companion, countess, or whatever else she was, had pigeoned him. To this suspicion were added some others of a still darker kind; but in their first shape, rather the exaggerated reflections of his fury, ready to believe anything, than well-defined conjectures.

At length an accident had placed the Colonel very nearly upon the right scent; a chance, possibly lucky for himself, had apprised the scoundrel Planard that the conspirators—himself among the number—were in danger. The result was that he made terms for himself, became an informer, and concerted with the police this visit made to the Château de la Carque, at the critical moment when every measure had been completed that was necessary to construct a perfect case against his guilty accomplices.

I need not describe the minute industry or forethought with which the police agents collected all the details necessary to support the case. They had brought an able physician, who, even had Planard failed, would have supplied the necessary medical evidence.

My trip to Paris, you will believe, had not turned out quite so agreeably as I had anticipated. I was the principal witness for the prosecution in this *cause célèbre*, with all the *agrémens** that attend that enviable position. Having had an escape, as my friend Whistlewick said, 'with a squeak' for my life, I innocently fancied that I should have been an object of considerable interest to Parisian society; but, a good deal to my mortification, I discovered that I was the object of a good-natured but contemptuous merriment. I was a *balourd*, a *benêt*, *un âne*,* and figured even in caricatures. I became a sort of public character, a dignity,

'Unto which I was not born,'

and from which I fled as soon as I conveniently could, without even paying my friend the Marquis d'Harmonville a visit at his hospitable château.

The Marquis escaped scot-free. His accomplice, the Count, was executed. The fair Eugenie, under extenuating circumstances—consisting, so far as I could discover, of her good looks—got off for six years' imprisonment.

Colonel Gaillarde recovered some of his brother's money, out of the not very affluent estate of the Count and *soi-disant** Countess. This, and the execution of the Count, put him in high good humour. So far from insisting on a hostile meeting, he shook me very graciously by the hand, told me that he looked upon the wound on his head, inflicted by the knob of my stick, as having been received in an honourable, though irregular duel, in which he had no disadvantage or unfairness to complain of.

I think I have only two additional details to mention. The bricks discovered in the room with the coffin, had been packed in it, in straw, to supply the weight of a dead body, and to prevent the suspicions and contradictions that might have been excited by the arrival of an empty coffin at the château.

Secondly, the Countess's magnificent brilliants were examined by a lapidary, and pronounced to be worth about five pounds to a tragedy-queen, who happened to be in want of a suite of paste.*

The Countess had figured some years before as one of the cleverest actresses on the minor stage of Paris, where she had been picked up by the Count and used as his principal accomplice.

She it was who, admirably disguised, had rifled my papers in the carriage on my memorable night-journey to Paris. She also had figured as the interpreting magician of the palanquin at the ball of Versailles. So far as I was affected by that elaborate mystification it was intended to re-animate my interest, which, they feared, might flag in the beautiful Countess. It had its design and action upon other intended victims also; but of them there is, at present, no need to speak. The introduction of a real corpse—procured from a person who supplied the Parisian anatomists—involved no real danger, while it heightened the mystery and kept the prophet alive in the gossip of the town and in the thoughts of the noodles with whom he had conferred.

I divided the remainder of the summer and autumn between Switzerland and Italy.

As the well-worn phrase goes, I was a sadder if not a wiser man. A great deal of the horrible impression left upon my mind was due, of course, to the mere action of nerves and brain. But serious feelings of another and deeper kind remained. My after life was ultimately formed by the shock I had then received. Those impressions led me—but not till after many years—to happier though not less serious thoughts; and I have deep reason to be thankful to the all-merciful Ruler of events, for an early and terrible lesson in the ways of sin.

CARMILLA

PROLOGUE

UPON a paper attached to the Narrative which follows, Doctor Hesselius has written a rather elaborate note, which he accompanies with a reference to his Essay on the strange subject which the MS illuminates.

This mysterious subject he treats, in that Essay, with his usual learning and acumen, and with remarkable directness and condensation. It will form but one volume of the series of that extraordinary man's collected papers.

As I publish the case, in these volumes, simply to interest the 'laity', I shall forestall the intelligent lady, who relates it, in nothing; and, after due consideration, I have determined, therefore, to abstain from presenting any *précis** of the learned Doctor's reasoning, or extract from his statement on a subject which he describes as 'involving, not improbably, some of the profoundest arcana of our dual existence, and its intermediates'.*

I was anxious, on discovering this paper, to re-open the correspondence commenced by Doctor Hesselius, so many years before, with a person so clever and careful as his informant seems to have been. Much to my regret, however, I found that she had died in the interval.

She, probably, could have added little to the Narrative which she communicates in the following pages, with, so far as I can pronounce, such a conscientious particularity.

CHAPTER I

AN EARLY FRIGHT

In Styria,* we, though by no means magnificent people, inhabit a castle, or schloss. A small income, in that part of the world, goes a great way. Eight or nine hundred a year does wonders. Scantily enough ours would have answered among wealthy people at home. My father is English, and I bear an English name, although I never saw England. But here, in this lonely and primitive place, where everything is so marvellously cheap, I really don't see how ever so much more money would at all materially add to our comforts, or even luxuries.

My father was in the Austrian service, and retired upon a pension and his patrimony, and purchased this feudal residence, and the small estate on which it stands, a bargain.

Nothing can be more picturesque or solitary. It stands on a slight eminence in a forest. The road, very old and narrow, passes in front of its drawbridge, never raised in my time, and its moat, stocked with perch, and sailed over by many swans, and floating on its surface white fleets of water-lilies.

Over all this the schloss shows its many-windowed front; its towers, and its Gothic chapel.

The forest opens in an irregular and very picturesque glade before its gate, and at the right a steep Gothic bridge carries the road over a stream that winds in deep shadow through the wood.

I have said that this is a very lonely place. Judge whether I say truth. Looking from the hall door towards the road, the forest in which our castle stands extends fifteen miles to the right, and twelve to the left. The nearest inhabited village is about seven of your English miles to the left. The nearest inhabited schloss of any historic associations, is that of old General Spielsdorf, nearly twenty miles away to the right.

I have said 'the nearest *inhabited* village', because there is, only three miles westward, that is to say in the direction of General Spielsdorf's schloss, a ruined village, with its quaint little church, now roofless, in the aisle of which are the mouldering tombs of the proud family of Karnstein, now extinct, who once owned the equally desolate château which, in the thick of the forest, overlooks the silent ruins of the town.

Respecting the cause of the desertion of this striking and melancholy spot, there is a legend which I shall relate to you another time.

I must tell you now, how very small is the party who constitute the inhabitants of our castle. I don't include servants, or those dependants who occupy rooms in the buildings attached to the schloss. Listen, and wonder! My father, who is the kindest man on earth, but growing old; and I, at the date of my story, only nineteen. Eight years have passed since then. I and my father constituted the family at the schloss. My mother, a Styrian lady, died in my infancy, but I had a good-natured governess, who had been with me from, I might almost say, my infancy. I could not remember the time when her fat, benignant face was not a familiar picture in my memory. This was Madame Perrodon, a native of Berne, whose care and good nature in part supplied to me the loss of my mother, whom I do not even remember, so early I lost her. She made a third at our little dinner party. There was a fourth, Mademoiselle De Lafontaine, a lady such as you term, I believe, a 'finishing governess'. She spoke French and German, Madame Perrodon French and broken English, to which my father and I added English, which, partly to prevent its becoming a lost language among us, and partly from patriotic motives, we spoke every day. The consequence was a Babel, at which strangers used to laugh, and which I shall make no attempt to reproduce in this narrative. And there were two or three young lady friends besides, pretty nearly of my own age, who were occasional visitors, for longer or shorter terms; and these visits I sometimes returned.

These were our regular social resources; but of course there were chance visits from 'neighbours' of only five or six leagues distance. My life was, notwithstanding, rather a solitary one, I can assure you.

My gouvernantes had just so much control over me as you might conjecture such sage persons would have in the case of a rather spoiled girl, whose only parent allowed her pretty nearly her own way in everything.

The first occurrence in my existence, which produced a terrible impression upon my mind, which, in fact, never has been effaced, was one of the very earliest incidents of my life which I can recollect. Some people will think it so trifling that it should not be recorded here. You will see, however, by-and-by, why I mention it. The nursery, as it was called, though I had it all to myself, was a large room in the upper storey of the castle, with a steep oak roof. I can't have been more than six years old, when one night I awoke, and looking round the room from my bed, failed to see the nursery-maid. Neither was my nurse there; and I thought myself alone. I was not frightened, for I was one of those happy children who are studiously kept in ignorance of ghost stories, of fairy tales, and of all such lore as makes us cover up our heads when the door creaks suddenly, or the flicker of an expiring candle makes the shadow of a bed-post dance upon the wall, nearer to our faces. I was vexed and insulted at finding myself, as I conceived, neglected, and I began to whimper, preparatory to a hearty bout of roaring; when to my surprise, I saw a solemn, but very pretty face looking at me from the side of the bed. It was that of a young lady who was kneeling, with her hands under the coverlet. I looked at her with a kind of pleased wonder, and ceased whimpering. She caressed me with her hands, and lay down beside me on the bed, and drew me towards her, smiling; I felt immediately delightfully soothed, and fell asleep again. I was wakened by a sensation as if two needles ran into my breast very deep at the same moment, and I cried loudly. The lady started back, with her eyes fixed on me, and then slipped down upon the floor, and, as I thought, hid herself under the bed.

I was now for the first time frightened, and I yelled with all my might and main. Nurse, nursery-maid, housekeeper, all came running in, and hearing my story, they made light of it, soothing me all they could meanwhile. But, child as I was, I could perceive that their faces were pale with an unwonted look of anxiety, and I saw them look under the bed, and about the room, and peep under tables and pluck open cupboards;

and the housekeeper whispered to the nurse: 'Lay your hand along that hollow in the bed; some one *did* lie there, so sure as you did not; the place is still warm.'

I remember the nursery-maid petting me, and all three examining my chest, where I told them I felt the puncture, and pronouncing that there was no sign visible that any such thing had happened to me.

The housekeeper and the two other servants who were in charge of the nursery, remained sitting up all night; and from that time a servant always sat up in the nursery until I was about fourteen.

I was very nervous for a long time after this. A doctor was called in; he was pallid and elderly. How well I remember his long saturnine face, slightly pitted with small-pox, and his chestnut wig. For a good while, every second day, he came and gave me medicine, which of course I hated.

The morning after I saw this apparition I was in a state of terror, and could not bear to be left alone, daylight though it was, for a moment.

I remember my father coming up and standing at the bedside, and talking cheerfully, and asking the nurse a number of questions, and laughing very heartily at one of the answers; and patting me on the shoulder, and kissing me, and telling me not to be frightened, that it was nothing but a dream and could not hurt me.

But I was not comforted, for I knew the visit of the strange woman was *not* a dream; and I was *awfully* frightened.

I was a little consoled by the nursery-maid's assuring me that it was she who had come and looked at me, and lain down beside me in the bed, and that I must have been half-dreaming not to have known her face. But this, though supported by the nurse, did not quite satisfy me.

I remember, in the course of that day, a venerable old man, in a black cassock,* coming into the room with the nurse and housekeeper, and talking a little to them, and very kindly to me; his face was very sweet and gentle, and he told me they were going to pray, and joined my hands together, and desired me to say, softly, while they were praying, 'Lord hear all good prayers for us, for Jesus' sake.' I think these were the very words, for I often repeated them to myself, and my nurse used for years to make me say them in my prayers.

I remember so well the thoughtful sweet face of that white-haired old man, in his black cassock, as he stood in that rude, lofty, brown room, with the clumsy furniture of a fashion three hundred years old about him, and the scanty light entering its shadowy atmosphere through the small lattice. He kneeled, and the three women with him, and he prayed aloud with an earnest quavering voice for, what appeared to me, a long time. I forget all my life preceding that event, and for some time after it is all obscure also, but the scenes I have just described stand out vivid as the isolated pictures of the phantasmagoria* surrounded by darkness.

CHAPTER II

A GUEST

I am now going to tell you something so strange that it will require all your faith in my veracity to believe my story. It is not only true, nevertheless, but truth of which I have been an eye-witness.

It was a sweet summer evening, and my father asked me, as he sometimes did, to take a little ramble with him along that beautiful forest vista which I have mentioned as lying in front of the schloss.

'General Spielsdorf cannot come to us so soon as I had hoped,' said my father, as we pursued our walk.

He was to have paid us a visit of some weeks, and we had expected his arrival next day. He was to have brought with him a young lady, his niece and ward, Mademoiselle Rhein-feldt, whom I had never seen, but whom I had heard described as a very charming girl, and in whose society I had promised myself many happy days. I was more disappointed than a young lady living in a town, or a bustling neighbourhood can possibly imagine. This visit, and the new acquaintance it promised, had furnished my day dream for many weeks.

'And how soon does he come?' I asked.

'Not till autumn. Not for two months, I dare say,' he answered. 'And I am very glad now, dear, that you never knew Mademoiselle Rheinfeldt.'

'And why?' I asked, both mortified and curious.

'Because the poor young lady is dead,' he replied. 'I quite forgot I had not told you, but you were not in the room when I received the General's letter this evening.'

I was very much shocked. General Spielsdorf had mentioned in his first letter, six or seven weeks before, that she was not so well as he would wish her, but there was nothing to suggest the remotest suspicion of danger.

'Here is the General's letter,' he said, handing it to me. 'I am afraid he is in great affliction; the letter appears to me to have been written very nearly in distraction.'

We sat down on a rude bench, under a group of magnificent lime-trees. The sun was setting with all its melancholy splendour behind the sylvan horizon, and the stream that flows beside our home, and passes under the steep old bridge I have mentioned, wound through many a group of noble trees, almost at our feet, reflecting in its current the fading crimson of the sky. General Spieldorf's letter was so extraordinary, so vehement, and in some places so self-contradictory, that I read it twice over—the second time aloud to my father—and was still unable to account for it, except by supposing that grief had unsettled his mind.

It said,

'I have lost my darling daughter, for as such I loved her. During the last days of dear Bertha's illness I was not able to write to you. Before then I had no idea of her danger. I have lost her, and now learn *all*, too late. She died in the peace of innocence, and in the glorious hope of a blessed futurity. The fiend who betrayed our infatuated hospitality has done it all. I thought I was receiving into my house innocence, gaiety, a charming companion for my lost Bertha. Heavens! what a fool have I been! I thank God my child died without a suspicion of the cause of her sufferings. She is gone without so much as conjecturing the nature of her illness, and the accursed passion of the agent of all this misery. I devote my remaining days to tracking and extinguishing a monster. I am told I may hope to accomplish my righteous and merciful purpose. At present there is scarcely a gleam of light to guide me. I curse my conceited incredulity, my despicable affectation of superiority, my blindness, my obstinacy—all—too late. I cannot write or talk collectedly now. I am distracted. So soon as I shall have a little recovered, I mean to devote myself for a time to enquiry, which may possibly lead me as far as Vienna. Some time in the autumn, two months hence, or earlier if I live, I will see you—that is, if you permit me; I will then tell you all that I scarce dare put upon paper now. Farewell. Pray for me, dear friend.'

In these terms ended this strange letter. Though I had never seen Bertha Rheinfeldt my eyes filled with tears at the sudden intelligence; I was startled, as well as profoundly disappointed.

The sun had now set, and it was twilight by the time I had returned the General's letter to my father.

It was a soft clear evening, and we loitered, speculating upon the possible meanings of the violent and incoherent sentences which I had just been reading. We had nearly a mile to walk before reaching the road that passes the schloss in front, and by that time the moon was shining brilliantly. At the drawbridge we met Madame Perrodon and Mademoiselle De Lafontaine, who had come out, without their bonnets, to enjoy the exquisite moonlight.

We heard their voices gabbling in animated dialogue as we approached. We joined them at the drawbridge, and turned about to admire with them the beautiful scene.

The glade through which we had just walked lay before us. At our left the narrow road wound away under clumps of lordly trees, and was lost to sight amid the thickening forest. At the right the same road crosses the steep and picturesque bridge, near which stands a ruined tower which once guarded that pass; and beyond the bridge an abrupt eminence rises, covered with trees, and showing in the shadows some grey ivy-clustered rocks.

Over the sward and low grounds a thin film of mist was

stealing, like smoke, marking the distances with a transparent veil; and here and there we could see the river faintly flashing in the moonlight.

No softer, sweeter scene could be imagined. The news I had just heard made it melancholy; but nothing could disturb its character of profound serenity, and the enchanted glory and vagueness of the prospect.

My father, who enjoyed the picturesque, and I, stood looking in silence over the expanse beneath us. The two good governesses, standing a little way behind us, discoursed upon the scene, and were eloquent upon the moon.

Madame Perrodon was fat, middle-aged, and romantic, and talked and sighed poetically. Mademoiselle De Lafontaine— in right of her father, who was a German, assumed to be psychological, metaphysical, and something of a mystic—now declared that when the moon shone with a light so intense it was well known that it indicated a special spiritual activity. The effect of the full moon in such a state of brilliancy was manifold. It acted on dreams, it acted on lunacy, it acted on nervous people; it had marvellous physical influences connected with life. Mademoiselle related that her cousin, who was mate of a merchant ship, having taken a nap on deck on such a night, lying on his back, with his face full in the light of the moon, had wakened, after a dream of an old woman clawing him by the cheek, with his features horribly drawn to one side; and his countenance had never quite recovered its equilibrium.

'The moon, this night,' she said, 'is full of odylic and magnetic influence*—and see, when you look behind you at the front of the schloss, how all its windows flash and twinkle with that silvery splendour, as if unseen hands had lighted up the rooms to receive fairy guests.'

There are indolent states of the spirits in which, indisposed to talk ourselves, the talk of others is pleasant to our listless ears; and I gazed on, pleased with the tinkle of the ladies' conversation.

'I have got into one of my moping moods to-night,' said my father, after a silence, and quoting Shakespeare, whom, by way of keeping up our English, he used to read aloud, he said:

' "In truth I know not why I am so sad:
It wearies me; you say it wearies you;
But how I got it—came by it."*

'I forget the rest. But I feel as if some great misfortune were hanging over us. I suppose the poor General's afflicted letter has had something to do with it.'

At this moment the unwonted sound of carriage wheels and many hoofs upon the road, arrested our attention.

They seemed to be approaching from the high ground overlooking the bridge, and very soon the equipage emerged from that point. Two horsemen first crossed the bridge, then came a carriage drawn by four horses, and two men rode behind.

It seemed to be the travelling carriage of a person of rank; and we were all immediately absorbed in watching that very unusual spectacle. It became, in a few moments, greatly more interesting, for just as the carriage had passed the summit of the steep bridge, one of the leaders, taking fright, communicated his panic to the rest, and after a plunge or two, the whole team broke into a wild gallop together, and dashing between the horsemen who rode in front, came thundering along the road towards us with the speed of a hurricane.

The excitement of the scene was made more painful by the clear, long-drawn screams of a female voice from the carriage window.

We all advanced in curiosity and horror; my father in silence, the rest with various ejaculations of terror.

Our suspense did not last long. Just before you reach the castle drawbridge, on the route they were coming, there stands by the roadside a magnificent lime-tree, on the other side stands an ancient stone cross, at sight of which the horses, now going at a pace that was perfectly frightful, swerved so as to bring the wheel over the projecting roots of the tree.

I knew what was coming. I covered my eyes, unable to see it out, and turned my head away; at the same moment I heard a cry from my lady-friends, who had gone on a little.

Curiosity opened my eyes, and I saw a scene of utter confusion. Two of the horses were on the ground, the carriage lay upon its side with two wheels in the air; the men were busy removing the traces, and a lady, with a commanding air and figure, had got out, and stood with clasped hands, raising the handkerchief that was in them every now and then to her eyes. Through the carriage door was now lifted a young lady, who appeared to be lifeless. My dear old father was already beside the elder lady, with his hat in his hand, evidently tendering his aid and the resources of his schloss. The lady did not appear to hear him, or to have eyes for anything but the slender girl who was being placed against the slope of the bank.

I approached; the young lady was apparently stunned, but she was certainly not dead. My father, who piqued himself on being something of a physician, had just had his fingers to her wrist and assured the lady, who declared herself her mother, that her pulse, though faint and irregular, was undoubtedly still distinguishable. The lady clasped her hands and looked upward, as if in a momentary transport of gratitude; but immediately she broke out again in that theatrical way which is, I believe, natural to some people.

She was what is called a fine-looking woman for her time of life, and must have been handsome; she was tall, but not thin, and dressed in black velvet, and looked rather pale, but with a pround and commanding countenance, though now agitated strangely.

'Was ever being so born to calamity?' I heard her say, with clasped hands, as I came up. 'Here am I, on a journey of life and death, in prosecuting which to lose an hour is possibly to lose all. My child will not have recovered sufficiently to resume her route for who can say how long. I must leave her; I cannot, dare not, delay. How far on, sir, can you tell, is the nearest village? I must leave her there; and shall not see my darling, or even hear of her till my return, three months hence.'

I plucked my father by the coat, and whispered earnestly in his ear: 'Oh! papa, pray ask her to let her stay with us—it would be so delightful. Do, pray.'

'If Madame will entrust her child to the care of my daughter, and of her good gouvernante, Madame Perrodon, and permit her to remain as our guest, under my charge, until her return, it will confer a distinction and an obligation upon us, and we shall treat her with all the care and devotion which so sacred a trust deserves.'

'I cannot do that, sir, it would be to task your kindness and chivalry too cruelly,' said the lady, distractedly.

'It would, on the contrary, be to confer on us a very great kindness at the moment when we most need it. My daughter has just been disappointed by a cruel misfortune, in a visit from which she had long anticipated a great deal of happiness. If you confide this young lady to our care it will be her best consolation. The nearest village on your route is distant, and affords no such inn as you could think of placing your daughter at; you cannot allow her to continue her journey for any considerable distance without danger. If, as you say, you cannot suspend your journey, you must part with her to-night, and nowhere could you do so with more honest assurances of care and tenderness than here.'

There was something in this lady's air and appearance so distinguished, and even imposing, and in her manner so engaging, as to impress one, quite apart from the dignity of her equipage, with a conviction that she was a person of consequence.

By this time the carriage was replaced in its upright position, and the horses, quite tractable, in the traces* again.

The lady threw on her daughter a glance which I fancied was not quite so affectionate as one might have anticipated from the beginning of the scene; then she beckoned slightly to my father, and withdrew two or three steps with him out of hearing; and talked to him with a fixed and stern countenance, not at all like that with which she had hitherto spoken.

I was filled with wonder that my father did not seem to perceive the change, and also unspeakably curious to learn what it could be that she was speaking, almost in his ear, with so much earnestness and rapidity.

Two or three minutes at most I think she remained thus employed, then she turned, and a few steps brought her to where her daughter lay, supported by Madame Perrodon. She knelt beside her for a moment and whispered, as Madame supposed, a little benediction in her ear; then hastily kissing her she stepped into her carriage, the door was closed, the footmen in stately liveries jumped up behind, the outriders spurred on, the postillions cracked their whips, the horses plunged and broke suddenly into a furious canter that threatened soon again to become a gallop, and the carriage whirled away, followed at the same rapid pace by the two horsemen in the rear.

CHAPTER III

WE COMPARE NOTES

We followed the *cortège**** with our eyes until it was swiftly lost to sight in the misty wood; and the very sound of the hoofs and the wheels died away in the silent night air.

Nothing remained to assure us that the adventure had not been an illusion of a moment but the young lady, who just at that moment opened her eyes. I could not see, for her face was turned from me, but she raised her head, evidently looking about her, and I heard a very sweet voice ask complainingly, 'Where is mamma?'

Our good Madame Perrodon answered tenderly, and added some comfortable assurances.

I then heard her ask:

'Where am I? What is this place?' and after that she said, 'I don't see the carriage; and Matska,* where is she?'

Madame answered all her questions in so far as she understood them; and gradually the young lady remembered how the misadventure came about, and was glad to hear that no one in, or in attendance on, the carriage was hurt; and on learning that her mamma had left her here, till her return in about three months, she wept.

I was going to add my consolations to those of Madame Perrodon when Mademoiselle De Lafontaine placed her hand upon my arm, saying:

'Don't approach, one at a time is as much as she can at

present converse with; a very little excitement would possibly overpower her now.'

As soon as she is comfortably in bed, I thought, I will run up to her room and see her.

My father in the meantime had sent a servant on horseback for the physician, who lived about two leagues away; and a bed-room was being prepared for the young lady's reception.

The stranger now rose, and leaning on Madame's arm, walked slowly over the drawbridge and into the castle gate.

In the hall, servants waited to receive her, and she was conducted forthwith to her room.

The room we usually sat in as our drawing-room is long, having four windows, that looked over the moat and draw-bridge, upon the forest scene I have just described.

It is furnished in old carved oak, with large carved cabinets, and the chairs are cushioned with crimson Utrecht velvet. The walls are covered with tapestry, and surrounded with great gold frames, the figures being as large as life, in ancient and very curious costume, and the subjects represented are hunt-ing, hawking, and generally festive. It is not too stately to be extremely comfortable; and here we had our tea, for with his usual patriotic leanings my father insisted that the national beverage should make its appearance regularly with our coffee and chocolate.

We sat here this night, and with candles lighted, were talking over the adventure of the evening.

Madame Perrodon and Mademoiselle De Lafontaine were both of our party. The young stranger had hardly lain down in her bed when she sank into a deep sleep; and those ladies had left her in the care of a servant.

'How do you like our guest?' I asked, as soon as Madame entered. 'Tell me all about her.'

'I like her extremely,' answered Madame, 'she is, I almost think, the prettiest creature I ever saw; about your age, and so gentle and nice.'

'She is absolutely beautiful,' threw in Mademoiselle, who had peeped for a moment into the stranger's room.

'And such a sweet voice!' added Madame Perrodon.

'Did you remark a woman in the carriage, after it was set

up again, who did not get out,' inquired Mademoiselle, 'but only looked from the window?'

'No, we had not seen her.'

Then she described a hideous black woman, with a sort of coloured turban on her head, who was gazing all the time from the carriage window, nodding and grinning derisively towards the ladies, with gleaming eyes and large white eye-balls, and her teeth set as if in fury.

'Did you remark what an ill-looking pack of men the servants were?' asked Madame.

'Yes,' said my father, who had just come in, 'ugly, hang-dog looking fellows, as ever I beheld in my life. I hope they mayn't rob the poor lady in the forest. They are clever rogues, however; they got everything to rights in a minute.'

'I dare say they are worn out with too long travelling,' said Madame. 'Besides looking wicked, their faces were so strangely lean, and dark, and sullen. I am very curious, I own; but I dare say the young lady will tell us all about it to-morrow, if she is sufficiently recovered.'

'I don't think she will,' said my father, with a mysterious smile, and a little nod of his head, as if he knew more about it than he cared to tell us.

This made me all the more inquisitive as to what had passed between him and the lady in the black velvet, in the brief but earnest interview that had immediately preceded her departure.

We were scarcely alone, when I entreated him to tell me. He did not need much pressing.

'There is no particular reason why I should not tell you. She expressed a reluctance to trouble us with the care of her daughter, saying she was in delicate health, and nervous, but not subject to any kind of seizure—she volunteered that—nor to any illusion; being, in fact, perfectly sane.'

'How very odd to say all that!' I interpolated. 'It was so unnecessary.'

'At all events it *was* said,' he laughed, 'and as you wish to know all that passed, which was indeed very little, I tell you. She then said, "I am making a long journey of *vital* import-ance"—she emphasized the word—"rapid and secret; I shall return for my child in three months; in the meantime, she will be silent as to who we are, whence we come, and whither we are travelling." That is all she said. She spoke very pure French. When she said the word "secret", she paused for a few seconds, looking sternly, her eyes fixed on mine. I fancy she makes a great point of that. You saw how quickly she was gone. I hope I have not done a very foolish thing, in taking charge of the young lady.'

For my part, I was delighted. I was longing to see and talk to her; and only waiting till the doctor should give me leave. You, who live in towns, can have no idea how great an event the introduction of a new friend is, in such a solitude as surrounded us.

The doctor did not arrive till nearly one o'clock; but I could no more have gone to my bed and slept, than I could have overtaken, on foot, the carriage in which the princess in black velvet had driven away.

When the physician came down to the drawing-room, it was to report very favourably upon his patient. She was now sitting up, her pulse quite regular, apparently perfectly well. She had sustained no injury, and the little shock to her nerves had passed away quite harmlessly. There could be no harm certainly in my seeing her, if we both wished it; and, with this permission, I sent, forthwith, to know whether she would allow me to visit her for a few minutes in her room.

The servant returned immediately to say that she desired nothing more.

You may be sure I was not long in availing myself of this permission.

Our visitor lay in one of the handsomest rooms in the schloss. It was, perhaps, a little stately. There was a sombre piece of tapestry opposite the foot of the bed, representing Cleopatra with the asp to her bosom;* and other solemn classic scenes were displayed, a little faded, upon the other walls. But there was gold carving, and rich and varied colour enough in the other decorations of the room, to more than redeem the gloom of the old tapestry.

There were candles at the bed-side. She was sitting up; her slender pretty figure enveloped in the soft silk dressing gown, embroidered with flowers, and lined with thick quilted silk, which her mother had thrown over her feet as she lay upon the ground.

What was it that, as I reached the bed-side and had just begun my little greeting, struck me dumb in a moment, and made me recoil a step or two from before her? I will tell you.

I saw the very face which had visited me in my childhood at night, which remained so fixed in my memory, and on which I had for so many years so often ruminated with horror, when no one suspected of what I was thinking.

It was pretty, even beautiful; and when I first beheld it, wore the same melancholy expression.

But this almost instantly lighted into a strange fixed smile of recognition.

There was a silence of fully a minute, and then at length *she* spoke; *I* could not.

'How wonderful!' she exclaimed, 'Twelve years ago, I saw your face in a dream, and it has haunted me ever since.'

'Wonderful indeed!' I repeated, overcoming with an effort the horror that had for a time suspended my utterances. 'Twelve years ago, in vision or reality, *I* certainly saw you. I could not forget your face. It has remained before my eyes ever since.'

Her smile had softened. Whatever I had fancied strange in it, was gone, and it and her dimpling cheeks were now delightfully pretty and intelligent.

I felt reassured, and continued more in the vein which hospitality indicated, to bid her welcome, and to tell her how much pleasure her accidental arrival had given us all, and especially what a happiness it was to me.

I took her hand as I spoke. I was a little shy, as lonely people are, but the situation made me eloquent, and even bold. She pressed my hand, she laid hers upon it, and her eyes glowed, as, looking hastily into mine, she smiled again, and blushed.

She answered my welcome very prettily. I sat down beside her, still wondering; and she said:

'I must tell you my vision about you; it is so very strange that you and I should have had, each of the other so vivid a dream, that each should have seen, I you and you me, looking as we do now, when of course we both were mere children. I was a child, about six years old, and I awoke from a confused and troubled dream, and found myself in a room, unlike my nursery, wainscoted clumsily in some dark wood, and with cupboards and bedsteads, and chairs, and benches placed about it. The beds were, I thought, all empty, and the room itself without anyone but myself in it; and I, after looking about me for some time, and admiring especially an iron candlestick, with two branches, which I should certainly know again, crept under one of the beds to reach the window; but as I got from under the bed, I heard some one crying; and looking up, while I was still upon my knees, I saw *you*—most assuredly you—as I see you now; a beautiful young lady, with golden hair and large blue eyes, and lips—your lips—you, as you are here. Your looks won me; I climbed on the bed and put my arms about you, and I think we both fell asleep. I was aroused by a scream; you were sitting up screaming. I was frightened, and slipped down upon the ground, and, it seemed to me, lost consciousness for a moment; and when I came to myself, I was again in my nursery at home. Your face I have never forgotten since. I could not be misled by mere resemblance. You *are* the lady whom I then saw.'

It was now my turn to relate my corresponding vision, which I did, to the undisguised wonder of my new acquaintance.

'I don't know which should be most afraid of the other,' she said, again smiling—'If you were less pretty I think I should be very much afraid of you, but being as you are, and you and I both so young, I feel only that I have made your acquaintance twelve years ago, and have already a right to your intimacy; at all events it does seem as if we were destined, from our earliest childhood, to be friends. I wonder whether you feel as strangely drawn towards me as I do to you; I have never had a friend—shall I find one now?' She sighed, and her fine dark eyes gazed passionately on me.

Now the truth is, I felt rather unaccountably towards the beautiful stranger. I did feel, as she said, 'drawn towards her', but there was also something of repulsion. In this ambiguous feeling, however, the sense of attraction immensely prevailed. She interested and won me; she was so beautiful and so indescribably engaging.

I perceived now something of langour and exhaustion stealing over her, and hastened to bid her good night.

'The doctor thinks', I added, 'that you ought to have a maid to sit up with you to-night; one of ours is waiting, and you will find her a very useful and quiet creature.'

'How kind of you, but I could not sleep, I never could with an attendant in the room. I shan't require any assistance—and, shall I confess my weakness, I am haunted with a terror of robbers. Our house was robbed once, and two servants murdered, so I always lock my door. It has become a habit—and you look so kind I know you will forgive me. I see there is a key in the lock.'

She held me close in her pretty arms for a moment and whispered in my ear, 'Good night, darling, it is very hard to part with you, but good-night; to-morrow, but not early, I shall see you again.'

She sank back on the pillow with a sigh, and her fine eyes followed me with a fond and melancholy gaze, and she murmured again 'Good-night, dear friend.'

Young people like, and even love, on impulse. I was flattered by the evident, though as yet undeserved, fondness she showed me. I liked the confidence with which she at once received me. She was determined that we should be very near friends.

Next day came and we met again. I was delighted with my companion; that is to say, in many respects.

Her looks lost nothing in daylight—she was certainly the most beautiful creature I had ever seen, and the unpleasant remembrance of the face presented in my early dream, had lost the effect of the first unexpected recognition.

She confessed that she had experienced a similar shock on seeing me, and precisely the same faint antipathy that had mingled with my admiration of her. We now laughed together over our momentary horrors.

CHAPTER IV

I told you that I was charmed with her in most particulars.
There were some that did not please me so well.

She was above the middle height of women. I shall begin by
describing her. She was slender, and wonderfully graceful.
Except that her movements were languid—*very* languid—
indeed, there was nothing in her appearance to indicate an
invalid. Her complexion was rich and brilliant; her features
were small and beautifully formed; her eyes large, dark, and
lustrous; her hair was quite wonderful, I never saw hair so
magnificently thick and long when it was down about her
shoulders; I have often placed my hands under it, and laughed
with wonder at its weight. It was exquisitely fine and soft, and
in colour a rich very dark brown, with something of gold. I
loved to let it down, tumbling with its own weight, as, in her
room, she lay back in her chair talking in her sweet low voice,
I used to fold and braid it, and spread it out and play with it.
Heavens! If I had but known all!

I said there were particulars which did not please me. I
have told you that her confidence won me the first night I saw
her; but I found that she exercised with respect to herself, her
mother, her history, everything in fact connected with her life,
plans, and people, an ever wakeful reserve. I dare say I was
unreasonable, perhaps I was wrong; I dare say I ought to have
respected the solemn injunction laid upon my father by the
stately lady in black velvet. But curiosity is a restless and
unscrupulous passion, and no one girl can endure, with
patience, that her's should be baffled by another. What harm
could it do anyone to tell me what I so ardently desired to
know? Had she no trust in my good sense or honour? Why
would she not believe me when I assured her, so solemnly,
that I would not divulge one syllable of what she told me to
any mortal breathing?

There was a coldness, it seemed to me, beyond her years, in

her smiling melancholy persistent refusal to afford me the least ray of light.

I cannot say we quarrelled upon this point, for she would not quarrel upon any. It was, of course, very unfair of me to press her, very ill-bred, but I really could not help it; and I might just as well have let it alone.

What she did tell me amounted, in my unconscionable estimation—to nothing.

It was all summed up in three very vague disclosures:

First.—Her name was Carmilla.

Second.—Her family was very ancient and noble.

Third.—Her home lay in the direction of the west.

She would not tell me the name of her family, nor their armorial bearings, nor the name of their estate, nor even that of the country they lived in.

You are not to suppose that I worried her incessantly on these subjects. I watched for opportunity, and rather insinuated than urged my inquiries. Once or twice, indeed, I did attack her more directly. But no matter what my tactics, utter failure was invariably the result. Reproaches and caresses were all lost upon her. But I must add this, that her evasion was conducted with so pretty a melancholy and deprecation, with so many, and even passionate declarations of her liking for me, and trust in my honour, and with so many promises that I should at last know all, that I could not find it in my heart long to be offended with her.

She used to place her pretty arms about my neck, draw me to her, and laying her cheek to mine, murmur with her lips near my ear, 'Dearest, your little heart is wounded; think me not cruel because I obey the irresistible law of my strength and weakness; if your dear heart is wounded, my wild heart bleeds with yours. In the rapture of my enormous humiliation I live in your warm life, and you shall die—die, sweetly die— into mine. I cannot help it; as I draw near to you, you, in your turn, will draw near to others, and learn the rapture of that cruelty, which yet is love; so, for a while, seek to know no more of me and mine, but trust me with all your loving spirit.'

And when she had spoken such a rhapsody, she would press

me more closely in her trembling embrace, and her lips in soft kisses gently glow upon my cheek.

Her agitations and her language were unintelligible to me.

From these foolish embraces, which were not of very frequent occurrence, I must allow, I used to wish to extricate myself; but my energies seemed to fail me. Her murmured words sounded like a lullaby in my ear, and soothed my resistance into a trance, from which I only seemed to recover myself when she withdrew her arms.

In these mysterious moods I did not like her. I experienced a strange tumultuous excitement that was pleasurable, ever and anon, mingled with a vague sense of fear and disgust. I had no distinct thoughts about her while such scenes lasted, but I was conscious of a love growing into adoration, and also of abhorrence. This I know is paradox, but I can make no other attempt to explain the feeling.

I now write, after an interval of more than ten years, with a trembling hand, with a confused and horrible recollection of certain occurrences and situations, in the ordeal through which I was unconsciously passing; though with a vivid and very sharp remembrance of the main current of my story. But, I suspect, in all lives there are certain emotional scenes, those in which our passions have been most wildly and terribly roused, that are of all others the most vaguely and dimly remembered.

Sometimes after an hour of apathy, my strange and beautiful companion would take my hand and hold it with a fond pressure, renewed again and again; blushing softly, gazing in my face with languid and burning eyes, and breathing so fast that her dress rose and fell with the tumultuous respiration. It was like the ardour of a lover; it embarrassed me; it was hateful and yet overpowering; and with gloating eyes she drew me to her, and her hot lips travelled along my cheek in kisses; and she would whisper, almost in sobs, 'You are mine, you *shall* be mine, you and I are one for ever.' Then she has thrown herself back in her chair, with her small hands over her eyes, leaving me trembling.

'Are we related,' I used to ask; 'what can you mean by all this? I remind you perhaps of some one whom you love; but you must not, I hate it; I don't know you—I don't know myself when you look so and talk so.'

She used to sigh at my vehemence, then turn away and drop my hand.

Respecting these very extraordinary manifestations I strove in vain to form any satisfactory theory—I could not refer them to affectation or trick. It was unmistakably the momentary breaking out of suppressed instinct and emotion. Was she, notwithstanding her mother's volunteered denial, subject to brief visitations of insanity; or was there here a disguise and a romance? I had read in old story books of such things. What if a boyish lover had found his way into the house, and sought to prosecute his suit in masquerade, with the assistance of a clever old adventuress? But there were many things against this hypothesis, highly interesting as it was to my vanity.

I could boast of no little attentions such as masculine gallantry delights to offer. Between these passionate moments there were long intervals of common-place, of gaiety, of brooding melancholy, during which, except that I detected her eyes so full of melancholy fire, following me, at times I might have been as nothing to her. Except in these brief periods of mysterious excitement her ways were girlish; and there was always a langour about her, quite incompatible with a masculine system in a state of health.

In some respects her habits were odd. Perhaps not so singular in the opinion of a town lady like you, as they appeared to us rustic people. She used to come down very late, generally not till one o'clock. She would then take a cup of chocolate, but eat nothing; we then went out for a walk, which was a mere saunter, and she seemed, almost immediately, exhausted, and either returned to the schloss or sat on one of the benches that were placed, here and there, among the trees. This was a bodily langour in which her mind did not sympathize. She was always an animated talker, and very intelligent.

She sometimes alluded for a moment to her own home, or mentioned an adventure or situation, or an early recollection, which indicated a people of strange manners, and described customs of which we knew nothing. I gathered from these chance hints that her native country was much more remote than I had at first fancied.

As we sat thus one afternoon under the trees a funeral passed us by. It was that of a pretty young girl, whom I had often seen, the daughter of one of the rangers of the forest. The poor man was walking behind the coffin of his darling; she was his only child, and he looked quite heartbroken. Peasants walking two-and-two came behind, they were singing a funeral hymn.

I rose to mark my respect as they passed, and joined in the hymn they were very sweetly singing.

My companion shook me a little roughly, and I turned surprised.

She said brusquely, 'Don't you perceive how discordant that is?'

'I think it very sweet, on the contrary,' I answered, vexed at the interruption, and very uncomfortable, lest the people who composed the little procession should observe and resent what was passing.

I resumed, therefore, instantly, and was again interrupted. 'You pierce my ears,' said Carmilla, almost angrily, and stopping her ears with her tiny fingers. 'Besides, how can you tell that your religion and mine are the same; your forms wound me, and I hate funerals. What a fuss! Why *you* must die—*everyone* must die; and all are happier when they do. Come home.'

'My father has gone on with the clergyman to the church-yard. I thought you knew she was to be buried to day.'

'*She*? I don't trouble my head about peasants. I don't know who she is,' answered Carmilla, with a flash from her fine eyes.

'She is the poor girl who fancied she saw a ghost a fortnight ago, and has been dying ever since, till yesterday, when she expired.'

'Tell me nothing about ghosts. I shan't sleep to-night if you do.'

'I hope there is no plague or fever coming; all this looks very like it,' I continued. 'The swineherd's young wife died only a week ago, and she thought something seized her by the throat as she lay in her bed, and nearly strangled her. Papa says such horrible fancies do accompany some forms of fever. She was quite well the day before. She sank afterwards, and died before a week.'

'Well, *her* funeral is over, I hope, and *her* hymn sung; and our ears shan't be tortured with that discord and jargon. It has made me nervous. Sit down here, beside me; sit close; hold my hand; press it hard—hard—harder.'

We had moved a little back, and had come to another seat.

She sat down. Her face underwent a change that alarmed and even terrified me for a moment. It darkened, and became horribly livid; her teeth and hands were clenched, and she frowned and compressed her lips, while she stared down upon the ground at her feet, and trembled all over with a continued shudder as irrepressible as ague. All her energies seemed strained to suppress a fit, with which she was then breathlessly tugging; and at length a low convulsive cry of suffering broke from her, and gradually the hysteria subsided. 'There! That comes of strangling people with hymns!' she said at last. 'Hold me, hold me still. It is passing away.'

And so gradually it did; and perhaps to dissipate the sombre impression which the spectacle had left upon me, she became unusually animated and chatty; and so we got home.

This was the first time I had seen her exhibit any definable symptoms of that delicacy of health which her mother had spoken of. It was the first time, also, I had seen her exhibit anything like temper.

Both passed away like a summer cloud; and never but once afterwards did I witness on her part a momentary sign of anger. I will tell you how it happened.

She and I were looking out of one of the long drawing-room windows, when there entered the court-yard, over the draw-bridge, a figure of a wanderer whom I knew very well. He used to visit the schloss generally twice a year.

It was the figure of a hunchback, with the sharp lean features that generally accompany deformity. He wore a pointed black beard, and he was smiling from ear to ear, showing his white fangs. He was dressed in buff, black, and scarlet, and crossed with more straps and belts than I could count, from which hung all manner of things. Behind, he carried a magic-lantern, and two boxes, which I well knew, in one of which was a salamander, and in the other a mandrake. These monsters used to make my father laugh. They were compounded of parts of monkeys, parrots, squirrels, fish, and hedgehogs, dried and stitched together with great neatness and startling effect. He had a fiddle, a box of conjuring apparatus, a pair of foils and masks attached to his belt, several other mysterious cases dangling about him, and a black staff with copper ferrules in his hand. His companion was a rough spare dog, that followed at his heels, but stopped short suspiciously at the drawbridge, and in a little while began to howl dismally.

In the meantime, the mountebank, standing in the midst of the court-yard, raised his grotesque hat, and made us a very ceremonious bow, paying his compliments very volubly in execrable French, and German not much better. Then, disengaging his fiddle, he began to scrape a lively air, to which he sang with a merry discord, dancing with ludicrous airs and activity, that made me laugh, in spite of the dog's howling.

Then he advanced to the window with many smiles and salutations, and his hat in his left hand, his fiddle under his arm, and with a fluency that never took breath, he gabbled a long advertisement of all his accomplishments, and the resources of the various arts which he placed at our service, and the curiosities and entertainments which it was in his power, at our bidding, to display.

'Will your ladyships be pleased to buy an amulet against the oupire,* which is going like the wolf, I hear, through these woods,' he said, dropping his hat on the pavement. 'They are dying of it right and left, and here is a charm that never fails; only pinned to the pillow, and you may laugh in his face.'

These charms consisted of oblong slips of vellum, with cabalistic ciphers and diagrams upon them.

Carmilla instantly purchased one, and so did I.

He was looking up, and we were smiling down upon him, amused; at least, I can answer for myself. His piercing black eye, as he looked up in our faces, seemed to detect something that fixed for a moment his curiosity.

In an instant he unrolled a leather case, full of all manner of odd little steel instruments.

'See here, my lady,' he said, displaying it, and addressing me, 'I profess, among other things less useful, the art of dentistry. Plague take the dog!' he interpolated. 'Silence, beast! He howls so that your ladyships can scarcely hear a word. Your noble friend, the young lady at your right, has the sharpest tooth,—long, thin, pointed, like an awl, like a needle; ha, ha! With my sharp and long sight, as I look up, I have seen it distinctly; now if it happens to hurt the young lady, and I think it must, here am I, here are my file, my punch, my nippers; I will make it round and blunt, if her ladyship pleases; no longer the tooth of a fish, but of a beautiful young lady as she is. Hey? Is the young lady displeased? Have I been too bold? Have I offended her?'

The young lady, indeed, looked very angry as she drew back from the window.

'How dares that mountebank insult us so? Where is your father? I shall demand redress from him. My father would have had the wretch tied up to the pump, and flogged with a cart-whip, and burnt to the bones with the castle brand!'

She retired from the window a step or two, and sat down, and had hardly lost sight of the offender, when her wrath subsided as suddenly as it had risen, and she gradually recovered her usual tone, and seemed to forget the little hunchback and his follies.

My father was out of spirits that evening. On coming in he told us that there had been another case very similar to the two fatal ones which had lately occurred. The sister of a young peasant on his estate, only a mile away, was very ill, had been, as she described it, attacked very nearly in the same way, and was now slowly but steadily sinking.

'All this,' said my father, 'is strictly referable to natural causes. These poor people infect one another with their superstitions, and so repeat in imagination the images of terror that have infested their neighbours.'

'But that very circumstance frightens one horribly,' said Carmilla.

'How so?' inquired my father.

'I am so afraid of fancying I see such things; I think it would be as bad as reality.'

'We are in God's hands; nothing can happen without His permission, and all will end well for those who love Him. He is our faithful creator; He has made us all, and will take care of us.'

'Creator! *Nature!*' said the young lady in answer to my gentle father. 'And this disease that invades the country is natural. Nature. All things proceed from Nature—don't they? All things in the heaven, in the earth, and under the earth, act and live as Nature ordains? I think so.'

'The doctor said he would come here to-day,' said my father, after a silence. 'I want to know what he thinks about it, and what he thinks we had better do.'

'Doctors never did me any good,' said Carmilla.

'Then you have been ill?' I asked.

'More ill than ever you were,' she answered.

'Long ago?'

'Yes, a long time. I suffered from this very illness; but I forget all but my pain and weakness, and they were not so bad as are suffered in other diseases.'

'You were very young then?'

'I dare say; let us talk no more of it. You would not wound a friend?' She looked languidly in my eyes, and passed her arm round my waist lovingly, and led me out of the room. My father was busy over some papers near the window.

'Why does your papa like to frighten us?' said the pretty girl, with a sigh and a little shudder.

'He doesn't, dear Carmilla, it is the very furthest thing from his mind.'

'Are you afraid, dearest?'

'I should be very much if I fancied there was any real danger of my being attacked as those poor people were.'

'You are afraid to die?'

'Yes, every one is.'

'But to die as lovers may—to die together, so that they may live together. Girls are caterpillars while they live in the world, to be finally butterflies when the summer comes; but in the meantime there are grubs and larvae, don't you see—each with their peculiar propensities, necessities and structure. So says Monsieur Buffon,* in his big book, in the next room.'

Later in the day the doctor came and was closeted with papa for some time. He was a skilful man, of sixty and upwards. He wore powder, and shaved his pale face as smooth as a pumpkin. He and papa emerged from the room together, and I heard papa laugh, and say as they came out:

'Well, I do wonder at a wise man like you. What do you say to hippogriffs* and dragons?'

The doctor was smiling, and made answer, shaking his head—

'Nevertheless life and death are mysterious states, and we know little of the resources of either.'

And so they walked on, and I heard no more. I did not then know what the doctor had been broaching, but I think I guess it now.

CHAPTER V

A WONDERFUL LIKENESS

This evening there arrived from Gratz the grave, dark-faced son of the picture cleaner, with a horse and cart laden with two large packing cases, having many pictures in each. It was a journey of ten leagues,* and whenever a messenger arrived at the schloss from our little capital of Gratz, we used to crowd about him in the hall, to hear the news.

This arrival created in our secluded quarters quite a sensation. The cases remained in the hall, and the messenger was taken charge of by the servants till he had eaten his supper. Then with assistants, and armed with hammer, ripping-chisel, and turnscrew, he met us in the hall, where we had assembled to witness the unpacking of the cases.

Carmilla sat looking listlessly on, while one after the other the old pictures, nearly all portraits, which had undergone the process of renovation, were brought to light. My mother was of an old Hungarian family, and most of these pictures, which were about to be restored to their places, had come to us through her.

My father had a list in his hand, from which he read, as the artist rummaged out the corresponding numbers. I don't know that the pictures were very good, but they were, undoubtedly, very old, and some of them very curious also. They had, for the most part, the merit of being now seen by me, I may say, for the first time; for the smoke and dust of time had all but obliterated them.

'There is a picture that I have not seen yet,' said my father. 'In one corner, at the top of it, is the name, as well as I could read, "Marcia Karnstein", and the date "1698"; and I am curious to see how it has turned out.'

I remembered it; it was a small picture, about a foot and a half high, and nearly square, without a frame; but it was so blackened by age that I could not make it out.

The artist now produced it, with evident pride. It was quite beautiful; it was startling; it seemed to live. It was the effigy of Carmilla!

'Carmilla, dear, here is an absolute miracle. Here you are, living, smiling, ready to speak, in this picture. Isn't it beautiful, papa? And see, even the little mole on her throat.'

My father laughed, and said 'Certainly it is a wonderful likeness,' but he looked away, and to my surprise seemed but little struck by it, and went on talking to the picture cleaner, who was also something of an artist, and discoursed with intelligence about the portraits or other works, which his art had just brought into light and colour, while *I* was more and more lost in wonder the more I looked at the picture.

'Will you let me hang this picture in my room, papa?' I asked.

'Certainly, dear,' said he, smiling, 'I'm very glad you think it so like. It must be prettier even than I thought it, if it is.'

The young lady did not acknowledge this pretty speech, did not seem to hear it. She was leaning back in her seat, her fine eyes under their long lashes gazing on me in contemplation, and she smiled in a kind of rapture.

'And now you can read quite plainly the name that is written in the corner. It is not Marcia; it looks as if it was done in gold. The name is Mircalla, Countess Karnstein, and this is a little coronet over it, and underneath AD 1698. I am descended from the Karnsteins; that is, mamma was.'

'Ah!' said the lady, languidly, 'so am I, I think, a very long descent, very ancient. Are there any Karnsteins living now?'

'None who bear the name, I believe. The family were ruined, I believe, in some civil wars, long ago, but the ruins of the castle are only about three miles away.'

'How interesting!' she said, languidly. 'But see what beautiful moonlight!' She glanced through the hall-door, which stood a little open. 'Suppose you take a little ramble round the court, and look down at the road and river.'

'It is so like the night you came to us,' I said.

She sighed, smiling.

She rose, and each with her arm about the other's waist, we walked out upon the pavement.

In silence, slowly we walked down to the drawbridge, where the beautiful landscape opened before us.

'And so you were thinking of the night I came here?' she almost whispered. 'Are you glad I came?'

'Delighted, dear Carmilla,' I answered.

'And you asked for the picture you think like me, to hang in your room,' she murmured with a sigh, as she drew her arm closer about my waist, and let her pretty head sink upon my shoulder.

'How romantic you are, Carmilla,' I said. 'Whenever you tell me your story, it will be made up chiefly of some one great romance.'

She kissed me silently.

'I am sure, Carmilla, you have been in love; that there is, at this moment, an affair of the heart going on.'

'I have been in love with no one, and never shall,' she whispered, 'unless it should be with you.'

How beautiful she looked in the moonlight!

Shy and strange was the look with which she quickly hid her face in my neck and hair, with tumultuous sighs, that seemed almost to sob, and pressed in mine a hand that trembled.

Her soft cheek was glowing against mine. 'Darling, darling,' she murmured, 'I live in you; and you would die for me, I love you so.'

I started from her.

She was gazing on me with eyes from which all fire, all meaning had flown, and a face colourless and apathetic.

'Is there a chill in the air, dear?' she said drowsily. 'I almost shiver; have I been dreaming? Let us come in. Come; come; come in.'

'You look ill, Carmilla; a little faint. You certainly must take some wine,' I said.

'Yes, I will. I'm better now. I shall be quite well in a few minutes. Yes, do give me a little wine,' answered Carmilla, as we approached the door. 'Let us look again for a moment; it is the last time, perhaps, I shall see the moonlight with you.'

'How do you feel now, dear Carmilla? Are you really better?' I asked.

I was beginning to take alarm, lest she should have been stricken with the strange epidemic that they said had invaded the country about us.

'Papa would be grieved beyond measure,' I added, 'if he thought you were ever so little ill, without immediately letting us know. We have a very skilful doctor near this, the physician who was with papa to-day.'

'I'm sure he is. I know how kind you all are; but, dear child, I am quite well again. There is nothing ever wrong with me, but a little weakness. People say I am languid; I am incapable of exertion; I can scarcely walk as far as a child of three years old; and every now and then the little strength I have falters, and I become as you have just seen me. But after all I am very easily set up again; in a moment I am perfectly myself. See how I have recovered.'

So, indeed, she had; and she and I talked a great deal, and very animated she was; and the remainder of that evening passed without any recurrence of what I called her infatuations. I mean her crazy talk and looks, which embarrassed, and even frightened me.

But there occurred that night an event which gave my thoughts quite a new turn, and seemed to startle even Carmilla's languid nature into momentary energy.

CHAPTER VI

When we got into the drawing-room, and had sat down to our coffee and chocolate, although Carmilla did not take any, she seemed quite herself again, and Madame, and Mademoiselle De Lafontaine, joined us, and made a little card party, in the course of which papa came in for what he called his 'dish of tea'.

When the game was over he sat down beside Carmilla on the sofa, and asked her, a little anxiously, whether she had heard from her mother since her arrival.

She answered 'No'.

He then asked whether she knew where a letter would reach her at present.

'I cannot tell,' she answered ambiguously, 'but I have been thinking of leaving you; you have been already too hospitable and too kind to me. I have given you an infinity of trouble, and I should wish to take a carriage to-morrow, and post in pursuit of her; I know where I shall ultimately find her, although I dare not yet tell you.'

'But you must not dream of any such thing,' exclaimed my father, to my great relief. 'We can't afford to lose you so, and I won't consent to your leaving us, except under the care of your mother, who was so good as to consent to your remaining with us till she should herself return. I should be quite happy if I knew that you heard from her; but this evening the accounts of the progress of the mysterious disease that has invaded our neighbourhood, grow even more alarming; and my beautiful guest, I do feel the responsibility, unaided by advice from your mother, very much. But I shall do my best; and one thing is certain, that you must not think of leaving us without her distinct direction to that effect. We should suffer too much in parting from you to consent to it easily.'

'Thank you, sir, a thousand times for your hospitality,' she answered, smiling bashfully. 'You have all been too kind to me; I have seldom been so happy in all my life before, as in your beautiful château, under your care, and in the society of your dear daughter.'

So he gallantly, in his old-fashioned way, kissed her hand, smiling and pleased at her little speech.

I accompanied Carmilla as usual to her room, and sat and chatted with her while she was preparing for bed.

'Do you think', I said at length, 'that you will ever confide fully in me?'

She turned round smiling, but made no answer, only continued to smile on me.

'You won't answer that?' I said. 'You can't answer pleasantly; I ought not to have asked you.'

'You were quite right to ask me that, or anything. You do not know how dear you are to me, or you could not think any confidence too great to look for. But I am under vows, no nun half so awfully, and I dare not tell my story yet, even to you. The time is very near when you shall know everything. You will think me cruel, very selfish, but love is always selfish; the more ardent the more selfish. How jealous I am you cannot know. You must come with me, loving me, to death; or else hate me and still come with me, and *hating* me through death and after. There is no such word as indifference in my apathetic nature.'

'Now, Carmilla, you are going to talk your wild nonsense again,' I said hastily.

'Not I, silly little fool as I am, and full of whims and fancies; for your sake I'll talk like a sage. Were you ever at a ball?'

'No; how you do run on. What is it like? How charming it must be.'

'I almost forget, it is years ago.'

I laughed.

'You are not so old. Your first ball can hardly be forgotten yet.'

'I remember everything about it—with an effort. I see it all, as divers see what is going on above them, through a medium, dense, rippling, but transparent. There occurred that night what has confused the picture, and made its colours faint. I was all but assassinated in my bed, wounded *here*,' she touched her breast, 'and never was the same since.'

'Were you near dying?'

'Yes, very—a cruel love—strange love, that would have taken my life. Love will have its sacrifices. No sacrifice without blood. Let us go to sleep now; I feel so lazy. How can I get up just now and lock my door?'

She was lying with her tiny hands buried in her rich wavy hair, under her cheek, her little head upon the pillow, and her glittering eyes followed me wherever I moved, with a kind of shy smile that I could not decipher.

I bid her good-night, and crept from the room with an uncomfortable sensation.

I often wondered whether our pretty guest ever said her prayers. *I* certainly had never seen her upon her knees. In the morning she never came down until long after our family prayers were over, and at night she never left the drawing-room to attend our brief evening prayers in the hall.

If it had not been that it had casually come out in one of our careless talks that she had been baptized, I should have doubted her being a Christian. Religion was a subject on which I had never heard her speak a word. If I had known the world better, this particular neglect or antipathy would not have so much surprised me.

The precautions of nervous people are infectious, and persons of a like temperament are pretty sure, after a time, to imitate them. I had adopted Carmilla's habit of locking her bed-room door, having taken into my head all her whimsical alarms about midnight invaders and prowling assassins. I had also adopted her precaution of making a brief search through her room, to satisfy herself that no lurking assassin or robber was 'ensconced'.

These wise measures taken, I got into my bed and fell asleep. A light was burning in my room. This was an old habit, of very early date, and which nothing could have tempted me to dispense with.

Thus fortified I might take my rest in peace. But dreams come through stone walls, light up dark rooms, or darken light ones, and their persons make their exits and their entrances as they please, and laugh at locksmiths.

I had a dream that night that was the beginning of a very strange agony.

I cannot call it a nightmare, for I was quite conscious of being asleep. But I was equally conscious of being in my room, and lying in bed, precisely as I actually was. I saw, or fancied I saw, the room and its furniture just as I had seen it last, except that it was very dark, and I saw something moving round the foot of the bed, which at first I could not accurately distinguish. But I soon saw that it was a sooty-black animal that resembled a monstrous cat. It appeared to me about four or five feet long, for it measured fully the length of the hearth-rug as it passed over it; and it continued toing and froing with the lithe sinister restlessness of a beast in a cage. I could not cry out, although as you may suppose, I was terrified. Its pace was growing faster, and the room rapidly darker and darker, and at length so dark that I could no longer see anything of it but its eyes. I felt it spring lightly on the bed. The two broad eyes approached my face, and suddenly I felt a stinging pain as if two large needles darted, an inch or two apart, deep into my breast. I waked with a scream. The room was lighted by the candle that burnt there all through the night, and I saw a female figure standing at the foot of the bed, a little at the right side. It was in a dark loose dress, and its hair was down and covered its shoulders. A block of stone could not have been more still. There was not the slightest stir of respiration. As I stared at it, the figure appeared to have changed its place, and was now nearer the door; then, close to it, the door opened, and it passed out.

I was now relieved, and able to breathe and move. My first thought was that Carmilla had been playing me a trick, and that I had forgotten to secure my door. I hastened to it, and found it locked as usual on the inside. I was afraid to open it—I was horrified. I sprang into my bed and covered my head up in the bed-clothes, and lay there more dead than alive till morning.

CHAPTER VII

DESCENDING

It would be vain my attempting to tell you the horror with which, even now, I recall the occurrence of that night. It was no such transitory terror as a dream leaves behind it. It seemed to deepen by time, and communicated itself to the room and the very furniture that had encompassed the apparition.

I could not bear next day to be alone for a moment. I should have told papa, but for two opposite reasons. At one time I thought he would laugh at my story, and I could not bear its being treated as a jest; and at another, I thought he might fancy that I had been attacked by the mysterious complaint which had invaded our neighbourhood. I had myself no misgivings of the kind, and as he had been rather an invalid for some time, I was afraid of alarming him.

I was comfortable enough with my good-natured companions, Madame Perrodon, and the vivacious Mademoiselle La Fontaine. They both perceived that I was out of spirits and nervous, and at length I told them what lay so heavy at my heart.

Mademoiselle laughed, but I fancied that Madame Perrodon looked anxious.

'By-the-by,' said Mademoiselle, laughing, 'the long lime-tree walk, behind Carmilla's bedroom-window, is haunted!'

'Nonsense!' exclaimed Madame, who probably thought the theme rather inopportune, 'and who tells that story, my dear?'

'Martin says that he came up twice, when the old yard-gate was being repaired, before sunrise, and twice saw the same female figure walking down the lime-tree avenue.'

'So he well might, as long as there are cows to milk in the river fields,' said Madame.

'I daresay; but Martin chooses to be frightened, and never did I see fool *more* frightened.'

'You must not say a word about it to Carmilla, because she

can see down that walk from her room window,' I interposed, 'and she is, if possible, a greater coward than I.'

Carmilla came down rather later than usual that day.

'I was so frightened last night,' she said, so soon as were together, 'and I am sure I should have seen something dreadful if it had not been for that charm I bought from the poor little hunchback whom I called such hard names. I had a dream of something black coming round my bed, and I awoke in a perfect horror, and I really thought, for some seconds, I saw a dark figure near the chimney-piece, but I felt under my pillow for my charm, and the moment my fingers touched it, the figure disappeared, and I felt quite certain, only that I had it by me, that something frightful would have made its appearance, and, perhaps, throttled me, as it did those poor people we heard of.'

'Well, listen to me,' I began, and recounted my adventure, at the recital of which she appeared horrified.

'And had you the charm near you?' she asked, earnestly.

'No, I had dropped it into a china vase in the drawing-room, but I shall certainly take it with me to-night, as you have so much faith in it.'

At this distance of time I cannot tell you, or even understand, how I overcame my horror so effectually as to lie alone in my room that night. I remember distinctly that I pinned the charm to my pillow. I fell asleep almost immediately, and slept even more soundly than usual all night.

Next night I passed as well. My sleep was delightfully deep and dreamless. But I wakened with a sense of lassitude and melancholy, which, however, did not exceed a degree that was almost luxurious.

'Well, I told you so,' said Carmilla, when I described my quiet sleep, 'I had such delightful sleep myself last night; I pinned the charm to the breast of my night-dress. It was too far away the night before. I am quite sure it was all fancy, except the dreams. I used to think that evil spirits made dreams, but our doctor told me it is no such thing. Only a fever passing by, or some other malady, as they often do, he said, knocks at the door, and not being able to get in, passes on, with that alarm.'

'And what do you think the charm is?' said I.

'It has been fumigated or immersed in some drug, and is an antidote against the malaria,' she answered.

'Then it acts only on the body?'

'Certainly; you don't suppose that evil spirits are frightened by bits of ribbon, or the perfumes of a druggist's shop? No, these complaints, wandering in the air, begin by trying the nerves, and so infect the brain, but before they can seize upon you, the antidote repels them. That I am sure is what the charm has done for us. It is nothing magical, it is simply natural.'

I should have been happier if I could have quite agreed with Carmilla, but I did my best, and the impression was a little losing its force.

For some nights I slept profoundly; but still every morning I felt the same lassitude, and a languor weighed upon me all day. I felt myself a changed girl. A strange melancholy was stealing over me, a melancholy that I would not have interrupted. Dim thoughts of death began to open, and an idea that I was slowly sinking took gentle, and, somehow, not unwelcome, possession of me. If it was sad, the tone of mind which this induced was also sweet. Whatever it might be, my soul acquiesced in it.

I would not admit that I was ill, I would not consent to tell my papa, or to have the doctor sent for.

Carmilla became more devoted to me than ever, and her strange paroxysms of languid adoration more frequent. She used to gloat on me with increasing ardour the more my strength and spirits waned. This always shocked me like a momentary glare of insanity.

Without knowing it, I was now in a pretty advanced stage of the strangest illness under which mortal ever suffered. There was an unaccountable fascination in its earlier symptoms that more than reconciled me to the incapacitating effect of that stage of the malady. This fascination increased for a time, until it reached a certain point, when gradually a sense of the horrible mingled itself with it, deepening, as you shall hear, until it discoloured and perverted the whole state of my life.

The first change I experienced was rather agreeable. It was

very near the turning point from which began the descent to Avernus.*

Certain vague and strange sensations visited me in my sleep. The prevailing one was of that pleasant, peculiar cold thrill which we feel in bathing, when we move against the current of a river. This was soon accompanied by dreams that seemed interminable, and were so vague that I could never recollect their scenery and persons, or any one connected portion of their action. But they left an awful impression, and a sense of exhaustion, as if I had passed through a long period of great mental exertion and danger. After all these dreams there remained on waking a remembrance of having been in a place very nearly dark, and of having spoken to people whom I could not see; and especially of one clear voice, of a female's, very deep, that spoke as if at a distance, slowly, and producing always the same sensation of indescribable solemnity and fear. Sometimes there came a sensation as if a hand was drawn softly along my cheek and neck. Sometimes it was as if warm lips kissed me, and longer and more lovingly as they reached my throat, but there the caress fixed itself. My heart beat faster, my breathing rose and fell rapidly and full drawn; a sobbing, that rose into a sense of strangulation, supervened, and turned into a dreadful convulsion, in which my senses left me and I became unconscious.

It was now three weeks since the commencement of this unaccountable state. My sufferings had, during the last week, told upon my appearance. I had grown pale, my eyes were dilated and darkened underneath, and the languor which I had long felt began to display itself in my countenance.

My father asked me often whether I was ill; but, with an obstinacy which now seems to me unaccountable, I persisted in assuring him that I was quite well.

In a sense this was true. I had no pain, I could complain of no bodily derangement. My complaint seemed to be one of the imagination, or the nerves, and, horrible as my sufferings were, I kept them, with a morbid reserve, very nearly to myself.

It could not be that terrible complaint which the peasants called the oupire, for I had now been suffering for three weeks, and they were seldom ill for much more than three days, when death put an end to their miseries.

Carmilla complained of dreams and feverish sensations, but by no means of so alarming a kind as mine. I say that mine were extremely alarming. Had I been capable of comprehending my condition, I would have invoked aid and advice on my knees. The narcotic of an unsuspected influence was acting upon me, and my perceptions were benumbed.

I am going to tell you now of a dream that led immediately to an odd discovery.

One night, instead of the voice I was accustomed to hear in the dark, I heard one, sweet and tender, and at the same time terrible, which said, 'Your mother warns you to beware of the assassin.' At the same time a light unexpectedly sprang up, and I saw Carmilla, standing, near the foot of my bed, in her white nightdress, bathed, from her chin to her feet, in one great stain of blood.

I wakened with a shriek, possessed with the one idea that Carmilla was being murdered. I remember springing from my bed, and my next recollection is that of standing in the lobby, crying for help.

Madame and Mademoiselle came scurrying out of their rooms in alarm; a lamp burned always on the lobby, and seeing me, they soon learned the cause of my terror.

I insisted on our knocking at Carmilla's door. Our knocking was unanswered. It soon became a pounding and an uproar. We shrieked her name, but all was vain.

We all grew frightened, for the door was locked. We hurried back, in panic, to my room. There we rang the bell long and furiously. If my father's room had been at that side of the house, we would have called him up at once to our aid. But, alas! he was quite out of hearing, and to reach him involved an excursion for which we none of us had courage.

Servants, however, soon came running up the stairs; I had got on my dressing-gown and slippers meanwhile, and my companions were already similarly furnished. Recognizing the voices of the servants on the lobby, we sallied out together; and having renewed, as fruitlessly, our summons at Carmilla's door, I ordered the men to force the lock. They did so, and we stood, holding our lights aloft, in the doorway, and so stared into the room.

We called her by name; but there was still no reply. We looked round the room. Everything was undisturbed. It was exactly in the state in which I had left it on bidding her good-night. But Carmilla was gone.

CHAPTER VIII

SEARCH

At sight of the room, perfectly undisturbed except for our violent entrance, we began to cool a little, and soon recovered our senses sufficiently to dismiss the men. It had struck Mademoiselle that possibly Carmilla had been wakened by the uproar at her door, and in her first panic had jumped from her bed, and hid herself in a press, or behind a curtain, from which she could not, of course, emerge until the majordomo and his myrmidons* had withdrawn. We now recommenced our search, and began to call her by name again.

It was all to no purpose. Our perplexity and agitation increased. We examined the windows, but they were secured. I implored of Carmilla, if she had concealed herself, to play this cruel trick no longer—to come out, and to end our anxieties. It was all useless. I was by this time convinced that she was not in the room, nor in the dressing-room, the door of which was still locked on this side. She could not have passed it. I was utterly puzzled. Had Carmilla discovered one of those secret passages which the old house-keeper said were known to exist in the schloss, although the tradition of their exact situation had been lost. A little time would, no doubt, explain all—utterly perplexed as, for the present, we were.

It was past four o'clock, and I preferred passing the remaining hours of darkness in Madame's room. Daylight brought no solution of the difficulty.

The whole household, with my father at its head, was in a state of agitation next morning. Every part of the château was searched. The grounds were explored. Not a trace of the missing lady could be discovered. The stream was about to be dragged; my father was in distraction; what a tale to have to tell the poor girl's mother on her return. I, too, was almost beside myself, though my grief was quite of a different kind.

The morning was passed in alarm and excitement. It was now one o'clock, and still no tidings. I ran up to Carmilla's room, and found her standing at her dressing-table. I was astounded. I could not believe my eyes. She beckoned me to her with her pretty finger, in silence. Her face expressed extreme fear.

I ran to her in an ecstasy of joy; I kissed and embraced her again and again. I ran to the bell and rang it vehemently, to bring others to the spot, who might at once relieve my father's anxiety.

'Dear Carmilla, what has become of you all this time? We have been in agonies of anxiety about you,' I exclaimed. 'Where have you been? How did you come back?'

'Last night has been a night of wonders,' she said.

'For mercy's sake, explain all you can.'

'It was past two last night,' she said, 'when I went to sleep as usual in my bed, with my doors locked, that of the dressing-room, and that opening upon the gallery. My sleep was uninterrupted, and, so far as I know, dreamless; but I awoke just now on the sofa in the dressing-room there, and I found the door between the rooms open, and the other door forced. How could all this have happened without my being wakened? It must have been accompanied with a great deal of noise, and I am particularly easily wakened; and how could I have been carried out of my bed without my sleep having been interrupted, I whom the slightest stir startles?'

By this time, Madame, Mademoiselle, my father, and a number of the servants were in the room. Carmilla was, of course, overwhelmed with inquiries, congratulations, and welcomes. She had but one story to tell, and seemed the least able of all the party to suggest any way of accounting for what had happened.

My father took a turn up and down the room, thinking. I

saw Carmilla's eye follow him for a moment with a sly, dark glance.

When my father had sent the servants away, Mademoiselle having gone in search of a little bottle of valerian and sal-volatile,* and there being no one now in the room with Carmilla, except my father, Madame, and myself, he came to her thoughtfully, took her hand very kindly, led her to the sofa, and sat down beside her.

'Will you forgive me, my dear, if I risk a conjecture, and ask a question?'

'Who can have a better right?' she said. 'Ask what you please, and I will tell you everything. But my story is simply one of bewilderment and darkness. I know absolutely nothing. Put any question you please. But you know, of course, the limitations mamma has placed me under.'

'Perfectly, my dear child. I need not approach the topics on which she desires our silence. Now, the marvel of last night consists in your having been removed from your bed and your room, without being wakened, and this removal having occurred apparently while the windows were still secured, and the two doors locked upon the inside. I will tell you my theory, and first ask you a question.'

Carmilla was leaning on her hand dejectedly; Madame and I were listening breathlessly.

'Now, my question is this. Have you ever been suspected of walking in your sleep?'

'Never, since I was very young indeed.'

'But you did walk in your sleep when you were young?'

'Yes; I know I did. I have been told so often by my old nurse.'

My father smiled and nodded.

'Well, what has happened is this. You got up in your sleep, unlocked the door, not leaving the key, as usual, in the lock, but taking it out and locking it on the outside; you again took the key out, and carried it away with you to some one of the five-and-twenty rooms on this floor, or perhaps up-stairs or down-stairs. There are so many rooms and closets, so much heavy furniture, and such accumulations of lumber, that it would require a week to search this old house thoroughly. Do you see, now, what I mean?'

'I do, but not all,' she answered.

'And how, papa, do you account for her finding herself on the sofa in the dressing-room, which we had searched so carefully?'

'She came there after you had searched it, still in her sleep, and at last awoke spontaneously, and was as much surprised to find herself where she was as any one else. I wish all mysteries were as easily and innocently explained as yours, Carmilla,' he said, laughing. 'And so we may congratulate ourselves on the certainty that the most natural explanation of the occurrence is one that involves no drugging, no tampering with locks, no burglars, or poisoners, or witches—nothing that need alarm Carmilla, or any one else, for our safety.'

Carmilla was looking charmingly. Nothing could be more beautiful than her tints. Her beauty was, I think, enhanced by that graceful languor that was peculiar to her. I think my father was silently contrasting her looks with mine, for he said:

'I wish my poor Laura was looking more like herself;' and he sighed.

So our alarms were happily ended, and Carmilla restored to her friends.

CHAPTER IX

THE DOCTOR

As Carmilla would not hear of an attendant sleeping in her room, my father arranged that a servant should sleep outside her door, so that she could not attempt to make another such excursion without being arrested at her own door.

That night passed quietly; and next morning early, the doctor, whom my father had sent for without telling me a word about it, arrived to see me.

Madame accompanied me to the library; and there the

grave little doctor, with white hair and spectacles, whom I mentioned before, was waiting to receive me.

I told him my story, and as I proceeded he grew graver and graver.

We were standing, he and I, in the recess of one of the windows, facing one another. When my statement was over, he leaned with his shoulders against the wall, and with his eyes fixed on me earnestly, with an interest in which was a dash of horror.

After a minute's reflection, he asked Madame if he could see my father.

He was sent for accordingly, and as he entered, smiling, he said:

'I dare say, doctor, you are going to tell me that I am an old fool for having brought you here; I hope I am.'

But his smile faded into shadow as the doctor, with a very grave face, beckoned him to him.

He and the doctor talked for some time in the same recess where I had just conferred with the physician. It seemed an earnest and argumentative conversation. The room is very large, and I and Madame stood together, burning with curiosity, at the further end. Not a word could we hear, however, for they spoke in a very low tone, and the deep recess of the window quite concealed the doctor from view, and very nearly my father, whose foot, arm, and shoulder only could we see; and the voices were, I suppose, all the less audible for the sort of closet which the thick wall and window formed.

After a time my father's face looked into the room; it was pale, thoughtful, and, I fancied, agitated.

'Laura, dear, come here for a moment. Madame, we shan't trouble you, the doctor says, at present.'

Accordingly I approached, for the first time a little alarmed; for, although I felt very weak, I did not feel ill; and strength, one always fancies, is a thing that may be picked up when we please.

My father held out his hand to me, as I drew near, but he was looking at the doctor, and he said:

'It certainly *is* very odd; I don't understand it quite. Laura, come here, dear; now attend to Doctor Spielsberg, and recollect yourself.'

'You mentioned a sensation like that of two needles piercing the skin, somewhere about your neck, on the night when you experienced your first horrible dream. Is there still any soreness?'

'None at all,' I answered.

'Can you indicate with your finger about the point at which you think this occurred?'

'Very little below my throat—*here*,' I answered.

I wore a morning dress, which covered the place I pointed to.

'Now you can satisfy yourself,' said the doctor. 'You won't mind your papa's lowering your dress a very little. It is necessary, to detect a symptom of the complaint under which you have been suffering.'

I acquiesced. It was only an inch or two below the edge of my collar.

'God bless me!—so it is,' exclaimed my father, growing pale.

'You see it now with your own eyes,' said the doctor, with a gloomy triumph.

'What is it?' I exclaimed, beginning to be frightened.

'Nothing, my dear young lady, but a small blue spot, about the size of the tip of your little finger; and now,' he continued, turning to papa, 'the question is, what is best to be done?'

'Is there any danger?' I urged, in great trepidation.

'I trust not, my dear,' answered the doctor. 'I don't see why you should not recover. I don't see why you should not begin *immediately* to get better. That is the point at which the sense of strangulation begins?'

'Yes,' I answered.

'And—recollect as well as you can—the same point was a kind of centre of that thrill which you described just now, like the current of a cold stream running against you?'

'It may have been; I think it was.'

'Ay, you see?' he added, turning to my father. 'Shall I say a word to Madame?'

'Certainly,' said my father.

He called Madame to him, and said:

'I find my young friend here far from well. It won't be of any great consequence, I hope; but it will be necessary that some steps be taken, which I will explain by-and-by; but in the meantime, Madame, you will be so good as not to let Miss Laura be alone for one moment. That is the only direction I need give for the present. It is indispensable.'

'We may rely upon your kindness, Madame, I know,' added my father.

Madame satisfied him eagerly.

'And you, dear Laura, I know you will observe the doctor's direction.'

'I shall have to ask your opinion upon another patient, whose symptoms slightly resemble those of my daughter, that have just been detailed to you—very much milder in degree, but I believe quite of the same sort. She is a young lady—our guest; but as you say you will be passing this way again this evening, you can't do better than take your supper here, and you can then see her. She does not come down till the afternoon.'

'I thank you,' said the doctor. 'I shall be with you, then, at about seven this evening.'

And then they repeated their directions to me and to Madame, and with this parting charge my father left us, and walked out with the doctor; and I saw them pacing together up and down between the road and the moat, on the grassy platform in front of the castle, evidently absorbed in earnest conversation.

The doctor did not return. I saw him mount his horse there, take his leave, and ride away eastward through the forest.

Nearly at the same time I saw the man arrive from Dranfeld* with the letters, and dismount and hand the bag to my father.

In the meantime, Madame and I were both busy, lost in conjecture as to the reasons of the singular and earnest direction which the doctor and my father had concurred in imposing. Madame, as she afterwards told me, was afraid the doctor apprehended a sudden seizure, and that, without prompt assistance, I might either lose my life in a fit, or at least be seriously hurt.

This interpretation did not strike me; and I fancied, perhaps luckily for my nerves, that the arrangement was prescribed simply to secure a companion, who would prevent my taking too much exercise, or eating unripe fruit, or doing any of the fifty foolish things to which young people are supposed to be prone.

About half-an-hour after my father came in—he had a letter in his hand—and said:

'This letter has been delayed; it is from General Spielsdorf. He might have been here yesterday, he may not come till to-morrow, or he may be here to-day.'

He put the open letter into my hand; but he did not look pleased, as he used when a guest, especially one so much loved as the General, was coming. On the contrary, he looked as if he wished him at the bottom of the Red Sea. There was plainly something on his mind which he did not choose to divulge.

'Papa, darling, will you tell me this?' said I, suddenly laying my hand on his arm, and looking, I am sure, imploringly in his face.

'Perhaps,' he answered, smoothing my hair caressingly over my eyes.

'Does the doctor think me very ill?'

'No, dear; he thinks, if right steps are taken, you will be quite well again, at least, on the high road to a complete recovery, in a day or two,' he answered, a little drily. 'I wish our good friend, the General, had chosen any other time; that is, I wish you had been perfectly well to receive him.'

'But do tell me, papa,' I insisted, '*what* does he think is the matter with me?'

'Nothing; you must not plague me with questions,' he answered, with more irritation than I ever remember him to have displayed before; and seeing that I looked wounded, I suppose, he kissed me, and added, 'You shall know all about it in a day or two; that is, all that *I* know. In the meantime you are not to trouble your head about it.'

He turned and left the room, but came back before I had done wondering and puzzling over the oddity of all this; it was merely to say that he was going to Karnstein, and had ordered the carriage to be ready at twelve, and that I and Madame should accompany him; he was going to see the priest who lived near those picturesque grounds, upon business, and as Carmilla had never seen them, she could follow, when she came down, with Mademoiselle, who would bring materials for what you call a pic-nic, which might be laid for us in the ruined castle.

At twelve o'clock, accordingly, I was ready, and not long after, my father, Madame and I set out upon our projected drive.

Passing the drawbridge we turn to the right, and follow the road over the steep Gothic bridge, westward, to reach the deserted village and ruined castle of Karnstein.

No sylvan drive can be fancied prettier. The ground breaks into gentle hills and hollows, all clothed with beautiful woods, totally destitute of the comparative formality which artificial planting and early culture and pruning impart.

The irregularities of the ground often lead the road out of its course, and cause it to wind beautifully round the sides of broken hollows and the steeper sides of the hills, among varieties of ground almost inexhaustible.

Turning one of these points, we suddenly encountered our old friend, the General, riding towards us, attended by a mounted servant. His portmanteaus were following in a hired waggon, such as we term a cart.

The General dismounted as we pulled up, and, after the usual greetings, was easily persuaded to accept the vacant seat in the carriage, and send his horse on with his servant to the schloss.

CHAPTER X

BEREAVED

It was about ten months since we had last seen him; but that time had sufficed to make an alteration of years in his appearance. He had grown thinner; something of gloom and anxiety had taken the place of that cordial serenity which used to characterize his features. His dark blue eyes, always penetrating, now gleamed with a sterner light from under his shaggy grey eyebrows. It was not such a change as grief alone usually induces, and angrier passions seemed to have had their share in bringing it about.

We had not long resumed our drive, when the General began to talk, with his usual soldierly directness, of the bereavement, as he termed it, which he had sustained in the death of his beloved niece and ward; and he then broke out in a tone of intense bitterness and fury, inveighing against the 'hellish arts' to which she had fallen a victim, and expressing, with more exasperation than piety, his wonder that Heaven should tolerate so monstrous an indulgence of the lusts and malignity of hell.

My father, who saw at once that something very extraordinary had befallen, asked him, if not too painful to him, to detail the circumstances which he thought justified the strong terms in which he expressed himself.

'I should tell you all with pleasure,' said the General, 'but you would not believe me.'

'Why should I not?' he asked.

'Because', he answered testily, 'you believe in nothing but what consists with your own prejudices and illusions. I remember when I was like you, but I have learned better.'

'Try me,' said my father; 'I am not such a dogmatist as you suppose. Besides which, I very well know that you generally require proof for what you believe, and am, therefore, very strongly pre-disposed to respect your conclusions.'

'You are right in supposing that I have not been led lightly into a belief in the marvellous—for what I have experienced *is*

marvellous—and I have been forced by extraordinary evidence
to credit that which ran counter, diametrically, to all my
theories. I have been made the dupe of a preternatural
conspiracy.'

Notwithstanding his professions of confidence in the
General's penetration, I saw my father, at this point, glance at
the General, with, as I thought, a marked suspicion of his
sanity.

The General did not see it, luckily. He was looking gloomily
and curiously into the glades and vistas of the woods that were
opening before us.

'You are going to the ruins of Karnstein?' he said. 'Yes, it is
a lucky coincidence; do you know I was going to ask you to
bring me there to inspect them. I have a special object in
exploring. There is a ruined chapel, ain't there, with a great
many tombs of that extinct family?'

'So there are—highly interesting,' said my father. 'I hope
you are thinking of claiming the title and estates?'

My father said this gaily, but the General did not recollect
the laugh, or even the smile, which courtesy exacts for a
friend's joke; on the contrary, he looked grave and even fierce,
ruminating on a matter that stirred his anger and horror.

'Something very different,' he said, gruffly. 'I mean to
unearth some of those fine people. I hope, by God's blessing,
to accomplish a pious sacrilege here, which will relieve our
earth of certain monsters, and enable honest people to sleep in
their beds without being assailed by murderers. I have strange
things to tell you, my dear friend, such as I myself would have
scouted as incredible a few months since.'

My father looked at him again, but this time not with a
glance of suspicion—with an eye, rather, of keen intelligence
and alarm.

'The house of Karnstein', he said, 'has been long extinct: a
hundred years at least. My dear wife was maternally
descended from the Karnsteins. But the name and title have
long ceased to exist. The castle is a ruin; the very village is
deserted; it is fifty years since the smoke of a chimney was seen
there; not a roof left.'

'Quite true. I have heard a great deal about that since I last saw you; a great deal that will astonish you. But I had better relate everything in the order in which it occurred,' said the General. 'You saw my dear ward—my child, I may call her. No creature could have been more beautiful, and only three months ago none more blooming.'

'Yes, poor thing! when I saw her last she certainly was quite lovely,' said my father. 'I was grieved and shocked more than I can tell you, my dear friend; I knew what a blow it was to you.'

He took the General's hand, and they exchanged a kind pressure. Tears gathered in the old soldier's eyes. He did not seek to conceal them. He said:

'We have been very old friends; I knew you would feel for me, childless as I am. She had become an object of very near interest to me, and repaid my care by an affection that cheered my home and made my life happy. That is all gone. The years that remain to me on earth may not be very long; but by God's mercy I hope to accomplish a service to mankind before I die, and to subserve the vengeance of Heaven upon the fiends who have murdered my poor child in the spring of her hopes and beauty!'

'You said, just now, that you intended relating everything as it occurred,' said my father. 'Pray do; I assure you that it is not mere curiosity that prompts me.'

By this time we had reached the point at which the Drunstall* road, by which the General had come, diverges from the road which we were travelling to Karnstein.

'How far is it to the ruins?' inquired the General, looking anxiously forward.

'About half a league,' answered my father. 'Pray let us hear the story you were so good as to promise.'

CHAPTER XI

THE STORY

'With all my heart,' said the General, with an effort; and after a short pause in which to arrange his subject, he commenced one of the strangest narratives I ever heard.

'My dear child was looking forward with great pleasure to the visit you had been so good as to arrange for her to your charming daughter.' Here he made me a gallant but melancholy bow. 'In the meantime we had an invitation to my old friend the Count Carlsfeld, whose schloss is about six leagues to the other side of Karnstein. It was to attend the series of fêtes which, you remember, were given by him in honour of his illustrious visitor, the Grand Duke Charles.'*

'Yes; and very splendid, I believe, they were,' said my father.

'Princely! But then his hospitalities are quite regal. He has Aladdin's lamp.* The night from which my sorrow dates was devoted to a magnificent masquerade. The grounds were thrown open, the trees hung with coloured lamps. There was such a display of fireworks as Paris itself had never witnessed. And such music—music, you know, is my weakness—such ravishing music! The finest instrumental band, perhaps, in the world, and the finest singers who could be collected from all the great operas in Europe. As you wandered through these fantastically illuminated grounds, the moon-lighted château throwing a rosy light from its long rows of windows, you would suddenly hear these ravishing voices stealing from the silence of some grove, or rising from boats upon the lake. I felt myself, as I looked and listened, carried back into the romance and poetry of my early youth.

'When the fireworks were ended, and the ball beginning, we returned to the noble suite of rooms that were thrown open to the dancers. A masked ball, you know, is a beautiful sight; but so brilliant a spectacle of the kind I never saw before.

'It was a very aristocratic assembly. I was myself almost the only "nobody" present.

'My dear child was looking quite beautiful. She wore no mask. Her excitement and delight added an unspeakable charm to her features, always lovely. I remarked a young lady, dressed magnificently, but wearing a mask, who appeared to me to be observing my ward with extraordinary interest. I had seen her, earlier in the evening, in the great hall, and again, for a few minutes, walking near us, on the terrace under the castle windows, similarly employed. A lady, also masked, richly and gravely dressed, and with a stately air, like a person of rank, accompanied her as a chaperon. Had the young lady not worn a mask, I could, of course, have been much more certain upon the question whether she was really watching my poor darling. I am now well assured that she was.

'We were now in one of the *salons*. My poor dear child had been dancing, and was resting a little in one of the chairs near the door; I was standing near. The two ladies I have mentioned had approached, and the younger took the chair next my ward; while her companion stood beside me, and for a little time addressed herself, in a low tone, to her charge.

'Availing herself of the privilege of her mask, she turned to me, and in the tone of an old friend, and calling me by my name, opened a conversation with me, which piqued my curiosity a good deal. She referred to many scenes where she had met me—at Court, and at distinguished houses. She alluded to little incidents which I had long ceased to think of, but which, I found, had only lain in abeyance in my memory, for they instantly started into life at her touch.

'I became more and more curious to ascertain who she was, every moment. She parried my attempts to discover very adroitly and pleasantly. The knowledge she showed of many passages in my life seemed to me all but unaccountable; and she appeared to take a not unnatural pleasure in foiling my curiosity, and in seeing me flounder, in my eager perplexity, from one conjecture to another.

'In the meantime the young lady, whom her mother called by the odd name of Millarca, when she once or twice addressed her, had, with the same ease and grace, got into conversation with my ward.

'She introduced herself by saying that her mother was a

very old acquaintance of mine. She spoke of the agreeable audacity which a mask rendered practicable; she talked like a friend; she admired her dress, and insinuated very prettily her admiration of her beauty. She amused her with laughing criticisms upon the people who crowded the ballroom, and laughed at my poor child's fun. She was very witty and lively when she pleased, and after a time they had grown very good friends, and the young stranger lowered her mask, displaying a remarkably beautiful face. I had never seen it before, neither had my dear child. But though it was new to us, the features were so engaging, as well as lovely, that it was impossible not to feel the attraction powerfully. My poor girl did so. I never saw anyone more taken with another at first sight, unless, indeed, it was the stranger herself, who seemed quite to have lost her heart to her.

'In the meantime, availing myself of the licence of a masquerade, I put not a few questions to the elder lady.

'"You have puzzled me utterly," I said, laughing. "Is that not enough? Won't you, now, consent to stand on equal terms, and do me the kindness to remove your mask?"

'"Can any request be more unreasonable?" she replied. "Ask a lady to yield an advantage! Beside, how do you know you should recognize me? Years make changes."

'"As you see," I said, with a bow, and, I suppose, a rather melancholy little laugh.

'"As philosophers tell us," she said; "and how do you know that a sight of my face would help you?"

'"I should take chance for that," I answered. "It is vain trying to make yourself out an old woman; your figure betrays you."

'"Years, nevertheless, have passed since I saw you, rather since you saw me, for that is what I am considering. Millarca, there, is my daughter; I cannot then be young, even in the opinion of people whom time has taught to be indulgent, and I may not like to be compared with what you remember me. You have no mask to remove. You can offer me nothing in exchange."

'"My petition is to your pity, to remove it."

'"And mine to yours, to let it stay where it is," she replied.

'"Well, then, at least you will tell me whether you are French or German; you speak both languages so perfectly."

'"I don't think I shall tell you that, General; you intend a surprise, and are meditating the particular point of attack."

'"At all events, you won't deny this," I said, "that being honoured by your permission to converse, I ought to know how to address you. Shall I say Madame la Comtesse?"

'She laughed, and she would, no doubt, have met me with another evasion—if, indeed, I can treat any occurrence in an interview every circumstance of which was pre-arranged, as I now believe, with the profoundest cunning, as liable to be modified by accident.

'"As to that," she began; but she was interrupted, almost as she opened her lips, by a gentleman, dressed in black, who looked particularly elegant and distinguished, with this drawback, that his face was the most deadly pale I ever saw, except in death. He was in no masquerade—in the plain evening dress of a gentleman; and he said, without a smile, but with a courtly and unusually low bow:

'"Will Madame la Comtesse permit me to say a very few words which may interest her?"

'The lady turned quickly to him, and touched her lip in token of silence; she then said to me, "Keep my place for me, General; I shall return when I have said a few words."

'And with this injunction, playfully given, she walked a little aside with the gentleman in black, and talked for some minutes, apparently very earnestly. They then walked away slowly together in the crowd, and I lost them for some minutes.

'I spent the interval in cudgelling my brains for a conjecture as to the identity of the lady who seemed to remember me so kindly, and I was thinking of turning about and joining in the conversation between my pretty ward and the Countess's daughter, and trying whether, by the time she returned, I might not have a surprise in store for her, by having her name, title, château, and estates at my fingers' ends. But at this moment she returned, accompanied by the pale man in black, who said:

'"I shall return and inform Madame la Comtesse when her carriage is at the door."

'He withdrew with a bow.'

CHAPTER XII

A PETITION

'"Then we are to lose Madame la Comtesse, but I hope only for a few hours," I said, with a low bow.

'"It may be that only, or it may be a few weeks. It was very unlucky his speaking to me just now as he did. Do you now know me?"

'I assured her I did not.

'"You shall know me," she said, "but not at present. We are older and better friends than, perhaps, you suspect. I cannot yet declare myself. I shall in three weeks pass your beautiful schloss, about which I have been making enquiries. I shall then look in upon you for an hour or two, and renew a friendship which I never think of without a thousand pleasant recollections. This moment a piece of news has reached me like a thunderbolt. I must set out now, and travel by a devious route, nearly a hundred miles, with all the dispatch I can possibly make. My perplexities multiply. I am only deterred by the compulsory reserve I practise as to my name from making a very singular request of you. My poor child has not quite recovered her strength. Her horse fell with her, at a hunt which she had ridden out to witness, her nerves have not yet recovered the shock, and our physician says that she must on no account exert herself for some time to come. We came here, in consequence, by very easy stages—hardly six leagues a day. I must now travel day and night, on a mission of life and death—a mission the critical and momentous nature of which I shall be able to explain to you when we meet, as I hope we shall, in a few weeks, without the necessity of any concealment."

'She went on to make her petition, and it was in the tone of a person from whom such a request amounted to conferring, rather than seeking a favour. This was only in manner, and, as it seemed, quite unconsciously. Than the terms in which it was expressed, nothing could be more deprecatory. It was simply that I would consent to take charge of her daughter during her absence.

'This was, all things considered, a strange, not to say, an audacious request. She in some sort disarmed me, by stating and admitting everything that could be urged against it, and throwing herself entirely upon my chivalry. At the same moment, by a fatality that seems to have predetermined all that happened, my poor child came to my side, and, in an undertone, besought me to invite her new friend, Millarca, to pay us a visit. She had just been sounding her, and thought, if her mamma would allow her, she would like it extremely.

'At another time I should have told her to wait a little, until, at least, we knew who they were. But I had not a moment to think in. The two ladies assailed me together, and I must confess the refined and beautiful face of the young lady, about which there was something extremely engaging, as well as the elegance and fire of high birth, determined me; and, quite overpowered, I submitted, and undertook, too easily, the care of the young lady, whom her mother called Millarca.

'The Countess beckoned to her daughter, who listened with grave attention while she told her, in general terms, how suddenly and peremptorily she had been summoned, and also of the arrangement she had made for her under my care, adding that I was one of her earliest and most valued friends.

'I made, of course, such speeches as the case seemed to call for, and found myself, on reflection, in a position which I did not half like.

'The gentleman in black returned, and very ceremoniously conducted the lady from the room.

'The demeanour of this gentleman was such as to impress me with the conviction that the Countess was a lady of very much more importance than her modest title alone might have led me to assume.

'Her last charge to me was that no attempt was to be made to learn more about her than I might have already guessed, until her return. Our distinguished host, whose guest she was, knew her reasons.

'"But here", she said, "neither I nor my daughter could safely remain for more than a day. I removed my mask imprudently for a moment, about an hour ago, and, too late, I fancied you saw me. So I resolved to seek an opportunity of talking a little to you. Had I found that you *had* seen me, I should have thrown myself on your high sense of honour to keep my secret for some weeks. As it is, I am satisfied that you did not see me; but if you now *suspect*, or, on reflection, *should* suspect, who I am, I commit myself, in like manner, entirely to your honour. My daughter will observe the same secresy, and I well know that you will, from time to time, remind her, lest she should thoughtlessly disclose it."

'She whispered a few words to her daughter, kissed her hurriedly twice, and went away, accompanied by the pale gentleman in black, and disappeared in the crowd.

'"In the next room", said Millarca, "there is a window that looks upon the hall door. I should like to see the last of mamma, and to kiss my hand to her."

'We assented, of course, and accompanied her to the window. We looked out, and saw a handsome old-fashioned carriage, with a troop of couriers and footmen. We saw the slim figure of the pale gentleman in black, as he held a thick velvet cloak, and placed it about her shoulders and threw the hood over her head. She nodded to him, and just touched his hand with hers. He bowed low repeatedly as the door closed, and the carriage began to move.

'"She is gone," said Millarca, with a sigh.

'"She is gone," I repeated to myself, for the first time—in the hurried moments that had elapsed since my consent— reflecting upon the folly of my act.

'"She did not look up," said the young lady, plaintively.

'"The Countess had taken off her mask, perhaps, and did not care to show her face," I said; "and she could not know that you were in the window."

'She sighed, and looked in my face. She was so beautiful that I relented. I was sorry I had for a moment repented of my hospitality, and I determined to make her amends for the unavowed churlishness of my reception.

'The young lady, replacing her mask, joined my ward in persuading me to return to the grounds, where the concert was soon to be renewed. We did so, and walked up and down the terrace that lies under the castle windows. Millarca became very intimate with us, and amused us with lively descriptions and stories of most of the great people whom we saw upon the terrace. I liked her more and more every minute. Her gossip, without being ill-natured, was extremely diverting to me, who had been so long out of the great world. I thought what life she would give to our sometimes lonely evenings at home.

'This ball was not over until the morning sun had almost reached the horizon. It pleased the Grand Duke to dance till then, so loyal people could not go away, or think of bed.

'We had just got through a crowded *salon*, when my ward asked me what had become of Millarca. I thought she had been by her side, and she fancied she was by mine. The fact was, we had lost her.

'All my efforts to find her were vain. I feared that she had mistaken, in the confusion of a momentary separation from us, other people for her new friends, and had, possibly, pursued and lost them in the extensive grounds which were thrown open to us.

'Now, in its full force, I recognized a new folly in my having undertaken the charge of a young lady without so much as knowing her name; and fettered as I was by promises, of the reasons for imposing which I knew nothing, I could not even point my inquiries by saying that the missing young lady was the daughter of the Countess who had taken her departure a few hours before.

'Morning broke. It was clear daylight before I gave up my search. It was not till near two o'clock next day that we heard anything of my missing charge.

'At about that time a servant knocked at my niece's door, to say that he had been earnestly requested by a young lady, who appeared to be in great distress, to make out where she could find the General Baron Spieldsdorf and the young lady his daughter, in whose charge she had been left by her mother.

'There could be no doubt, notwithstanding the slight inaccuracy, that our young friend had turned up; and so she had. Would to heaven we had lost her!

'She told my poor child a story to account for her having failed to recover us for so long. Very late, she said, she had got to the housekeeper's bedroom in despair of finding us, and had then fallen into a deep sleep which, long as it was, had hardly sufficed to recruit her strength after the fatigues of the ball.

'That day Millarca came home with us. I was only too happy, after all, to have secured so charming a companion for my dear girl.

CHAPTER XIII

THE WOOD-MAN

'There soon, however, appeared some drawbacks. In the first place, Millarca complained of extreme languor—the weakness that remained after her late illness—and she never emerged from her room till the afternoon was pretty far advanced. In the next place, it was accidentally discovered, although she always locked her door on the inside, and never disturbed the key from its place till she admitted the maid to assist at her toilet, that she was undoubtedly sometimes absent from her room in the very early morning, and at various times later in the day, before she wished it to be understood that she was stirring. She was repeatedly seen from the windows of the schloss, in the first faint grey of the morning, walking through the trees, in an easterly direction, and looking like a person in a trance. This convinced me that she walked in her sleep. But this hypothesis did not solve the puzzle. How did she pass out from her room, leaving the door locked on the inside? How did she escape from the house without unbarring door or window?

'In the midst of my perplexities, an anxiety of a far more urgent kind presented itself.

'My dear child began to lose her looks and health, and that in a manner so mysterious, and even horrible, that I became thoroughly frightened.

'She was at first visited by appalling dreams; then, as she fancied, by a spectre, sometimes resembling Millarca, some-times in the shape of a beast, indistinctly seen, walking round the foot of her bed, from side to side. Lastly came sensations.

One, not unpleasant, but very peculiar, she said, resembled the flow of an icy stream against her breast. At a later time, she felt something like a pair of large needles pierce her, a little below the throat, with a very sharp pain. A few nights after, followed a gradual and convulsive sense of strangulation; then came unconsciousness.'

I could hear distinctly every word the kind old General was saying, because by this time we were driving upon the short grass that spreads on either side of the road as you approach the roofless village which had not shown the smoke of a chimney for more than half a century.

You may guess how strangely I felt as I heard my own symptoms so exactly described in those which had been experienced by the poor girl who, but for the catastrophe which followed, would have been at that moment a visitor at my father's château. You may suppose, also, how I felt as I heard him detail habits and mysterious peculiarities which were, in fact, those of our beautiful guest, Carmilla!

A vista opened in the forest; we were on a sudden under the chimneys and gables of the ruined village, and the towers and battlements of the dismantled castle, round which gigantic trees are grouped, overhung us from a slight eminence.

In a frightened dream I got down from the carriage, and in silence, for we had each abundant matter for thinking; we soon mounted the ascent, and were among the spacious chambers, winding stairs, and dark corridors of the castle.

'And this was once the palatial residence of the Karnsteins!' said the old General at length, as from a great window he looked out across the village, and saw the wide, undulating expanse of forest. 'It was a bad family, and here its blood-stained annals were written,' he continued. 'It is hard that they should, after death, continue to plague the human race with their atrocious lusts. That is the chapel of the Karnsteins, down there.'

He pointed down to the grey walls of the Gothic building, partly visible through the foliage, a little way down the steep. 'And I hear the axe of a woodman,' he added, 'busy among the trees that surround it; he possibly may give us the information of which I am in search, and point out the grave of Mircalla, Countess of Karnstein. These rustics preserve the local traditions of great families, whose stories die out among the rich and titled so soon as the families themselves become extinct.'

'We have a portrait, at home, of Mircalla, the Countess Karnstein; should you like to see it?' asked my father.

'Time enough, dear friend,' replied the General. 'I believe that I have seen the original; and one motive which has led me to you earlier than I at first intended, was to explore the chapel which we are now approaching.'

'What! see the Countess Mircalla,' exclaimed my father; 'why, she has been dead more than a century!'

'Not so dead as you fancy, I am told,' answered the General.

'I confess, General, you puzzle me utterly,' replied my father, looking at him, I fancied, for a moment with a return of the suspicion I detected before. But although there was anger and detestation, at times, in the old General's manner, there was nothing flighty.

'There remains to me', he said, as we passed under the heavy arch of the Gothic church—for its dimensions would have justified its being so styled—'but one object which can interest me during the few years that remain to me on earth, and that is to wreak on her the vengeance which, I thank God, may still be accomplished by a mortal arm.'

'What vengeance can you mean?' asked my father, in increasing amazement.

'I mean, to decapitate the monster,' he answered, with a fierce flush, and a stamp that echoed mournfully through the hollow ruin, and his clenched hand was at the same moment raised, as if it grasped the handle of an axe, while he shook it ferociously in the air.

'What?' exclaimed my father, more than ever bewildered.

'To strike her head off.'

'Cut her head off!'

'Aye, with a hatchet, with a spade, or with anything that can cleave through her murderous throat. You shall hear,' he answered, trembling with rage. And hurrying forward he said:

'That beam will answer for a seat; your dear child is

fatigued; let her be seated, and I will, in a few sentences, close my dreadful story.'

The squared block of wood, which lay on the grass-grown pavement of the chapel, formed a bench on which I was very glad to seat myself, and in the meantime the General called to the woodman, who had been removing some boughs which leaned upon the old walls; and, axe in hand, the hardy old fellow stood before us.

He could not tell us anything of these monuments; but there was an old man, he said, a ranger of this forest, at present sojourning in the house of the priest, about two miles away, who could point out every monument of the old Karnstein family; and, for a trifle, he undertook to bring him back with him, if we would lend him one of our horses, in little more than half-an-hour.

'Have you been long employed about this forest?' asked my father of the old man.

'I have been a woodman here,' he answered in his *patois*, 'under the forester, all my days; so has my father before me, and so on, as many generations as I can count up. I could show you the very house in the village here, in which my ancestors lived.'

'How came the village to be deserted?' asked the General.

'It was troubled by *revenants*, sir; several were tracked to their graves, there detected by the usual tests, and extinguished in the usual way, by decapitation, by the stake, and by burning;* but not until many of the villagers were killed.

'But after all these proceedings according to law,' he continued—'so many graves opened, and so many vampires deprived of their horrible animation—the village was not relieved. But a Moravian nobleman,* who happened to be travelling this way, heard how matters were, and being skilled—as many people are in his country—in such affairs, he offered to deliver the village from its tormentor. He did so thus: There being a bright moon that night, he ascended, shortly after sunset, the tower of the chapel here, from whence he could distinctly see the churchyard beneath him; you can see it from that window. From this point he watched until he saw the vampire come out of his grave, and place near it the linen clothes in which he had been folded, and then glide away towards the village to plague its inhabitants.

'The stranger, having seen all this, came down from the steeple, took the linen wrappings of the vampire, and carried them up to the top of the tower, which he again mounted. When the vampire returned from his prowlings and missed his clothes, he cried furiously to the Moravian, whom he saw at the summit of the tower, and who, in reply, beckoned him to ascend and take them. Whereupon the vampire, accepting his invitation, began to climb the steeple, and so soon as he had reached the battlements, the Moravian, with a stroke of his sword, clove his skull in twain, hurling him down to the church-yard, whither, descending by the winding stairs, the stranger followed and cut his head off, and next day delivered it and the body to the villagers, who duly impaled and burnt them.*

'This Moravian nobleman had authority from the then head of the family to remove the tomb of Mircalla, Countess Karnstein, which he did effectually, so that in a little while its site was quite forgotten.'

'Can you point out where it stood?' asked the General, eagerly.

The forester shook his head and smiled.

'Not a soul living could tell you that now,' he said; 'besides, they say her body was removed; but no one is sure of that either.'

Having thus spoken, as time pressed, he dropped his axe and departed, leaving us to hear the remainder of the General's strange story.

CHAPTER XIV

THE MEETING

'My beloved child,' he resumed, 'was now growing rapidly worse. The physician who attended her had failed to produce the slightest impression upon her disease, for such I then supposed it to be. He saw my alarm, and suggested a consultation. I called in an abler physician, from Gratz. Several days elapsed before he arrived. He was a good and pious, as well as a learned man. Having seen my poor ward together, they withdrew to my library to confer and discuss. I, from the adjoining room, where I awaited their summons, heard these two gentlemen's voices raised in something sharper than a strictly philosophical discussion. I knocked at the door and entered. I found the old physician from Gratz maintaining his theory. His rival was combating it with undisguised ridicule, accompanied with bursts of laughter. This unseemly manifestation subsided and the altercation ended on my entrance.

'"Sir," said my first physician, "my learned brother seems to think that you want a conjuror, and not a doctor."

'"Pardon me," said the old physician from Gratz, looking displeased, "I shall state my own view of the case in my own way another time. I grieve, Monsieur le Général, that by my skill and science I can be of no use. Before I go I shall do myself the honour to suggest something to you."

'He seemed thoughtful, and sat down at a table and began to write. Profoundly disappointed, I made my bow, and as I turned to go, the other doctor pointed over his shoulder to his companion who was writing, and then, with a shrug, significantly touched his forehead.

'This consultation, then, left me precisely where I was. I walked out into the grounds, all but distracted. The doctor from Gratz, in ten or fifteen minutes, overtook me. He apologized for having followed me, but said that he could not conscientiously take his leave without a few words more. He told me that he could not be mistaken; no natural disease exhibited the same symptoms; and that death was already very near. There remained, however, a day, or possibly two, of life. If the fatal seizure were at once arrested, with great care and skill her strength might possibly return. But all hung now upon the confines of the irrevocable. One more assault might extinguish the last spark of vitality which is, every moment, ready to die.

'"And what is the nature of the seizure you speak of?" I entreated.

'"I have stated all fully in this note, which I place in your hands upon the distinct condition that you send for the nearest clergyman, and open my letter in his presence, and on no account read it till he is with you; you would despise it else, and it is a matter of life and death. Should the priest fail you, then, indeed, you may read it."

'He asked me, before taking his leave finally, whether I would wish to see a man curiously learned upon the very subject, which, after I had read his letter, would probably interest me above all others, and he urged me earnestly to invite him to visit him there; and so took his leave.

'The ecclesiastic was absent, and I read the letter by myself. At another time, or in another case, it might have excited my ridicule. But into what quackeries will not people rush for a last chance, where all accustomed means have failed, and the life of a beloved object is at stake?

'Nothing, you will say, could be more absurd than the learned man's letter. It was monstrous enough to have consigned him to a madhouse. He said that the patient was suffering from the visits of a vampire! The punctures which she described as having occurred near the throat, were, he insisted, the insertion of those two long, thin, and sharp teeth which, it is well known, are peculiar to vampires; and there could be no doubt, he added, as to the well-defined presence of the small livid mark which all concurred in describing as that induced by the demon's lips, and every symptom described by the sufferer was in exact conformity with those recorded in every case of a similar visitation.

'Being myself wholly sceptical as to the existence of any such portent as the vampire, the supernatural theory of the good doctor furnished, in my opinion, but another instance of learning and intelligence oddly associated with some one hallucination. I was so miserable, however, that, rather than try nothing, I acted upon the instructions of the letter.

'I concealed myself in the dark dressing-room, that opened upon the poor patient's room, in which a candle was burning, and watched there till she was fast asleep. I stood at the door, peeping through the small crevice, my sword laid on the table beside me, as my directions prescribed, until, a little after one, I saw a large black object, very ill-defined, crawl, as it seemed to me, over the foot of the bed, and swiftly spread itself up to the poor girl's throat, where it swelled, in a moment, into a great, palpitating mass.

'For a few moments I had stood petrified. I now sprang forward, with my sword in my hand. The black creature suddenly contracted toward the foot of the bed, glided over it, and, standing on the floor about a yard below the foot of the bed, with a glare of skulking ferocity and horror fixed on me, I saw Millarca. Speculating I know not what, I struck at her instantly with my sword; but I saw her standing near the door, unscathed. Horrified, I pursued, and struck again. She was gone; and my sword flew to shivers against the door.

'I can't describe to you all that passed on that horrible night. The whole house was up and stirring. The spectre Millarca was gone. But her victim was sinking fast, and before the morning dawned, she died.'

The old General was agitated. We did not speak to him. My father walked to some little distance, and began reading the inscriptions on the tombstones; and thus occupied, he strolled into the door of a side-chapel to prosecute his researches. The General leaned against the wall, dried his eyes, and sighed heavily. I was relieved on hearing the voices of Carmilla and Madame, who were at that moment approaching. The voices died away.

In this solitude, having just listened to so strange a story, connected, as it was, with the great and titled dead, whose monuments were mouldering among the dust and ivy round us, and every incident of which bore so awfully upon my own mysterious case—in this haunted spot, darkened by the towering foliage that rose on every side, dense and high above its noiseless walls—a horror began to steal over me, and my heart sank as I thought that my friends were, after all, not about to enter and disturb this triste and ominous scene.

The old General's eyes were fixed on the ground, as he leaned with his hand upon the basement* of a shattered monument.

Under a narrow, arched doorway, surmounted by one of those demoniacal grotesques in which the cynical and ghastly fancy of old Gothic carving delights, I saw very gladly the beautiful face and figure of Carmilla enter the shadowy chapel.

I was just about to rise and speak, and nodded smiling, in answer to her peculiarly engaging smile; when with a cry, the old man by my side caught up the woodman's hatchet, and started forward. On seeing him a brutalized change came over her features. It was an instantaneous and horrible transformation, as she made a crouching step backwards. Before I could utter a scream, he struck at her with all his force, but she dived under his blow, and unscathed, caught him in her tiny grasp by the wrist. He struggled for a moment to release his arm, but his hand opened, the axe fell to the ground, and the girl was gone.

He staggered against the wall. His grey hair stood upon his head, and a moisture shone over his face, as if he were at the point of death.

The frightful scene had passed in a moment. The first thing I recollect after, is Madame standing before me, and impatiently repeating again and again, the question, 'Where is Mademoiselle Carmilla?'

I answered at length, 'I don't know—I can't tell—she went there,' and I pointed to the door through which Madame had just entered; 'only a minute or two since.'

'But I have been standing there, in the passage, ever since Mademoiselle Carmilla entered; and she did not return.'

She then began to call 'Carmilla', through every door and passage and from the windows, but no answer came.

'She called herself Carmilla?' asked the General, still agitated.

'Carmilla, yes,' I answered.

'Aye,' he said; 'that is Millarca. That is the same person who long ago was called Mircalla, Countess Karnstein. Depart from this accursed ground, my poor child, as quickly as you can. Drive to the clergyman's house, and stay there till we come. Begone! May you never behold Carmilla more; you will not find her here.'

CHAPTER XV

ORDEAL AND EXECUTION

As he spoke one of the strangest-looking men I ever beheld, entered the chapel at the door through which Carmilla had made her entrance and her exit. He was tall, narrow-chested, stooping, with high shoulders, and dressed in black. His face was brown and dried in with deep furrows; he wore an oddly-shaped hat with a broad leaf.* His hair, long and grizzled, hung on his shoulders. He wore a pair of gold spectacles, and walked slowly, with an odd shambling gait, with his face sometimes turned up to the sky, and sometimes bowed down toward the ground, and seemed to wear a perpetual smile; his long thin arms were swinging, and his lank hands, in old black gloves ever so much too wide for them, waving and gesticulating in utter abstraction.

'The very man!' exclaimed the General, advancing with manifest delight. 'My dear Baron, how happy I am to see you, I had no hope of meeting you so soon.' He signed to my father, who had by this time returned, leading the fantastic old gentleman, whom he called the Baron, to meet him. He introduced him formally, and they at once entered into earnest conversation. The stranger took a roll of paper from his pocket, and spread it on the worn surface of a tomb that stood by. He had a pencil case in his fingers, with which he traced imaginary lines from point to point on the paper, which from their often glancing from it, together, at certain points of the building, I concluded to be a plan of the chapel. He accompanied, what I may term, his lecture, with occasional readings from a dirty little book, whose yellow leaves were closely written over.

They sauntered together down the side aisle, opposite to the spot where I was standing, conversing as they went; then they began measuring distances by paces, and finally they all stood together, facing a piece of the side-wall, which they began to examine with great minuteness; pulling off the ivy that clung over it, and rapping the plaster with the ends of their sticks, scraping here, and knocking there. At length they ascertained the existence of a broad marble tablet, with letters carved in relief upon it.

With the assistance of the woodman, who soon returned, a monumental inscription, and carved escutcheon,* were disclosed. They proved to be those of the long lost monument of Mircalla, Countess Karnstein.

The old General, though not I fear given to the praying mood, raised his hands and eyes to heaven, in mute thanksgiving for some moments.

'To-morrow', I heard him say; 'the commissioner will be here, and the Inquisition will be held according to law.'*

Then turning to the old man with the gold spectacles, whom I have described, he shook him warmly by both hands and said:

'Baron, how can I thank you? How can we all thank you? You will have delivered this region from a plague that has scourged its inhabitants for more than a century. The horrible enemy, thank God, is at last tracked.'

My father led the stranger aside, and the General followed. I knew that he had led them out of hearing, that he might relate my case, and I saw them glance often quickly at me, as the discussion proceeded.

My father came to me, kissed me again and again, and leading me from the chapel, said:

'It is time to return, but before we go home, we must add to our party the good priest, who lives but a little way from this; and persuade him to accompany us to the schloss.'

In this quest we were successful: and I was glad, being unspeakably fatigued when we reached home. But my satisfaction was changed to dismay, on discovering that there were no tidings of Carmilla. Of the scene that had occurred in the ruined chapel, no explanation was offered to me, and it was clear that it was a secret which my father for the present determined to keep from me.

The sinister absence of Carmilla made the remembrance of the scene more horrible to me. The arrangements for that night were singular. Two servants, and Madame were to sit up in my room that night; and the ecclesiastic with my father kept watch in the adjoining dressing-room.

The priest had performed certain solemn rites that night, the purport of which I did not understand any more than I comprehended the reason of this extraordinary precaution taken for my safety during sleep.

I saw all clearly a few days later.

The disappearance of Carmilla was followed by the discontinuance of my nightly sufferings.

You have heard, no doubt, of the appalling superstition that prevails in Upper and Lower Styria, in Moravia, Silesia, in Turkish Servia,* in Poland, even in Russia; the superstition, so we must call it, of the Vampire.

If human testimony, taken with every care and solemnity, judicially, before commissions innumerable, each consisting of many members, all chosen for integrity and intelligence, and constituting reports more voluminous perhaps than exist upon any one other class of cases, is worth anything, it is difficult to deny, or even to doubt the existence of such a phenomenon as the Vampire.*

For my part I have heard no theory by which to explain what I myself have witnessed and experienced, other than that supplied by the ancient and well-attested belief of the country.

The next day the formal proceedings took place in the Chapel of Karnstein. The grave of the Countess Mircalla was opened; and the General and my father recognized each his perfidious and beautiful guest, in the face now disclosed to view. The features, though a hundred and fifty years had passed since her funeral, were tinted with the warmth of life. Her eyes were open; no cadaverous smell exhaled from the coffin. The two medical men, one officially present, the other on the part of the promoter of the inquiry, attested the marvellous fact, that there was a faint but appreciable respiration, and a corresponding action of the heart. The limbs were perfectly flexible, the flesh elastic; and the leaden coffin floated with blood, in which to a depth of seven inches, the body lay immersed. Here then, were all the admitted signs and proofs of vampirism. The body, therefore, in accordance with the ancient practice, was raised, and a sharp stake driven through the heart of the vampire, who uttered a piercing shriek at the moment, in all respects such as might escape from a living person in the last agony. Then the head was struck off, and a torrent of blood flowed from the severed neck. The body and head were next placed on a pile of wood, and reduced to ashes, which were thrown upon the river and borne away, and that territory has never since been plagued by the visits of a vampire.

My father has a copy of the report of the Imperial Commission, with the signatures of all who were present at these proceedings, attached in verification of the statement. It is from this official paper that I have summarized my account of this last shocking scene.*

CHAPTER XVI

CONCLUSION

I write all this you suppose with composure. But far from it; I cannot think of it without agitation. Nothing but your earnest desire so repeatedly expressed, could have induced me to sit down to a task that has unstrung my nerves for months to come, and reinduced a shadow of the unspeakable horror which years after my deliverance continued to make my days and nights dreadful, and solitude insupportably terrific.

Let me add a word or two about that quaint Baron Vordenburg, to whose curious lore we were indebted for the discovery of the Countess Mircalla's grave.

He had taken up his abode in Gratz, where, living upon a mere pittance, which was all that remained to him of the once princely estates of his family, in Upper Styria, he devoted himself to the minute and laborious investigation of the marvellously authenticated tradition of Vampirism. He had at his fingers' ends all the great and little works upon the subject: 'Magia Posthuma', 'Phlegon de Mirabilibus', 'Augustinus de curâ pro Mortuis', 'Philosophicae et Christianae Cogitationes de Vampiris', by John Christofer Harenberg;* and a thousand others, among which I remember only a few of those which he lent to my father. He had a voluminous digest of all the judicial cases, from which he had extracted a system of principles that appear to govern—some always, and others occasionally only—the condition of the vampire. I may mention, in passing, that the deadly pallor attributed to that sort of *revenants*, is a mere melodramatic fiction. They present, in the grave, and when they show themselves in human society, the appearance of healthy life. When disclosed to light in their coffins, they exhibit all the symptoms that are enumerated as those which proved the vampire-life of the long-dead Countess Karnstein.

How they escape from their graves and return to them for certain hours every day, without displacing the clay or leaving any trace of disturbance in the state of the coffin or the cerements, has always been admitted to be utterly inexplicable.* The amphibious existence of the vampire is sustained by daily renewed slumber in the grave. Its horrible lust for living blood supplies the vigour of its waking existence. The vampire is prone to be fascinated with an engrossing vehemence, resembling the passion of love, by particular persons. In pursuit of these it will exercise inexhaustible patience and stratagem, for access to a particular object may be obstructed in a hundred ways. It will never desist until it has satiated its passion, and drained the very life of its coveted victim. But it will, in these cases, husband and protract its murderous enjoyment with the refinement of an epicure, and heighten it by the gradual approaches of an artful courtship. In these cases it seems to yearn for something like sympathy and consent. In ordinary ones it goes direct to its object, overpowers with violence, and strangles and exhausts often at a single feast.

The vampire is, apparently, subject, in certain situations, to special conditions. In the particular instance of which I have given you a relation, Mircalla seemed to be limited to a name which, if not her real one, should at least reproduce, without the omission or addition of a single letter, those, as we say, anagrammatically, which compose it. *Carmilla* did this; so did *Millarca*.

My father related to the Baron Vordenburg, who remained with us for two or three weeks after the expulsion of Carmilla, the story about the Moravian nobleman and the vampire at

Karnstein churchyard, and then he asked the Baron how he had discovered the exact position of the long-concealed tomb of the Countess Millarca? The Baron's grotesque features puckered up into a mysterious smile; he looked down, still smiling, on his worn spectacle-case and fumbled with it. Then looking up, he said:

'I have many journals, and other papers, written by that remarkable man; the most curious among them is one treating of the visit of which you speak, to Karnstein. The tradition, of course, discolours and distorts a little. He might have been termed a Moravian nobleman, for he had changed his abode to that territory, and was, beside, a noble. But he was, in truth, a native of Upper Styria. It is enough to say that in very early youth he had been a passionate and favoured lover of the beautiful Mircalla, Countess Karnstein. Her early death plunged him into inconsolable grief. It is the nature of vampires to increase and multiply, but according to an ascertained and ghostly law.

'Assume, at starting, a territory perfectly free from that pest. How does it begin, and how does it multiply itself? I will tell you. A person, more or less wicked, puts an end to himself. A suicide, under certain circumstances, becomes a vampire. That spectre visits living people in their slumbers; *they* die, and almost invariably, in the grave, develop into vampires. This happened in the case of the beautiful Mircalla, who was haunted by one of those demons. My ancestor, Vordenburg, whose title I still bear, soon discovered this, and in the course of the studies to which he devoted himself, learned a great deal more.

'Among other things, he concluded that suspicion of vampirism would probably fall, sooner or later, upon the dead Countess, who in life had been his idol. He conceived a horror, be she what she might, of her remains being profaned by the outrage of a posthumous execution. He has left a curious paper to prove that the vampire, on its expulsion from its amphibious existence, is projected into a far more horrible life; and he resolved to save his once beloved Mircalla from this.

'He adopted the stratagem of a journey here, a pretended removal of her remains, and a real obliteration of her monument. When age had stolen upon him, and from the vale of years he looked back on the scenes he was leaving, he considered, in a different spirit, what he had done, and a horror took possession of him. He made the tracings and notes which have guided me to the very spot, and drew up a confession of the deception that he had practised. If he had intended any further action in this matter, death prevented him; and the hand of a remote descendant has, too late for many, directed the pursuit to the lair of the beast.'

We talked a little more, and among other things he said was this:

'One sign of the vampire is the power of the hand. The slender hand of Mircalla closed like a vice of steel on the General's wrist when he raised the hatchet to strike. But its power is not confined to its grasp; it leaves a numbness in the limb it seizes, which is slowly, if ever, recovered from.'

The following Spring my father took me a tour through Italy. We remained away for more than a year. It was long before the terror of recent events subsided; and to this hour the image of Carmilla returns to memory with ambiguous alternations—sometimes the playful, languid, beautiful girl; sometimes the writhing fiend I saw in the ruined church; and often from a reverie I have started, fancying I heard the light step of Carmilla at the drawing-room door.

EXPLANATORY NOTES

GREEN TEA

Green Tea was serialized in four successive issues of *All the Year Round*, then edited by Charles Dickens. The story was divided as follows: Preface and Chapters 1–2 (*AYR* vol. 2, Number 47 new series; 23 October 1869); Chapters 3–5 (48: 30 October); Chapters 6–8 (49: 6 November); Chapters 9–10 and Conclusion (50: 13 November).

5 *Martin Hesselius*: like many learned men in Germany, The Netherlands, and Scandinavia (*c.*1500–1800), Hesselius has Latinized his name (cf. Celsius, Gryphius, Benzelius). Given the role of Swedenborg's *Arcana Caelestia* in the story, Le Fanu may have named him for Andreas Hesselius, Swedenborg's cousin.

6 *Van Loo of Leyden*: Van Loo is imaginary, but Le Fanu may have remembered the famous and versatile Sebald Justinus Brugmans (1763–1819), Professor of Botany at the University of Leiden from 1786, and later also Professor of Natural History and Chemistry. Brugmans was Rector Magnificus during the French occupation.

6 *high-church*: since the story is taking place about 1805, Le Fanu is not suggesting the leaning toward ritualism or 'Roman' practices that the term came to connote during the Tractarian Movement of the 1830s and early 1840s. Here it suggests a clergyman committed to maintaining the Church of England in all its privileges. Le Fanu adds a commitment to neatness, in keeping with a sense of a high calling.

6 *Lady Mary Heyduke's*: Heyduke is an unlikely English family name. A heyduke or heyduck (Serbian *hajduk*) is usually a brigand, but sometimes an irregular soldier. Le Fanu would have found references to Serbian Heyducqs in Dom Augustin Calmet's *The Phantom World*, one of his sources for 'Carmilla'.

7 *funds*: long-term interest-bearing government bonds.

7 *Kenlis*: there is no English place so named, but Kenlis (Irish *Cean-lis*, head fort) is an old name for Kells in County Meath.

7 *vestry-room*: a room adjacent to the sanctuary in a church, where the clergy put on their vestments.

11 *vicar*: in the Church of England, the priest in charge of a parish.

11 *Dawlbridge*: not a real place, but echoing Dawlish in Devon, site of a ford over the Dalch ('black') river, originally Dawlish river.

11 *green tea*: tea that has not been fermented. The leaves are steamed. It is usually drunk without milk, sugar, or lemon.

13 *Turkey carpet*: a rectangular deep-piled carpet from Turkey or Iran, with a broad border and usually a pattern of abstract botanical forms.

14 *Swedenborg's Arcana Caelestia*: Emanuel Swedenborg's *Arcana caelestia* [or *Coelestia*] *quae in Scriptura Sacra, seu Verbo Domini sunt detecta; nempe quae in Genesi et Exodo, una cum mirabilis quae visa sunt in Mundo Spiritum, et in Coelo Angelorum* (Heavenly Secrets which are in Holy Scripture, or the Word of the Lord, revealed; specifically those which are in Genesis and Exodus, together with wonders seen in the World of Spirits and in the Heaven of the Angels). Jennings has the first edition, in eight volumes, published in London by John Lewis (1749–56). The *Arcana* contains the texts of Genesis and Exodus, with Swedenborg's lengthy commentary thereon, and a further narrative commentary describing Swedenborg's visions, which enabled him to see and talk with angels and spirits, and so understand the hidden or allegorical meanings of Scripture.

14 *'When man's interior sight . . . and so on'*: in the *Arcana* the biblical text is in numbered verses, as in Bibles. Swedenborg's double commentary is in numbered paragraphs. 'When man's interior sight . . . bodily sight' is *Arcana Caelestia* 1619; 'By the internal sight . . . and so on' is *AC* 994. See *Arcana Coelestia/The Heavenly Arcana*, 10 vols. (New York: American Swedenborg Printing and Publishing Society, 1870). That Dr Hesselius's translation coincides word for word with the standard translation is one more proof of his remarkable powers. He may have checked against John Clowes's translation (London, 1802–16).

14 *'There are . . . evil spirits'*: a basic Swedenborgian idea, though I have not found this exact phrasing. See *AC* 5977–8, 5993.

15 *'With wicked genii . . . eternal ruin'*: 'With wicked genii . . . within it' (*AC* 1760; genii are spirits in Hell); 'The evil spirits . . . their former state' (*AC* 5852); 'If evil spirits . . . the good of faith' (*AC* 5863); 'Nothing is more carefully . . . destroy him' (I have not found this phrasing in *Arcana*, but see Swedenborg's *Heaven and Hell*, 292: 'The Lord takes exceeding care that spirits may not

know that they are with man; for if they knew they would speak with him, and then evil spirits would destroy him. For evil spirits, because they are conjoined with hell, desire nothing more than to destroy man'); 'The delight ... eternal ruin' (*AC* 5864).

15 *bestial forms*: this partly echoes *AC* 3646. Swedenborg does not include monkeys among the 'bestial forms'.

16 *Dr Harley*: many prominent physicians have traditionally had their consulting-rooms in London's Harley Street, so that 'Harley Street' often designates the medical profession.

17 *hippish*: in low spirits, suffering from hypochondria, considered a form of melancholy.

19 *people*: relatives.

19 *season*: the London social season (May–July). Brighton, on the English Channel, was then a fashionable resort.

19 *Richmond*: a small town in Surrey, about ten miles from central London, then in the country but now a London suburb.

21 *Schalken's*: Godfried Schalken (1643–1706), a Dutch painter admired for his contrasts of light and darkness, and especially for his candle-light effects. He is the protagonist of Le Fanu's 'Strange Event in the Life of Schalken the Painter' (*Dublin University Magazine*, May 1839), a story of marriage with the dead. In Le Fanu's *The Rose and the Key* (1871), Mr Damian is 'exhibited, like a figure of Schalken's, partly in deep shadow, and partly in the oblique candle-light' (chapter 85).

21 *nemesis*: the Greek goddess of just punishment or vengeance.

22 *City*: the oldest part of London, originally enclosed with walls.

25 *skance*: sideways, askance.

32 *"paries"*: wall, partition (Latin).

32 *Dee*: a Welsh/English river, flowing through Chester and into the Irish Sea.

THE FAMILIAR

Apart from a few slight verbal changes and omissions, and a change of title, 'The Familiar' is a reprinting of 'The Watcher' from Le Fanu's *Ghost Stories and Tales of Mystery* (Dublin: J. McGlashan, 1851).

'The Watcher' is not divided into chapters, and its paragraphs are much longer.

In *Ghost Stories*, 'The Watcher' had an epigraph: 'How long wilt thou not depart from me? Thou terrifiest me through visions: so that my soul chooseth strangling rather than my life.' Le Fanu has adapted Job 7: 13–15: 'When I say, My bed shall comfort me, my couch shall ease my complaint; Then thou scarest me with dreams, and terrifiest me through visions: So that my soul chooseth strangling, and death rather than my life.'

The 1851 'Watcher' had a different opening paragraph:

> It is now more than fifty years since the occurrences which I am about to relate caused a strange sensation in the gay society of Dublin. The fashionable world, however, is no recorder of traditions; the memory of selfishness seldom reaches far; and the events which occasionally disturb the polite monotony of its pleasant and heartless progress, however stamped with the characters of misery and horror, scarcely ever outlive the gossip of a season; and, except perhaps in the remembrance of a few more directly interested in the consequences of the catastrophe, are in a little time lost to the recollection of all. The appetite for scandal, or for horror, has been sated; the incident can yield no more of interest or of novelty; curiosity, frustrated by impenetrable mystery, gives over the pursuit in despair; the tale has ceased to be new, grows stale and flat; and so, in a few years, inquiry subsides into indifference, and all is forgotten.

Here and elsewhere the narrator is presented as having personally witnessed some of the story's incidents. Paragraph 2 of 'The Watcher' begins, as here, 'Somewhere about the year 1794 . . .'

42 *the American War*: the American Revolution (1776–81).

43 *south side of the town*: that part of Dublin south of the River Liffey. Since Barton's way home brought him past the wall bounding Trinity College Park, he presumably lived in or near Merrion Square, laid out about 1769.

43 *free-thinker*: one who rejected the authority of the Bible and the teachings of any church in religious matters.

43 *gaming*: gambling.

43 *Dowager Lady L——*: Dowager Lady Rochdale in 'The Watcher'.

43 *reigning toast*: a young woman known for her beauty, and so often toasted by gallants.

44 *street . . . laid out*: Lady L—— probably lived in or near Mountjoy Square, then very fashionable. Barton would cross the Liffey by either the Carlisle (now O'Connell) Bridge (1794), or the Essex (now Grattan) Bridge (1676; rebuilt 1755), and presumably makes his way toward the Liffey along Gardiner Street, laid out about 1787.

45 *evidences of revelation*: evidence that Christian doctrine, as revealed in the Bible and taught in the churches, is true. They may be discussing William Paley's newly published *View of the Evidences of Christianity* (1794), which argued that design in the universe implied a divine rational mind.

45 *'French principles' . . . Whiggism*: a sceptical attitude toward any traditional authority, political or religious, presumably based on the ideas of Voltaire and the Encyclopaedists, by 1794 considered responsible for the French Revolution. The Whig Party, which preferred Parliamentary power to royal power, welcomed the earlier stages of the French Revolution.

47 *a thumb*: in 'The Watcher' a coarse thumb.

48 *Crow-street*: the Theatre Royal, Crow Street, opened in 1758, and closed in the 1820s. The theatre played a small part in Le Fanu's family history: its 1758 opening and early success forced his great-grandfather, Thomas Sheridan (1719–88), manager of the older Smock Alley Theatre, to move to London.

48 *the College*: Trinity College.

49 *the College Park*: Barton is walking along Nassau Street. The 'dead wall' was replaced by iron railings in 1842.

50 *House of Commons . . . his and mine*: though subject to the British Crown, Ireland had its own parliament from 1295 until 1800; the Irish Parliament was independent of the British Parliament 1782–1800. The Irish Houses of Parliament (Lords and Commons), now the Bank of Ireland, stand in College Green, an open space in front of the main entrance to Trinity College. In 'The Watcher' the Member is identified as 'a Mr Norcott;' the narrator is not present, nor does he claim to know Norcott or Barton. 'The Watcher' text reads: 'As they walked down together, he was observed to become absent and silent, and to a degree so marked as scarcely to consist with good breeding; and this, in one who was obviously, in all his habits, so perfectly a gentleman, seemed to argue the pressure of some urgent and absorbing anxiety. It was afterwards known that, during the whole of that walk . . .'.

52 *in Chancery*: involved in a civil lawsuit, presumably over inherited property, or a disputed will.

52 *Dr R——*: Dr Richards in 'The Watcher'.

53 *lock-jaw*: a form of tetanus, during which muscular contraction prevents moving the jaws.

53 *Naples*: Lisbon in 'The Watcher'.

54 *foremast-man*: a sailor assigned to work the upper rigging on the mast nearest the ship's bow. A frigate was a fast three-masted warship, usually carrying 30 to 40 guns.

54 *Dame Street*: a continuation of College Green westward, toward Dublin Castle.

58 *blue devils*: low spirits.

58 *Dr——*: Dr Macklin in 'The Watcher'.

63 *prince of the powers of the air*: the devil, who rules a host of invisible evil spirits. 'Wherein in time past ye walked according to the course of this world, according to the prince of the powers of the air, the spirit that now worketh in the children of disobedience' (Ephesians 2: 2).

63 *'resist . . . flee from thee'*: James 4: 7.

66 *whipped . . . at the cart's tail*: malefactors were sometimes tied behind a slow-moving cart and whipped through the principle streets.

66 *a rump and a dozen*: a rump of beef and a dozen bottles of claret, then a common wager.

67 *at fault*: at a loss.

67 *runs like a lamp-lighter*: like a flash or streak of light. A common eighteenth-century phrase, it does not refer to any special swiftness among the men who lit street lamps.

68 *packet*: a ship that sails on a regular schedule, here one crossing the English Channel.

69 *provincial patois*: a dialect of a language, often with peculiarities of vocabulary and pronunciation.

69 *personnel*: personal appearance.

70 *jockey*: manipulate, outsmart.

70 *Clontarf*: then a small village on Dublin Bay, two miles north of the central city; now part of the city.

72 *receipts*: recipes or formulae for herbal remedies.

77 *Requiescat*: may he/she rest (in peace), often the first word of a
Latin epitaph.

77 *heart-broken*: 'The Watcher' reads: 'heart-broken; a circumstance
which, for the sentimental purposes of our tale, is much to be
deplored. But truth must be told, especially in a narrative,
whose chief, if not only, pretensions to interest consist in a rigid
adherence to facts, or what are so reported to have been.'

81 *Plymouth*: a port on the English Channel, headquarters of the
British Navy's Channel Fleet.

82 *ipsissima verba*: the very own words.

MR JUSTICE HARBOTTLE

'Mr Justice Harbottle' appeared as 'The Haunted House in Westminster', without chapter divisions, in *Belgravia* (January 1872), then
edited by Mary Elizabeth Braddon, the author of *Lady Audley's Secret*
(1861–2; World's Classics), *Aurora Floyd* (1863), and other Victorian
sensational novels. The story is a drastic revision of Le Fanu's 'An
Account of Some Strange Disturbances in Aungier Street' (*Dublin
University Magazine*, December 1853).

84 *annuity . . . quarter-day*: an annuity is a fixed yearly income,
payable in installments on each of the year's four quarter-days.

85 *Westminster*: that part of London immediately west of 'the City',
containing the Houses of Parliament, Westminster Abbey, and
many government buildings.

85 *wainscoted*: panelled in wood.

85 *Hogarth*: William Hogarth (1697–1764), painter and engraver,
is particularly known for his many prints portraying life in
eighteenth-century London. Mr Harbottle's character and
appearance recall the coarseness, greed, sensuality, and cruelty
Hogarth often depicts.

85 *sensuality and villainy*: Le Fanu may be remembering the central
figure in Hogarth's 'The Bench' (1758), portraying the then
Chief Justice Sir John Willes, 'who allied learning with lechery'.
S. M. Ellis has suggested that Harbottle owes something to
Macaulay's description of George Jeffreys (1648–89), lord chan-
cellor under James II:

The depravity of this man has passed into a proverb . . . He
was a man of quick and vigorous parts, but constitutionally

prone to insolence and to the angry passions ... he became the most consummate bully ever known in his profession. Tenderness for others and respect for himself were feelings alike unknown to him ... The profusion of maledictions and vituperative epithets which composed his vocabulary could hardly have been rivalled in the fishmarket ... Impudence and ferocity sate upon his brow. The glare of his eyes had a fascination for the unhappy victim on whom they were fixed ... His yell of fury ... sounded like the thunder of the judgment day ... There was a fiendish exultation in the way in which he pronounced sentence on offenders ... he loved to scare them into fits by dilating with luxuriant amplification on all the details of what they were to suffer ... He frequently poured forth on plaintiffs and defendants, barristers and attorneys, witnesses and jurymen, torrents of frantic abuse, intermixed with oaths and curses ... His evenings were ordinarily given to revelry ... He was constantly surrounded on such occasions by buffoons selected ... from among the vilest pettifoggers ... He joined in their ribald talk, sang catches with them, and, when his head grew hot, hugged and kissed them in an ecstasy of drunken fondness.

See Thomas Babington Macaulay, *History of England from the Accession of James II*, ch. 4 (1849; repr. New York: John Wurtele Lovell, n.d.), i. 406–9.

85 *perukes*: wigs.

86 *Court of Common Pleas*: a court for civil cases between private parties, fixed at Westminster (abolished 1873). Harbottle, however, also hears criminal cases and goes on circuit, perhaps reflecting aspects of the Irish legal system. There was a Chief Judge of Common Pleas, and four subordinate judges.

86 *'winter tales'*: tales traditionally told by the fireside in winter, usually about supernatural or marvellous events.

87 *letting value*: the rent that can be charged to a tenant.

87 *Turkey merchant ... James I*: a member of the Turkey or Levant Company, chartered by James I (King 1603–25) and given exclusive rights to conduct British trade with the Turkish Empire.

87 *flambeaux ... chairs*: footmen with torches (flambeaux) escorted coaches or sedan-chairs through the unlit streets of seventeenth- and eighteenth-century cities.

87 *well-staircase*: the stairwell, or space occupied by the stairs.

88 *session of 1746*: the parliamentary session. The date partly explains Harbottle's alertness to a possible political conspiracy. In July 1745, Bonnie Prince Charlie landed in Scotland, rallied many of the clans and their chieftains to his side, captured Edinburgh, and invaded England, intending to gain the throne for his father, 'James III', the Stuart claimant, by driving out the Protestant George II, of the House of Hanover. The Prince reached Derby before opposing forces had gathered to attack him; he retreated, and was finally defeated at Culloden (16 April 1746).

88 *division . . . order*: the Lords and Commons vote by 'dividing', members leaving their places to enter the aye or the no lobby. Harbottle's order is the legal or judicial profession.

89 *roquelaure*: a heavy knee-length cloak.

90 *Circean enchantment*: in the *Odyssey* (book 10), the sorceress Circe treats Odysseus' sailors to a lavish banquet, which turns them into swine.

90 *now-a-days*: like many Victorians, Le Fanu saw the eighteenth century as a time of unrestrained social and verbal behaviour that would be acceptable 'now' only in a barracks.

91 *livery*: a distinctive uniform or costume, worn by male servants.

92 *Privy Council*: originally the sovereign's appointed advisers, but Harbottle probably means the prime minister and cabinet.

92 *Jacobite plot*: a plot to restore the Stuarts in the person of 'James III' (Latin *Jacobus*). See note to p. 88.

92 *State prisoners*: those accused of high treason.

92 *Whig name*: Whigs supported the Protestant Hanoverian succession; Stuart supporters were Tories. An earlier Hugh Peters (1598–1660) was one of the Puritan judges who condemned the Stuart King Charles I to death in 1649.

92 *Thames-street . . . Three Kings*: facing, across from, an inn or tavern named for the Three Magi. Thames Street, now divided at London Bridge into Upper and Lower Thames Street, runs beside the Thames from Blackfriars Bridge to the Tower of London. Harbottle's joke suggests that, with two claimants to the throne, Britain already has one king too many.

93 *king's attorney-general*: the chief law officer of the Crown.

94 *guinea*: then a gold coin (last minted 1813), worth 21 shillings (£1. 1*s*.).

94 *ran like a lamplighter*: see note to p. 67.

94 *watchman*: one appointed to patrol the streets at night.

94 *broad street ... lash*: see note to p. 66. Those condemned to death in London travelled from Newgate prison, adjacent to the Old Bailey, the court where criminals were tried, to Tyburn, at the Hyde Park end of Edgware Road, where they were publicly executed. Sometimes the condemned were tied to a cart and whipped throughout the journey.

94 *'affidavit man' or footpad*: an affidavit man was a professional witness, who would swear to anything. Footpads held up and robbed pedestrians.

95 *pharisaical*: rigorous, self-righteous, observing the letter rather-than the spirit of the law.

96 *saque*: a loose gown.

97 *Rhadamanthus*: in Greek myth, a son of Zeus, so revered for his probity that he became one of the judges of the dead in the underworld.

97 *in furore*: enraged.

97 *Mother Carey's chickens*: stormy petrels, sea birds whose appearance indicates that a storm is coming.

97 *registrar ... crown solicitor*: a registrar is a clerk who keeps track of a court's docket of cases. The crown solicitor is the government's legal adviser.

98 *circuit*: judges travel through an assigned district, holding 'sittings' (assizes) at designated cities and towns.

99 *Assizes*: court sessions held periodically to hear criminal or civil cases.

99 *scarlet and ermine*: Harbottle's official dress was a scarlet robe trimmed with ermine.

100 *epicurean*: originally a follower of the Greek philosopher Epicurus (342?–270 BC), who taught that the good life was one of rational and moderate pleasure; later, as here, the term came to mean one addicted to eating, drinking, and other sensual pleasures.

100 *crier*: a court attendant, whose duties include calling for order, summoning witnesses, and sometimes loudly repeating the judge's commands.

100 *attracted*: 'He has the usual . . . he has attracted' in *Belgravia* and Bentley first edition.

101 *tipstaff*: a bailiff, who escorts and controls prisoners at court sessions. A gown and short staff or wand were his signs of office.

101 *sheriff*: the sheriff was in charge of all arrangements for trials. Crier and tipstaff served under him.

102 *scrivinary*: handwriting.

103 *'Sblood!*: a euphemistic oath 'by God's blood'.

103 *advocate . . . at the bar*: before becoming a judge, Harbottle had been a barrister, arguing cases in court; his language and behaviour sometimes provoked a duel.

103 *'piggins full'*: a piggin is a small wooden bucket.

104 *[What of the paper . . . my belief.]*: the bracketed passage does not appear in *Belgravia*.

104 *Drury Lane*: then one of London's two licensed theatres; the present theatre is the fourth on the site. Le Fanu was proud of his relationship to the playwright Richard Brinsley Sheridan (1751–1816), his great-uncle, lessee and manager of Drury Lane 1776–1809.

104 *Lincoln's Inn*: one of the Inns of Court, containing lawyers' offices, and serving also as a law school and bar association.

104 *Thavies*: Thavie's Inn was a subordinate Inn of Court.

105 *Mrs Abington*: Frances Abington (1737–1815) was the leading actress at Drury Lane in 1764–82, later than the time of the story; she made her debut in 1755. She was the first to play Lady Teazle in Sheridan's *School for Scandal* (1777) and Betty Hoyden in his *A Trip to Scarborough* (1777).

105 *Bow Street officers*: members of London's eighteenth-century police force, attached to the Bow Street Magistrate's court in Westminster. They were also called Bow Street Runners, and, because of their red waistcoats, Robin Redbreasts. They were replaced by the Metropolitan Police in 1839.

105 *check-string*: a cord by which a coach passenger can signal the driver to stop.

106 *depended . . . by their chains*: the bodies of executed criminals were often left hanging on the gallows as a warning to others, until they rotted and fell apart. Cere-clothes were cloth shrouds waterproofed with wax, for wrapping corpses.

106 '*Idle Apprentice*': 'The Idle 'Prentice Executed at Tyburn' is Plate xi of 'Industry and Idleness', a series of twelve plates 'designed and engraved' by Hogarth (1747). The series depicts the contrasting fortunes of the Industrious Apprentice (who becomes Lord Mayor of London in Plate xii) and the Idle Apprentice. In the background of Plate xi, the hangman with the pipe sits atop the 'Triple Tree', the Tyburn gallows, a triangle of beams held up by three tall posts. The borders of Plate xi show two skeletons hung in chains.

107 *brutum fulmen*: literally an irrational thunderbolt, and so an outburst of rage.

107 *porte-cochère*: a covered entrance to a building, under which a coach could be driven.

107 *They looked . . . their shoes*: the sentence is not in *Belgravia*.

107 *temple of Themis*: Themis was the Greek goddess of justice, often portrayed holding scales.

107 *with . . . their pens*: not in *Belgravia*.

107 *king's counsel*: a senior barrister who can represent the Crown, or prosecution, in court proceedings.

108 *that shook . . . the corridors*: not in *Belgravia*.

108 *in limine*: at the bar, literally 'on the threshold'.

108 *acclamation*: 'like a deafening peal of thunder' (*Belgravia*); the next phrase ('he saw nothing . . . and grin') is not in *Belgravia*.

108 *enhanced awfully*: enchanced awfully in power (*Belgravia*).

109 *coldly*: not in *Belgravia*, which reads 'shining, as it were phosphorically, out . . .'.

109 *lumen . . . eyes*: 'lumen of the strange eyes' in *Belgravia*; lumen is light reflected off the pupil of the eye.

110 *gyves*: fetters, or chains and shackles, for the wrists and ankles.

110 *marriage à-la-mode case*: presumably some scandal in high life, but Le Fanu is also alluding to another series of plates by Hogarth, *Marriage-à-la-Mode* (1745; six plates), depicting the course of an arranged and loveless marriage; the husband dies in a duel with his wife's lover, the lover is executed, and the wife commits suicide.

111 *vapours . . . Buxton*: vapours are a state of depression. Buxton, a Derbyshire health resort with mineral waters, hot and cold

springs, and baths, was often recommended in cases of rheumatism or gout.

111   *what stuff dreams are*: an echo of Prospero (*Tempest* iv. i. 156–7): 'We are such stuff | As dreams are made on.' Prospero is explaining that what Ferdinand and Miranda have seen was illusory, the 'actors . . . all spirits'.

111   *maggot*: a whim.

111   *The copy of the*: *Belgravia* reads 'The parchment . . .'.

111   *chalk-stones*: calcium deposits that form in the joints of sufferers from gout.

112   *Odsbud! odsheart!*: God's blood! God's heart!

112   *blue devils*: see note to p. 58.

112   *Aesculapius*: the Greek god of medicine.

113   *in their own salutary way*: not in *Belgravia*.

114   *Southwark fair*: an annual fair, featuring acrobats, theatrical performances, and waxworks, held for fourteen days in early September in the London borough of Southwark, south of the Thames. Often disorderly, the fair was suppressed in 1762. Hogarth depicted the fair in a well-known engraving (1733).

114   *She stopped . . . child's hand*: not in *Belgravia*.

115   *posset*: a hot spicy drink of milk beaten with wine.

115   *Judge's*: not in *Belgravia*.

116   *vally*: value.

116   *The old house . . . the housekeeper*: in *Belgravia*, the paragraph following 'measureless scorn' reads 'But this sceptical heroine, at near twelve o'clock, being the only person awake and about, and the house within quite still, except for the uncertain wailing of the wintry winds, audible from outside, piping high among the roofs and chimneys, or rumbling at intervals, in under gusts, through the narrow channels of the streets, was herself destined to be more terrified than even was the housekeeper.'

116   *strokes*: 'she heard a sound like the strokes of a hammer on metal' (*Belgravia*).

116   *She walked out softly into the passage*: not in *Belgravia*.

116   *The room seemed thick with smoke*: not in *Belgravia*.

116   *Looking in . . . a chain*: in *Belgravia* this paragraph and the following paragraph read as follows:

Looking in, she beheld a monstrous figure, black as soot, over a furnace, beating with a mighty hammer the rings and rivets of a long iron chain, which he shifted on the huge stone of a disused jack that served him for an anvil.

The strokes, swift and heavy as they looked, sounded faint and distant. The man fixed his red eyes on her, and pointed to a coarse cloth which lay upon the flags, spread like a coverlet, with a great bulk like a huge bale stretched under it.

She said something in her panic to the unknown smith, who seemed to await only that to speak. What he said she did not tell; but he drew the cloth down from the feet, slowly disclosing the bloated features and body of the old Judge, lying flat on his back, with his eyes open, and quite dead. She remarked no more; but the servants in the room close by, startled from their sleep by a hideous scream, found her in a swoon on the flags where she had just witnessed this ghastly vision.

117 *having first searched . . . house*: not in *Belgravia*.

117 *atrabilious state*: melancholia or hypochondria.

118 '*the rich man died, and was buried*': 'the rich man also died, and was buried' (Luke 16: 22), from Christ's parable about the rich man 'clothed in purple and fine linen' who 'fared sumptuously every day', but went to hell, and the beggar Lazarus, who went to heaven.

THE ROOM IN THE DRAGON VOLANT

'The Room in the Dragon Volant' was serialized in *London Society: An Illustrated Magazine of Light and Amusing Literature for the Hours of Relaxation* (vol. 21): Chapters 1–6 (February 1872); 7–12 (March); 13–16 (April); 18–21 (May); 22–6 (June).

119 '*Mortis Imago*' . . . *Thessaliae:* 'Mortis Imago' means the appearance or semblance of death. The Latin names of the catalepsy-inducing potions can be translated as follows: *Vinum letiferum*, wine of Lethe (oblivion), death-bringing wine; *Beatifica*, the blessed, ironically because it can bring the victim to heaven; *Somnus Angelorum*, the sleep of angels; *Hypnus Sagarum*, the sleep of wise-women; *Aqua Thessaliae*, water of Thessaly, a district in Greece famous for witches. None of these appear in the histories of drugs, toxicology, or catalepsy I have consulted; they are

almost certainly Le Fanu's own concoctions. I am grateful to Professor Francis Schiller, MD, of the University of California, San Francisco, for assistance with this question.

119   *consols*: stocks and bonds (consolidated annuities) issued and guaranteed by the British government.

120   *first fall of Napoleon . . . Waterloo*: after numerous defeats, Napoleon abdicated as emperor of the French (11 April 1814), and was exiled to the island of Elba. Louis XVIII, brother of the guillotined Louis XVI, became king of France. After eleven months, Napoleon escaped from Elba, landed in France (1 March 1815), and marched on Paris, joined by the troops sent to arrest him. His second reign lasted for the 'Hundred Days'. The powers which had defeated him in 1814 mobilized their armies, and Napoleon set out to intercept them in Belgium, where his forces were defeated at Waterloo (18 June) by an allied army commanded by the Duke of Wellington.

120   *frontier side*: the frontier between France and the kingdom of the Netherlands, of which Belgium was then a part.

120   *leaders*: the two horses leading a four- or six-horse team.

120   *tournure*: shape.

121   *carmine . . . supporters*: the coat-of-arms shows a red stork against a gold background (field or). Supporters are figures of men or animals at either side of a coat-of-arms.

121   *Dobbin's*: Dobbin is the traditional name for a slow steady horse; in Thackeray's *Vanity Fair* (1847–8), Colonel Dobbin is Amelia's endlessly patient and loyal admirer. Le Fanu's mother was Emma Dobbin, of a prominent Anglo-Irish family.

122   *envious veil*: a jealous veil, because it keeps her beauty to itself.

122   *cabriole-table*: an eighteenth-century table, with legs curving outward, then inward to a claw holding a ball.

126   *Napoleon*: a gold coin bearing the image of Napoleon I, worth 20 francs.

126   *razors set*: given a sharper edge.

127   *petit souper*: a light evening meal.

127   *valet*: Beckett remembers such assertive and impudent servants as Sganarelle in Molière's *Dom Juan* (1665), Scapin in his *Les Fourberies de Scapin* (1671), and Figaro in Beaumarchais's *Le Barbier de Séville* (1775) and *Le Mariage de Figaro* (1778).

127 *devil's tattoo*: drumming impatiently with one's fingers.

128 *rug*: a lap-robe.

128 *'choker'* ... *Brummel*: a wide linen cloth wrapped tightly around the neck, as worn by Beau (George Bryan) Brummel (1778–1840), who set the style for Englishmen eager to be considered fashionably dressed during the Regency period (1811–20).

128 *chevelure*: head of hair.

128 *Scott's romances*: *Waverley*, the first of Sir Walter Scott's historical romances, appeared in 1814.

130 *Philomel*: in Greek legend, a rape victim who was turned into a nightingale.

130 *table-d'hote*: the inn's common table, where guests would eat together, as opposed to being served in a private room.

132 *seat* ... *attacked*: someone is to run against you for your seat in Parliament.

132 *MP*: Member of Parliament.

134 *gudgeons*: small minnow-like fish.

134 *undress*: an ordinary rather than a full dress uniform. Since we later learn that the officer is a colonel of dragoons, he would here be wearing a swallow-tailed green coat, scarlet *reverse* superimposed on the coat and attached with gold buttons, white breeches and stockings (or possibly since he is travelling, white gaiters and black boots), and a 'fore and aft' hat (with front and rear brims looped up), possibly bearing a black plume. Different regiments had different facings (collar, cuffs, coat-lining); since the colonel's are scarlet, he belonged to one of the first six dragoon regiments. In Napoleon's army, dragoons (French *dragons*) were cavalrymen, but were sometimes employed as infantry. Dragoons were probably so called because in the seventeenth century they were armed with a short musket called a dragon. But Le Fanu is also punning: the colonel himself is a *dragon volant* (and *violent*). See Commandant Bucquoy, *Dragons et guides* (Paris: Grancher, 1980), volume 6 of his *Les Uniformes du premier empire*. For information about Napoleonic uniforms, including those of the Imperial Guard and the Prussian hussars, I am greatly indebted to David Gilson.

134 *parbleu!*: by Jove!

136 *by play*: by gambling.

136 *habitués*: those who regularly frequent a place.

137 *bourgeois*: the middle class.

138 *pigeoned*: deceived, swindled.

139 *Mâcon*: red or white wine from the department of Saône-et-Loire, in eastern France.

139 *ichor*: the fluid in the veins of the Greek gods, which guarantees their immortality.

139 *fine-draw*: to patch so carefully that the patch cannot be distinguished from the original cloth.

139 *Madrid . . . Arcola*: Napoleon's troops occupied Madrid 1808–12. The convent, Saint Mary of Chastity, is oddly Italian *Castità*, not Spanish *Castidad*. Napoleon defeated the Austrians at Arcola, near Verona in northern Italy, 15–17 November 1796.

139 *congreve rocket*: a rocket fired from a cannon, invented by Sir William Congreve (1772–1828).

139 *'Bravo! . . . gallant uomo!'*: well done! extremely well done! [literally: a brave man! an extremely brave man!] By [the god] Bacchus! a gallant fellow!

140 *Ligny*: a Belgian village, site of an important battle of the Waterloo campaign (16 June 1815). Napoleon defeated the Prussians under Blücher, but failed to destroy the Prussian army. Its reappearance at Waterloo ensured Napoleon's defeat.

140 *sacré bleu!*: damn it!

140 *vin ordinaire*: inexpensive table wine.

140 *'Garçon'*: waiter!

140 *facings*: the collar, cuffs, and lining of a military uniform coat, usually contrasting with the coat's colour. The facings' colour identified the wearer's regiment.

141 *Henry IV*: king of France 1589–1610.

141 *revenant*: a ghost or vampire, literally one who comes back.

142 *catafalque*: a platform or framework, usually draped in black, used to support a coffin.

142 *demi-tasse of café noir*: a small cup of black coffee.

144 *ennui*: boredom.

146 *condign punishment*: a punishment suitable to the offence.

147 *Eylau*: a town in East Prussia, where Napoleon defeated the armies of Russia and Prussia (8 February 1807).

148 *upon the tapis*: literally 'on the carpet', that is, made it the subject of discussion.

150 *wooden shoes*: some peasant, wearing the traditional wooden *sabots*.

153 *an imperial*: a narrow pointed beard below the lower lip, so called after Napoleon III (emperor 1852–70).

155 *coquin*: rascal.

155 *Hôtel*: the town house of a nobleman.

156 *second restoration of the Bourbons*: the Bourbons were the French royal family, restored again after Waterloo in the person of Louis XVIII (king 1814–15, 1815–24).

160 *bal masqué . . . cards*: a costume ball, where participants would also be disguised with masks. Cards are invitations.

160 *'bifstek'*: properly *bifteck* (beefsteak), the supposed national dish of England.

161 *Greenwich*: an outlying London borough, on the Thames south east of the City. A steamboat ride to Greenwich and dinner there in one of the many riverside restaurants was a popular outing for nineteenth-century Londoners. See Dickens, *Our Mutual Friend*, bk. 2, ch. 8.

162 *trottoir*: the sidewalk or footpath.

163 *Murat . . . tactique*: Joachim Murat (1767–1815) was the most dashing and impetuous of Napoleon's cavalry commanders. Helmuth von Moltke (1800–91) was a careful planner of strategy (*tactique*), the architect of Prussian victory in the Austro-Prussian War (1866) and the Franco-Prussian War (1870–1).

164 *Caen stone*: a pale yellow building stone, quarried near Caen in Normandy.

164 *the Flying Dragon*: the dragon, combined with the architecture of the inn, suggests it dates from the reign of Francis I of France (king 1515–47), whose personal emblem was a salamander.

164 *domino*: a loose hooded garment, which thoroughly conceals the wearer.

164 *red cross . . . Englishman*: the red cross is the insignia of St George, patron saint of England, and so appropriate for Beckett.

165 *milord*: my lord, then the common term for wealthy Englishmen travelling on the Continent.

166 *Château de la Carque*: carque (Old French) means load, burden.

166 *Père la Chaise*: usually Père-Lachaise, a large cemetery in north-eastern Paris, laid out in 1804 on Jesuit-owned land, and named for the Jesuit Père [Father] de la Chaise (1624–1709), after 1674 confessor of Louis XIV.

166 *Wandering Jew*: a legendary figure, who insulted Christ as He went to be crucified, and was punished by being condemned to live on, unable to settle anywhere, until Christ's second coming.

166 *sous*: a *sou* was the least valuable French coin.

168 *par ma foi! . . . Vive la bagatelle!*: indeed! [literally 'by my faith!'] . . . Long live [what] doesn't matter!

168 *master-of-the-horse . . . lost his head*: the Master of the Horse or Grand Écuyer was an important official of the French royal household, in charge of the king's retinue as well as of horses, carriages and coaches, and the stables. The late king, Louis XVI, reigned 1774–92, and was guillotined in 1793.

168 *Peter the Great . . . eau de vie*: Peter the Great, emperor of Russia, died in 1725; *eau de vie* (literally 'water of life') is brandy.

169 *curé*: a French parish priest.

169 *'Grande Galerie des Glaces'*: the Hall of Mirrors, a splendid room (236 feet long) in the Palace of Versailles, completed in 1684. Seventeen large windows overlooking the gardens are matched by seventeen large mirrors; the walls are decorated with paintings celebrating events in the reign of Louis XIV (1643–1715). Writing soon after another Napoleon had been defeated and exiled, Le Fanu would remember that, after the defeat of Napoleon III and the French armies in the Franco-Prussian war (1870–71), King William of Prussia was proclaimed German emperor in this room on 18 January 1871.

169 *fête*: a gala celebration or entertainment.

170 *'Celestial'*: Chinese in style, since China was traditionally the 'Celestial Empire' ruled by the 'Son of Heaven'.

170 *dervish*: a member of an Islamic religious fraternity, whose ritual often included whirling or dancing.

170 *cabalistic devices*: occult or mystical emblems.

171 *d'Argensaque*: money bag.

173 *Imperial Guard*: the élite corps of Napoleon's army, eventually divided into the Old, Middle, and Young Guard. Members of the Old Guard were usually veterans. The colonel may have served in the Guard earlier in his career, or have chosen this uniform deliberately as a provocative costume at a ball honouring Napoleon's conquerors. He wears a blue swallow-tailed coat lined in red, with red cuffs and white cuff patches attached with gold buttons; red epaulets; tight white breeches; white gaiters; white vest; white *reverse* superimposed on the coat and attached with gold buttons; a tall bearskin *bonnet à poil* with red plume, fronted with a plate showing the imperial eagle; and a saber. Each arm displayed a corporal's chevron of two *aurore* (a pinky orange) stripes piped in scarlet.

174 *Prussian hussar*: a light cavalryman. A hussar wore a dolman (short jacket) with elaborate gold or silver braiding, tight trousers, and usually a pelisse (a loose over-jacket, braided and fur-trimmed); the pelisse was often worn hanging from the left shoulder, with sleeves empty.

174 *mon sorcier*: my wizard.

175 *shako*: a tall visored hat; the colonel actually wears the Guard's bearskin *bonnet*.

175 *pelisse*: here a long loose outer cloak or coat.

176 *rara avis*: literally, a rare bird; a kind of person rarely encountered.

177 *Confu*: presumably short for Confucius, or Kung Fu-tse (557?–479 BC), the Chinese sage.

178 *'Salon d'Apollon'*: one of Louis XIV's 'grands appartements' (once the throne room) at Versailles, connected with the Galerie des Glaces by the Salon de la Guerre. The Salons de Vénus, Diane, Mars, Mercure, and Apollon (Apollo) make up this series of decorated and intercommunicating rooms. The ceiling of the Salon d'Apollon shows Apollo in a four-horse chariot escorted by the Four Seasons.

179 *Collignan's . . . portrait of . . . de la Vallière*: Louise de La Vallière (1644–1710) was Louis XIV's mistress from 1660 or 1661 to about 1667. There are many portraits of her, but there is no record of the painter Collignan or of the portrait described. Le Fanu never visited France, but may somewhere have seen a print or copy of Pierre Mignard's full-length portrait of Mme de La Vallière, showing her with her two children by the King,

painted shortly before she entered a convent in 1674. She is richly dressed in a white silk bodice and gown with gold-lace trimmed bouffant sleeves. There is a rose silk stole across her lap. She wears pearl earrings and a ruby and pearl brooch. The picture allegorically bids farewell to the world's vanities: she points to a purse full of gold pieces, an open casket of jewels, a mask, playing-cards—the ace of hearts is conspicuous—a globe, and a guitar. The pillar behind her is inscribed 'Sic Transit Gloria Mundi' (So passes the glory of the world). In her right hand she holds a white rose, which is shedding its petals. The picture presents an image of disillusion with the world of appearances comparable to Beckett's eventual mood, and the gold coins, jewel-box, mask, and white rose all have their place in Le Fanu's story.

Le Fanu probably knew the elaborate descriptions of La Vallière's beauty in *La Duchesse de La Vallière* (1804) by Mme de Genlis, and in Alexandre Dumas's *Dix ans plus tard, ou le vicomte de Bragelonne* (26 parts, 1848–50). a second sequel to *Les Trois Mousquetaires* (*The Three Musketeers*, 1844).

179 *precious stone* . . . '*Arabian Nights*': such jewels are frequent in the *Arabian Nights*, notably in the story of Aladdin and the lengthy story of the Porter and the Three Girls.

184 '*circumbendibus*': the long way around, pseudo-Latin combining *circum* (Latin 'around'), English *bend,* and the Latin ending -*ibus*.

186 *émigré* . . . *Napoleon*: an *émigré* was one who had fled France during the Revolution. Carmaignac starts to say emperor, then corrects himself and says Napoleon, because the regime of Louis XVIII, which he now serves, considered Napoleon a revolutionary upstart, and did not recognize his status as emperor.

188 *fiacre*: a small carriage, for hire by the public.

188 *Count Chateau Blassemare*: Carmaignac calls him Chevalier earlier.

189 *harlequin*: a mischievous nimble charactger from traditional pantomime. He wears close-fitting multi-coloured clothes, and usually carries a wooden sword.

189 *sage femme*: a wise woman, learned in herbal medicines.

190 *embroidered hat* . . . *mandarin's*: mandarins were the civil servants of Imperial China, divided into nine ranks, the rank indicated by a jewel 'button' in the broad-brimmed hat that was part of their official costume.

193 *hearse-plumes*: hearses were decorated with ostrich feathers dyed black.

193 *grotto . . . Egeria*: Egeria was a water-nymph who advised Numa, a legendary king of Rome.

196 *Oh! Richard! Oh, my king!*: Beckett's name is Richard, but the Countess is quoting a well-known song, 'Ô Richard, Ô mon Roi, l'univers t'abandonne' (O Richard, O my King, the whole world forsakes thee), from André Ernest Modest Grétry's opera *Richard Côeur-de-Lion* (1784). The song was sung by royalists at a Versailles dinner (1 October 1789), which became a demonstration of loyalty to Louis XVI and Marie Antoinette and of opposition to the Revolution. News of this event led to a mob march on Versailles and the enforced transfer of the royal family to Paris. The episode is vividly described by Carlyle (*French Revolution*, pt. I, bk. 7, ch. 2). In the opera, the loyal minstrel Blondel sings the song to the imprisoned King Richard.

198 *contre-temps*: a misfortune, a mishap.

198 *funeste*: depressing.

198 *Père la Chaise*: see note to p. 166.

200 *insult the Allies*: Great Britain, Austria, Russia, and Prussia, who had combined to overthrow Napoleon.

200 *necromancy*: foretelling the future by communicating with the dead.

201 *never found out*: A group of masquers in Chinese costume, carrying their 'chief' in a palanquin, appeared at a St Petersburg ball in 1834. They set the palanquin in the middle of a room, danced around it for a time, then mingled with the company:

> After awhile they began gradually to disappear unnoticed, slipping out of the room one or two at a time. At last they were all gone, but their chief still remained sitting motionless in dignified silence in his palanquin in the middle of the room. The ball began to thin, and the attention of those who remained was wholly drawn to the silent figure of the Chinese mask.
>
> The master of the house at length went up to him, and told him that his companions were all gone; politely begging him at the same time to take off his mask, that he and his guests might know to whom they were indebted for all the pleasure which the exhibition had afforded them. The Chinaman, however, gave no reply by word or sign, and a feeling of

uneasy curiosity gradually drew around him the guests who remained in the ball-room. He still took no notice of all that was passing around him, and the master of the house at length, with his own hand, took off the mask, and discovered to the horrified by-standers the face of a corpse.

The police were immediately sent for, and on a surgical examination of the body, it appeared to be that of a man who had been strangled a few hours before. Nothing could be discovered, either at the time or afterwards, which could lead to the identifying of the dead man, or to the discovery of the actors in this extraordinary scene, and no clue has ever been obtained. It was found on inquiry that they arrived at the house where they deposited the dead body in a handsome equipage with masked servants.

See John Timbs, *English Eccentrics and Eccentricities* (London: R. Bentley, 1866), ii. 127–8. Timbs's source, a clergyman named Venables, heard the story from a General Bontourlin. In his book, Timbs also described Beau Brummell and his 'choker'. S. M. Ellis credits E. H. W. Meyerstein with noting Le Fanu's use of Timbs's anecdote; see S. M. Ellis, *Wilkie Collins, Le Fanu and Others* (London: Constable, 1931), 170.

201 *Bacchus*: Roman god of revelry and wine.

202 *modicum bonum*: a moderate but sufficient fortune.

202 *Dutch courage*: bravery instigated by alcohol.

203 *Henriade*: an epic poem by Voltaire, celebrating the life and deeds of Henri IV of France.

206 *farouche*: fierce, angry.

206 *stile*: an arrangement of steps to assist in getting over a wall or fence.

209 *porte-cochère*: see note to p. 107.

211 *sabreur*: swashbuckler.

212 *high-cauld cap*: a tall cap of netting, worn by Scottish women.

212 *Countess d'Aulnois ... genius loci*: Countess d'Aulnoy (*c.* 1650–1705) compiled *Contes des fées* (1698), a collection of fairy tales popular at the Court of Versailles, and later in the nurseries of France and England. *Genius loci* means the spirit haunting a particular place.

213 *beldame*: an old woman, often one ugly or grotesque (*belle*: beautiful).

213   *Spessart*: a forested district in southern Germany, often the setting for legends of ghosts and demons.

216   *Conciergerie . . . Sainte Chapelle*: the Palace of Justice consists of a number of buildings in central Paris, not far from Notre-Dame. Once a royal palace, it has housed France's chief law courts since the thirteenth century. The Conciergerie is a prison adjoining the courts, where Marie Antoinette and many other victims of the Revolution were confined. The Sainte-Chapelle, once the palace chapel, is a splendid Gothic structure (1245–8).

216   *Canon Fulbert . . . Eloise*: Éloise or Héloïse, niece of Canon Fulbert of Notre-Dame cathedral, and Peter Abelard (1079–1142), priest, scholastic philosopher, and also a canon, became lovers. Pregnant, she declined a secret marriage lest this injure his career. When they did marry, the secret was badly kept, and Eloise fled to a convent. Fulbert had Abelard seized and castrated.

216   *bull's eye*: a thick pane of glass.

219   *dulcinea*: a woman idealized and loved, from Don Quixote's Dulcinea del Toboso, a peasant girl he insisted was a great lady, and in whose name he performed his chivalric deeds.

224   *noyeau*: a cordial, properly *noyau*.

226   *crape*: a band of thin black cloth, to indicate mourning.

226   *Ma foi!*: Really! After all! (literally '[by] my faith').

226   *mignonne*: my pet, my darling.

227   *ma chère*: my dear.

228   *Rouleaux*: rolls (plural) of coins.

230   *gold-beater's leaf*: thin membrane from an ox's intestine, used to separate thin 'leaves' of gold (gold leaf) used for gilding.

230   *stethoscope*: a slight anachronism. the stethoscope was invented in 1817 by Théophile-René-Hyacinthe Laennec (1781–1826). In its early form it was a wooden rod for listening to the heart, and a wooden tube for the lungs, each fitted with a small 'cup' for the doctor's ear and a flattened 'bell' of bone to place against the chest.

233   *catalepsy*: a loss of feeling and ability to move or speak; the muscles become rigid.

236   *legerdemain*: sleight of hand, trickery.

236   *perpendicular*: Beckett is actually horizontal.

237   *Berkley Square*: usually Berkeley, a fashionable London address in the eighteenth and nineteenth centuries.

238   '*judge the secrets of men*': Romans 2: 16.

238   *gasconading*: blustering.

240   *cause célèbre . . . agrémens*: a notorious case . . . agreeable features.

240   *balourd . . . benêt, un âne*: a numskull, a booby, a jackass.

240   *soi-disant*: supposed, self-styled.

241   *lapidary . . . paste*: a lapidary is an expert in precious stones; paste is hard glass used in making artificial jewelry, including the jewels worn by stage royalty.

CARMILLA

'Carmilla' appeared in four successive issues of *The Dark Blue*, vols. 2–3: Chapters 1–3 (December 1871); 4–6 (January 1872); 7–10 (February); 11–16 (March).

243   *précis*: a brief summary.

243   *arcana . . . dual existence . . . intermediates*: arcana are secrets; our dual existence is, as in Swedenborg's teachings, in the spiritual and material worlds. Swedenborg describes 'The world of spirits' as 'a place intermediate between heaven and hell, and . . . also the intermediate state of man after death'. It is a kind of posthumous purgatory or testing place, where humanity is purged and the individual inclines toward heaven or hell. Hesselius seems to posit a similar state between life and death where the 'undead' exist; Carmilla can apparently materialize and dematerialize.

244   *Styria*: an Austrian province, on the Hungarian border.

247   *cassock*: a long close-fitting garment often worn by clergymen.

248   *phantasmagoria*: a magic lantern, which projected pictures on the wall of a darkened room.

251   *odylic . . . influence*: a mysterious force (od) supposed to pervade nature, and manifesting itself through magnetism, hypnotic influence, chemical reactions, and the like; sensitive individuals can detect it. The notion was promulgated by Baron Karl von Reichenbach (1788–1869).

252   '*In truth . . . came by it*': *Merchant of Venice* I. i. 1–3. The speech begins 'In sooth', and line 3 is 'But how I caught it, found it, or

came by it', but the speaker here is quoting from memory. In the play, Antonio is speaking, and goes on: 'What stuff 'tis made of, whereof it is born, | I am to learn.'

254 *traces*: straps connecting the horses' harnesses to the coach.

255 *cortège*: a group of attendants.

255 *Matska*: a feminine diminutive, suggesting a Czech or Polish servant.

258 *Cleopatra . . . asp to her bosom*: Cleopatra committed suicide by provoking the bite of a poisonous snake. A picture of the same event hangs in a gloomy antechamber in Le Fanu's *The Rose and the Key* (1871: ch. 87).

268 *oupire*: vampire. The word is a Slavic variant of Magyar *vampyr*; cf. Russian *upír*; Polish *upíor*; Czech *upír*; Ruthenian *opyr*.

271 *Buffon*: Georges Louis Leclerc de Buffon (1707–88), the great French naturalist, devised a system for classifying animals.

271 *hippogriffs*: mythical creature, half-horse and half-griffin.

271 *Gratz . . . ten leagues*: Gratz or Graz, a cathedral and university town, provincial capital of Styria. A league was about three English miles.

282 *Avernus*: Hades, the realm of the dead.

284 *majordomo . . . myrmidons*: a majordomo is the butler or other upper servant in charge of a household; myrmidons, originally warriors led by Achilles in the Trojan War, are any group of subordinates.

286 *valerian . . . sal volatile*: valerian is a sedative, sal volatile (smelling-salts) a restorative.

290 *Dranfeld*: a imaginary place.

295 *Drunstall*: imaginary.

296 *Grand Duke Charles*: presumably the reigning monarch of a small German state.

296 *Aladdin's lamp*: a magic lamp in the *Arabian Nights*. Rubbing it summons a genie who will fulfil any wish.

307 *usual tests . . . burning*: the tests involved examining buried corpses for evidence that they had moved after burial, that hair and nails continued to grow, or that corruption had not begun. Suspected vampires were 'extinguished' when the head was cut off, a stake driven through the heart, the corpse burned, and the ashes scattered. See Paul Barber, *Vampires, Burial, and Death:*

Folklore and Reality (New Haven, Conn.: Yale University Press, 1988).

307   *a Moravian nobleman*: Moravia, then an Austrian province, is now part of Czechoslovakia.

308   *impaled and burnt them*: Le Fanu adapted the forester's story from an account in *Traité sur les Apparitions des Esprits, et sur les Vampires, ou les Revenans de Hongrie, de Moravie, etc.* (A Treatise on the Apparitions of Spirits, and on the Vampires or Revenants of Hungary, Moravia, etc.), by Dom Augustin Calmet (Paris, 1751); Le Fanu probably read Calmet as translated into English by Henry Christmas: *The Phantom World: or, the Philosophy of Spirits, Apparitions, etc.*, 2 vols. (London: Richard Bentley, 1850). Calmet attributes the story to 'a sensible priest' who accompanied Canon Jeanin of the cathedral at Olmütz (Olomouc) to the Moravian village of Liebava 'to take information concerning the fact of a certain famous vampire, which had caused much confusion in this village . . . some years before'. The priests examine witnesses, who testify that the vampire 'had often disturbed the living in their beds at night, that he had come out of the cemetery, and had appeared in several houses three or four years ago; that his troublesome visits had ceased because a Hungarian stranger, passing through the village at the time of these reports, had boasted that he could put an end to them, and make the vampire disappear. To perform his promise, he mounted on the church steeple, and observed the moment when the vampire came out of his grave, leaving near it the linen clothes in which he had been enveloped, and then went to disturb the inhabitants of the village.

The Hungarian, having seen him come out of his grave, went down quickly from the steeple, took up the linen envelops of the vampire, and carried them with him up the tower. The vampire having returned from his prowlings, cried loudly against the Hungarian, who made him a sign from the top of the tower that if he wished to have his clothes again he must fetch them; the vampire began to ascend the steeple, but the Hungarian threw him down backwards from the ladder, and cut his head off with a spade. Such was the end of this tragedy' (*Phantom World*, ii. 209–10).

311   *basement*: foundation.

313   *leaf*: hat-brim (Irish-English).

314 *escutcheon*: a coat-of-arms.

314 *commissioner . . . Inquisition . . . law*: Calmet describes the Austrian legal proceedings for exhuming and destroying the body of
a suspected vampire. An imperial commissioner presided, villagers were sworn and testified, and cross-examination was
permitted. Inquisition here means a formal inquiry.

315 *Silesia . . . Servia*: Silesia is an area north-east of Bohemia and
Moravia, or of modern Czechoslovakia. Servia (Serbia) was
then under Turkish rule.

315 *If human testimony . . . Vampire*: Calmet emphasizes the number
of reports from commissions, doctors, lawyers, and public
officials, especially in early eighteenth-century Hungary,
describing cases of vampirism.

316 *shocking scene*: Le Fanu's details are drawn from Calmet, especially from chapter 46, which describes the exhumation and
destruction of a vampire named Peter Plogojovitz. See also
Barber, pp. 5–9.

316 '*Magia Posthuma . . . Harenberg*: *Magia Posthuma* [Sorcery after
Death] by Charles Ferdinand de Schertz (Olmütz, 1706); *De
Mirabilibus* [Concerning Marvels], a Latin version of the Greek
Peri thaumasion by Phlegon of Tralles, a freedman of the Emperor
Hadrian; St Augustine, *De cura pro Mortuis* [On caring for the
dead], a treatise on respect for the dead, which also warns
against excessive mourning; *Philosophicae et Christianae Cogitationes
de Vampiris* [Philosophical and Christian Reflections on Vam-
pires] by John Christian [not Christofer] Harenberg (Wolfen-
büttel, 1739). Calmet refers to all of these works.

317 *inexplicable*: Calmet, who is learned and intelligent, is sceptical
about most of the wonders he narrates, but notes the testimony
of reliable witnesses and is willing to extend a provisional belief.
He admits his bafflement at the vampire's mobility, and also his
doubts, finally conceding that the devil may be at work.

The Oxford World's Classics Website

www.worldsclassics.co.uk

- Browse the full range of Oxford World's Classics online

- Sign up for our monthly e-alert to receive information on new titles

- Read extracts from the Introductions

- Listen to our editors and translators talk about the world's greatest literature with our Oxford World's Classics audio guides

- Join the conversation, follow us on Twitter at OWC_Oxford

- Teachers and lecturers can order inspection copies quickly and simply via our website

www.worldsclassics.co.uk

American Literature

British and Irish Literature

Children's Literature

Classics and Ancient Literature

Colonial Literature

Eastern Literature

European Literature

Gothic Literature

History

Medieval Literature

Oxford English Drama

Poetry

Philosophy

Politics

Religion

The Oxford Shakespeare

A complete list of Oxford World's Classics, including Authors in Context, Oxford English Drama, and the Oxford Shakespeare, is available in the UK from the Marketing Services Department, Oxford University Press, Great Clarendon Street, Oxford OX2 6DP, or visit the website at www.oup.com/uk/worldsclassics.

In the USA, visit www.oup.com/us/owc for a complete title list.

Oxford World's Classics are available from all good bookshops. In case of difficulty, customers in the UK should contact Oxford University Press Bookshop, 116 High Street, Oxford OX1 4BR.